Barbara and the Smiley People

The Army Cadets

C.R. Cummings

Also By
CHRISTOPHER CUMMINGS

The Boy and the Battleship

The Green Idol of Kanaka Creek

Ross River Fever

Train to Kuranda

The Mudskipper Cup

Davey Jones's Locker

Air Cadet

Below Bartle Frere

Bowling Green Bay

Airship Over Atherton

Cockatoo

The Cadet Corporal

Stannary Hills

Coast of Cape York

Kylie and the Kelly Gang

Beyond the Barrier Reef

Behind Mt. Baldy

The Cadet Sergeant Major

Cooktown Christmas

Secret in the Clouds

Mischief at Mingela

The Word of God

The Cadet Under-Officer

Through the Devil's Eye

Barbara in the Bush

*Barbara and the Smiley People

Barbara at her Best

Barbara's Bivouac

Barbara and the Smiley People

The Army Cadets

C.R. Cummings

DoctorZed
Publishing
www.doctorzed.com

Copyright © 2021 by Christopher Cummings

All rights reserved. No part of this book may be used or reproduced by any means, graphic, electronic, or mechanical, including photocopying, recording, taping or by any information storage retrieval system without the written permission of the publisher except in the case of brief quotations embodied in critical articles and reviews.

This 2nd edition Published 2021 by DoctorZed Publishing

DoctorZed Publishing books may be ordered through booksellers or by contacting:

DoctorZed Publishing
10 Vista Ave
Skye, South Australia 5072
www.doctorzed.com

ISBN: 978-0-6451840-3-7 (hc)
ISBN: 978-0-6451840-2-0 (sc)
ISBN: 978-0-6451840-1-3 (ebk)

National Library of Australia Cataloguing-in-Publication entry

    Author: Cummings, C. R., author.

    Title: Barbara and the Smiley People/ Christopher Cummings.

    ISBN: 9780645184037 (hardcover)

    Series: Cummings, C. R. The army cadets.

    Target Audience: For young adults.

    Subjects: Adventure stories, Australian.

    Military cadets--Queensland--Fiction.

This is a work of fiction. Names, characters, places, events, and dialogues are creations of the author or are used fictitiously. Any resemblance to any individuals, alive or dead, is purely coincidental. The views expressed in this work are solely those of the author and do not necessarily reflect the views of the publisher, and the publisher hereby disclaims any responsibility for them.

Cover image © Talashow | Dreamstime.com
Cover design © Scott Zarcinas

Printed in Australia, UK & USA

DoctorZed Publishing rev. date: 30/08/2021

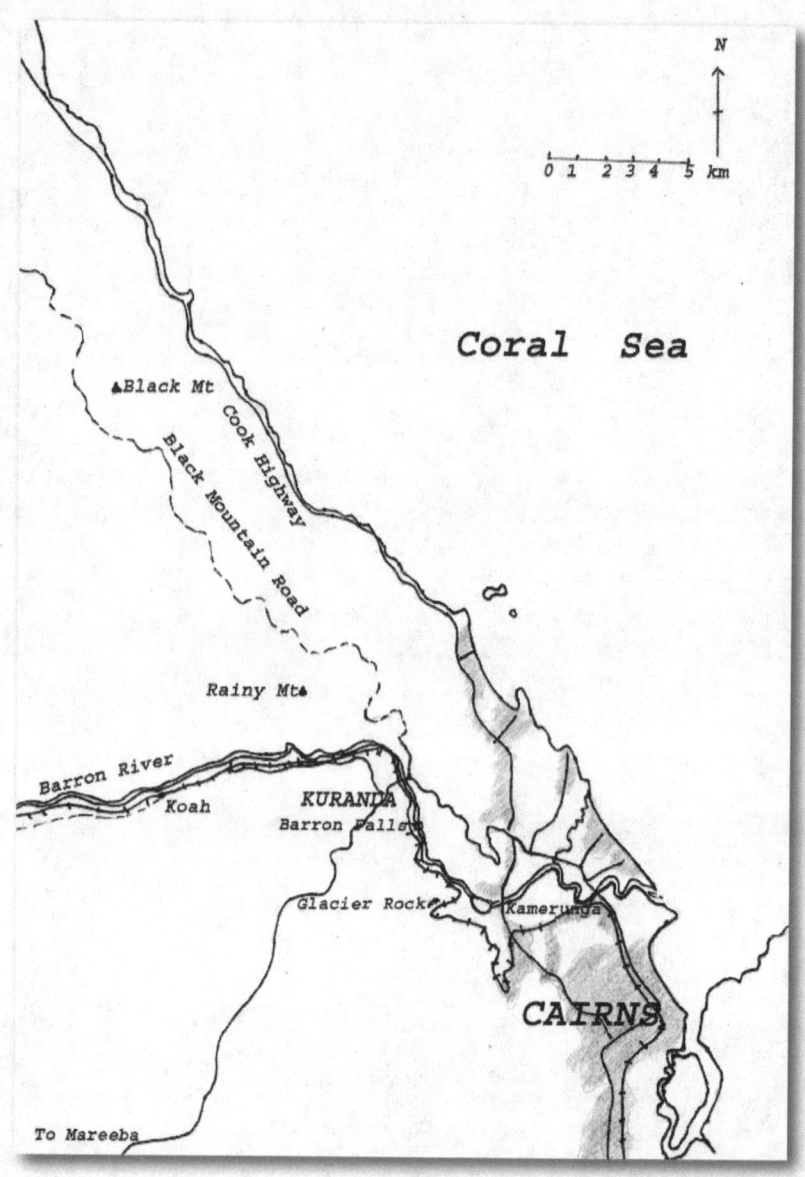

N

0 1 2 3 4 5 km

Coral Sea

▲Black Mt

Cook Highway

Black Mountain Road

Rainy Mt▲

Barron River

Koah

KURANDA

Barron Falls

Glacier Rock

Kamerunga

CAIRNS

To Mareeba

Chapter 1

FIONA IS MISSING

At a High School, Cairns, North Queensland. Friday 12th June.

Seventeen-year-old Barbara Brassington shook her head and slumped down on the seat beside her friend Wendy. For a few moments Barbara sat silent.

Then she shook her head and said, "Fiona's gone. She's not at home. There's no-one there."

She shivered and bit her lower lip. Tears were very close, but she held them back. She didn't want to cry in front of the boys.

Wendy placed a sympathetic hand on Barbara's arm. "Maybe the family have just gone somewhere on a visit?" she suggested.

"No," Barbara replied, shaking her head emphatically. "She would have told me. Besides, we've got our end of term exams starting today. Fiona wouldn't miss those. They are too important."

The thought of those exams weighed heavily on Barbara. It was near the end of her Third Semester in her Senior Year. As a Year 12 at high school the results would play a major part in determining her final grading. Her future plans to attend university would partly depend on them. And exams were the last thing she felt capable of doing. Her best friend, Fiona Davies, was missing.

Barbara had visited Fiona at her home the previous afternoon. On the way to school that morning she had called in as usual, so they could ride to school together on their bicycles. To Barbara's surprise Fiona's house had been all closed up.

Vanished overnight! Barbara thought.

It just didn't seem credible. Ugly possibilities crept into her consciousness, like cockroaches appearing while the lights are still on. She shook her head again to try to drive them away. But her fears made her feel sick in the stomach.

Wendy gave Barbara's arm a gentle squeeze. "Don't get too upset Barb, or you won't do well in your exams," she said.

7

Barbara forced a smile and put her hand over Wendy's. "It's alright for you. Your exams aren't as important." She said that because Wendy was only in Year 11, although both girls were only a few months apart in age.

A male voice interrupted Barbara's thoughts. "What's the matter with you two?" the voice asked. "You both look down in the dumps."

Barbara looked up. It was Roger Dunning. Roger was in her class and like herself was one of the four Cadet Under-Officers in the school's Army Cadet Unit. Four years of part-time training, camps and adventures had made them close. Barbara liked Roger. He was always kind and considerate. Her grey-green eyes met his blue eyes and read the concern in them. Poor old Roger! It was a pity he was chubby in build.

"It's Fiona. She is missing," Barbara replied.

"Fiona! Missing!" Roger cried. "Does Lofty know?"

Lofty Ward, a strapping big lad to match his name, was another CUO, as was Fiona. At that moment he was walking towards them across the playground, a cheerful grin all over his face. Lofty was in love with Fiona but thought nobody else knew.

Barbara shook her head. "I don't think he knows," she answered. She pictured the two together; Fiona with her sparkling blue eyes and blonde beauty next to Lofty with his rugged good-looks, brown hair, and hazel eyes.

They would make a good couple, if only Fiona would stop getting silly ideas, Barbara thought.

Roger glanced around and saw Lofty coming. "Then don't tell him. We've both got a science exam in ten minutes and it will upset him," he said.

Lofty joined them. "G'day gang, how's tricks? You pair look pretty cosy. You fallen in love or something?" he joked.

"Don't be horrible, Lofty," Wendy retorted. "I'm just cheering Barbara up. She's not looking forward to her exam."

"Nor am I. Can I have a little cuddle too?" Lofty replied light-heartedly.

"You can have a little smack for being too fresh," Wendy replied, but she smiled.

"That's not a very respectful way to speak to your senior officer Sergeant Werribee," Lofty laughed.

8

He was Platoon Commander of Number 1 Platoon and Wendy was his 2ic and Platoon Sergeant. They had been a team for three years now. Lofty had been Wendy's Section Commander when she was a 'First Year' cadet; then her platoon sergeant the previous year when Wendy was a corporal. The pair had several times fallen in and out of love. They were the best of friends and indulged in good-natured teasing all the time. Barbara had a suspicion that Roger was in love with Wendy and that he was hurt by her closeness with Lofty.

Wendy poked her tongue at Lofty. They weren't in army uniform or 'on duty'. She said, "Give Roger a hug if you need one."

Lofty threw up his hands in mock horror. "Fair go! I'm not like that," he replied.

"Nor am I," Roger added, a distinct blush mottling his neck and ears.

Barbara looked up at them. Men! They were all the same. Even when they weren't thinking about sex it was the only thing on their mind! She snorted in exasperation but couldn't really get angry. They were nice boys really.

Then Lofty sent her anxiety level shooting up by asking, "Does anyone know where Fiona is?'"

Barbara felt her stomach churn. She looked up at Lofty's cheerful, freckled face. For a moment she hesitated, not wanting to hurt him. After biting her lip she said, "We don't know. She is missing. I went to her house this morning and there was no-one there."

"Perhaps the family has just gone somewhere for the day?" Lofty suggested, worry clouding his face.

"That's what I suggested," Wendy said.

"But they wouldn't do that with her major exams starting today," Lofty replied.

Roger spoke next. "Could be some sort of family crisis. Fiona's been having a few problems at home recently," he said.

Barbara nodded. The morning sunlight glinted on her ginger hair. Family crisis was the least of it. Fiona had told her in confidence of the terrible rows her parents had been having when her father discovered her mother was having an affair with another man. Barbara knew that Fiona's family was being torn apart. She had been intensely distressed. In the resulting battle Fiona had sided with her father. To Barbara it was sickeningly familiar. Her own parents had gone through exactly the same crisis three years before, when she was in Year 9. Her own mother had left and ever since she had lived with her father.

It was memories of her own experience which worried Barbara so much. She remembered how emotionally disturbed she had been, of the black despair, erratic, and irrational behaviour, of the deep depression and thoughts of suicide. In the end she had run away. It had been these people, and Fiona in particular, who had saved her. They were why she had joined the Army Cadets. And Cadets had been very important in helping her. For those critical teenage years it had given her a group to belong to and had helped rebuild her confidence.

She looked up to find the others silently waiting, looking at her.

"Sorry, I was thinking," she said.

"You know what Fiona's problem is, don't you?" Lofty asked quietly.

Barbara nodded. "Yes I do. Fiona told me. But I'm not sure if I can tell you."

"You may as well," Roger said. "It will all come out anyway if something serious has happened. Besides, I think we all have some idea anyway."

Wendy agreed. "Yes Barbara. We will only imagine the worst. Besides, people will make things up. The truth is better. You know the horrible things people have been saying about you and Fiona lately," she said.

Barbara bit her lip and nodded sadly. She knew alright. Half the school openly accused them of being lesbian lovers. The thought made her aware she was holding Wendy's hand. Hot anger surged through her.

People can be so cruel! It isn't like that! she thought.

Or is it?

Barbara brushed the niggling doubt aside. She knew she did enjoy the company of girls more than boys. And she did like being touched by them. But she had never done anything like... well... like that. And she certainly didn't like men much. Over the last few years she had suffered some truly terrifying experiences at the hands of men. There had been five attempted rapes, mostly with some physical violence. The memories made her feel as though she wanted to vomit.

Contrariwise she silently cursed herself for being so attractive to men. She knew this wasn't just vanity on her part. She had a strong but pretty face and a well-shaped body. She thought her legs too long but knew from constant experience of the way men's eyes travelled that they liked what they saw. She looked down and sighed. The heave of her shirt front reminded her of how prominent her breasts were. She thought them much too big, but at least they weren't as large as Wendy's. Hers were so big her school nickname was 'Wobbles'.

Barbara glanced down at where Wendy's right breast pressed gently against her arm. It felt nice. *Am I like that?* she wondered. The thought made her uncomfortable.

In exasperation, and embarrassed at her own thoughts, she shook herself free and stood up. "I will think about it. Wait till this afternoon. Fiona might have turned up by then. I'm going to get ready for my exam," she said.

The others agreed, Lofty with obvious reluctance. He looked so downcast, in contrast to his cheerfulness of a few minutes before, that Barbara wished she could do something. She felt an urge to hug him. Tears prickled in her eyes. To hide them she turned and walked away.

Most of Barbara's morning was taken up by a two-hour Economics exam. She found it very hard to concentrate. Worry over Fiona dominated her thoughts. Where was she? Was she alright? Was she with her father? What if...?

As the minutes of the exam ticked rapidly by Barbara forced herself to work. She could not drive the concern away but at least she managed to push it to one side so that it ranked with an aching tooth as a distraction. Somehow, she managed to fill the pages of paper with handwriting but later could not remember whether what she wrote made much sense or not.

As soon as the exam was over Barbara rushed to put her bag in her locker, then she tried to call Fiona on her mobile phone. It rang out, adding to Barbara's anxiety. Feeling a sick sense of dread she hurried to the bike racks. Students were not supposed to leave the school grounds without permission during the day, but Barbara ignored this, was barely conscious of it in fact. She got her bicycle and set off, pedalling as fast as she could towards Fiona's.

Being June, which in tropical North Queensland is 'winter', it was just cold enough for the exertion to be pleasantly warming. Fiona's house was only a kilometre from the school along pleasant, tree-lined streets. As Barbara pedalled towards it her eyes searched between the trees lining the footpath for some sign that people were there. But the house, a well maintained, high-set, 'Old Queenslander' was shut up. It appeared the same as when she had called that morning.

Barbara stopped and swallowed her disappointment. What had happened? Where was Fiona? The family car was gone and the doors of the carport closed. But had Fiona gone with her father?

Perhaps she has done what I did and run away and the family have gone to look for her? Barbara speculated, but in her heart she felt that was not the answer. She had spoken to Fiona for several hours the previous day and there had been no hint of any such inner turmoil. Fiona had been upset but not obviously distressed.

Then a terrible thought crept into Barbara's mind. Maybe Fiona had been alone in the house, her father having gone away. Perhaps she was still inside the house?

What if...? Barbara thought anxiously.

Into here mind crept horrible stories from the news about family tragedies that resulted from such break-ups: suicides and murders. As Barbara thought this, she pictured ghastly images of her friend's body and hastily suppressed them. But the morbid thoughts returned, along with a host of other possibilities.

She might be inside the house and be sick; or perhaps she has had an accident, fallen in the bath or something; or perhaps she has cut her wrists or taken an overdose of sleeping pills?

Feeling quite distressed, her heart pounding from concern as much as from pedalling so fast, Barbara placed her bicycle against the fence and opened the gate. Feeling sick with anxiety she walked along the pathway and up the stairs to the front door of the high-set 'Old Queenslander'. She rang the doorbell.

"Fiona!"

Barbara rang a second time. No answer. She called again. Still no response. She waited a full minute then rang and called loudly. When there was still no response, she went down the stairs and around to the back of the house. The back yard looked quite normal. She went up to the back door and knocked.

"Fiona!"

The name came out almost as a sob. Emotion was constricting her throat. Barbara gnawed at her knuckles and wiped away a tear. She knocked again. The sound echoed in the closed-up house. Again she waited, but there was still no response. Next, she tried the door handle. It was locked. Her gaze checked the back windows. They were all shut tight. The door leading under the house was also locked.

Barbara returned to the street and went to the house next door on the right. No-one was home there either. Feeling even more upset and worried Barbara went to the house on the other side.

A woman answered her knock. Barbara had seen her before when visiting Fiona but couldn't remember her name. In answer to Barbara's questions the woman returned surly negatives. She had seen and heard nothing. Yes, she thought Fiona had been there the previous day but wasn't sure. No, she hadn't seen her today. The woman did not seem very concerned, which annoyed Barbara.

Out on the footpath once more Barbara checked her watch. Unsure what to do next she rode back to school. Her friends were waiting in their usual place. Because of teasing by the majority of the student body most of the older cadets formed a social group. The corporals and lance corporals, most of whom were Year 10s, formed two more such groups. Except when they were attending one of the weekly cadet 'Home Training' parades after school, or a camp, the cadets did not wear army uniform. At school they wore the school uniform. They were only 'part-time' volunteers.

The group of older cadets included Lofty, Roger and Wendy, Dan Russell, who was Barbara's own platoon sergeant, and Fiona's platoon sergeant Don Blake. Both were Year 11s. Barbara was the commander of Number 4 Platoon, the 'senior' cadet platoon. It was something she was very proud of.

Lofty spoke first. "Where have you been?" he asked.

"To Fiona's," Barbara replied. "No-one home. And the lady next door was no help. Oh, I am so worried!"

"Aren't we getting a bit ahead of things?" Roger suggested. "She might just be away for the day and all this worry might be for nothing."

Barbara shook her head. "I don't think so. I was talking to her yesterday afternoon, and she was studying for these exams today. She didn't say anything to suggest she wasn't coming to school today."

Wendy then put Barbara on a spot by saying, "What about her parents? Did they say anything?"

13

Barbara hesitated before answering. She didn't really want to go into the details of Fiona's personal life. But after a moment's thought she sighed. It was obvious that some at least had to come out. She said, "They weren't there. Fiona has been living on her own."

"Living on her own!" Lofty cried. "But.... but where are her parents?"

"Her mother left two weeks ago. She walked out on Fiona's father, with another man," Barbara explained.

There was shocked silence for a minute.

"And her father, where is he?" Lofty asked anxiously.

"He went a week ago. But he said he would come back."

Roger frowned. "Then that is where Fiona is. She has followed them," he said. "Do know where the parents went?"

Barbara shook her head. "I'm not sure. I think Fiona's mum and her... her boyfriend (Barbara said the word with sour distaste) went down south to Sydney. That's where he came from."

"And her dad? Did he follow her?" Lofty asked.

"I don't think so. He was terribly downcast by it all. Fiona said he was absolutely shattered and that he was very depressed. She was ...was worried he might commit suicide," Barbara replied. She knew exactly what it was like. She remembered what a stunning blow it had been to her and her own father when the adultery was unmasked. The feeling of rejection, betrayal and worthlessness had been all but overwhelming.

"But where did he go then?" Lofty persisted.

"Fiona said he was going off with some religious group; just for a short while, to think things out," Barbara replied.

Roger nodded. "That sound sensible," he commented. "The church can be very helpful at times like that. A 'retreat' is a good idea. So why are we worried? That is probably where Fiona is too."

"You could be right," Barbara agreed. She had already considered the idea but had not liked it. Fiona was upset but she had never been all that religious.

"We can easily check surely. Which church is it?" Lofty asked.

"It's not a proper church I don't think," Barbara replied. She paused while she tried to remember what little she had been told. She was angry with herself now for not having listened more carefully. "It's not like the old established churches like the Catholics or the Anglicans. It's some sort of new church with one of those charismatic guru type leaders."

"You mean some sort of sect? Like the 'Orange People' or the 'Hari Krishnas' or something?" Dan Russell asked.

Barbara nodded. "I think so. Only not as big. They follow someone called the... er... the Grand Jubo or something."

"Grand Ju-jube!" Roger quipped with a laugh.

Barbara frowned. She wasn't in the mood for jokes. "Something like that," she agreed.

"Are they Christians?" Wendy asked.

Barbara shrugged and said, "I'm not sure. I think it's one of those mixtures of Christianity and bits of other religions."

"What is the name of this sect?" Lofty asked.

Barbara shrugged. "I can't remember. It has a long title like 'The true and happy way to God', or 'The path to happy enlightenment' or something. Fiona called them 'The Smiley People' because they all wore a little yellow 'Smiley' badge."

Lofty stood up. "Then let's go and see the Smiley People and ask the Grand Jumbo where Fiona is," he said.

Chapter 2

MISSING PERSON

"After school. We have another exam this afternoon," Roger reminded them.

Barbara bit her lip. Tears suddenly welled up. She hung her head. Wendy put her arm around her and patted her. Barbara made an effort and controlled her emotions. "Sorry. I didn't mean to get upset. I don't know the name of this church or where it is," she said.

Roger patted her shoulder. "Don't worry. We will find out," he replied.

"Thanks Roger. Oh heavens! Look at the time. Oh! I don't feel up to doing an exam," Barbara exclaimed. She took out her handkerchief, wiped her eyes and blew her nose. Feeling thoroughly miserable she walked off towards the exam room.

When she arrived there Barbara met another of the males in her life: Willy Williams. When he spoke to her Barbara experienced a brief spurt of annoyance which quickly changed to a sort of grudging admiration and liking. Willy was in the same class and she saw him every school day. Three years earlier, in Year 9, Willy had developed an almost obsessive crush on her, which she had found very upsetting, but since then Willy had developed a torrid relationship with a girl who was one year younger. Marjorie was a blousy blonde with freckles and big boobs and she and Willy were notorious around the school for their heated encounters. Despite this, Willy had remained smitten by Barbara and was her strongest admirer. Now the relationship was one of wary friendship, bolstered by the fact that it was Willy who had saved Barbara from a maniac during a terrifying chase at Mt Mulligan earlier in the year.

Another thing that made her tolerate Willy's friendship was that he was a 5th Year Air Cadet and a Warrant Officer. Willy was also a trained pilot. He looked at her quizzically and said, "You okay, Barbara? You look a bit down."

Barbara nodded but then said, "I'm just very worried about Fiona. I don't know where she is." She explained the situation.

16

Roger joined them. "G'day Willy, how are the 'Blue Orchids'?"

Willy snorted. "Better than being a 'grunt'," he replied.

"I heard you were going to some sort of parade in Sydney during the holidays. Is that right?" Roger asked.

Willy nodded. "Yes. The Air Force Cadets are being presented with a new banner. I have been selected to be in the guard."

Roger snorted. "Huh! They must be bloody hard up then," he teased.

Barbara sensed that the banter had an edge to it so she said, "Are you still doing your CUO's course in the second week of the holidays?"

Willy nodded. "Yes. After the week in Sydney we fly to Townsville and do a weeklong CUO Course. I will be the same rank as you then."

Barbara knew it was one of the bones of contention between the two cadet services that the army cadets seemed to get promoted younger and more easily.

She smiled and said, "That will be good."

Roger snorted and said, "We are just smarter and don't take as long to learn simple skills."

"They would need to be simple for you blokes to master them," Willy retorted.

Once again Barbara detected the undercurrent of tension. To change the subject she said, "We are going to the Townsville area during the second week of the holidays."

"Oh, yes? What for?" Willy asked.

"An army cadet field exercise. We are joining 130 Army Cadet Unit for one of their 'Senior' Exercises," Barbara explained.

Willy nodded. "Lucky you. I have heard they are really great, very challenging. Is it going to be like the one we were the opposing force for in Year 9?"

Barbara nodded but went red. During that exercise she'd been part of a recon patrol that had observed Willy and Marjorie being very naughty indeed, and the memory made her feel both uncomfortable and aroused.

"Yes," she replied.

Willy nodded. "What are you doing during the first week of the holidays?" he asked.

"A hike to get fit, ready for the exercise," Barbara answered.

Willy went to speak, but the bell rang and a teacher told them to move into the exam room so that ended the conversation. It was a Maths exam. For Barbara that was alright. She could recall the formulae easily enough and then it was just mechanical. She was able to cope in spite of being very upset. Still, she found it a great relief to leave the room two hours later.

She met Roger, Lofty and Wendy at the bike racks.

Lofty asked, "What do we do now?"

"Go to Fiona's first and see if she has come home," Barbara replied.

The friends mounted their bicycles and rode off. Ten minutes later they stood on the footpath at Fiona's gate. Barbara went up to the front door and rang the doorbell. There was no response. She tried again. Still none. A third attempt still received no answer. Sadly she walked back down the front steps.

"No-one home," she told them, trying to sound calm.

Lofty took out his mobile phone. "Have you tried ringing her?" he asked.

Barbara nodded. "Both her home phone and her mobile but no result," she replied.

"I'll try again," Lofty replied.

He began using his mobile. As he did, Barbara observed Wendy looking at him with a hurt and wistful look on her face. *Wendy must still like Lofty,* she mused. Then she realised that Lofty had Fiona's phone numbers in his phone and that made her wonder as well.

Lofty listened and then tried the other number before shaking his head. "No answer," he said.

"What do we do now?" Wendy asked.

"What about that church you were talking about?" Lofty suggested.

Roger frowned. "I'm not sure. Perhaps we should wait a bit longer before we start pushing the panic button," he cautioned. "If they've just gone away for the day and we make a big fuss it will cause a lot of worry for nothing. I think we should wait until tomorrow."

Barbara didn't really agree. She wanted to start looking at once, but she saw the point of Roger's argument. Reluctantly she assented. The group parted and went their separate ways. Barbara pedalled slowly home. When she got there, she lay on her bed with a Geography text book and tried to study for the next exam.

When her father came home from work, he immediately noted her mood. "What's the matter, Bubs?" he asked.

Barbara made them both a cup of coffee and sat opposite him at the kitchen table, then told him. When she finished, she asked, "What do you think we should do dad?"

"Get the police to contact her relatives and see if they know anything. There isn't much we can do ourselves. I will do that now if you like?" he replied.

"Thanks Dad. Please."

Barbara's father went to the telephone while Barbara made more coffee. He called out once to check Fiona's address and made answers like 'yes' and 'I see' and 'I realise that' and 'I don't know'; then said, 'Thank you' and hung up. He sat down and shook his head. "They were very polite but as we aren't relations, they aren't going to open a 'Missing Persons' inquiry yet. However they did say they would do a check and would try to locate the relatives. Do you know any?"

"I think she has an uncle on the Atherton Tablelands; and she sometimes mentions cousins in Mackay," Barbara replied. She was angry with herself for not having listened more carefully when her friend had been talking.

"Well, that's all we can do for the moment. You go and study while I get dinner," her father said.

Barbara smiled at him with affection. *Poor dad! He has aged so much since Mum left. But he tries very hard,* she thought.

She went to her room and settled to work. The notion that maybe her father needed another woman in his life came to her again, but she pushed it aside as being disloyal to her mother. It also raised thoughts about men and women being intimate and that was too uncomfortable to think about.

All evening worry niggled at Barbara. Once she went and rang Fiona's home number on the telephone, but nobody answered. Then she tried Fiona's mobile phone. Again no answer. That sent her spirits plummeting.

Surely Fiona would have her mobile, especially if she is away from home? she pondered.

She found it very difficult to concentrate after that and had trouble falling asleep. Once she had drifted off bad dreams crept in to disturb her.

Twice she woke up, aware that she had been having a nightmare but quite unable to remember the details. She slipped off into restless sleep and another dream. This time it was erotic. In the dream she found herself naked in Fiona's house and enjoying it when Fiona looked at her. She woke up feeling very hot and aroused. Lingering memories gave her some uncomfortable thoughts.

Am I really like that? Barbara worried.

Ashamed of herself she sprang out of bed and went to the shower. Touching her own body while she soaped herself brought the memories and doubts back. At the back of her mind she recognised the emotion of fear.

"I'm scared I'm not normal," she whispered to herself. *Oh curse this stupid body and sex! It makes life so complicated!*

Then she remembered that Fiona was missing and forgot about herself.

After breakfast she rang Fiona's number. The monotonous *chrrrrp-chrrrrp-chrrrrp-chrrrrp* of the dial tone seemed to squeeze her heart as it went on. No answer. She bit her lip and hung up. For a moment she contemplated phoning the police to ask if they had any news but decided not to. Depression gripped her.

For a while Barbara walked around, unable to think straight. She picked things up and put them down after wondering what they were doing in her hand. Being a Saturday she set herself to do the usual chores she shared with her father. This included sweeping out under the house, helping with the washing, vacuuming her room and mowing the front lawn.

After lunch she was able to get away on her bike to check if Fiona had arrived home. She hadn't. Knocking on both the front and back doors elicited no response. Feeling very despondent Barbara rode home again and lay on her bed. She tried to study but her mind and emotions were in too much turmoil to take much in.

Her father tried to help by keeping her busy and by getting her to cook the evening meal. Because it was the middle of the exam period she was not allowed to go out to any parties or social functions and nor were most of her friends, so she sat at home and watched TV or pretended to study.

She slept badly that night and was restless, anxious, and washed out the next day. Her first thought was to phone Fiona but again the phone rang out with no answer. This left her even more depressed, but she had to accept that her father might be right, that Fiona might just be away for the weekend. From then on Sunday seemed to drag and the only relief was when her father took her for a drive around some of the new suburbs. At Barbara's insistence they drove to Fiona's and Barbara went in to check. But the house was closed up and there was no answer.

This time there were tears and when her father comforted her she insisted that he again phone the police to see if they had any information. But as before there was no news. The police would not say what they were doing, which annoyed Barbara.

Sunday night was another period of tension and distress. In the evening she again phoned both Fiona's numbers but again got no response. As a result she had another night of poor sleep and dimly remembered bad dreams. On Monday morning she woke up feeling drained and apprehensive. Once again, she phoned and once again there was no answer. That put her in a very edgy and depressed mood and she fidgeted around the house, only half her mind on her own preparations for the day.

Feeling utterly wretched Barbara started for school but forgot her school bag and had to pedal back two blocks to get it. As she pedalled, she was consumed by impatience to get to Fiona's to check if she had come home. In her anxiety she pedalled so fast she was panting and perspiring by the time she got there. The house looked exactly the same. Once again, she rang the doorbell and called out. There was no response and her hopes crashed. Sick with worry she pedalled slowly to school.

Lofty met her, a troubled look on his face. "Fiona's not home yet," he said.

Barbara nodded. "I know. I've just checked. I'm so worried."

"What can we do?"

"My dad called the police last night," Barbara said.

Lofty's eyes lit up with hope. "Have they found out anything?"

Barbara shook her head. "They didn't call back. I don't know. Oh Lofty, I'm so worried!" she cried. She felt so upset she thought she was going to throw up.

"We've got a Geography exam now," Lofty reminded.

The two of them walked slowly to the classroom. As they went up the stairs, they met Roger but he had no news. A teacher arrived and they were moved into the exam room and placed one to a desk. Barbara sat and stared out the window. Her vision seemed to swim and she felt exhausted.

A voice beside her said, "Are you alright Barbara?"

Barbara looked up. It was her Geography teacher, Mr Conkey. He was a cheerful, tubby man of middle-age. And he was one of the most important people in Barbara's life because he was also the captain of the school's army cadet unit.

Barbara shook her head. "I didn't sleep very well sir. I'm worried about Fiona."

Capt Conkey looked around. "Fiona? Yes, where is she? She should be here for this exam."

"We don't know sir. She was at home on Thursday but was missing on Friday. And she hasn't been home all weekend. I checked at her house half a dozen times on Friday and over the weekend and again this morning. Her house is all closed up and she is gone."

Capt Conkey's blue eyes were filled with concern. She knew he cared deeply about his cadets. As her emotions welled up, she was unable to stop her own watering with tears.

Capt Conkey said, "That sounds unusual. She didn't say anything to me about going away. Aren't you kids going camping together during the first week of the holidays?"

"Yes sir. Some of the other CUOs from Townsville, Sarina and Broadsound are coming up on Friday," Barbara replied.

"Yes, I know that. You look very down. Do you feel up to doing this exam? I can defer it if you like," Capt Conkey offered.

"No sir. I'll be alright. I will try," Barbara replied. Next to her father she thought Capt Conkey was the nicest man alive, and she felt very grateful for all he had done for her over the years.

He smiled. "Good on you! I'll keep it in mind when I mark the paper. I tell you what I'll do. While the exam is on I will check with the office and see if they know where Fiona is."

Barbara smiled. "Thanks sir." She felt a surge of affection.

The exam was started and Barbara was able to settle down to solid work with an easier mind. She noted Capt Conkey leave the room and felt much happier and more optimistic.

As soon as the exam was over Capt Conkey met her on the veranda. Lofty and Roger joined them. In their capacity as the cadet platoon commanders they met constantly with him. They had all served in the cadets for four years and there was a strong bond of shared experience.

Capt Conkey was now as worried as them. "I've checked with the office. They know nothing about why Fiona is absent. I've had them phone her home and also her father's work address. All they could say was that Mr Davies is on sick leave. I have to say that I am surprised and worried. I'm going to ask the principal to make an official enquiry to the police."

"My father phoned them last night," Barbara said. She explained what her father had been told.

Capt Conkey pulled at his chin. "Hmmm. Yes. Well, we aren't relations, but the school certainly needs to know where she is in an official capacity. Come on."

They followed him to the main office. He went in to see the principal. A few minutes later he re-appeared and went to the school's records computer. The office lady typed for a few moments and both peered at the screen. A printer chattered and he took a copy of Fiona's Personal File back into the principal's office.

Ten minutes later Capt Conkey came out. "Okay. The principal has made an official request to the police to find out where Fiona is. I will let you know as soon as we have something, provided it isn't confidential."

Barbara heaved a sigh of relief. "Thank you, sir."

Feeling much better she went downstairs to tell Wendy. On the way she detoured to the tuck shop as she suddenly felt very hungry. After a good lunch she felt even better.

There was another exam that afternoon. It was English and Barbara was able to relax and let her pen flow. She managed an essay of five pages plus a critique of a play and an analysis of a poem during the two hours. When she came out of the room, she was sure she had done well.

She went directly to Capt Conkey's staffroom and asked if he had any news about Fiona. He was busy marking exam papers but at once went with her to the office to ask. His face as he came out of the principal's office told the story. Barbara felt her heart lurch.

Capt Conkey shook his head and said, "I'm sorry Barbara. The police have contacted some relations, but they do not know anything. The police have now begun an official investigation. They have checked the house and found nothing suspicious."

Capt Conkey tried to sound optimistic, but Barbara knew him too well.

"You don't sound too sure sir," she said.

"No. Well, we can only hope. The police have a lot on their plate. I'm sure they will do their best."

"Thanks sir," Barbara said. Hastily she turned and walked away before he could see the tears forming. She didn't want him to see his senior platoon commander cry.

None of her friends were in the school yard so she got her bicycle and pedalled to Fiona's. There was still no-one at home. By this time Barbara was imagining the worst and was deeply distressed. She went home and sat deep in thought, considering all the possibilities.

Her father found her sitting in the lounge room when he came home. "What's this? Sitting in the dark!" he said, turning on the light.

Barbara looked up in surprise. She had not noticed the evening shadows. Her father came and sat on the sofa beside her and gave her a gentle hug.

"What's the matter old girl? Is your friend still missing?"

"Yes Dad. I asked at school. Capt Conkey went to the principal and the school notified the police. The police contacted some of Fiona's relations, but they didn't know anything. She is still not home. I checked. Oh dad! I'm so worried."

"Well, let's hope the police find something," her father said, patting her hair.

"Oh dad! You sound just like Captain Conkey. You are trying to re-assure me but you don't think the police will find her. I can tell!"

Her father was silent. He pursed his lips and nodded. "Sorry, Bubs. I was just being realistic. The police have lots of things to worry about and lots of people go missing. I don't want to alarm you but I read in the paper a few weeks ago that 15,000, or maybe it was 17,000 people, go missing in Australia each year. Most go missing deliberately and about 90% turn up again after a short while."

Barbara considered this but did not find it at all heartening. It sounded an incredibly large figure and after a moment's thought she was even more depressed.

"But that is hundreds of people every day!" she cried.

Her father agreed. "That's right, but it is Australia wide, not just in one place. Fiona is probably the only person reported missing in Cairns today."

"And her dad," Barbara replied. She had vivid flashbacks to when she had run away three years earlier and how the cadets had saved her from the escaped criminals who were going to rape her.

Her father shook his head. "People go missing for lots of reasons," he pointed out. "Young people like yourself running away from home, criminals on the run, debtors, husbands deserting wives, or, in this case, vice-versa." He paused for a moment and Barbara sensed the bitter regret in his voice. "Or people who are kidnapped or murdered."

That was the black pit Barbara had been brooding over already and another look into it only deepened her depression.

"The police won't find her," she said flatly.

"They might. Or she might just be with her father and quite safe. Now stop working yourself into a fit of the dejections and come and help me prepare dinner. How did your exams go today?"

He hoisted her to her feet and led her into the kitchen and resolutely changed the subject.

For Barbara it was an awful night. She was so worried she could not concentrate to study, and she was poor company for her father. That he was also concerned on her account was obvious. Over supper they sat and discussed the situation again, but it was just raking over old bones.

Barbara went to bed thoroughly depressed but, to her own surprise, slept soundly all night. The last two days had quite drained her.

She woke the next morning feeling fresh and happy and it was only while preparing her breakfast that she remembered, with a guilty start, that she had quite forgotten Fiona. She at once descended into gloom. Before she left for school, she dialled Fiona's numbers but there was no answer. She then telephoned the police and asked if they had learnt anything.

The policeman at the other end was very polite. "Are you a relation, Miss? No? Only a friend. I see. All I can tell you is that are enquiries are proceeding."

Barbara hung up, feeling resentful and angry. She felt that the adults weren't taking things seriously enough. As far as she was aware there hadn't even been anything broadcast on the radio or TV asking people for information.

She rode to school feeling sick at heart and annoyed. On the way she passed Fiona's but did not stop. The house was still shut up. At school she met Wendy and they discussed the situation for a few minutes before going to their respective exam rooms. The exam was Modern History. At the door Barbara met Capt Conkey, who was her teacher for that subject.

"Have you heard anything about Fiona Barb?" he asked.

Barbara was disappointed. She had been hoping he might have news. The question needled her anxiety into anger.

"No sir. I phoned the police, but they wouldn't tell me anything because I'm not a relative. I don't think they care. It is just another job to them. I don't think they are trying hard enough," she snapped.

"Now Barbara, be fair. You don't know what the police have done," Capt Conkey chided. "I'm sure they are doing their best."

"Well I'm not!" Barbara cried, stamping her foot. To her mortification a large tear formed and trickled down her right cheek before she could prevent it.

Capt Conkey pretended not to notice. "Even so, you'd better calm down. Fiona wouldn't want you to spoil your exam by getting upset."

Feeling quite wretched Barbara nodded. More tears came. She pulled out her handkerchief to dab at them.

Capt Conkey asked, "Do you feel up to sitting the exam?" His face clearly registered his concern.

"I'll be alright sir," Barbara replied. She made her way to her seat, blew her nose and composed herself. Roger gave her a sympathetic greeting from the next row.

As was usual the teacher who set the exam supervised the last hour. This was Capt Conkey. As he collected the papers for marking, he told Barbara she was wanted at the office straight away. On seeing her face light up with hope he shook his head.

"It is the police. They want to interview you as part of their inquiry," he explained.

Barbara went with Capt Conkey to the principal's office. There was a male constable there who looked only a few years older than herself. It reinforced her perception that the police weren't treating the matter very seriously.

Her feelings were further aggravated while she was being introduced.

She noticed the way the young constable's eyes appraised her. His gaze travelled rapidly from head to toe, then lingered on her bosom. She pursed her lips from resentment and sat down, hunching forward and folding her arms to make her breasts less noticeable. His attitude made her hostile.

Men! she thought angrily. *They're all the same!*

In the presence of the principal and Capt Conkey Barbara told the policeman all she knew. It appeared she was the last person to have seen Fiona. The constable wrote it down and asked a few questions, his eyes straying from time to time to her legs or breasts. Barbara was so annoyed she could barely restrain herself.

"Have you interviewed all the neighbours?" she asked.

"Yes Miss. Well, most of them. A few weren't home when we called," the constable replied.

"And what about this church, this religious cult? What have they got to say?"

"I can't tell you that," the young policeman replied.

He looks embarrassed, Barbara thought. *They haven't asked these religious people anything. They probably didn't even know about them until I mentioned them a minute ago!*

Angrily she snapped, "Who are they anyway?"

The constable went poker-faced. "I'm sorry. I can't say," he said.

"That's because you don't know! In twenty-four hours you haven't found out anything. You aren't trying! And Fiona could be in terrible trouble!" she cried.

The young policeman reddened with embarrassment. Capt Conkey and the principal both spoke up to calm the situation. Barbara pressed her lips together to stop them trembling. Then she said, "I'm sorry. I'm very worried, that's all."

Capt Conkey nodded. "So are we, even if we don't show it," he replied.

The young policeman agreed, "We will do all we can to find her," he promised. Barbara sniffed and gave him a doubting look.

After the interview she made her way downstairs to where her friends were waiting. Roger stood up as she approached.

"You don't look very happy," he observed as she joined them. "No luck I gather?"

"That's right, I'm not happy," Barbara replied. "I don't think the police are really trying. Finding Fiona is just one more routine chore to them. Well it isn't for me. I'm going to find her!"

"How will you do that?" Lofty asked.

"I will ask her neighbours and I will go and see these religious people," Barbara replied.

"Be careful Barbara," Wendy cautioned.

"I will be. Who is going to come with me?" Barbara asked.

"We've got exams this afternoon," Dan Russell reminded.

"So have I. I'm going as soon as school is finished. Who will come with me?"

Roger, Lofty and Wendy all said they would. Dan and Pat Sheehan, the Company Sergeant Major, both said they had things on after school. Dan had to go home and Pat had a part-time job.

At 3:30pm the four pulled up outside Fiona's house and parked their bicycles against the fence.

Chapter 3

THE SMILEY PEOPLE

"Right," Barbara said, "Roger, you go and ask the neighbours on that side. Wendy, you and Lofty go and ask at the houses across the road. I will ask at the house on this side."

They dispersed to this task. Barbara went to the same house as previously. In answer to her knock the woman came to the door. The woman scowled and muttered, "Oh it's you again. What do you want this time?"

"I wondered if you had remembered any more about Fiona and her dad?" Barbara replied, trying to keep her irritation at the woman's manner from showing on her face.

"No I haven't. What are you asking for? I've just had a policeman here asking the same thing. What have the Davies been up to eh?"

"Nothing. They are just missing," Barbara replied.

The woman sneered. "Bah! That Mrs Davies, she was a right tart that one. She had a real string of gentlemen callers. Every day I would see them. It's a wonder it took the silly man so long to twig what was going on," she replied.

Barbara blushed. She didn't want to hear the woman's ugly gossip. "So you don't remember seeing anything unusual on last Thursday evening or Friday morning?"

"I told you that didn't I!" the woman snapped. She rudely shut the door in Barbara's face, leaving her seething with dislike. She returned to the street and met Roger.

He shook his head. "No luck. They didn't notice anything."

Barbara nodded. She was amazed how quickly her hopes could turn into fears. Her emotions shot up and down. Chewing her lip with anxiety she stood beside Roger and watched Lofty and Wendy walk towards them.

Lofty spoke first, "The lady over there said she saw a car here on Sunday afternoon: a large white car driven by a well-dressed man. She said she had seen it here before and recognised the man. He is in his

29

thirties, good looking, suntanned, fit, with a short haircut. He was wearing a suit and tie; a light grey suit."

"Did Fiona go with him?" Barbara asked.

"No. He went inside. When the lady looked later she saw the man drive off alone."

"Did she tell this to the police?"

"Yes. She said a young constable had been around only an hour ago," Lofty replied.

They stood for a minute considering this.

Roger asked, "So how do we find a man in a grey suit in a white car? White cars are the most common on the road."

Barbara chewed her lip. It certainly was a problem. It seemed they were pushing at a wall of nothingness.

Wendy spoke next. "I'll bet he was from that religious group," she offered. They all looked at her so she went on, "Well, who else would be wearing a suit in Cairns on a Sunday afternoon?"

"Yeah, that'd be right," Lofty agreed. "Now, how do we track this character down?"

"Go to his church?" Roger suggested.

"But we don't know where it is," Wendy said.

Inspiration came to Barbara. "We can look in the phone book," she said, snapping her fingers. She was filled with an urge to move.

"My place," Lofty said. He only lived in the next street.

A few minutes later they were seated in the lounge of Lofty's house with their heads together over the Telephone Directory. Lofty flicked the pages, mumbling as he did, "C... C... Ch... Church... here we are, 'churches'," he said.

Barbara ran her finger down the column. "Church Resource Directories... No, Church of Christ... No. It didn't have a name like that."

"What about 'The Church of Jesus Christ of the Latter Day Saints'?" Wendy asked, pointing.

"No, they are the Mormons I think," Roger replied. "The one we are looking for isn't an established church. It's some new sect."

"Church of the Modern Apostles?" Lofty read.

"No." Barbara bit her lip again. She could not see anything that sounded right. She read down the column, then went back to the top of the page, "Christian Education Centre... No, Christian Literature Crusade...

No, Christian Outreach Centre..." She paused and shook her head. "No. Christian Projects... No. It's none of these."

She could not find a name that seemed right. That left her feeling baffled and dejected.

"The police will know," Lofty suggested.

"They won't tell us," Barbara replied.

"Maybe this cult has another name," Roger put in. "I mean, we don't even know if they are Christians." He pulled the book towards him, his forehead wrinkled in concentration.

"Look under 'Guru'," Lofty suggested.

They did but there was nothing listed. Then they searched under words like 'Faith' and 'Gospel'.

"Gospel Centre ... No; Gospel Chapel... Oh! How can we tell?" Barbara cried.

"We could phone them all and ask," Lofty suggested.

Roger clicked his fingers. "I know. I'll go and ask Father George. He might know."

"Who is he?" Lofty asked.

"My parish priest," Roger answered.

"Oh Roger! That's brilliant," Barbara cried. She knew that Roger was one of the few people her age who actually went to a church and who was brave enough to say so. "Come on. Let's go!"

"Hang on!" Lofty said. "Look at the time. I'd better ask my mum first."

Wendy looked at the clock. "Heavens! Four thirty. I'd better get home or my mum will start to worry."

A few minutes later Barbara set off with Lofty and Roger. Wendy went the other way. As they pedalled quickly along Lofty said, "You go to church don't you Roger?"

Roger nodded. "Yes. I am a regular church-goer,"

"Are you Catholic?"

"Anglican," Roger answered.

Lofty nodded. "Just wondered. This Father George, who is he? Have you known him long?"

Roger smiled and said, "I've known Father George all my life; or rather he has known me. He Christened me."

By then they had reached the church buildings and they parked their

31

bikes against the fence and Roger led the others unhesitatingly to the door of the Rectory.

Father George was middle-aged, chubby and cheerful. He welcomed them in. Roger acted as spokesperson and explained the situation. The priest listened and nodded, then said, "I know the group you mean, and the man as well. They go under the nickname of 'The Smiley people' or 'The Happy People', because of their badges. They make all sorts of promises about saving souls and bringing happiness, not only in the life to come but in this life as well. I don't like to think ill of people or want you to think I am being jealous of another religious group, but I have grave doubts about them myself."

"Why is that Father?" Roger asked.

"I've heard a few stories. I know it is not fair to listen to stories and people will just say it is professional jealousy or rivalry, but a couple of my parishioners have had experiences with these Smiley People. They come across as all friendly and loving but I suspect they are not sincere. In one case I know of, they befriended a very distressed woman. She thought they were wonderful. They visited her in hospital, organised people to keep her yard and garden and feed her pets and sent her cards and flowers. After she came out of hospital, they drew her into a social group which gave her emotional support and friendship. She was very grateful and happy."

Father George paused and shook his head. "Then she was asked to make donations to help with the sect's expenses. She says they were very nice about it but when she told them how little money she actually had the visits and social calls died away. After a while they stopped visiting. At least that was her experience."

Lofty asked, "So you think they just befriend people for their money?"

"It is a suspicion," Father George replied.

Roger asked, "Is Fiona rich?"

Barbara nodded. "Her dad has a lot of investments, real estate and shares and things like that, on top of his income as a Barrister."

"Yes, they've got a nice house. They don't look poor," Lofty agreed.

Roger turned to Father George. "Are these Smiley People Christians Father?"

"After a fashion. From what I gather they believe in a mixture of things: mostly Christian but with bits of Hinduism. There are also hints of Voodoo and Black Magic. It is that aspect which worries me most."

"Voodoo? Isn't that from the West Indies?" Lofty asked.

"Yes. Originally from Africa. The Negro slaves brought it with them, and their descendants still worship it in some places, notably in Haiti," Father George explained.

"Voodoo!" Roger exclaimed. "Aren't they the mob that believe in zombies? You know, the walking dead, like we saw in that horror movie."

Father George nodded. "Yes, that's right. Although there is no evidence such things as zombies actually exist. At least no-one has ever been able to produce one for examination by non-believers," he replied. "They also go in for witchcraft, spells and trances, with lots of drum music, dancing and sacrifices."

"Sacrifices!" Barbara gasped.

"Oh, only goats and poultry and things like that," Father George reassured her. "I've never heard of them sacrificing people."

Barbara curled her lips in distaste. "It sounds disgusting. I can't imagine Fiona or her father being involved in that sort of thing," she said.

Father George nodded. "I agree. We have digressed. I only said there were hints of Voodoo and Black Magic. Several members of the sect are West Indian Negroes."

"The man who visited Fiona wasn't black," Barbara said.

"No. From the description he is the 'Reverend', sorry if I smile when I use the title; I doubt if he earned it at a reputable theological college; the 'Reverend' Simon Ditchburn. He is their local man,"

"Is he the Great Onjumbo?" Lofty asked.

"No. The Grand Oojoombie is the sect's leader. He is some sort of prophet or guru type person," Father George replied.

"Who is he? Where is he?" Barbara asked.

Father George shook his head. "I don't know. I don't think he is here. The sect has its headquarters in America. I know they have a branch in Florida. As for who the Grand Oojoombie is, I can't tell you. I've never heard his name or seen a picture of him. He's not like those charismatic leaders who make a personality cult part of their faith."

"You mean like the Baghwan and so on?" Roger asked.

Father George nodded. "That's right."

"You seem to know a lot about these people," Barbara said.

"It is my business to protect my flock," the priest replied. "Know thine enemy the Good Book says!"

"So you don't like them?"

"No, I do not. Nor do I trust them."

"But you have no proof," Lofty challenged.

"No direct proof; only circumstantial and hearsay," Father George agreed.

"You said the Reverend Simon whatever was their local man. Have they got other people in Australia?" Roger asked.

"Yes. They have set up a whole network of branches in all the capital cities. It has been causing some concern to the church. These people also have some sort of Commune or 'Faith Centre for Joy' up near Kuranda. That seems to be their main base in Australia," Father George explained.

"This is all very interesting," Lofty said, "but it may have nothing at all to do with Fiona's disappearance."

Barbara disagreed. "It has! I'm sure of it," she said. She felt quite certain of that. "Besides, it's the only solid clue we have."

That made them smile. Father George said, "Like the man searching under the lamppost because the light was better."

"But you said Fiona wasn't interested in religion," Lofty reminded Barbara.

"She wasn't. It was her dad. And this Reverend Simon Dickburn was at her house the day she went missing," Barbara said.

"Ditchburn," Father George corrected.

Barbara blushed. "Yes, him. Do you know his address Father? I'd like to ask him a few questions."

"I do. He has a house in Mooney Street."

"Mooney Street!" Roger laughed. "Get it? Moonies! Remember them? They are some sort of religion, aren't they?"

"Yes Roger," Barbara replied flatly. She wasn't in the mood for jokes. She stood up.

Father George showed them to the door. "Now, you children be careful. Don't just barge in asking silly questions or making a lot of accusations. Keep in mind that there may be no mystery at all; that your friend might not be with these people; or might have gone with them of her own free will. In that case it is none of your business and you should respect their privacy."

34

"Yes Father, thank you," Barbara replied. She led the way downstairs. As they collected their bikes Roger pointed to his watch.

"It's after five o'clock. I'm going to have to go home."

Lofty agreed, "I'd better go home. Let's postpone this until tomorrow. None of us has any exams then."

Barbara was most reluctant to do this but knew her own father would start to worry if she was home late. She had several kilometres to pedal and, as it was 'winter', darkness would be setting in by 6pm.

She pedalled part of the way with Lofty, then said goodbye and set off on her own. But she had not gone far when the thought came to her: *If I detour a bit I can ride along Mooney Street. It's not far out of my way and it won't hurt to have a quick look.*

Having thought of it she was then consumed by curiosity. What did this Reverend Simon look like? What did the house look like?

At the next intersection she turned left.

Chapter 4

REVEREND SIMON

When Barbara reached Mooney Street she realised she had been along it hundreds of times but had not taken note of its name. It was a typical Cairns residential street, wide and with a wide grass footpath on each side. It was lined on either side with trees and with a mixture of high and low-set houses. Most had nice gardens. The footpaths were neatly mowed lawn.

Barbara picked out the house almost at once, the low-set one third along. She had seen it many times, but it had nothing particular about it to mark it apart from its neighbours. As she pedalled past, she looked out of the corner of her eye, pretending no special interest.

In the driveway beside the house was a white car. Someone was at home! "Should I stop now and ask about Fiona?" Barbara muttered. It was a powerful temptation. Torn by indecision she rode on past the next house then stopped. She dismounted and looked back.

Should I or shouldn't I? He's home now; or someone is. He may not be there tomorrow. But what will I say? I can't just ask or he will get suspicious. And what if...? No, I'm being silly. I'm on my own and nobody knows where I am.

Fretting with indecision she looked around. Not a soul was in sight. The evening shadows were already making it quite gloomy under the trees. At that moment the front door of the house opened. Barbara felt her heart leap in fright. For a flustered moment she stood there feeling guilty. Then she bent down to pretend she was doing something to her bike.

To her surprise a youth in the uniform of her school came out. He stood on the doorstep talking to someone inside.

Why it's that stuck-up dead-head Cyril from 11B! Barbara noted. Then it clicked. *Of course! He's always going on about religion and putting up posters advertising revival meetings and visiting evangelists.*

A man appeared in the doorway: slim build, fit, grey trousers, white long-sleeved shirt and tie, clean cut. *Could be described as handsome,* Barbara considered. *Bit hard to tell at this distance. I'd better get going or they will get suspicious. I don't want Cyril to recognise me. Oh blast! Now I've got grease on my fingers!*

Keeping her head averted Barbara mounted and rode on, not daring to look back. She was sure their eyes must be on her. It made the back of her neck come up in goose bumps. Thankfully she turned the corner and increased speed.

Heavens! The streetlights are on. Dad will be worried.

Spurred on by that worry she pedalled as hard as she could and was home within five minutes. Her father turned from the stove to greet her as she ran upstairs. He was busy cooking. The smell of frying onions filled the air.

"Hello Bubs! I was starting to worry about you. How did it go today? Any news of Fiona?"

"No Dad. Sorry I'm late. I'll have a wash and tell you after tea," Barbara replied.

After the meal father and daughter sat and faced each other over the kitchen table. Mr Brassington considered what Barbara had just told him, then said, "I think you'd better leave it all to the police. They are obviously now on the job," he said, adding, "I don't want you taking risks or making trouble."

"No Dad, I wouldn't."

Her father leaned back and laughed aloud. "No Dad! You wouldn't! You never get into trouble! Not much! What about those escaped convicts a few years ago? Or the bloke you shot at Bunyip River during cadet camp last year? Or the two pig hunters who kidnapped you before Christmas? Never mind that maniac who tried to abduct you at Mount Mulligan two months ago! You have been in more strife than any other person I know!"

"Fair go Dad! I didn't ask to get into trouble," Barbara replied.

"I know. It just seems to seek you out. That's why I'm worried now. Don't you go stirring up more, particularly with religious types. They tend to be a bit fanatical and irrational."

"I want to find Fiona," Barbara answered stubbornly. She could feel her temper rising.

"I know. Leave it to the police. They are paid to do it and know what they are doing. Now, how did your exams go today?"

"Don't change the subject, Dad."

"I'm going to. How did your exams go?"

"Okay," Barbara replied. She reluctantly described each exam. "Capt Conkey said he would take Fiona's disappearance into account when he marks the papers," she added.

"That's decent of him. Now, what about these friends of yours who are coming from the south for this camping holiday; are they still coming?"

"I think so," Barbara replied. She realised with a guilty start that she had quite forgotten about them over the last few days.

Her father said, "If they are due to arrive on Friday you had better check. That is only three days away."

"Oh Dad! Karen Harvey, she's a CUO from Heatley Cadet Unit in Townsville, is supposed to be staying with Fiona on Friday night!"

"You had better get on the phone right away. She can stay here. Who are the others?"

"Jennifer Bladen, she's a CUO from Sarina Cadet Unit. She is staying with Wendy. The other one is Gordon Farr. He is a CUO from Broadsound. Do you remember him?" Barbara asked anxiously.

Her father nodded. "Of course I do. He saved you from that revolting pig-hunter."

There were a few moments of silence while memories of that dreadful experience flooded back. Barbara had gone to the Bunyip River Army Camp the previous December for her 12 day Cadet Under-Officers Course. While there she had met and fallen in love with Gordon.

Was it love? Or was it just strong emotion? She pictured Gordon as she remembered him: tall, tanned, muscular and healthy, a good-natured grin on his handsome, friendly face. Those clear blue eyes. She sighed. They had not seen each other since. It was just too far and there had been no opportunity. They had written and Gordon had phoned and said he loved her, but...

Barbara shook her head. *We don't really know each other at all,* she mused. Several times she had feared it had just been a fleeting holiday romance. Now she wasn't sure how she felt, other than a bit apprehensive. *No, I'm a little scared,* she admitted.

It had been Fiona's idea to invite the other cadets to come up for an unofficial camp during the first week of the June school holidays. She said it would be a good chance for them all to get together, but Barbara suspected she was really trying to 'match-make' her with Gordon.

Barbara had let her do the planning. In the end only three had said they would come. Now it was all spoilt. Fiona was missing.

Barbara's father interrupted her thoughts, "Don't worry. It will all work out. If it's not love it will soon be obvious."

"Oh Dad! It's not like that," Barbara replied, blushing crimson.

"Of course it is! And so it should be at your age. True Romance, that's the thing. We all need it," he said with a grin.

Barbara smiled but detected the far-off look in her father's eyes. It twisted her heart. Poor Dad! He still loved mum and missed her terribly, even after four years and in spite of all the pain she had caused him.

He needs love more than I do, she thought. Barbara wasn't even sure if she wanted it at all.

Her father asked, "Do you have a program for this camping trip?"

"Not in detail, Dad. We were going to wait till the others got here and see what they wanted to do," Barbara answered. She knew it was an enormous vote of confidence by the parents to allow them to go off camping, boys and girls together, without direct adult supervision.

"You'd better make those phone calls. I'll do the washing up," her father said.

Barbara went to the phone with her address book. For a full minute she sat, composing herself and working out what to say. Then she started. Karen Harvey first, she would be the easiest to tell.

Forty minutes later it was done. Each had been pleased she had phoned. Each had said they had just been about to call. All were still coming on the bus on Friday, and all were surprised at Fiona's disappearance. Jennifer had sounded very upset. Gordon? He had sounded cool and detached. Did he care?

Barbara then dialled Fiona's number. Still no answer. She then rang Wendy to tell her of the latest developments. The two girls talked for half an hour until Wendy said her dad was grumbling she was sending him poor and wearing out the wires.

Barbara made herself a cup of coffee and sat in the lounge to think over the day's events. She felt very tense and deeply worried. The coming visit by the other cadets, particularly by Gordon, was just added stress. She wasn't really looking forward to it at all. Rather than go camping she felt she just wanted to find Fiona.

That night she lay awake for a long time. She could not remember when she had ever been so deeply troubled. It was Gordon's impending arrival, she decided, that was at the nub of her fear. Was she queer? Did she prefer women to men? True she had been strongly attracted to Gordon last December. And she had been glad when he had embraced her then.

"But I would have welcomed almost anyone's embrace at that time," she told herself, remembering those awful moments when the pig-hunters had her prisoner.

I would have hugged anyone who rescued me, she told herself.[1]

She had rejected all male advances since then. In most cases she had found them so repugnant she had felt physically sick.

How will I react to Gordon if he wants to kiss me? I feel ill now, just worrying about it. And what if he wants more? What will I do if he suggests sex? she worried.

Barbara writhed in her bed at the thought. To test her reactions she ran her hands ran down over her breasts and waist. She tried to imagine how she would react.

I'm not even sure if I will ever want to do it or not! she moaned. Tears came. It was at times like this she most missed her mother. Who could she turn to for comfort and advice?

Not dad. That would be unfair. Oh!

Sleep slowly claimed her but it was a restless night from which she woke feeling wrung out and tense. Wednesday was to be another day of exams but was also the day on which the cadets had their two hour 'Home Training' parade. That required Barbara to do some lesson preparation and that helped keep her mind occupied. As she had every other morning, she tried Fiona's phone before she left home and then she rode her bike there.

On the way she again rode along Mooney Street. As she passed the Reverend Ditchburn's house she studied it as carefully as she could without making it obvious. But there was no sign of anyone there and it looked closed up. The car that had been in the driveway the previous afternoon was gone. But thinking about Cyril Wenkle gave her the germ of an idea.

When she got to Fiona's Barbara placed her bike against the fence and went up to the front door. Just knocking made her heart feel like lead and she had a horrible sensation that things were very wrong. There was

---

[1] Read *Barbara in the Bush* by C. R. Cummings.

no answer, so she made her way to the back door. As she did another ghastly thought came to her. It was one that had fleetingly crossed her mind before, but which was so horrible she had resisted thinking about it. Now she did. As she walked around the house she made a conscious effort to sniff to see if there was any odour of death.

She had never smelt a decaying corpse but she had read what it should smell like, so she made the effort. To her relief there was no unusual odour. She was relieved but the actions and the ugly idea behind it made her feel nauseous. But it so upset her she had to pause at the gate and lean on the fence while her stomach heaved and her heart and breathing steadied.

Then Barbara rode on to school and another maths exam. This one was mostly geometry, and she did it easily. As soon as she was released from the room after the exam Barbara hurried to where her friends gathered. Lofty, Roger and Wendy were there but they had no news. Once again Barbara's hopes slumped, and she had to fight back tears.

By this time her emotions were so sensitive that it took very little to upset her. Thus, when Willy strolled over to join them a few minutes later with Marjorie on his arm Barbara felt a sharp stab of hurt. While Willy and Marjorie stood talking to them Barbara ran her eyes over Marjorie and experienced a deep sense of insecurity.

Marjorie had pasty white legs which were thick at the ankles. She had a broad waist and big boobs and her face was only average pretty and covered with freckles. And her mousy fair hair had its usual rumpled rat's nest look. Barbara considered herself to be far more beautiful than Marjorie, yet Willy had chosen Marjorie.

Why? What's wrong with me? Barbara thought. But despite her jealousy, she liked Marjorie and was able to talk to her easily.

"Are you going to this Air Cadet Banner Parade in Sydney Marjorie?" she asked.

Marjorie shook her head. "No. My drill's not good enough. They only picked four from each squadron."

Barbara knew that Marjorie was a corporal. She asked, "Are you going on a promotion course?"

Again Marjorie shook her head. "Not in June. We only run our CUOs Course in June. I have to wait till next January to do my sergeant's course."

At that Lofty laughed and said, "Then Willy will be safe for a couple of weeks!"

The others laughed and Marjorie poked her tongue. She said, "I will be at Garbutt too. Instead of a promotion course we have a GST camp."

"GST?" Lofty asked.

"General Service Training. I will be doing my ATA Course," Marjorie replied.

The cadets discussed the differences between army cadet and air cadet training for a while before Willy said, "Do you have any news of Fiona?"

At that Barbara burst into tears. Wendy and Marjorie both hugged her and the boys looked at each other. After a minute or so Barbara calmed down and they again discussed what might have happened to Fiona. But she was undecided what to do.

The afternoon session was taken up with another exam, this time Ancient History. Barbara really enjoyed the subject and had no doubts that she did well. It seemed to be over quickly, even though the session was three hours long.

After school was the cadet parade. Normally this was one of the highlights of the week for Barbara but this parade she found distressing because of Fiona's absence. This was really noticeable when they did the first parade and the officers lined up on the side. The gap where Fiona should have been was a depressing reminder and seeing it again caused Barbara's eyes to well with tears.

But she wasn't going to cry in front of her platoon, so she bit her trembling lip and braced up. When the officers were fallen in by Capt Conkey she was dry eyed and straight backed. She was able to march on and take over from Dan, now in uniform and in his other role of platoon sergeant. He gave her a sympathetic look as he saluted, and Barbara managed a wry grin in return.

The training was easy. Period 1 was Drill for the platoon. Dan did this. During that Capt Conkey took the platoon commanders and section commanders for a map planning exercise on how to do a recon patrol. Second period was map reading for the cadets, taught by Barbara. Third period was administration for the up-coming Senior Exercise. Twenty of the leaders were attending and Capt Conkey wanted them well prepared. He emphasised that they needed to be fit.

"I know that the CUOs are doing some hiking with packs next week to get ready. I recommend that you all do a lot of walking. Major Wickham usually includes a twenty-kilometre march as part of his exercises and they usually cover seventy or eighty kilometres in the seven days," he said.

Having done two Senior Exercises with 130ACU Barbara knew that and normally she would have relished the challenge. But this time she felt like lead in the stomach and the usual excitement was missing.

After cadets the friends briefly discussed Fiona but as it was already 1745hrs and getting dark they did not linger. Barbara rode quickly home, her mind still full of ugly possibilities and a few vague ideas of how to find out more. That evening she was at a bit of a loose end. Exams were over so there was no study. Instead she watched TV and read. Then she lay on her bed and agonized over what she could do to find Fiona. Once again, she was moved to tears but she stifled these so as not to upset her father.

At length she fell into a restless sleep. This was broken by a nightmare. She dreamt she was walking next to a swamp (was it at Centenary Lakes near the cemetery?) when a hand emerged from black, slimy water. Fear rooted her to the spot. Then a head surfaced. She knew at once it was a dead body, but it was rising up, wading towards her. A zombie! She tried to cry out, but her throat choked up. She tried to run but her muscles refused to move. The hideous thing, all green and black rotting flesh, moved inexorably towards her. Its hands went up in a strangler's grasp. She tried to scream but a gasping moan was all she could achieve.

Barbara woke up to find herself sweat-soaked and shaking. It was 4am. By an effort of will power she calmed herself. Then she made herself pluck up the courage to walk through the darkened house to go to the toilet. Back in her bed she felt the terror rising again and she was sure she would remain awake for the rest of the night. Instead she lapsed into a deep, dreamless sleep.

Her father roused her at 7:30am. "Wake up sleepy head. You will be late for school."

"Mmmm. Doesn't matter. We've finished all our exams. Nothing much will happen today," Barbara replied.

"Never mind. Up you get. I'm off to work. See you this afternoon," her father said. He bent and kissed her cheek and gave her hair an affectionate ruffle, then left.

When her father had gone Barbara had a shower. Afterwards she stood in front of the mirror nude and critically examined herself. It was a fully developed woman's body she saw. There was still a hint of adolescent awkwardness, but she knew she was on the threshold of womanhood. Gently she ran her hands over her skin. It felt very pleasant and she enjoyed the sensation.

But is it a man's hands or a woman's hands I want to do it?

That reminded her of Fiona. They had certainly never been intimate in any way physically, and Barbara had never imagined or wanted any such relationship but she had had some uncomfortable thoughts. Without bothering to dress she went to the phone and dialled Fiona's number. There was no answer. Feeling sharply dejected she next phoned the police.

They were quite blunt. She was told they were continuing their enquiries and that was that. The rebuff made Barbara see red. She snorted and slammed the phone down. Simmering with anger she walked through to the kitchen and prepared her breakfast, still naked and enjoying the sensual pleasure of being so.

By twenty past eight she was dressed and on her bike pedalling towards school.

I'll just check out the Reverend Simon's place on the way, she thought. So she turned into Mooney Street. As she rode along the street, she saw that the car was in the driveway. *He's at home. I should ask him now. He might be out later,* she thought.

She knew it was a silly risk for her to go to a man's house on her own but she seemed to be drawn to it. On an impulse she stopped and parked her bicycle against the fence then walked up to the front door. By then her heart was pounding furiously and her palms had gone sweaty. She wiped them on her skirt, straightened her blouse and tried to calm her breathing.

Nervously she knocked.

There was no immediate response. For a few moments she felt relieved and considered walking away. Instead she forced herself to knock again, harder this time. Only then did she notice the button for a door bell.

Even as she pressed it she heard footsteps. She felt foolish as well as scared. The door opened. A man stood there in a shiny light grey suit.

He is handsome, Barbara thought. But she also felt his welcoming smile was a bit artificial. She cleared her throat and asked, "Hello. Are you the Reverend... er... the Reverend Simon... er." She couldn't remember his surname.

"Yes ma'am, I surely am," the man replied in a very pleasant Southern American drawl. "And whom do I have the pleasure of meeting?"

"I'm Barbara Brassington. My friend... is...Cyril (Cyril what was his name?)...Wenkle is a friend of mine. We go to the same school. He suggested you might be able to help."

"Oh sure. I am always ready to help," Reverend Simon said, "Would you like to come in?"

He really has a nice voice. Maybe I'm mistaken? Barbara thought. Then she cautioned herself. *No. He'd have to be convincing to be a con-man.*

But there was no way she was going into a strange man's house. Feeling a mild stab of fear she said, "No thanks. I can't stay long. I'll be late for school." She was annoyed at feeling such a surge of flustered panic.

Reverend Simon gave her a smile which displayed a set of shiny white teeth. "How can I help you?"

"I was interested in your church. My friend said they were very nice people and a great comfort to her. I'm well, I'm in a lot of trouble and I come from a broken home, and I don't know where to turn."

The lie came easily to Barbara's lips, and she was ashamed of herself.

The Reverend Simon wrinkled his brow. "Her? I thought you said Cyril was your friend?"

"Oh, I did. He is," Barbara replied. She cursed herself for being careless. "It was another friend who said your church was very helpful."

Reverend Simon smiled again. "That's nice. One of our missions is to help people. That is the main aim of my ministry, praise the Lord!"

Barbara's mind raced, trying to think what to say next. "Could you tell me more please? Perhaps I could attend your services? When are they? I..." She stopped and pretended to be upset and to cry; and found she didn't have to act at all. She burst into tears.

"Now, now! Dry your eyes my poor lamb. Here, I will give you the times of our gatherings. Our Bible study groups and prayer circles we hold most often, as well as group therapy sessions for people in need to help each other," Reverend Simon said soothingly.

He sounded very friendly and his voice filled with such warm sympathy that Barbara began to relax. She wiped her eyes while he opened a briefcase and took out a small pamphlet. On the top was a small 'Smiley' face logo. He said, "Here are the times. We usually meet here but sometimes at the houses of friends. We are only a small church yet but we try to be one happy family. We believe there can be joy in this life too; if we smile a lot and help each other. Now smile and see if you don't feel better." As he said this, he flashed another smile.

Barbara found the set of perfect white teeth a bit off-putting, but she couldn't help it. She smiled back. To hide her confusion she glanced at the timings on the pamphlet.

Reverend Simon pointed at a time. "Here, 7:30 this evening. That is a social gathering for young people like yourself. That might be a good introduction."

"Oh! I don't know. I am a bit shy," Barbara replied.

"Come with your friend. That will make it easier. Is she a member of our church?"

"I'm not sure. She might be," Barbara said.

"What is her name?"

Barbara had been hoping he wouldn't ask that. She cast around for a suitable name but finally answered, "Fiona."

"Fiona? I don't know any Fionas," Reverend Simon replied. "Fiona who?"

"Fiona Davies."

"Sorry, never heard of her."

Barbara noted the change in the man's voice, a distinctly harder inflexion. *Am I imagining it? Or did his eyes go hostile above that plastic smile?* she wondered.

There was a moment's uncomfortable silence, then Barbara said, "It might have been her father then, Harry Davies?"

"Sorry. Don't know him either. Never met him," Reverend Simon replied brusquely.

"You do so!" Barbara said. "Fiona told me. She said you used to visit them often."

"You are mistaken. I don't know these people; and I have never been to their house," Reverend Simon insisted. The smile was gone now. Reverend Simon radiated irritation.

"You have so! You were seen there last Sunday!" Barbara cried angrily. She only just bit back the accusation of 'liar'.

Reverend Simon looked hard at her. "Excuse me. I have business to attend to. I don't think I can help you." He stepped back, gave Barbara a searching stare and closed the door firmly.

Barbara stood on the doorstep, seething with anger; mostly directed at herself. *You fool! You stupid person! Why did you mention Fiona?* she mentally berated herself. *Now I won't be able to go ahead with my plan to infiltrate the sect. Oh, if only I could control my temper and my tongue!*

Furious at herself she walked back to her bicycle and pedalled off, sure she was being watched. "What a Mister Smoothy! He was lying, I'm sure. He does know Fiona. And he must know where she is!"

But how to find out?

Chapter 5

A CHANGE OF PLAN

On her way to school Barbara again detoured to pass Fiona's. The house was still closed up but she was resigned to this now and was not so sharply downcast. She did not stop to check but pedalled on to school.

The bell was just ringing for morning classes when she arrived. Lofty, Roger and Wendy were waiting for her.

Wendy ran over to her as she wheeled her bike in the gate. "Where have you been Barbara? You are late," she said.

"I've just been to see the Reverend Simon."

Lofty joined them. "What did he say?" he asked.

Barbara began describing the meeting. At that moment, grumpy old Mr Burgomeister came along and growled at them, "You people are late for class. Get moving!"

"Yes sir," Barbara replied. "I'll tell you all at morning break."

She headed for her classroom with Roger and Lofty. Once there she sat in her usual seat. The seat beside her was vacant. It was where Fiona usually sat. Lofty sat there instead and Roger sat behind them.

"Keep going Barb. Tell us," Lofty insisted. In spite of annoyed glances from the teacher Barbara continued describing how the Reverend Simon had reacted. The class was English and their teacher, Mrs Ramsey, had already marked their exams and was returning the papers. She then began to discuss how students could have improved their marks.

After a few minutes Mrs Ramsey stopped her dissertation to the class and turned to the friends. "If it is so interesting Barbara, why don't you share it with the whole class?"

"Sorry, Miss," Barbara replied. She sat and tried to curb her impatience until the end of the lesson. Her own paper had been awarded an 'A' but the fact barely registered.

Between periods she completed her story. Lofty then said, "So you reckon the good reverend knows something?"

"I do. His manner changed so abruptly the moment I mentioned

48

Fiona's name. He tried not to show it but it did. He was lying, I'm sure. He knows where she is, and I think I do too."

"You do! Where?" Roger asked.

"At this Commune of Joy place near Kuranda," Barbara replied.

Lofty looked doubtful. "Maybe. What proof have you got?" he asked.

Barbara shrugged. "None really, but unless she's locked up in a house somewhere, where else could she be?"

"Lots of places," Lofty replied. He said it so flatly and with such a dejected expression Barbara couldn't help reaching out to touch his arm.

"Don't lose heart Lofty. We will find her."

"How?" Lofty said. His voice broke as he said it.

Barbara could see he was fighting back tears. "I am going to look for her," she said.

"Barbara! Don't be silly," Roger cautioned.

"I'm not," she replied stubbornly.

"Besides, we don't have enough information," Roger persisted.

"I'm going to get some. I am going to talk to that Cyril Wenkle at morning break," Barbara replied.

"Do you want us to come?" Lofty asked

Barbara considered this. As she did a wicked thought flashed through her mind. "No. I'll talk to him alone."

Roger grinned. "Strewth! I don't like the sound of that Lofty," he said. "I think poor old Cyril is going to be the victim of feminine wiles. Rather him than me."

Barbara flushed as the dart had been close to the truth. "Don't be a nong, Roger. He will talk more freely to one person, that's all. Now let's get to Maths."

At morning break Barbara quickly located Cyril. He was sitting alone reading a book. *Supercilious dork!* she thought as she walked towards him.

She felt a bit ashamed of herself at what she planned but was determined to get the information. In preparation she had hitched her skirt as high as she dared and undone the top two buttons on her blouse.

Barbara stopped in front of him. Cyril glanced up from his reading. From the way his eyes dilated, then travelled upwards, she was sure she had his attention.

In her sweetest purr, she said, "Excuse me Cyril. I'm Barbara."

Cyril blinked and blushed, pretending he hadn't ogled her thighs. "Er... er... yes. Yes, I know."

"Can I talk to you for a moment?" Barbara asked, making her voice low and husky. Without waiting for an answer she sat down so that she was half turned towards him. She leaned forward to feign being very interested, but in reality to allow the front of her blouse to sag open. His eyes instantly swivelled to look. She pretended not to notice.

Cyril blinked and licked his lips. "Wh...what do you want?" he asked, clearly flustered.

"You belong to a religious group, don't you?"

"Yes. Yes, I do," Cyril replied, his gaze alternating between her face and her cleavage. To make it more pronounced Barbara squeezed her breasts together with her arms.

"I've been told they are a really nice church who help people who are in trouble," she said.

Cyril again licked his lips and his eyes flickered from her front to her face and back again. "Yes. Yes, we do. That is one of our most important missions. Are you... sorry, I shouldn't pry."

"Am I in trouble?" Barbara said. She hung her head, ostensibly in sadness but actually to hide a smile. She bit her lip to kill the expression and went on, "Well, I have done some wicked things. But now I want to change and I realise I am not strong enough to do it on my own. I need friends who will help me instead of pulling me down. I heard your group were the sort of people who might help me."

Barbara raised her head, pretending distress and even managed to make her eyes water. Cyril began to talk earnestly and excitedly about what a wonderful church he belonged to. Barbara was easily able to keep him going with expressions of interest and some more lavish praise. Cyril became quite eloquent about the 'Happy People' and their 'Way Stations on the Road to Joy and God'.

The flow of information and evangelising became a bit much for Barbara very quickly, but it was what she wanted to know. Even so she felt uncomfortable and ashamed of herself as she could see his eyes continually flicking to the front of her blouse and he kept licking his lips.

You poor bastard! she thought. *You think I'm a fallen woman and you think you can save me, then have me. You are having evil thoughts which your 'goody-goody' religious conscience is tormenting you over!*

Barbara endured his enthusiastic monologue for ten minutes, frequently smiling and nodding. It rapidly became obvious that he was a humourless fanatic with all sorts of peculiar ideas and obsessions. Several times she had to restrain herself from laughing at the way the jargon words came out: 'Praise the Lord', 'Thanks be to God', 'Saviour', 'Path to Enlightenment and eternal happiness'. He said these things with such apparent sincerity she was amazed.

When the bell went to return to class, she asked him if she could talk to him again at lunch time. He preened himself and smiled and said yes.

Barbara went off to her own class, adjusting her clothing as she went. Roger met her at the door.

"How did it go?" he asked.

"Incredible. It was like listening to a recording of a revival meeting. I'm going to talk to him again at lunch time. I'll try to pump him for information then."

"That's what he's hoping he can do to you, but not for information," Roger replied.

Barbara pursed her lips. "Don't be crude, Roger."

"Fair go, Barb! We could see what you were doing. Lofty had to bite his thumb to stop laughing out loud at the way poor old Cyril was pretending not to ogle down your blouse."

Barbara blushed. "Yes, well. I'm not very proud of myself."

"All in a good cause. Don't feel bad about it," Roger replied.

The next class was Geography. Capt Conkey was their teacher. He handed back their exam papers and proceeded to go over the answers with them. Barbara noted that she had done well, a borderline between an A and a B. However, her mind was busy sorting out the clues she had gleaned about Fiona, so she barely listened.

At the end of the lesson, Capt Conkey called the two CUOs over. "Any news of Fiona?" he asked.

"No sir," Barbara replied. "We were hoping you might have some."

"Sorry, no."

"Well, I'm going to keep on looking. I reckon I know where she is," Barbara said.

"Oh yes! Where?" Capt Conkey queried.

"At the commune these Smiley People run near Kuranda."

Capt Conkey looked worried. "Why do you think that?" he asked.

51

Barbara explained what she knew, but didn't mention the conversation with Cyril.

Capt Conkey frowned. "Now see here Barbara, even if she is at this commune it may be of her own free will and with her father's permission, if not actually with him. You can't just go poking your nose into other people's business."

"No sir," Barbara replied.

She set her jaw. She didn't believe Fiona had gone missing of her own free will. They had been close friends for too long for Fiona not to have said something about it. Not to even hint what she was going to do was completely out of character.

Capt Conkey set his mouth in a firm line. "No sir indeed! Don't you get all stubborn Barbara, and don't you go off and do silly things like barging into this commune. You leave it to the police. I will make sure they know about it. Which reminds me, I spoke to the OCs of the other cadet units on the phone last night about their cadets who are coming up here for the holidays. They have asked me to keep an eye on them, even though it is not an official cadet activity. Do you lot have some sort of itinerary or plan?"

"Not yet, sir. We were going to decide when the others get here. We are meeting the bus tomorrow evening and will then meet at my place to discuss what they want to do," Barbara replied.

"Where were you thinking of going?"

Barbara paused then made a wry face. She couldn't deceive Capt Conkey. He had been too good to her over the years.

"Kuranda," she murmured.

"Oh are we!" Roger exclaimed. "I thought we were going to the Mulgrave Valley."

Capt Conkey laughed. Then he looked Barbara straight in the eye. "Kuranda, eh? Just remember what I said."

"Yes sir," Barbara replied. But she blushed as she did because she had every intention of disobeying Capt Conkey.

During the lunch break she sought out Cyril again. As she walked towards him his face lit up in what she assumed was a hopeful smile, causing her a twinge of guilt. She did not normally use people. She was also annoyed at Lofty and Roger who could be seen squirming with mirth in the distance.

It took her twenty minutes to lead Cyril's verbal flood around to discussing the local Smiley Organisation.

"There is our Pastor, Reverend Simon. You'll like him," Cyril said.

Barbara had to smile at that. She gathered that Reverend Simon was the only member of the Smiley 'clergy' in Cairns, but that there was another in Kuranda and more at the commune.

"What's this commune?" she asked.

"It's a wonderful place. Everyone is friendly. They help each other and share. It is where we all want to go," Cyril explained enthusiastically.

"Where exactly is it?" Barbara asked.

"Somewhere up near Kuranda."

"How do you get there?" Barbara persisted.

Cyril looked worried. "I'm not sure. Only those who are baptised to the 'Third Order' are allowed to go there. The location is kept secret."

"Why?"

"Because we suffer a lot from people who are jealous of our happiness, or who fear our truth. There are many religious bigots who harass us. We even have to hire security guards to protect ourselves."

Barbara was surprised by this. "Have you been there?" she asked.

"No. I am only baptised to the 'First Order'," Cyril replied. "But soon I'll be raised to the 'Second Order'. I'm being re-baptised this weekend."

Cyril stopped and seemed to go into a trance of ecstasy. He stared past Barbara as if she did not exist. She waited for a moment, then leaned forward and put her hand on his arm.

Cyril jumped as though he had been burned. He stared at Barbara's breasts, and she saw a blush suffusing his ears and cheeks. To increase the pressure she placed her hand on his thigh. In a husky voice she asked, "How do you get raised from one order to the next? Is it very hard?"

"You must learn the words of the Grand Oojoombie by rote and know their mystical meanings. I am going on Saturday to do my pilgrimage where more of the secrets will be explained. We must do a walk on foot to make the flesh suffer, as a penance, and as a precursor to joy. It will go on for a day or two. Along the way we will be instructed and tutored, then tested. At the end we will be re-baptised at a special ceremony. After that there is to be a Festival of Happiness. I am told that the Grand Oojoombie himself will be there."

As he spoke Cyril's voice rose and rose in volume until he was almost shouting. Barbara was amazed at the emotion the boy was expressing. The words 'fanatic' and 'ecstasy' flitted at the back of her mind.

"Where does the pilgrimage go Cyril? It sounds really interesting," she asked, leaning forward and moving her arms to cause her breasts to bulge up.

Cyril stared at them, and his mouth hung open for a moment, his eyes glazed with lust. He licked his lips before answering, "I don't know. In the mountains somewhere. We are told it will be hard. All I know is that it starts at Kamerunga on Saturday morning."

"What time do you start? Can I come?"

Cyril looked concerned. "No. This is only for the novitiates of the Second Order. We will be taken there in a bus. I can't tell you anymore. I shouldn't have even told you that?"

Barbara smiled and moved her arms again, noting the shifting of his gaze as she did. His reactions made her feel both amused and ashamed. But she kept on with the tactic, saying, "That's alright. It was my fault. I won't tell. What about this festival, can I go to that?"

"It is at Kuranda but I'm sorry only baptised members can attend. We include secret ceremonies which outsiders are not allowed to observe. They are wonderful. They..." He paused and watched as Barbara crossed her legs, her skirt pulling right up her thighs. After licking his lips again he said, "Don't be sad. There will be other festivals. If you join us now, you could be initiated into the First Order by the September holidays."

Kuranda! Barbara thought. *I am definitely going to Kuranda, no matter what Capt Conkey or anyone else says,* she decided. In the hope of gaining more information she tried a few more questions, even asking about the Grand Oojoombie.

"Who is he?" she asked.

"He is our spiritual and mystic leader," Cyril replied.

"But who is he?"

"That is a secret," Cyril replied stiffly.

"Why?"

"To protect him. Lesser men and unbelievers threaten him. They are jealous and fear his powers," Cyril replied pompously.

Barbara must have let her scepticism show on her face as Cyril frowned. She decided she had learnt enough. *If I keep on asking questions, he will get suspicious,* she thought.

Now feeling distinctly uncomfortable under his lascivious gaze and at her own underhand tactics she said, "Thanks Cyril. That has all been very interesting. I've got a lot to think about. Thank you." She stood up.

Cyril gave her an oily smile. "I am happy to talk anytime," he replied. "I would like to see much more of you."

I'll bet you would! Barbara thought. Annoyed both with him and with herself, she snapped, "You've seen enough already! Goodbye. See you again." With that she turned and walked off.

Roger's head appeared around the corner of the next building then vanished. When she got there Barbara found him and Lofty clutching each other in convulsions of mirth.

"Here she is! The biblical temptress, Delilah!" Lofty cried.

"Jezebel, or Salome," Roger corrected.

Lofty shrugged. "One of them. Poor Cyril. What did you learn Barb?" he asked.

Barbara shook her head. "That he is a real dork. That he's a single minded, humourless fanatic, who's just full of himself, and a hypocrite. He spent all his time leering at me," she replied.

She then noticed that Roger and Lofty were trying not to look at her. That reminded her to adjust her clothing. She did this and felt no unease at the two boys watching. She was more embarrassed by the frown of disapproval she detected on the face of a Year 8 girl who was passing.

The friends joined a group of other cadets sitting under a tree: Wendy, Pat Sheehan, Don Blake, Dan Russell, and Allison Ashton. For the next quarter of an hour she related all she had learned.

When she finished, Lofty said, "How can Fiona be at this commune place if only these Third Order people are allowed there?"

"I don't know. But I still think she is there. I think she was taken there." Barbara replied.

Pat frowned. "Do you mean kidnapped?" he asked.

She nodded, and Loft said, "So what can we do about it?"

"I'm going there to find out," Barbara replied.

Roger shook his head with evident disapproval. "Barb, remember what Capt Conkey said," he cautioned.

Barbara set her jaw. "I know. And if this commune is really all innocent then no harm will be done. Anyway I'm going. I don't care what anyone says."

"You aren't going on your own," Roger replied flatly.

"I will if I have to," Barbara replied defiantly.

Lofty met her eyes. "You don't have to. I will come with you."

Roger nodded. "So will I," he added.

Barbara looked from one to the other. She felt a surge of emotion and had to blink back tears. She wanted to hug them both. "That's fine. Who else is coming?"

"I'd like to," Wendy said. "When are we going?"

"What about tomorrow? It's only the last day of term. There won't be any work done and no-one will notice," Barbara replied.

Lofty recoiled in mock horror. "Miss Brassington! You surely aren't suggesting we play truant? What about your academic career?"

Barbara swore. It was something she did so rarely it emphasised to the others just how strongly she felt. "Stuff school! Finding Fiona is ten times more important," she said heatedly.

"How are we doing this?" Roger asked.

Barbara turned to Lofty. "Do you think you might be able to borrow your dad's car? We could drive up to Kuranda tomorrow morning then."

"Where's there? We don't even know where this place is." Lofty answered.

"Yes, we do. It is near Kuranda somewhere."

"But where near Kuranda, on which road?" Lofty persisted.

"We can find out. People will know. We will ask when we get there," Barbara replied.

"We could find out from the Local Government offices or the government," Dan put in. "My uncle works for the Department of Natural Resources. They have that sort of info."

"Could you ask him?" Barbara asked eagerly.

Dan pulled a face. "Yes, but we need to go to town now. And I couldn't just ask a favour. I think you have to pay a fee."

"So? I'll pay. I don't care what it costs to find Fiona!" Barbara cried.

Roger looked worried. "What about this afternoon's lessons?"

Barbara snorted. "They don't matter! School isn't as important as Fiona. Besides, if we are taking tomorrow off as well the school won't do anything to us till after the holidays. You don't have to come. I will go on my own."

"We are coming," Lofty said.

Roger again shook his head. "There's no need for us all to go," he pointed out.

"So I will go with Lofty," Barbara said. "What about you Dan?"

"Yeah, I'll show you where. I'm only skipping Maths and I did okay at that."

"Let us know please," Roger requested.

Barbara nodded. "We will. Meet us after school so we can plan tomorrow," she agreed.

"Where?" Roger asked.

"My place." Lofty said. "It is the most central."

When the bell rang to return to classes Barbara, Lofty and Dan left school and pedalled their bikes to the main business area. At the government offices it took them a while to locate Dan's uncle. He queried why they weren't at school but only in a good-humoured way. Then he helped them to do a Title Search. This was complicated by the fact that they didn't have a survey map with its numbered allotments.

But the computer had maps on it and quickly found the numbers to look for. Dan's uncle pointed at the numbers and said, "There are two properties listed under the sect's name, this one here, and this other one, north of Kuranda."

He indicated them and Barbara made notes on a slip of notepaper, and they stared at the coloured computer map.

"What about this one?" Dan said, pointing to a small sub-division Southwest of Kuranda.

"That's not very big. It looks like it is only a house. It isn't big enough to be a farm or commune," Barbara said in disappointment.

"This other one is much bigger, a few square kilometres from the look of it," Lofty said, indicating an area well north of Kuranda. The property was wedged in between a State Forest, a Timber Reserve, and the sea.

"That looks more likely. We need a topo map to relate to," Barbara said.

"To the map shop. You got any money left?" Lofty asked.

"A few dollars," Barbara replied. She counted them, "Only six."

"Won't be enough," Lofty replied. He dug in his own pocket and found $5.20. Dan contributed $1.75.

"How much do we need?" Barbara asked.

57

"Fifteen dollars," Lofty replied.

Barbara felt a stab of disappointment so sharp she found she was on the edge of tears. The trivial obstruction to her search caused her emotions to boil. Frustration, anger, and depression coursed through her.

Lofty said, "I'll go and ask my dad. He just works down in the next street."

"In the street?" Dan quipped. "I thought he worked in an office!"

Lofty snorted and swung a mock punch at him. Barbara asked, "Won't he wonder why you aren't in school?"

"Probably. Don't worry. His policy is that I do what I like, but I pay the consequences. He trusts me," Lofty replied. He set off at a brisk walk.

Barbara forced a smile at Dan's weak attempt at humour. "Come on, let's select the maps we want," she said.

They walked to the map shop in Absell's Arcade and studied the wall charts listing the maps. These showed maps on different scales with their reference numbers.

"Let's look at a CAIRNS 1:100 000 and a KURANDA 1:50 000," Barbara decided.

They asked the very helpful shop proprietor for these and compared them with the Land Survey Map.

"I think we also need the next map up," Dan said.

So they also asked for the MACALISTAIR RANGE 1:50 000. This was spread out and they studied it. Lofty re-joined them.

"How's it going?" he asked.

"Good. What did your dad say?" Barbara asked.

"Asked me if I was playing the wag. I said yes and added that I was chasing a pretty girl. He just laughed and told me I'd need more than ten dollars in that case and gave me twenty, and some fatherly advice which I won't repeat in your pink little ears," Lofty answered. "Have you found this Joy camp?"

Barbara pointed. "Here, this area between Ellis Beach and Yule Point. I think this property must be the commune."

"It's a fair way from Kuranda," Lofty noted.

Barbara looked at the wall clock. "We will buy the two 1:50 000 scale maps. I'll pay you back Lofty. Now, let's go to your place and decide on a plan."

Wendy and Roger were waiting for them at Lofty's.

"Did you find the commune?" Roger asked as they trooped upstairs.

"Yes, we think so," Barbara replied.

"First things first," Lofty interrupted. "Let's have afternoon tea."

"Here, here!" Roger heartily agreed.

Ten minutes later, fortified with cordial, cakes and biscuits the friends sat around the maps which were spread on the dining room table. Lofty set to work with pencil, ruler and protractor to transfer the boundaries from the survey map to the topographical map.

"What's the plan Barbara?" Wendy asked.

Barbara thought for a moment, then said, "We could just drive to Kuranda and then follow this road going north, the Black Mountain Road." She traced her finger along it. "There is a side road here going to the commune. We could park the car and walk in."

"Why not drive all the way?" Dan asked.

"Because if Fiona has been kidnapped that would just alert these Smileys that we were looking," Barbara replied.

"Why should she be kidnapped? Why would they do that?" Roger queried.

"I don't know. But why else would Fiona just vanish?" Barbara replied.

This led them into a dispute over whether Fiona was following her father to Sydney or not. Barbara stubbornly insisted she was going to visit the commune.

"We can sneak in through the jungle," she said. "Then they won't know we have been there at all." They all understood what she meant. All had been trained in fieldcraft and the art of reconnaissance by the cadets.

"Are you serious?" Dan asked in astonishment. "You mean trespass on private property and spy on people?"

"Yes," Barbara replied.

They were silent for a moment while they considered this. That Barbara was determined was obvious to them all. They knew what she was like once she had set her mind on something. Lofty leaned over to study the map and did some quick measurements.

"If we really want to get in unseen, we could walk in from the sea. That would be only about half the distance. We could drive north along the Cook Highway to about here and go up this ridge."

"That means climbing over this mountain, Mt Burton," Roger said.

"All the better. They won't expect that. You don't have to come," Barbara replied.

Roger met her eyes. "I'll come. When are we doing this?"

"Tomorrow."

Wendy spoke, "But we have to meet the kids coming from the south tomorrow."

"That is not until the evening. We shouldn't take that long," Barbara replied, brushing aside the objection.

Lofty sucked his teeth. "I don't know. If we go up Mt Burton it is 600 metres. That will take an hour or two each way. Then it is 2 kilometres through the jungle. It could be slow going."

"We won't be carrying a pack, just water bottles," Barbara replied. "And there are tracks shown. We should be able to do it."

They settled to more detailed consideration of timings. Lofty said, "Don't forget we are supposed to see Capt Conkey tomorrow to give him a detailed program for our hike."

"Hike? I thought we were going camping," Dan said.

"No. It is a hike now," Barbara replied in a firm voice.

Wendy looked surprised. "If we are going hiking instead of camping, we need different gear. What about the kids from the south?"

"That's okay. I phoned them last night and told them to come prepared for cross-country marching," Barbara replied.

"Cross-country marching!" Roger cried. "I had visions of us lolling in the shade beside a cool stream."

They all laughed at that. Lofty said to Barbara, "I might have known. We are just pawns in your devious plans."

"Lofty you aren't!" Barbara replied. She met his eyes and felt a surge of affection and guilt. She did take her friends for granted sometimes, and they were good friends. Her eyes watered and she looked down at the map.

Lofty patted her shoulder. "It's okay Barbara. We don't mind. We agree with you."

She looked up and met his smile. He went on, "I want to find Fiona too. Now, let's plan tomorrow. It will mean an early start."

"Do we tell our parents?" Wendy asked. "I will have to explain why I'm not going to school. I... I don't want to... don't want to deceive them."

That made Barbara feel uncomfortable. She didn't want to be

responsible for people telling lies. 'Wagging' school that afternoon had been bad enough. "You don't have to. You can go to school."

"No way! If you go, I go!" Wendy said.

"We all do, parents or not," Lofty agreed. Barbara felt another surge of affection. She reached out and placed her hand on Wendy's arm. Tears prickled her eyes. She tried to hide them but Wendy leaned over and put her arm around her.

"It's okay Barb. We understand. We feel that way too," Wendy said. She hugged Barbara and the two of them had a good cry. Barbara found it very comforting. After a couple of minutes she squeezed Wendy with her arms, then wiped her eyes.

"Thanks. Now, I have an idea. We can do two things at once, that is if you can get the car Lofty, and don't mind a bit of extra driving?" She raised an eyebrow.

Lofty grinned. He had obtained his Driver's Licence the previous month and was very proud of his driving ability. "That'll be fine. What's the plan?"

"We do a recon of this commune from two directions at once. You drop some of us off near the turnoff on the Black Mountain Road. Then you drive back down the Kuranda Range and drop the rest of us on the coast road at Casuarina Beach. Then pick us up later."

Lofty studied the map and did some calculations. "It's a half hour drive to Kuranda. Then it would be half an hour each way along the Black Mountain Road. It would be nearly two hours before we dropped the second group. Then we would have to repeat that in the afternoon. It can't be done between 8am and 3pm. You'd never get over that mountain in time."

Again Barbara felt the sharp stab of disappointment. Her search for Fiona seemed to be thwarted at every turn. It made her angry and even more determined.

"We need two cars," Roger said. "Who else has a car?"

They pondered for a moment. Dan sat up suddenly. "Pat Sheehan drives to school."

"I'll ask him," Dan offered. "Can I use your phone Lofty?"

Chapter 6

MT BURTON

A few minutes later Dan put the phone down. "That's fixed. Pat is happy to help. He and I will go up the Black Mountain Road. I know where to go. I've been up there before with my old man."

"It's a pity Pat can't come on our hike," Lofty said.

"Why can't he?" Wendy asked.

"He has to work for his father during the holidays," Lofty replied.

Barbara turned to Dan. "Will just the two of you be enough? Should one of us come with you?"

"No. Two will do. You lot go over Mt Burton."

"What about maps?" Lofty asked.

"We will buy some tomorrow before we go," Dan answered.

Lofty turned to Roger. "You okay to go over this mountain Roger?"

Roger pursed his lips at the implication his chubbiness made him soft. "I've climbed plenty in the past," he said stiffly.

There was a moment's tense silence. Barbara knew that what he said was true. For years Roger had been the member of a group of four boys who nicknamed themselves 'The Hiking Team' and they had done many expeditions. The other three boys had been a year ahead and had now left school. She broke the tension by asking what other details they had to decide. It was agreed they would meet at school at 3pm the following afternoon to compare notes. Once all the details were agreed they dispersed.

As she pedalled her bicycle home Barbara felt much better. At last they seemed to be doing something, to be making real progress.

Her dad noted her improved mood and asked if she had heard good news about Fiona. Barbara shook her head. "No Dad," she replied. Then she hesitated. She didn't want to lie to him, or even to deceive him by omission. But she knew he would forbid her to do a reconnaissance of the commune. So she said, "I'm just looking forward to seeing my friends from the south again."

"I hope you all have a good camp," her father said.

Barbara nodded and met his eye. "Thank you for trusting us to go camping alone."

Mr Brassington wiped his hands on a dishcloth and faced her. "It is the only way, Bubs. If I haven't taught you to make sensible decisions by now, then it has all been a waste of time. Besides, if you wanted to play up you could just sneak away at any time."

There was an awkward silence for a moment. Her father broke it by asking about her exam results. Barbara related these and helped set the table for tea. Afterwards she washed up then phoned Karen Harvey from Heatley. Karen wanted to know if there was any news of Fiona. She said that her disappearance had been in the local news on TV. The police were appealing for information. Barbara mentioned this to her father later and he showed her an article in the *Cairns Post*, complete with a photo of Fiona. That jagged fiercely at Barbara's emotion.

It wasn't a very good photo but seeing it made Barbara choke up and tears came. Her father patted her shoulder. "There, you see, the police are working on it."

Barbara nodded but privately she thought that all the newspaper article showed was that the police didn't have a clue. It strengthened her resolve to search.

That night she had the best sleep in a week. She woke fresh and alert. As she showered, she thought of what the day might bring, and her mood changed to butterflies of apprehension in her stomach. They were going to sneak into the commune, and Gordon was arriving on the bus. That thought made her look down at her body. She studied her body and pondered what might develop. This left her confused and worried because she didn't know what she wanted, or would allow.

When her father left for work, she said to him, "Don't forget we have to meet my friends at the bus terminal at 6:45 this evening, Dad."

"I won't Bub. Have a good day at school. See you later," her father said. He kissed her cheek and went out.

Barbara blushed at her deceitfulness but set her jaw. *It is for Fiona,* she told herself.

She waited till her dad had driven off then quickly changed from school uniform into jeans, an old jungle green shirt, cloth hat and her army boots. She stuffed a change of clothes, cut lunch and a water bottle into a haversack. Then she checked she had her mobile phone, map, compass, protractor, pencil, assorted small items such as First Aid kit and a pair of secateurs. From long experience she knew that trying to hack a path through the jungle with a machete was a fool's game. It was noisy, inefficient and exhausting. The trick was to slip through the stuff with a quiet snick now and then with secateurs or scissors to cut a vine or a 'wait-a-while' tendril.

At 8:15 Lofty arrived driving his father's car. Barbara ran down the steps and hopped in. They drove to school to collect Roger and Wendy, both of whom were in school uniform with their bush gear in their school bags.

As they opened the car doors Barbara asked them, "Are you sure you don't mind getting into trouble?"

Roger snorted. "We won't get into trouble. It's the last day of term. Half the school was absent yesterday and it'll be worse today. No-one will even notice, and in two weeks time the admin will be too busy to worry about it," he said.

"Okay, let's go," Barbara said. She suddenly felt light-hearted and excited. They were off! They would find Fiona, she was sure of it!

Their route took them north across the Barron River and through Smithfield and along the Cook Highway. As they drove Barbara eyed the wall of jungle-covered mountains on their left.

Fiona is somewhere up there, she thought.

Determined to do things properly Barbara opened the maps and began to follow their progress in detail.

At Buchans Point the coastal plain ended. The car crested a rise and there ahead of them was the sea. The mountains fell steeply down to a fringe of beaches and rocky headlands. It was a glorious North Queensland winter day with not a cloud in the sky. The sea sparkled blue and inviting. The highway swept down to hug the base of the mountain. The Coral Sea sparkled in the morning sun on their right.

It was a beautiful drive. Barbara had done it many times and never tired of it, but this time her eyes were directed up the steep slopes on her left rather than at the sea. The car raced past Ellis Beach and on northwards. For the first time Barbara observed that the mountainsides were not covered with rainforest but were in fact quite open: dry savannah woodland, more grass than trees. The grass was dry and brown and there were numerous exposed rock faces.

At length they arrived at Casuarina Beach where there was a small settlement: a kiosk, some holiday huts and a caravan park.

"We'd better park here and walk," Lofty said. "I don't want to leave the old man's car parked on a bush track all day and come back to find it gone."

"No fear. We need wheels and things to get home," Roger agreed. As locals they held jaundiced views about the morals of the hordes of tourists who passed through the area.

The car was parked under a large tree across from the kiosk. Roger and Wendy went to nearby change rooms to put on their bush clothes. Lofty sauntered over to the shop and purchased four soft drinks while Barbara studied the map. She tried to pick out the ridge they planned to go up. Lofty handed them all a soft drink and Barbara smiled and said, "Thanks."

Good old Lofty, she thought. *He is always generous and helpful.*

It was 9:15 when they started walking. There was so much traffic on the highway they walked along the beach back past the caravan park, which was nestled among a grove of palm trees between the beach and the highway.

It was pleasant walking along the beach. A gentle breeze blew in from the sea. Small waves swashed up the golden sand. Sunlight sparkled on the wave tops. The triangle of a sail moved slowly across the pattern of shimmering blue sparkles well out to sea. The white sand of the beach ran uninterrupted and deserted for nearly a kilometre to where the highway curved around the base of a rocky headland. The four friends chattered happily as they walked. When a small dry creek led down across the beach Barbara consulted her map for the twentieth time and pointed.

"This is the one," she said. She peered up at the mountainside. The vegetation looked fairly open until near the top which was crowned by a dark mass of jungle.

Roger studied the slope and cried out in dismay, "Strewth! That looks bloody steep."

It did. But Barbara didn't hesitate. Fiona was up there. She led the way across the highway and plunged into head-high guinea grass at the bottom of the slope.

Five minutes of pushing into this convinced her she wasn't winning.

"This is no good. The grass is too hard to push through. Back out and we will go up the creek bed," she said, wiping perspiration and grass seeds off her face.

"I'm glad you said that," Roger agreed. "Anything could be lurking in this bloody long grass." (By 'anything' he meant Taipans and other large deadly snakes, but none of them wanted to articulate that fear).

Barbara silently agreed. She hadn't thought of snakes till she was actually in the grass and she had instantly regretted her decision.

They made their way along the highway ten metres to the bed of the small dry creek. It was a jumble of rocks lined with trees but was relatively open and easy going. They set off up it. Within a hundred paces the slope had changed to about 45° and the creek bed comprised either huge water-smoothed boulders or sheets of bedrock. Trees and bushes sprouted from crevices and provided a handhold.

Barbara clambered up as fast as she could go then slowed down as she realised Roger and Wendy were falling rapidly behind. She stopped and waited and realised she was puffing and perspiring herself. Lofty joined her and they watched the other two. Roger was nimble enough for all his bulk but was red in the face. Wendy appeared to be very awkward. Her jeans were obviously too tight, and Barbara couldn't help noticing just how much Wendy really did wobble. Roger stayed with her to help her up the steeper places.

They rested for five minutes, and all had a drink before Barbara's impatience drove her on up the slope. This time she moved at a slow pace, but Wendy still had trouble keeping up. During her struggles to haul herself over the rocks two buttons on Wendy's shirt popped undone, giving more than a glimpse of her breasts. Barbara had to smile at the way the boys both pretended not to notice, particularly Roger who was obviously very interested.

He's a real sweety, Barbara thought watching him give Wendy a helping hand. *It's a pity Wendy likes Lofty instead of him.*

They stopped again after what seemed like only a few minutes. While they had a drink Barbara drew Wendy's attention to the undone buttons. Wendy blushed and did them up but gave an impish smile. Then they resumed their climb. The slope became steeper and steeper so that they often had to haul themselves up hand and foot. The buttons worked their way undone again.

At their next rest Lofty commented, "This is getting a bit dangerous."

Barbara looked up. They were at the base of a sheet of smooth granite which would be a waterfall after rain. "We will have to get out of the creek bed," she said, eyeing the grassy ridges on either side. The covering of grass did not look either very high or very thick.

"Bloody hot!" Roger gasped, flopping down and mopping his forehead. Wendy lay down panting and for the tenth time did up the two buttons. Barbara had a drink and looked at her watch.

"Ten fifteen. And we aren't even halfway up."

"Not even a third of the way," Lofty said, fanning himself with his hat.

Roger groaned and had a big drink. "I've drunk half my water already," he said, measuring the contents of the plastic 2 Litre container he was carrying.

After a few minutes Barbara pushed on. She found it difficult to get out of the creek bed. The slope was so steep she had to haul herself from tree to tree. Her boots kept slipping on dead leaves and loose topsoil. The grass grew in sparse clumps and was mostly blady grass so they could not use it for handholds. The only other things which appeared to grow on the slope were clumps of prickly Lantana and an occasional grass tree.

A hundred metres and five minutes of exertion brought them to a halt again. They sat sweating and gasping on an outcrop of rocks. Wendy was last and her shirt was undone again. She sat down and took off her hat to fan her front. The boys looked away.

"This is hopeless," Roger grumbled. "It's too steep. You slip back as much as you go up."

"At least there's a bit of a breeze," Lofty said. He undid his shirt and held it open to allow the wind to cool him. Barbara wished she could do the same as trickles of sweat were running down between her breasts and her shirt clung to her back.

"It's a good view," she said.

Wendy re-buttoned her shirt and looked. "Oh, so it is!"

They gazed out over a vast vista of sunlit sea. The coastline trended off in both directions as a line of mountains until they vanished in the hazy distance a hundred kilometres away.

"Oh, there's a ship!" Wendy cried.

67

A large bulk-carrier stood out on the horizon like a tiny model. Otherwise the sea appeared deserted. The sailing boat had vanished off to the south.

"What are those islands?" Lofty asked, pointing to two dark elliptical shapes on the horizon to the Northeast.

"Low Isles I think," Barbara replied. She had been there once with her parents. It evoked a painful memory of her mother in a floral swimsuit laughing on the beach with her father, and of her own fear of sharks when she was first introduced to snorkelling.

They struggled on up. 11 o'clock came and went. The day got hotter and hotter. The slope actually got steeper until they had to claw their way up on hands and knees, slipping and cursing. Wendy gave up trying to keep her shirt done up. Dirt grimed their sweat streaked arms and faces.

A wall of exposed bedrock barred their path. They detoured along the base till they found a way round, up a fissure jumbled with rocks. The sight of the fat tail of a Death Adder slipping in under a rock made Barbara move with more caution. She warned the others and kept on climbing. By this time she was beginning to regret the whole plan as unworkable. For a while she toyed with giving up, with going back to the car and driving up to Kuranda and along the Black Mountain Road, or possibly to look at the other Smiley property Southwest of Kuranda.

On top of the rock wall they rested again and enjoyed the view. It was 11:15. Barbara bit her lip, studied the map and did calculations. Her mind told her they would not make it in time at the rate they were going. She could see they were all hot and tired, especially Wendy, and they had drunk nearly all of their water... but... they were at least two thirds of the way up, maybe even more. She studied the terrain. The slope did seem to be less steep. She pushed her doubts aside and stood up.

The going became a bit easier. There were more small trees and a noticeable increase in the number of grasstrees. A false crest raised the usual false hopes. Another rest and another false crest lured them on. Once over this they came abruptly to a wall of rainforest.

This cheered Barbara as it meant they were close to the top. She took the secateurs from her haversack, rolled down her sleeves and pushed into the jungle. It was dry rainforest and fairly open, so they made their way through it quite quickly. The gradient levelled out. Then the slope changed abruptly to a steep jumble of rocks. The rainforest gave way to a dense thicket of stunted trees, all twisted and bent by the wind. The easiest path was up over patches of exposed rock. On these they had a magnificent view along the coast in both directions, from Double Island to Port Douglas and beyond. Cape Tribulation showed as a hazy blue silhouette in the distance.

Suddenly Wendy jerked upright. "Green ants!" she shrieked.

Barbara stopped and looked back. Wendy began to scream and dance around, flailing at her hair and beating at her clothes.

"Aaaargh! Arh! Get them off! Get them off me!" Wendy shrilled.

The others stood in amazement and watched. To everyone's surprise Wendy began tugging at the buttons on her shirt. Barbara couldn't believe her eyes as Wendy stripped off her shirt and flung it aside. Shrieking and whimpering she began to scrape at her skin, trying to reach down the small of her back.

The boys stood gaping in astonished delight as Wendy unclipped her bra and pulled it off. She seemed quite beside herself. Her large breasts jerked and bobbled in the sunlight.

Barbara stared, then sprang into action. "Stop looking, you boys! Turn your backs!" she snapped.

They hastily did so. Barbara stepped beside Wendy and took hold of her arm. She began flicking green ants off Wendy's hair and shoulders.

"Calm down Wendy! They are only green ants. They won't kill you!"

Wendy began sobbing. Barbara shook her arm sharply. "Stop it Wendy! Calm down!"

Wendy looked at her from dilated eyes, then abruptly stopped writhing and stood trembling. "Barbara! Get them off. I hate them!"

"Hold still. There are only a few," Barbara replied firmly.

She proceeded to pick the ants off one by one, working her way down Wendy's back. Some of the green ants were biting and had their nippers firmly embedded in Wendy's skin. Barbara nipped these out with her fingernails. She then realised she had some crawling on herself. She flicked at them. Wendy turned and began helping to pick them off.

Roger brought her back to earth. "Can we look yet?"

"No. Wait a minute," Wendy replied, still brushing at ants on her front and on Barbara's. She suddenly seemed to become conscious of what she was doing. "Oh my goodness! I'm sorry Barbara."

Barbara smiled. "That's okay. Check my back and I'll check yours."

She turned and Wendy brushed her back. She then checked Wendy's.

Lofty cried, "Minutes up. You can look now Roger."

"Don't you dare!" Wendy shrieked.

She giggled and retrieved her clothing and dressed. In the process she hunted down a dozen more ants. As Wendy dressed Barbara tried not to appear interested or aware. Instead she turned away to have a drink. But her heart was pounding and she felt dry in the throat. She wiped sweaty palms and wondered, was that from climbing the mountain or was it in reaction to seeing Wendy? Was she really like that? She shook her head and felt confused.

Misery would have engulfed her if Roger and Lofty hadn't been playing the fool. Lofty laughed and said, "Remember that trick Roger, next time you want to get a girl's clothes off."

"I will. I'll keep some pet green ants in a container," Roger replied.

Barbara had to smile at that but then she looked at her watch. It was nearly midday. The incident cost them ten minutes. As she urged them on, she noticed Lofty check his watch and look at her quizzically but he said nothing.

He thinks we won't make it, she thought. She had doubts herself, but she didn't want to admit defeat.

The rough scrub gave way to more rainforest. There was almost no undergrowth, but the slope was very steep and they kept slipping on the thick carpet of dead leaves. The trees also cut out the breeze, making it very hot.

Barbara felt ready to give up. She bit her lip and checked the time. She looked up, and saw what appeared to be the top. *Oh, I hope that isn't another false crest!* she thought. She pushed her sore muscles hard and another two minutes of panting struggle had them on the crest.

To her surprise she came out on a vehicle track which ran along the ridge top. It was just an un-graded jeep track. Lofty joined her.

"A road!" he panted, wiping sweat from his face.

Barbara pulled out her map. "It's not marked on the map. We are about here, about a kilometre south of the highest point on Mt Burton."

The others joined them and looked around. All they could see through the thick foliage were glimpses of more jungle covered peaks to the West and Southwest. They tried to identify these. Barbara took out her compass.

"Do we go on?" Lofty asked, indicating the time. It was 12:05.

"We will take nearly as long going down," Roger reminded.

Barbara bit her lip. She didn't want to give up. "It is only two kilometres to this commune. It doesn't matter if we are a bit late."

"That is four kilometres there and back, and it is jungle. That could take two or three hours. It could be five o'clock before we even get back to here," Roger cautioned. He had a lot of experience at moving through jungle on previous adventures.

"I want to go on," Barbara replied.

"Why not follow this road?" Lofty suggested.

"It's not going the right way. We don't know where it leads. Besides, we might be seen by someone," Barbara said.

Lofty agreed, "There's been a vehicle along here recently," he said, pointing to tyre marks in the dust.

"This way," Barbara said, setting her compass on 250°. Without waiting to see if the others agreed she stepped off the track into the jungle and began slithering down a very steep slope. It was so steep she slid from tree to tree and used vines to retard her progress. There was little undergrowth and they made rapid progress.

"We have to come back up this," Roger commented gloomily.

"Good exercise," Lofty replied.

"What about lunch?" Roger grumbled.

"Later. When we have found this commune," Barbara replied. "Now keep quiet. We are in enemy territory."

That thought sobered them. Barbara felt tiny prickles of fear up the back of her neck. At the very least they were trespassing on private property, and if these Smiley People really had kidnapped Fiona, then they could be in real danger.

After twenty minutes the slope began to level out and the jungle became thicker. This slowed them down, but Barbara was feeling happier. They had covered at least 500 metres and had come down a long way. They were over the mountain. She now had to use her secateurs frequently and had to continually deviate from her compass course to avoid thickets of spiky bushes and clumps of 'wait-a-while'.

Progress became slow and the minutes seemed to race past. The infuriating and depressing thought that they would run out of time and have to turn back gnawed at her continually. She began to worry that she would cause her friends to be so late they would get into trouble from their parents. It even occurred to her that they might be so late they wouldn't be back in time to meet the bus. She kept checking her watch constantly and bit her lip in frustration and concern. Her determination began to waver.

It was very hot and sweaty, so heat exhaustion loomed as a possible problem. Roger was red in the face and Wendy looked very drawn and tired. Barbara decided they would have to turn back. She was about to voice this when a change in the pattern of sunlight ahead of her attracted her attention. She stayed silent and went on another twenty-five paces.

She came out onto an overgrown vehicle track.

Roger looked along it. "Probably a timber track from the days when they used to haul logs out of the forest," he suggested.

"That was years ago. Wouldn't it be more overgrown?" Wendy said.

Roger shook his head. "Not necessarily. Mr Conkey was telling us about it in Geography. Because the sunlight can't penetrate very well these tracks last for many years," he replied. "I've seen lots like it."

Barbara checked her compass. "It goes roughly the right way. I'm going to follow it," she said. She checked her watch again. 12:45. In her anxiety she chewed at her bottom lip. She knew it was stupid stubbornness to go on.

Roger thought so too as he said, "We are running out of time. We won't get back in time to meet the cadets coming on the bus."

"We can phone them and warn them," Lofty suggested.

"Do you have service?" Wendy asked.

Lofty took out his mobile phone and looked at it. Then he shook his head. "No, no service."

"These mountains must block it," Roger suggested.

Barbara shrugged. "Too bad. I am going on." Walking as fast as she could she hurried along the old track. This ran roughly West down a gentle spur. From time-to-time rotting logs or wait-a-while blocked it but mostly it was easy to follow, a shady tunnel with a floor of dead leaves and sticks. Once she paused as a movement caught her eye. An olive-brown snake about half a metre long slid off into the undergrowth.

Barbara just waited till it was gone and then resumed walking. Brightness ahead indicated a clearing. The track was partly blocked by a tangle of weeds, mostly wild raspberries with vicious thorns on their branches. They cut through these and came out into a plantation of mature pine trees.

"A pine forest!" Lofty exclaimed.

"Looks a bit neglected," Barbara observed, indicating the long grass and tangle of weeds under the trees.

"I don't like pine forests," Roger commented.

"Why not?" Wendy asked.

Roger visibly shivered and made a wry face. "It reminds me of the pine forest behind Mount Baldy near Atherton where we were hunted by those Kosarian Partisans two years ago."

Barbara nodded as she remembered the outline of the tale. "Is that when you and Graham rescued that princess and found a sacred icon?"

"Yes," Roger agreed. Then he shook his head. "I don't want to talk about it. It was horrible."[2]

Barbara saw him shiver and that caused her to come out in goose bumps herself. *A premonition?* she wondered.

But she shook the idea off and resumed walking. The vehicle track became a matt of knee-high grass with occasional patches of bare gravel or sand. Barbara hated walking in the long grass for fear of snakes, but it was easy going and she strode on. They came to a road junction where a side road joined from the left. This was in better condition. The grass had been crushed by two distinct wheel tracks. Barbara noted the track on her map with a pencil, guessing at its position, then continued on westwards.

The track dipped down to a concrete floodway over a small creek. A trickle of discoloured water ran from one overgrown pond to another through long grass.

"This must be Blacksnake Creek," Barbara decided. "That means the commune should only be another few hundred metres."

"Let's have a drink," Roger said.

"Will the water be safe to drink?" Wendy asked.

Roger nodded. "Yes. It is only that colour from algae or tannin or something. There's nothing upstream to pollute it, no farms or mines," he replied. He proceeded to fill his water bottle.

Barbara did the same. She eyed the tea-coloured water with distaste. It was full of suspended black particles of decaying vegetation. But she was very thirsty.

---

[2] Read *Behind Mt Baldy* by C. R. Cummings

It might give me an upset stomach, but I need the water, she told herself. So she closed her eyes and forced herself to drink.

They moved on. Another road junction appeared ahead. Barbara slowed down and moved off the track into waist high grass and weeds beside the trees. The track they were on joined a well graded gravel road at a T-Junction. Barbara looked carefully both ways along the gravel road but could see nothing but forest. She crouched and studied the map.

"Left, or right?" Lofty asked.

"Right," Barbara replied. "I was deliberately aiming off and this track we followed took us even further away. The commune should be just along this road a short distance."

74

Chapter 7

THE COMMUNE OF JOY

Barbara checked her watch. Almost 1300hrs. Time was slipping away very quickly! After another careful look both ways along the gravel road she walked quickly across and into the jungle beyond. The others followed.

She found herself in flat, dry rainforest with an undergrowth of palms which offered plenty of concealment and were no real impediment to movement. She walked fifty paces in till she could just see the road. Turning right she set off as fast as she could walk, using the road as a guide.

After less than five minutes a patch of brighter sunlight off to the right indicated a clearing. Barbara angled over and saw that the pine forest on the other side of the road had given way to a small field of vegetables. This extended back into the forest for about a hundred metres. Two people dressed in some sort of yellow robes were working at the far end. One had a yellow scarf over their head which suggested the person might be a woman, but the person was too far away to be sure.

After a long, hard look Barbara backed into the jungle. Her heart was thumping with excitement. "We must be close," she whispered. The others nodded. Roger looked worried. Wendy looked anxious.

Barbara continued on, followed by the others. The vegetable patch gave way to more jungle across the road. The friends walked a hundred paces, two hundred paces. Brightness showed through the trees ahead. It was a clearing on their side of the road. They moved forward carefully from tree to tree and looked out from under cover.

It was the commune. No doubt about it. A large rectangular clearing in the jungle was studded with huts made of timber and corrugated iron. Rows of large hoop pines and a scattering of fruit trees provided shade. The whole clearing was carpeted with a well-kept lawn and flower gardens.

Barbara put her map away and took out notebook and pencil. She felt a fierce sense of achievement. She began to make a sketch map.

75

The clearing was only about a hundred metres wide but extended off along a gentle ridge to the left as far as she could see. She estimated this at about three hundred metres. There was not a soul in sight. Directly opposite them, standing in a tree-studded lawn, was a row of three small wooden huts. An entrance road led in past them on the other side. A sign near the first hut indicated it was an office. Opposite the huts was more lawn with a wall of jungle beyond. It all looked very pleasant and peaceful.

Barbara found it hard to imagine any sort of evil being present in such a nice place. She whispered to the others, "I'm going to do a recon of this place."

"Have we got time?" Roger asked, indicating his watch.

Barbara saw it was 1:15pm. "I don't care if we have or not. What's the point of coming all this way if we don't have a look?" she replied.

Roger shrugged. "Okay. I was just reminding you," he replied.

Barbara thought rapidly. Along with the other CUOs she had done tactical reconnaissance on exercises, and she knew it would take half an hour or more. It would be 2 o'clock at least before she finished.

Wendy nudged her. "Don't forget Gordon and the other kids coming from the South arrive at six o'clock."

"I haven't," Barbara replied. "I'll tell you what, why don't you and Roger start back. Go as far as where that timber track reaches the edge of the pine forest and wait there."

Roger and Wendy reluctantly agreed. Barbara could see that Roger was hurt by the implication that he was too unfit to move fast but she hardened her heart. The pair set off back the way they had come. Barbara sketched quickly with her pencil, then rose and skirted left, well back inside the jungle for a hundred metres. Lofty followed her. They crept forward to the edge of the clearing again.

Now they were opposite a large shed with several smaller ones in front of it and beyond it. They had a workshop, utilitarian look about them. A concrete slab, a vehicle ramp, fuel drums and a parked truck near a petrol pump added to this impression.

Lofty pointed at the buildings. "I think this place used to be a Forestry Barracks," he whispered.

At that moment, a chubby, middle-aged man wearing a dirty apron over white clothes came out of a door in the end of the large building. He was whistling cheerfully and tossed a bundle into a garbage can before vanishing back inside.

"The cook?" Lofty suggested.

Barbara shrugged, her attention now focused on another large building further along to the left, half hidden in a grove of large, shady trees. She moved back into the forest in another semi-circle to the left.

The building turned out to be a large open sided hall or meeting place. It had a concrete floor covered with rugs and carpet. A low dais at the far end indicated the place was important.

"It might be their temple or church," Lofty suggested.

Barbara nodded agreement. They scouted on. The gravel vehicle track through the commune passed on their side of the large shed and the meeting hall, then curled right to vanish into thick rainforest. On their left, between the gravel road and the edge of the jungle a hedge of brilliant flowers: violet, purple and pink Bougainvillea, formed the far end of the clearing. The roof of a house showed above the flowers.

The pair crept along to the end of the hedge and peered through. A very pleasant bungalow surrounded by lawns and gardens was backed onto the jungle. The house had wide, shady verandas and looked very cool and attractive. Behind the bungalow were septic tanks and a hen run beside a foot track which threaded off into the jungle. The two cadets crossed this and pushed through more jungle behind the bungalow to discover a sort of village of small huts.

Most of the undergrowth had been cleared and the vehicle track wound amongst the huts. Barbara counted the huts. She could see seven but decided there could be more. The huts were made of timber and stood on low wooden stumps. Their walls were half made of timber louvres, and they looked very Third World, like peasant's huts in Southeast Asia. Orange trees and lemon trees grew amongst the huts and there were small vegetable plots. Chickens scratching in the dirt added to the impression.

Barbara and Lofty crept through the belt of jungle which separated the 'village' from the meeting hall until they reached the vehicle track. They were now in the middle of the commune.

"Sssh!" Lofty warned, gripping Barbara's arm.

They moved behind a tree and peered out. The sound of female voices singing came to them from their left. Barbara heard murmuring, then a burst of laughter, followed by more singing, a melodious chanting rhythm with an oriental sound. From the direction of the huts two girls came into view carrying baskets of vegetables. Both were clad in white cheesecloth garments. They wore flowers in their hair and around their necks. One was slim and had long black hair. The other was more rounded and had brown hair. They walked past singing and vanished in the direction of the big shed.

When she was sure no-one else was around Barbara led the way across the track and through a belt of rainforest to the far side of the meeting hall. From inside this cover she carefully scrutinised the huts.

"I don't think anyone could be held prisoner in those huts," she whispered.

"I agree," Lofty replied. "They are all plywood and louvres. You would have to chain someone up to keep them in there."

"More people," Barbara observed.

In the distance between the huts two women in white and a man in khaki shirt and shorts appeared. They were talking and laughing. Barbara bit her lip as she watched them walk out of sight around a hut. The place looked so much like a holiday camp she feared she had come on a wild goose chase. She glanced at her watch and muttered in annoyance. They were nearly out of time.

Barbara turned right and continued the clockwise circumnavigation of the commune. This led them back towards the main gravel road. The two friends moved just inside the edge of the jungle. Keeping a thicket of banana trees between them and the meeting shed they passed behind it. This brought them to a pump house and steel girder tower topped by a huge, galvanised steel water tank. A rough vehicle track led off to the Northwest down a gentle slope into the jungle. A half-buried black plastic pipe beside the track indicated it led to a creek.

Barbara crossed the track and moved on along the fringe of the jungle to where two solid buildings stood between the big shed and the forest. Both had bars on their windows and were constructed of concrete blocks.

"This looks more promising," she thought.

After a quick check that no-one was around, she walked the ten paces to the back of the first building, reached up, gripped the bars and hauled herself up to look in. The building was a single room and had a door open on the other side. This allowed in plenty of light. A glance showed it was a workshop of some sort with machines on benches, tools and odd bits of machinery.

Barbara lowered herself to the ground and walked across to the second building. It was similar in construction. Again she hauled herself up by the bars. This time it was hard to see inside. Not only was the door shut so the room was in semi-darkness, but the window was dirty and covered in cobwebs. She brushed off some of the dirt and tried to shield the glass from the sky's reflection with one hand, only to be disappointed. It was a storeroom full of boxes and drums.

Feeling both frustrated and let down she lowered herself to the grass and stood trembling from the effort and reaction. A movement caught her eye. Lofty was pointing and gesticulating and he had a look of alarm on his face.

Barbara turned to look and was staggered to see a white-haired old man in faded blue overalls not ten metres away. He was kneeling side on to her and was weeding a flower garden while humming to himself.

For a moment Barbara froze, uncertain what to do. Clearly the man had not seen her. Quelling her rising panic, she walked the ten paces back to the banana trees. As she stepped thankfully into cover, she saw that the old man was still weeding. She did not stop but walked directly away from the commune into the jungle, moving as fast as she could without making too much noise. Lofty rose and followed her.

Once they were a hundred paces into the jungle, Barbara stopped and waited for Lofty. As she stood there, she felt suddenly weak at the knees and began to tremble. She wiped perspiration out of her eyes.

Lofty didn't help. "That was downright silly, Barb. If you had looked you would have seen that old bloke. What would you have done if he'd spotted you?"

Barbara made no reply. The criticism nettled her, even though she knew Lofty was right. She was angry with herself, and disappointed. There was no sign of Fiona in the commune.

Lofty looked at his watch, "It has gone two o'clock. We'd better start back. I don't think Fiona is here."

Barbara nodded. She felt a real stab of defeat and dejection, overlaid by concern that she had probably dragged her friends into a situation which could land them in trouble.

Because of my stubbornness we will get home late, and they will get into trouble with their parents, she thought. And it would not just be for wagging school. It would come out where they had been. *Some of us might even be grounded by our parents and not be allowed to go on the hike, Wendy for sure,* she thought wretchedly. The whole camping trip might be cancelled... and all because of her.

"Come on!" she snapped.

She pulled out her compass and started walking east. She pushed through the undergrowth as fast as she could, reasonably certain that no-one in the commune could hear them.

They will think it is just wild pigs, she reasoned.

After only a few minutes they came in sight of the main gravel road. Barbara paused and checked both ways before walking across, to plunge into the green tangle beyond. This patch of rain forest was a much thicker. There was a lot of wait-a-while and she hooked herself badly several times in her impatience. Once this drew a sharp cry of pain and she saw blood trickle from a scratch on her left forearm.

They pushed a hundred paces in, to get well away from the road, then turned right and headed south, parallel to it. After about 150 paces they came to an overgrown timber track which angled in from the left. Looking along it they could just see the clearing of the commune. They flitted across and continued on through more jungle for another 200 paces.

Barbara kept looking anxiously at her watch: 2:15, then 2:20, then 2:25. The minutes seemed to race past. She began to feel sick with anxiety. A right turn brought them to the gravel road just near the vegetable patch. After another careful look they crossed the road and were back where they had started the reconnaissance. Barbara turned left and began to retrace their route just inside the edge of the jungle.

Now she stopped worrying about noise. No-one was visible in the vegetable patch so she moved as fast as she could, ignoring bumps, bruises, and minor scratches. 2:30! Barbara was appalled at how fast time went. As soon as they were past the vegetable patch, she crashed her way out onto the gravel road and began to run along it. Lofty frowned but followed.

By running they reached the pine forest in just over one minute. Within two minutes they were at the side-track. Barbara turned and ran along it, ignoring the thumping of her heart and the beginnings of a stitch.

By 2:35 they were kneeling beside Blacksnake Creek gulping the murky water. Barbara splashed water over her face and neck and stood up.

"Come on, run!" she croaked.

She ran up the bank and on along the track. By 2:45 they had caught up with Wendy and Roger at the edge of the jungle. Although her heart was pounding furiously, and her throat raspy and dry, Barbara kept going although she slowed to a fast walk to gasp reassurance to the waiting pair.

"It's okay. We aren't being chased. We are just late."

She did not pause but pushed into the tangle of wild raspberries along the track they had made. Less than ten minutes' walk brought them to the end of the overgrown timber track at the base of the steep ridge they had come down.

Barbara went straight up the slope through the rainforest. She soon lost the sign of their inward track but wasn't worried by that. She plodded up as fast as she could go. It was only when Roger called on her to slow down that she looked back and saw that the others had fallen well behind.

She stopped and leaned on a tree. As she gulped air, she felt misery well up. To her dismay she found hot tears streaming down her cheeks. She tried to hide them as the others came up but her snuffles betrayed her.

Roger puffed up to her, concern all over his reddish face. He reached out and squeezed her shoulder. "It's alright Barbara. We will find her."

Barbara's eyes misted up again and more tears came. She was wracked by sobs. "I... I... (sob) I was so... (sob) so sure we would find... Fi... Fiona at the com... commune... (sob)!"

Roger put his arm around her and squeezed her gently. Wendy puffed up and hugged her as well.

After a moment Barbara felt ashamed and embarrassed, "Come on (sniffle). I'm alright. We must move fast, or we will be late."

She led them on up the slope in a determined, if miserable, plod. The others gamely followed. By 3:15 they stood on the jeep track on the razorback ridge. Barbara only paused for a couple of minutes for them to recover their breath. As she checked the time, she bit her lip. They were supposed to be back at school by this and they were still on the mountain!

As soon as the others looked ready, she went down the steep slope as fast as she dared, slipping and sliding from tree to tree, catching at vines and saplings. In a few minutes they were scrambling down the jumbled rocks through the stunted trees. A fabulous view of sea and coast lifted her spirits. A strong breeze helped cool them.

Down through more rainforest, across the ledge of grasstrees she went, almost at a run. There was a delay of a few minutes while they found a way down past the line of granite cliffs. Then they went slipping and sliding down a long grassy slope. It wasn't the same ridge they had come up, but Barbara did not care. Far below she could see the Kiosk and Caravan Park and she wanted to get there as quickly as possible.

From behind her Roger yelled, "Slow down Barbara! You'll break your neck."

She waved to show she heard but did not slow down. Then she slipped. She grabbed at the grass to stop her fall. It was blady grass and it resulted in several deep cuts in her fingers. They stung and that sobered her up. After that she went more carefully. She sucked blood from the cuts till the bleeding stopped. Salt stung her eyes as perspiration trickled into them and her leg muscles cried out in protest. But progress down was fast.

It took them just over half an hour. By 3:55 they were standing on the highway a few hundred metres from the caravan park. As soon as Wendy and Roger caught up, Barbara started walking towards the car.

Chapter 8

GORDON

At the kiosk they all bought a soft drink. Lofty opened the car. Barbara checked her watch.

"Ten past four. We'd better get going."

"We have to change back into our school uniforms first," Wendy said.

Barbara gestured to a nearby change shed. "There are showers in there."

"Be quick," Lofty added as they scooped up their clothes and towels. They tried to be quick, but it was still another ten minutes before they were all seated in the car in clean clothes. Lofty started the car and headed back towards Cairns, driving as fast as he dared. As they drove Barbara recounted to Roger and Wendy what they had seen at the commune. Then she sat and brooded, staring moodily up at the mountains.

The minutes seemed to slip away much faster than the kilometres. As they sped through Smithfield against the tide of afternoon traffic Barbara became more and more tense. Worry about the impending meeting with Gordon began to dominate her thoughts. This, on top of her anxiety about them being late and of possible trouble with parents made her shiver and feel sick in the stomach.

It was 5pm when they reached the school. The place was deserted and Wendy's bicycle was all alone in the bike racks. Barbara relaxed a little; 5 o'clock wasn't too bad.

We shouldn't have serious questions from parents, she decided.

Lofty stopped the car and looked around. "I wonder where Pat and Dan are?"

"Gone home I expect. We were supposed to meet them at three o'clock," Roger replied.

Wendy leaned forward. "If we are to meet the bus at six we will have to move fast."

"Strewth yes! Quick Wendy, grab your bike and stick it in the boot. I'll give you a lift home," Lofty said.

Wendy did so. Roger only lived a block away so he got out and waved them goodbye. Lofty turned the car and they set off.

As they drove along Barbara turned to Wendy. "What will you tell your parents if they ask you where you have been?" she asked.

Wendy shrugged. "That I have been for a drive with you to the beach," she replied. "But they might not be home yet. They both work."

Luckily, they weren't. Wendy heaved a sigh of relief at the sight of the empty car port. Lofty lifted her bike out and she promised to be ready by ten to six. Lofty then drove Barbara home. It was 5:25 when they arrived. Barbara also sighed with relief when she saw her dad was not home yet. She hated the idea of having to lie or deceive him. She thanked Lofty and ran inside to shower and change.

By then her thoughts were filled with worry about Gordon. In the shower she ran her hands over her body and wondered if she would allow him to do that. Did she want him to? She dried herself and walked nude to her bedroom and stood in front of the mirror. Her mind told her it was not just vanity. She had a good body.

Physically I am quite normal, she conceded, noting that she was also very attractive. It was a notion she tried to suppress, not wanting to be vain. *What will I do if Gordon wants to touch me?* she wondered anxiously. *Do I want him to? And do I want him to see me nude?*

She chewed her lip in indecision and turned to her wardrobe to select what to wear for the meeting. All the while she became more and more nervous and also aroused. To add to her anxiety she began to shiver but told herself it was only a reaction to the sun and the day's exertions. She certainly felt tired and sore. It took an effort for her not to bite her fingernails.

Finally she decided on a T-shirt and jeans. Then, seeing the scratches on her forearms, and feeling the evening chill, she added a white turtleneck sweater. As she brushed her hair, she looked at herself critically in the mirror.

"This is no good. It accentuates my bust too much. Gordon will think it is a 'come on'," she muttered.

Again she turned to study herself from the side and back. *Too curvy altogether,* she decided.

She paused, chewed her lip, then got stubborn. Banging down the hairbrush she cried, "Oh blast! I don't know what effect I want to create!"

Barbara felt tears prickling and her lip trembled. "It's all too much! I... Oh heck! That is dad."

The arrival of her father in his car decided her. She quickly worked on her makeup. Her father came upstairs and called to her.

"Come on, Bubs. We will have to fly if we are going to meet this bus on time."

"Coming dad," she called. Barbara cast a last anxious glance at her reflection then ran out to meet him.

"Sorry I'm late," he said. "I got caught up at work. Hmmm. You look lovely. Gordon will be pleased to see you."

"Oh Dad!" Barbara blushed. She ran down to the car feeling quite breathless and all 'a-flutter'.

Her father got in and started up. "Did you have a good day?" he asked as he reversed down the driveway.

"Mmmm. Yes," Barbara mumbled.

He glanced sharply at her. "Not so good, eh? You look a bit flushed and tired. Are you sick?"

"Not really. I'm just a bit nervous and upset."

Her father turned the car onto the street and asked, "Is it Fiona, or is it Gordon you are worrying about?"

"Both Dad."

"You'll be right. Your friends will cheer you up," he assured her.

"I hope so," Barbara replied doubtfully.

As they drove into town she tried to calm her fears, but her insides were in such turmoil she felt she was going to be ill.

At the bus terminal the first person she recognised was Wendy. She was standing with her parents and looked tired but normal. She also looked very pretty. Like Barbara she wore a pullover and the whole front of it seemed to bulge out. Barbara bit her lip, worried that she had noticed and that she found such a sight arousing and interesting.

While the adults were greeting each other Barbara raised an eyebrow. Wendy gave an almost imperceptible shake of her head.

"It's okay. They don't know," she murmured.

Barbara relaxed, then went tense again. Walking through the door was Capt Conkey! She trembled with apprehension. Capt Conkey eyed her and Wendy quizzically as he said, "Good evening."

Now the parents will discover we wagged school, Barbara thought.

To her relief, Capt Conkey said nothing about it. He greeted the parents and began talking to them. A few minutes later, when Barbara's dad was engrossed in conversation with Wendy's parents Capt Conkey drew Barbara and Wendy aside. Barbara felt sick. She knew what he was going to ask even before he spoke.

"Where were you lot today? You weren't at school."

"No sir," Barbara replied, reluctantly meeting his eye.

"So where did you go?"

"Have you heard anything about Fiona sir?" Barbara asked.

"Don't try to side-track me. Where did you go?" Capt Conkey insisted. He did not appear or sound angry, but Barbara knew from experience that he was only withholding judgement until he had the facts.

"We went to Casuarina Beach sir," Barbara replied.

"We?"

"Oh sir! I can't dob in my friends," Barbara replied.

"Your friends, eh?" Capt Conkey grinned.

Barbara blushed and felt foolish. He rubbed his chin, then looked at Wendy, then at the door. Barbara followed his gaze. Lofty and Roger had just walked in, laughing, and joking. They stopped so suddenly and looked so guilty when they saw Capt Conkey that he had to smile.

He turned to Barbara and said, "You don't have to dob anyone in. I think they just did it for themselves. Hello you two. Where were you today?"

The two boys looked at each other.

"We went for a drive," Lofty said.

"We... er... we went to the beach," Roger replied.

"Which beach?" Capt Conkey asked.

"Casuarina," Lofty replied.

"What did you do there?"

Barbara answered, "We walked along the beach."

Capt Conkey rubbed his chin thoughtfully. "Hmmm. It's very odd. All my platoon commanders, the CSM and half the sergeants all absent at the same time. You weren't up to any mischief, were you?"

"Oh, no sir!" they chorused.

"Hmmm. Well, don't forget I want an itinerary from you before you head off on this hike tomorrow," he said.

Capt Conkey then changed the subject, much to their relief. They had

86

all been squirming with worry that the parents would overhear. Barbara stood feeling that her mind and body were two separate things. She became more and more tense with every passing minute. Her thoughts and emotions struggled with each other: Where was Fiona? Will I like Gordon? Do I hate men? What will I do if he tries to kiss me? Was Fiona safe?

While standing there Barbara made an effort to keep smiling but her face felt like a plastic mask. She was so wrung out physically and emotionally she just wanted to slump down and go to sleep. Every few moments she kept glancing through the plate glass window and at the wall clock.

Roger called out and pointed. "Here's the bus," he said.

Barbara looked and seemed to have trouble focusing her eyes. Things started to happen too fast for her to properly prepare for them. She was swept outside with the others as the coach drew to a halt. Its doors hissed open and people began pouring out. Her eyes flicked to each in turn, then glanced up to scan the faces inside.

Karen Harvey appeared at the door, smiling and waving. Two strangers followed her, then Jennifer Bladen. Then Gordon stepped down. He looked tense and tired and was not smiling. Barbara felt her heart leap and her throat choke up. She gave a little sob. What should she do? Should she go and embrace him? Or...?

She found herself walking forward. Their eyes met. They stopped two paces apart, oblivious to the jostling crowd around them. He reached forward and she gave him both hands. He nodded with approval and gave a gentle smile. Then he drew her to him.

Gordon's arms enfolded her. Instinctively she put hers around him. He hugged her firmly, but gently. She trembled and tried to relax. She kept her head lowered, afraid of being kissed. He made no attempt to do so but patted her shoulder and hair, then released her.

Barbara stepped back, aware that Gordon was still holding her hands. Everything else was just a blur. She shivered. The only things in focus were his eyes, so blue, so calm. He gave her a wry smile, anxiety peeping through. The crinkling of his mouth into dimples made her catch her breath. She was not able to remember later whether she had smiled or not.

"You look lovely," he said.

The sound of his voice sent a thrill through her like a charge of electricity. She trembled. Her tongue seemed to be too heavy to move. Her mouth and lips felt dry. She was aware that her hands had become moist.

Jennifer saved her.

"Hello Barbara," she cried as she engulfed her in a strong hug and kissed her on the cheek. Barbara felt a surge of pleasure and warmth. To respond she released Gordon's hands and returned Jennifer's hug. After a few seconds they parted and she and Karen hugged.

Roger chuckled. "Don't we get a hug?" he asked.

Barbara released Karen. "Gordon, give Roger a hug."

Gordon and Roger recoiled from each other in mock horror, both laughing.

"Fair go! We aren't like that," Roger expostulated.

He turned to shake Gordon's hand. Karen gave Lofty a brief peck on the cheek then did the same to Roger. Jennifer put her arms around Lofty's neck, pressed herself hard against him and kissed him on the cheek. Barbara noticed a flicker of pain in Wendy's eyes.

Poor Wendy! She looks jealous! Does she still love Lofty? Barbara wondered.

Over the last few years they had been in and out of love with each other several times. Barbara watched Wendy carefully when Jennifer gave Roger a hug and a kiss. No, not the same reaction, just casual interest.

Roger cried with delight. "Oh I say! That's more like it! Hello Jennifer. Hop back on the bus and greet us again."

Jennifer stepped back smiling. "That's enough for now. Too much of anything is bad for you."

The others laughed. Parents were then introduced. As Gordon gravely shook hands with her father Barbara studied his profile. Yes, he certainly was handsome. And he had grown even taller. She only just topped his shoulder with her chin.

Capt Conkey greeted the three visitors. They knew him from the combined Promotion Courses each December when cadets and staff from all the North Queensland cadet units came together.

He explained, "Your OCs have asked me to keep an eye on you."

"We will be good sir," Gordon replied with a smile.

"I'm sure you will. It's not you I'm worried about. It is my lot. Don't let them lead you astray," Capt Conkey answered. He smiled as he said it, but Barbara was acutely aware of his underlying concern. He continued, "And don't forget I want that program. Now, have a good time. I had better get home or I will miss my tea. Goodnight."

Capt Conkey left to a chorus of 'Goodnights'. Luggage was collected and they all walked around to the car park. Barbara walked beside Gordon knowing that everyone expected her to. It was obvious that even her dad thought of him as her boyfriend. But she wasn't sure herself.

Do I love him? she wondered. She certainly liked him and found him attractive, but she was too jumbled up in her emotions to decide.

I hardly know him, she told herself as she watched him place his kitbag in the boot of the car. He gave the impression of being very grown up and self-assured as he talked to her father. *He looks much older and more mature than a Year 12,* she thought.

But his voice! It was so rich and deep. It seemed to vibrate right through to her very core. Was that important?

Suddenly she wanted to run away and hide.

They climbed into the car. Karen hopped in the front so that Gordon and Barbara were together in the back. Everyone just took it for granted. Barbara felt very tense. She sat over against the door and looked out to check that Jennifer was being looked after. She was going to stay with Wendy.

What will I do if he tries to hold my hand? Barbara thought.

Gordon moved on the seat and she tensed up. But he was just making himself comfortable. He gave her a quizzical look then began to chatter, drawing Karen and Barbara's father into general conversation about the coach trip, about going to school at Broadsound College, and asking questions about Cairns.

"I've heard a lot about the place, but I've never been here," he explained.

Barbara remained tense throughout the drive, thankful it was only ten minutes. She barely looked at Gordon during that time. He gave her a few worried glances but made no move to touch her.

Chapter 9

PLANS

When they arrived at Barbara's home Gordon and Karen were shown to their rooms. Barbara explained, "Bathroom and toilet that way. There are fresh towels for you. Freshen up while we organise tea, or rather while Dad does. He is the chef."

Barbara walked through to the lounge room feeling annoyed, tired and unhappy. She knew she was being very stand-offish with Gordon. *I don't mean to be. I just can't help it*, she thought.

She slumped into her favourite chair listening to every little sound from along the corridor. Gordon sounded as though everything was fine, but she did wonder if he wasn't feeling a bit strained. After five minutes she got up and went into the kitchen, but her father chased her out.

"You go back and entertain your guests. Get them to telephone their parents to let them know they have arrived safely," he said. "And Bubs, relax. It is always easier if you don't force things."

Barbara smiled and sighed. "I know. Thanks Dad."

She returned to the lounge room just as Gordon appeared. Pointing to the phone she said, "Father's orders. Ring your parents." Feeling quite tense she settled into her armchair and watched as Gordon made the call. He seemed to radiate confidence and manliness.

Karen joined them. She was a tall, slender girl with hazel eyes and brown hair. She also phoned her parents. Gordon moved to sit opposite Barbara.

He smiled gently and said, "I know we have come at a bad time. Is there any news of Fiona?"

"No. Nothing," Barbara replied.

Karen settled herself in another chair. "That's terrible. What can have happened to her?"

"I'll tell you later, after tea, when the others are here. I don't want to talk about it now," Barbara said. Then she forced a smile and said, "Tell me about your cadet unit. Do you still do all those extra camps and exercises?"

90

"Yes, we do," Karen agreed.

They fell to discussing their respective cadet units, comparing the training programs and the different experiences. This easily carried them through till dinner time. Barbara was a bit jealous because the Heatley Cadet Unit seemed to do so many bush exercises. It made her defensively proud of her own.

"We do more drill, and a lot more shooting. We win most of the rifle shooting competitions. Captain Conkey is very keen on that. He is a very good shot," Barbara enthused.

"I think he's a real old sweety," Karen said.

"You make him sound soft," Barbara laughed. "He can be very tough when he needs to be."

"Here's a car. This might be the others," Karen said.

Barbara listened. "Lofty's car," she said, levering herself out of her chair. She went to the door to greet the new arrivals. Lofty, Roger, and Dan came in. Barbara met Dan's eye. She badly wanted to ask him if he and Pat had discovered anything but at that moment her father came into the room.

"Dessert," he said. "Who wants ice-cream?"

Bowls of ice-cream and fruit salad were served and they gossiped about the coach trip while they waited. Barbara's father placed coffee and biscuits on the table then sat to chat with them. She could tell he was glad her friends had come to visit.

Twenty minutes later, Wendy and Jennifer were dropped off by Wendy's mum. They were ushered in and offered drinks. Barbara noticed that Jennifer had changed into a white silk blouse. The front was an open 'V' and as she moved the soft, white roundness of the tops of her breasts was plainly visible. When Jennifer bent down to move a chair, Barbara was able to see right down her front.

She is doing that deliberately, Barbara thought. She was both scandalised and, to her own shame and confusion, intensely interested. It was obvious to her that Jennifer was trying to make the boys take notice. *And they have!* she thought.

Jennifer seated herself beside Lofty and started to chatter away. Barbara watched Wendy's face. *No doubt about it. Wendy is jealous. She must still like Lofty. Oh, poor Roger!*

Barbara shook her head sadly. She looked up and saw Gordon

observing her gravely from across the table. He gave a quick smile which disarmed her irritation at once. His voice cut across all the others.

"Well Barbara, what is the plan? Where are we going?"

The others stopped talking and looked at her. The sound of dishes being washed told her where her father was, so she said, "I'm going looking for Fiona. You can come if you like."

There was a moment of silence then Gordon spoke. "Do you know where to look?" he asked.

Barbara nodded. She quickly related the events of the last four days then bit her lip. She said, "We thought we did. I thought she might be at this commune in the Jungle near Kuranda." She went on to describe the day's expedition. As she talked, she felt her eyes misting up. She hoped there would be no tears and bit her lip.

"The commune seemed to be deserted, hardly a soul in the place. I was so disappointed," she concluded.

Her lip trembled then and her eyes did water. She gripped her lower lip with her teeth and felt a hand on each shoulder, squeezing gently. It was Wendy on the left and Roger on her right.

Lofty turned to Dan. "What did you and Pat find? Did you reach the commune too?"

Dan shook his head. "No. We ran out of time, but I'll tell you what, the set-up looks mighty fishy to me."

"Fishy? How?" Barbara asked, brushing aside her tears.

"Well, we parked the car in an old timber track off the Black Mountain Road and walked a couple of kilometres to the commune turn-off," Dan explained. "There was a sign saying 'Private Property', and 'Trespassers will be Prosecuted'. We scouted around for a bit then followed the side road. After a while it crossed a cattle grid with more 'Keep out' signs."

"Then the road went round a curve and across a small timber bridge. Beyond it was a gate with a guard hut beside it and an armed man on duty. He wore a sort of khaki uniform. He didn't see us, so we did a detour through the jungle to bypass him. It took us an hour and boy, was the scrub thick! Bloody wait-a-while!"

Dan digressed to describe the rainforest before going on with the tale. "We crept up and had a look at the guard. He had a walkie-talkie radio on his belt and an orange badge on his shirt. There was a 4WD parked beside the hut. While we were watching a beeper sounded on the man's belt, and another in the hut. A minute or so late another 4WD arrived from the direction of Kuranda. The bloke driving it spoke to the guard like he was the boss, then drove on towards the commune."

"After that we went on along the road towards the commune till we ran out of time. We reached a track junction on the edge of Macalistairs Pocket. That's here." He pointed at the map. "It is a natural change of vegetation from rainforest to sheoaks but a lot of it has been cleared and turned into a pine plantation."

Barbara nodded, "We got to it, but on the northern side, a couple of kilometres further north." She indicated where on the map.

"So what did you think was fishy?" Lofty asked.

"Because they didn't like visitors and they had guards. And they had some sort of electronic warning system. We thought it was probably part of the cattle grid, or maybe the bridge, wired to sound when a vehicle went over it," Dan replied.

Barbara made a face. "Maybe, but that dork Cyril said they have the guards because they get harassed by religious bigots."

Gordon spoke, "So, if Fiona isn't at this commune, where do you think she is?"

"Probably at the other place the sect owns on the other side of Kuranda," Barbara replied.

Gordon frowned. "Are you suggesting that Fiona has been kidnapped by these people and is being held against her will?" When Barbara nodded, he added, "Why? She might be there because of her father."

Roger agreed, "Or she might be a convert to their cult."

Barbara shook her head. She explained again why she did not think so. "Anyway, I don't care what you say. I'm going to find out."

"But why on earth should these people kidnap Fiona?" Karen asked.

Barbara couldn't answer that. "I don't know. But the whole situation doesn't make sense."

"She might not be with them at all," Dan reminded her. "She might be anywhere."

"I know. But I'm still going to investigate these Smiley People first."

"Are these people liable to be dangerous?" Jennifer asked.

Roger answered that. "If they practice voodoo and have armed guards they might be. Most religious fanatics are dangerous."

"So we should leave it to the police," Jennifer said.

Barbara shook her head. "No. I'm going to look," she said.

"In that case we are going with you," Gordon said. He met Barbara's eyes and she found her own misting up again.

Lofty nodded. "We will have to. The only other option is to tell Barb's dad and then have her physically restrained."

Barbara snorted but she knew it was true. She was also annoyed at the way Jennifer was leaning forward so that Lofty could see her cleavage. What annoyed her most was the knowledge that she was being hypocritical. It was exactly what she had done at various times herself, most recently to Cyril.

Gordon's eyes flicked to Jennifer's front, then up to meet Barbara's gaze. To her own surprise she found she didn't mind.

He's a normal male, she thought.

He asked, "So who is going and what is the plan?"

Barbara replied at once, "Tomorrow morning we get dropped off at Kamerunga and we watch this religious group. When they head off on their pilgrimage, we follow them. That should lead us to this other place."

She gestured to the map on the coffee table and the others crowded around to study it. Barbara knelt on the floor. Karen knelt beside her. Wendy leaned on her from behind and Barbara became aware of Wendy's breast pressing on her shoulder. She also found herself staring straight down the front of Jennifer's blouse as she knelt opposite her. In spite of herself her eyes were drawn to look, and she was uncomfortably aware that she was excited by what she saw. She looked up and met Jennifer's eyes. Jennifer smiled.

She knows I'm looking and doesn't mind, Barbara thought.

The idea made her feel hot and confused. Wendy pressed against her and she noted she was also leaning on Lofty who crouched beside Barbara. Barbara shook her head to clear it. Blast sex! What a stupid complication! She bent to concentrate on the map.

After she had pointed out the likely routes they might take, the cadets resumed their seats. Barbara looked around the group.

"Are you all coming with me?"

Each in turn nodded or said 'yes.'

"That's marvellous!" she cried.

Lofty counted, "That's eight. A bit big for a recon patrol?"

Barbara again shook her head. "Safety in numbers. We can always break into smaller groups if we need to," she replied. She felt her spirits rising. *Now we can do something!*

Karen frowned. "What are we to wear? Are we going to wear cadet uniform?" she asked.

"No. It is not an official activity. But I am taking mine in case we have to do a bit of creeping and crawling," Barbara replied.

Roger looked doubtful. "What are we going to tell Captain Conkey?" he asked.

That put Barbara on a spot. She did not want to lie to Capt Conkey. "Let's work out a rough program working around Kuranda for a few days. Then, if need be, some of us can go off to search while the others follow the plan."

"Bit devious," Gordon commented.

Barbara blushed at the hint of disapproval in his voice. "You don't have to do it," she said.

Gordon raised an eyebrow. "I said I would. And I think Fiona is worth a bit of dinted integrity."

Barbara blushed again, fearing she had just lowered Gordon's opinion of her.

Karen spoke up, "What do we do if this pilgrimage doesn't go anywhere near Kuranda?"

Roger answered. "It must. At least for the first day or so," he said. He bent over and put his finger on the map. "Unless they walk along the bitumen roads the only foot tracks from Kamerunga go up over the mountains, either to Kuranda or to Speewah."

"How many tracks are there?" Jennifer asked. She leaned forward again, giving them all an eyeful while she studied the map.

"Three," Roger replied. "Two are old pack tracks blazed by the pioneers during the gold rushes back in the 1870s. There is Smith's track which goes up behind Stoney Creek Falls, past Yalbogie Hill and through here to Speewah, and this one, Douglas's Track, which goes up behind Glacier Rock and across to Speewah. The third is this power line access track which runs from Red Bluff to Kuranda."

"What is Glacier Rock?" Karen asked.

"A huge, exposed granite bluff above the railway. It sticks up a couple of hundred of metres high. It looks like rock formations in cold climates but there has never been a glacier here," Roger explained.

"What are these tracks like?" Jennifer asked.

She folded her arms, causing her breasts to be squeezed up so that they half bulged out. Barbara noted the boy's eyes widen with interest and felt herself torn between interest and disapproval.

Roger answered, "They are mostly well-maintained National Parks walking tracks and are easy enough to follow."

Jennifer looked worried. "We won't get lost? Have you been along them?" she asked.

Roger smiled and Barbara knew his mind was going back over several earlier adventures, a couple of them truly terrifying. He said, "Yes. I've been along them. We won't get lost."

They settled to plotting a rough program. Barbara jotted down Roger's suggestions on a note pad.

"We will need to do some shopping tomorrow to buy some canned food and stuff," Karen said.

That was a disappointment to Barbara. She had been hoping they could get going early the following morning, but she conceded that the change of plan meant different arrangements.

When the plan was agreed on Wendy let out a big yawn. That started the others off.

"Sorry," Wendy said. "It's been a big day."

"Ten o'clock," Barbara noted. "If we are going to start early, we had better get to bed."

Lofty agreed. "Yes, we've got another big day ahead. Come on you lot. Let's go home."

They said 'thanks' to Barbara's father before trooping downstairs. Barbara noted that Jennifer manoeuvred herself into the front of the car next to Lofty. Wendy gave her a hard look and hopped in the back next to Roger.

Oh dear! Barbara thought. She began to worry that Wendy might get hurt, or that ill-will might boil up and spoil their trip.

After Lofty had driven off Barbara, Gordon and Karen went back upstairs and sat talking for a while. Barbara's father joined them and was given a copy of the proposed program. He promised to help transport them to their start point at Kamerunga.

"I want you to phone me every day," he said.

"Yes Dad Of course," Barbara agreed.

She was now itching with an urge to get moving. He looked at her very thoughtfully for a moment and she feared he was going to ask some hard question but instead he just nodded and said 'sweet dreams'.

A few minutes later as Barbara said goodnight Gordon lingered in his bedroom doorway for a moment and looked at her. Karen flicked her gaze from one to the other and smiled. It made Barbara feel uncomfortable.

Everyone expects Gordon and I to be lovers! she thought.

At that moment, she did not feel like any intimacy. She just felt tired and impatient to start the search. She gave Gordon a nod, not wishing to encourage him, and went into her room.

To her annoyance she then found she could not sleep. Instead she tossed and turned with her mind in turmoil. Worrying thoughts scudded across her consciousness like storm clouds over a hard-pressed sailing ship: Am I normal? Do I like boys? Do I like Gordon? What will I do if he comes to my room now?

This last thought fairly nagged at her. She hoped he would not as she had not encouraged him or hinted at it. *What will I do if he does come in?* she wondered.

"I don't even know if I would be angry or frightened or if I would welcome him," she moaned.

She had a mental picture of reaching up to pull him down on top of her and of kissing him fiercely. She drove the picture from her mind, but it returned. Her breathing grew fast and she knew she was excited at the prospect.

As the fantasy glowed in her mind, she imagined what to say and what it might be like and wondered how far she would let him go, then realised what she was telling herself. She ran her hands over her naked body, enjoying the sensation and thinking of what it might be like if they were Gordon's hands. Unbidden, horrible memories of other men's hands crept into her mind. Then she remembered their cruel lust and revolting assaults and shivered.

The terrible memories cooled her. She rolled on her side and the tears came.

"I'm so mixed up! I just want to be normal, but I don't think I am!" she cried.

With her eyes wet with tears she slipped into a deep sleep.

* * *

"Wake up sleepy head!" a voice murmured in her ear.

Barbara opened her eyes to find it was daylight. Gordon was leaning over her smiling. For an instant fear gripped her as her vision took in his hairy chest and tanned muscles. Then she realised that Gordon had just had a shower and shave. He wore a towel around his waist, smelled of soap and After Shave and had wet hair. Her bedroom door was open and Karen was standing there wearing a bath wrap and grinning.

"It is seven o'clock Barbara," she said.

Barbara looked up into Gordon's eyes and marvelled at how bright they were. She reached up and gently felt his chin.

"You've just shaved. Isn't it smooth."

Then she remembered she slept nude and was aware that the bedclothes had pulled down so as to partly expose her breasts. She bunched the quilt up under her chin. Gordon smiled. *He wants to kiss me,* she decided.

For an instant she felt an urge to fling off the bedclothes, to wrap her arms around his neck. Something must have showed in her eyes or on her face. Gordon looked at her questioningly. He leaned forward.

Barbara suddenly turned her head away. "No. Please. Not yet," she whispered.

Gordon stopped at once. He stood up and smiled. "Later then. You'd better get up. It's time for breakfast."

"I will when you go away. Then I can get dressed," Barbara replied.

"Why? Aren't you dressed now?" Gordon asked, his eyes alive with interest. Karen giggled. Barbara blushed. She put out her arm and took his hand. He squeezed it gently and she smiled. Her eyes travelled over his body, noting that he looked good. He was tanned and fit. His waist was trim and well-muscled.

Gordon stood still while she examined him, a faint blush mottling his neck and cheeks. Then she smiled and said, "Go away. Let me get dressed. And you get dressed too."

Gordon nodded and let her hand go. He turned and went out. Karen gave her a mischievous wink, which made her blush, then closed the door. Barbara slipped out of bed and shrugged on her dressing gown, enjoying the whisper of silk on her bare skin. She felt hot and her heart beat rapidly.

"I need a cold shower!" she told herself.

But she had a hot one instead, stretching and easing stiff muscles. As she dressed, she felt much better. Today they would find Fiona.

If she wasn't at the commune, she must be at the other place between Kuranda and Speewah, she thought. "I'll find you Fiona," she promised.

Breakfast was a pleasant meal. Barbara was a bit tense as she walked to the table, but Gordon and her father were laughing and joking and Karen was bright and cheerful so she soon relaxed.

Once they had eaten Barbara went downstairs and dragged her cadet gear out of the storeroom. Pack and webbing were emptied onto the floor and the contents sorted. While she was doing this Gordon joined her. He sat and chatted while she repacked what she would need. Because her cadet unit did a lot of camping and hiking, she was quite experienced at this. As she worked, she was conscious that Gordon was studying her but was surprised to realise she did not mind.

After checking their gear the three of them walked along to the convenience store two blocks away to purchase food and other small items.

"Only get enough for three days," Barbara said. "We can buy more food in Kuranda."

Half an hour later they walked home laden with cans, packet soups, dehydrated noodles, chocolates, jellybeans, condensed milk, Milo, matches, torch batteries and a dozen other items. With something of an effort these were crammed into already bulging packs. As they did this a car pulled into the driveway.

"That'll be Lofty," Barbara said. She checked her watch. "Only nine thirty. He's a bit early. We said ten."

But it was not Lofty. It was Capt Conkey. He wore casual clothes and had his three young children with him. Barbara's father came down to meet him and the two men stood talking. Barbara ran upstairs to get the rough program. Feeling rather nervous she took this to Capt Conkey.

"It's a bit vague sir," she explained. "We weren't quite sure where we wanted to go and had trouble agreeing."

"That's not like you to be vague," Capt Conkey said. "Where will you be tonight?"

"Kuranda, we think," Barbara replied.

"You think?"

"We don't know if we will get that far sir."

Her father turned to her. "Kuranda for sure, even if you have to do a forced march. And you will phone me when you get there, or if there are any problems. Your mobile phone should have coverage in most of that area."

"Yes Dad"

Capt Conkey nodded, "And phone me too so I can tell parents where their offspring are. Now, where will you camp tonight?" he added.

"We haven't decided. We thought we would see how far we got," Barbara replied. She could see her secret plan of heading off to search the other Smiley property looking shaky.

Capt Conkey shook his head. "You can't just camp anywhere. It is either National Park or State Forest along the Barron Gorge. Do you have camping permits?" he asked.

"No sir."

"Then you camp in a proper campground," her father said. "There is a Caravan Park in Kuranda. I will phone and book you in."

"Two nights please Dad We plan to spend Sunday in Kuranda," Barbara said. She knew it was no good arguing.

Capt Conkey looked her firmly in the eye. "Now Barbara, promise me you won't go sneaking off to look at this commune. In fact, promise me you won't go north of Kuranda along the Black Mountain Road at all."

Barbara's heart leapt. She wouldn't have to lie or break a promise. "Yes sir. I promise."

Capt Conkey looked a bit surprised. He obviously hadn't expected her to give in so easily. He asked suspiciously, "You won't go off prying into other people's affairs and getting into trouble, will you?"

"I will try not to get into trouble," Barbara replied.

"I didn't say that," Capt Conkey snorted.

Gordon stepped forward, "We will keep her out of mischief sir, or at least we will try to."

Barbara's father added, "I agree with Captain Conkey Barbara. If you have any thoughts of going off to find Fiona then you will not go."

Barbara faced him, "You will have to lock me up then Dad I won't promise more than I have. If we find a lead, we will investigate it."

"No! Let the police know and tell us," her father said. He sighed. "If only you weren't so stubborn and strong-willed!" he cried.

The two men looked at each other, both slightly baffled. Barbara could see they were worried. "It's okay, Dad There are eight of us. You should be fretting about us being boys and girls together, you know...?"

"Well I'm not," her father said. "I know my little girl and I trust her."

Barbara blushed with both pleasure and doubt. Did he really know what she was like? Did he suspect? Was he not worried because he thought she wouldn't do anything because she didn't like boys? She noted that Gordon also went a bit pink about the ears.

The discussion was ended by the arrival of Lofty, Roger, Wendy and Jennifer, all crammed into a car with their gear. Lofty's mother was the driver. They all climbed out to say hello and Barbara was at once struck by the fact that Jennifer was wearing a white T-shirt which looked too small for her, and which emphasised her bust. She also wore tight jeans which accentuated her hips. Barbara found it unsettling and annoying.

Lofty was like his old cheerful self. "Hello sir. Hello Mr Brassington. Here we are, the brains and strength of the expedition. Is everyone ready to go?"

He looked happier than he had all week and it lifted Barbara's spirits to see him. She nodded and told herself that the previous days search had been a false trail but today they had solid clues to work on.

Now we will find Fiona!

Chapter 10

THE PATH TO ENLIGHTENMENT

By 10:30 that Saturday morning the eight cadets, clad in civilian clothes but with their issue webbing and packs, were standing near the southern end of the road bridge at Kamerunga.

Barbara's father and Lofty's mother had ferried the group there and, after further warnings to be careful and not to get into trouble, had driven off.

Barbara sniffed the air and looked around. It was a beautiful clear day, typical of North Queensland in winter. The temperature was just cool enough for them to be aware of it, but not cold enough to need a pullover. The cloudless sky was deep blue and the air was crisp and dry.

Jungle covered mountains rose like a wall less than a kilometre away. The sun picked out every possible shade of green and the effect was startling and brilliant. Barbara's gaze travelled up the slopes to where the railway to Kuranda curved out of sight halfway up the side of North Peak. Her eyes moved to take in the end of the Stoney Creek valley and then rested for a moment on the rugged grey mass of Glacier Rock. Below it the line of the railway re-appeared, to cut across the base of the rich red rock of Red Bluff, an artificial cliff formed by the railway cut. The railway then curved out of sight along the western side of the massive cleft of the Barron Gorge.

Barbara shifted her gaze back to her companions. Gordon was watching her. Their eyes met and he smiled. She smiled back. *He looks even more handsome with that khaki shirt on,* she thought.

She liked the way the rolled-up sleeves accentuated his tanned and muscular arms. He had a bush hat which he wore tilted to one side and which really suited him.

She sighed. If it wasn't for the fact that Fiona was missing, she felt she would be very happy. The other main irritant was Jennifer's too-tight T-shirt which the boys kept glancing at.

We don't need any sort of temptation to cause problems, she thought.

Barbara also felt quite stiff and sore from the exertions of the previous day. So did Roger and Wendy, both of whom moaned and grumbled and walked like old people.

Roger groaned and rubbed his back. He looked up at the mountains, "Well, which way do we go?"

"Up there I suppose," Barbara replied.

"I thought you might say that," Roger said glumly. "I've been up there. Can't we look somewhere where it is flat?"

They all laughed but the question bothered Barbara. She was not sure which way to go. After another look around, she unfolded her map and studied it. The others crowded round. Gordon stood close beside her.

"Where is a likely spot for people to hold a mass baptism?" he asked.

Dan Russell pointed, "The picnic area just upstream."

"How far is that?" Karen asked.

"Only a few hundred metres," Lofty answered.

"That is where we will go first then," Barbara said. She wasn't sure but it seemed better than just standing around doing nothing.

They hoisted on their webbing and packs and started walking, to the accompaniment of many groans as stiff muscles were called into use. Almost at once they began to sweat.

"Oh! Oh! Strewth I'm sore," Roger groaned. He wiped perspiration from his face. "This is supposed to be winter!"

"It is the tropics," Dan reminded him.

Five minutes later they stood on the road overlooking the picnic area at the lower end of Kamerunga Island where the two branches of the Barron River re-joined. Apart from a scattering of litter the place was deserted. Barbara found herself to be unreasonably depressed and baffled. She looked around for some clue as to where to go next.

Dan looked around. "No-one here," he said, stating the obvious.

Lofty nodded and frowned. "But are we too early or too late?" he asked.

Karen hoisted her pack to a more comfortable position. "So what do we do? Do we just sit and wait and hope these religious weirdos turn up or what?" Karen asked.

"We could ask someone," Roger suggested.

"Who?" Karen asked, looking around. There was not a soul in sight.

"There are houses just along there, a whole suburb," Lofty replied, pointing upstream. "It's called 'Rainforest Estate'."

For lack of a better plan they started walking that way, Barbara striding out in front. The road was cut out of the hillside with the river on their right and a steep slope covered with jungle up on their left. After about a hundred metres they came to a bitumen driveway going up to a building tucked in against the mountain.

"Up there," Roger suggested. "That will also tell us if they went up to the railway. There is an old pack track which starts just behind the left-hand end of that building."

"Have you been up this track?" Gordon asked as they turned off and went up the steep driveway.

Roger nodded. "Came down it a few years ago. It was a hike I will never forget I can tell you," he said. He shuddered at the memory.[3]

"Was that when you were chasing that Tarzan fellow?" Wendy asked.

"Yes. But I thought he was chasing us!" Roger replied with a laugh.

"Tarzan? Who's he?" Karen asked.

"A madman who lived in the jungle. I'll tell you the story later," Roger answered.

They came to a halt in front of the building. It looked all shut up.

"Nobody home," Lofty observed.

They knocked and called out but there was no response. Once again Barbara felt sharply depressed. Gordon looked around the corner of the building. "Where is this track? Maybe we can see if it has been used."

Roger led the way into a small, jungle-choked re-entrant. "There. It goes up in a zigzag. It is bench-cut into the hillside."

Lofty eyed the tall blady grass. "Well, no-one has been along this track for a while," he observed.

"Where do we go now?" Wendy asked.

Roger pointed back to the main road. "We check if they went up Smith's Track," he said.

"Smith's Track?" Gordon queried.

"An old pack track used by the early pioneers back in the 1870s," Roger explained. Now it's just a National Parks walking track."

They made their way back down to the road. As they did Barbara felt her thigh and calf muscles protesting at going downhill.

We certainly pushed ourselves yesterday, she thought ruefully.

---

[3] Read *Train to Kuranda* by C. R. Cummings

Roger turned left and led them 25 metres across a small bridge and then pointed to a muddy foot trail that wound its way up into the forest.

"Smith's Track," he said. "It goes up over the mountains to Speewah. There are cross tracks that connect to Douglas' Track."

Gordon and Dan both bent to study the muddy ground and leaf litter. Dan shook his head. "Nobody has been up there this morning," he observed.

Karen frowned. "So what do we do now?" she asked.

"Ask at one of the houses further along the road," Barbara said.

She stubbornly refused to be disheartened although she could not shake the nagging doubt that they were on another wild-goose chase. She led the way on along the road, stepping out so smartly she soon left most of the others behind.

After several hundred metres the road rounded a curve. Through the trees ahead the grey bulk of Glacier Rock towered up. On the right was a belt of trees on the bank of the river. On the left were houses nestled into the rainforest on the hillside.

The first few houses were closed up, their occupants presumably at work in Cairns. This irritated Barbara. She went to the next. It was half-hidden behind a wall of shrubbery and flowers. A stone-flagged path gave access to a rock garden beside the house. She dropped her pack and webbing and went in.

The whole garden gave Barbara such an impression of strangeness that she halted to look more closely. The garden was shady, almost gloomy, as it was set amongst rainforest trees. There was no lawn, only carefully constructed and artfully arranged rock gardens with pathways woven amidst them. Among the flowers, rocks and ferns stood small statues. These gave the place a distinctly oriental flavour being mostly dragons and dwarf-like men with slanted eyes and long beards.

While Barbara was gazing at this in some wonder, and with definite appreciation, the others joined her.

"Chinese or Japanese," Jennifer suggested.

Barbara began walking towards a door she had espied half-hidden by a fern covered boulder. When she was still a dozen paces from the door it swung open. A man stepped out and his appearance was so unexpected and unusual that she came to a standstill and gaped.

The man was a middle-aged Asian with a shaven head. He was

dressed in the orange robes of a Buddhist Monk and carried a stick with curious little wooden wheels on it. The monk stopped and gave a low bow.

As a reflex Barbara returned the bow and only later felt a bit embarrassed at having done so. A waft of incense reached her nostrils and the gentle tinkle of wind chimes made the setting feel complete. Before Barbara could gather her astonished thoughts, the monk spoke. He had a lilting accent she found musical but hard to follow.

"Greetings travellers. I give you peace. I am Lin Fay and this is my garden. You are welcome. May I ask what it is you seek?"

For a moment Barbara wondered if the monk was one of the 'Smiley People' and was at a loss what to say. While she groped for the right words Gordon stepped up beside her and bowed.

"Good morning sir. We are seeking after a group of people who are searching...who are searching for the true path to happiness and enlightenment."

A faint frown formed on the monk's brow, but he stood otherwise impassive. "I can help you a little along that path for I have travelled it for many years and have gathered a small amount of knowledge. But do not look for true happiness in this world. It will only be found in the next. There are many people who preach that true happiness can be found in this life but I do not believe them, except in that it comes from within and is an attitude of mind."

Gordon nodded. "The people you speak of are probably the ones we seek," he said. "Did they pass this way?"

No doubt this time, Barbara decided. *A distinct frown.* But the monk's eyes were quizzical rather than unfriendly.

He said, "But you are not of these people?"

"No sir. We are not. We search for one of our friends who may be with them," Gordon replied.

The monk bowed his head and muttered a prayer. After a minute he raised his eyes and searched Gordon's face. The cadets all stood in silence and waited. Next the monk raised his right hand, and said, "I am a servant of the Lord Buddha. I come from Tibet. I also search for the true meaning of God's word. These people you seek do not search for God's truth. They are bad people. There is much evil among them. I have felt this here (he touched his heart)...and here (touching his head)."

Barbara shivered. She swallowed and asked, "Have you seen these Smiley People? Did they come this way?"

The monk seemed to cringe, and a look of real fear crossed his face. "Hush! Do not speak their name aloud. Yes. They have passed this way. That is the way they went." He pointed up towards Glacier Rock across the valley. "There is a path which goes up the mountain. These people went that way early this morning."

"What do they look like? How will we know them?" Barbara asked.

"They are in a group, perhaps a dozen. They all wear yellow cloaks with a hood, and they are singing and laughing," the monk replied.

Lofty turned to go. "Come on then."

"Wait!" the monk commanded. He fixed them with an intent stare. Barbara shivered as his eyes seemed to bore into her skull. "I can tell that you are good people and that you are on a true quest. I must warn you. The way you go may be dangerous. These people are evil ones. They dabble with the dark forces. Be on your guard. There is much Godlessness in this country. Evil spirits are abroad."

Wendy gave a gasp. Barbara felt her pulse quicken and icy fingers ran down her spine. She shook her head. Gordon spoke, "We will be careful. Please tell us exactly where we have to go."

The monk stepped forward and again stared intently at Gordon's face. Then he pointed again. "I do not know where these people go but the path leads up that ridge to the railway and then on up to the top of the mountain. If you go that way you may meet a hermit. He also is a Holy Man by his own rights. But I tell you he is wrong. For he lives alone in the jungle and worships the trees."

"Is he one of the Smi... er, one of these people we are looking for?" Gordon asked.

The monk smiled. "Bless you no. He is just a poor hermit who has gone in the head. But he is a good man and will help you, unless he is mad. Then he can be violent. If you meet him be careful what you say. Do not mention these people you seek by name for he is afraid of them."

The friends looked at each other uncertainly, as though unable to believe their eyes and ears. The monk stepped close to Gordon. From inside his robes the monk drew out a metal medallion on a chain. It was about 15 centimetres in diameter and was engraved with what looked like

107

Chinese characters. He took this from around his own neck and placed it around Gordon's.

"This is a Sacred Amulet. It was blessed by the Abbot of my monastery in Tibet. It has great powers. It can ward off evil. I give it to you for you are good people on a dangerous quest. Keep it on you at all times and no harm will come to you. Now go, and God be with you."

The monk turned and walked to the door. He opened it and went through without looking back. The door closed.

For a few moments the friends stood in silence. Gordon stared at the amulet in his hand. Dan spoke first.

"What a load of eyewash! Evil spirits! Magic medals!"

"Don't be rude!" Wendy retorted. "It is a gift and well meant, even if it has no powers."

"Of course it hasn't got any powers!" Dan snorted.

"Let us go outside," Barbara said. "There is no need to argue and be rude in the monk's garden."

She firmly ushered them back out onto the road. Roger looked along it. "Well, at least we know that the Smiley People came this way."

"And went that way," Lofty said with a grin, pointing up at Glacier Rock.

Roger groaned. "Yes. Up there somewhere. At least the track doesn't go right to the top. The monk said this mad hermit lives somewhere in the jungle near the railway."

"Might be your old mate Tarzan, escaped and come back to his old haunts," Lofty said.

Roger went pale and shook his head. "Oh, don't say that! Kirk reckoned he saw Tarzan there one day."

"Never mind Tarzan. Let's get going," Barbara said. She looked at the others as she swung on her pack. Wendy pulled a face and looked decidedly pale. "You okay Wendy?" she asked.

"Yes. I'm very sore from yesterday and my shoulders are starting to hurt from carrying this pack." She paused then mentioned what was really on her mind. "I just had such an odd feeling then. I... I'm not... not really looking forward to meeting a mad hermit."

Gordon chuckled. "You will be okay. We will send Roger and Dan in first."

He tucked the amulet into his shirt and swung on his pack. Roger snorted and Dan told the joke about the wildlife photographers in Africa watching a lion which looked like it was about to attack.

"The first guy starts putting on his 'Reebok' running shoes yer see and the second guy says: 'Why bother, you can't outrun that lion.' And the first guy replies: 'I don't need to; I only need to outrun you!'"

Roger snorted again and they all laughed. Gordon and Barbara set off side-by-side and the others followed. Almost at once they came out into bright sunlight with ordinary houses on either side. A brilliant blue butterfly fluttered past. Flowers provided splashes of colour to set against the varied greens of the surrounding jungle. Some workmen drove past in a truck. A lady looked up from her gardening. Suddenly it all seemed so ordinary, so suburban.

"I feel silly hiking in a town," Lofty said. A woman hanging out the washing turned to stare at them. Small children called out.

The road curved left into the Stoney Creek valley. Steep slopes rose on three sides. It all appeared very ordinary, and very pretty.

"This is a lovely suburb," Karen commented.

"Yes," agreed Jennifer. "I love some of these houses. They are fabulous. And what a setting!"

They came to a roundabout. A side road to the right dipped down to cross Stoney Creek via a concrete bridge then climbed out of sight among the trees up the other side of the narrow valley. Nice houses lined both sides.

"That way," Barbara said. She led them down across the bridge. They all admired the crystal-clear water gurgling down the bed of the jungle stream.

"It looks like it would be good to swim in," Jennifer said.

"Be a bit cold at this time of year," Lofty replied.

"What about a break for lunch?" Roger protested as they started up the opposite slope.

"Too early. It's only 11:30," Barbara replied.

Now that they had a clue to follow, she was fired with the desire to catch up with the people in the yellow cloaks. She walked as fast as she could and was soon puffing and perspiring. The road went up a steep slope and the others began to string out and fall behind.

"Fair go, Barb! Slow down," Roger called.

She looked back and saw that Roger and Wendy were already fifty paces back and both were red in the face from the effort. Karen and Dan were in front of them, heads down and not talking. Jennifer was walking with Lofty and holding her pack straps with both hands in a way that squeezed her breasts together and made them more noticeable. Lofty kept glancing at them as he talked to her. Barbara compressed her lips. That made her glance at Gordon to see if he was looking at her.

He was. He met her glance with a grin. "We will be okay," he said.

Barbara smiled and suddenly felt happy. She lifted her eyes up to the encircling mountains. They were on the trail.

Now they would find Fiona.

Chapter 11

DOUGLAS TRACK

The bitumen road curved quite steeply up to the left between houses nestled among the rainforest. For a hundred metres the cadets walked straight towards the looming bulk of Glacier Rock. The bitumen road then ended and became an overgrown gravel road. This went on up through more rainforest. There were no more houses. After a few hundred paces the road abruptly switched back to the right. Barbara paused to allow the others to catch up. By then she was just high enough up the mountainside to be able to see back over the tree tops out to the sugar cane fields around Freshwater.

Roger panted up to join her. "Slow down Barbara. It isn't a bloody race!" he grumbled. Wendy looked even more puffed and was scarlet from exertion. They were all perspiring freely.

"I agree," Gordon added. "I came here for a holiday and I'd like a chance to view the scenery. This is very pretty country."

"Pretty bloody steep," Lofty added.

Barbara made no reply, but she did walk more slowly. She was feeling out of breath herself and her leg and shoulder muscles were starting to complain. The group plodded on up, stopping several times to drink and to catch their breath.

"Is this the right way?" Karen asked when they halted at a concrete reservoir at the end of the road.

"We have to go up this ridge the monk said," Barbara answered.

"Where to now?" Dan asked indicating the wall of jungle and weeds at the end of the road.

"There must be a track," Lofty said. "Yes. Over there." He led the way to the left of the reservoir to where a faint foot trail led into the fringe of the jungle. The track curved back through some spiky bushes and came to a clearing covered in shoulder high molasses grass and lantana. A trampled line in the grass showed clearly which way to go. As they rounded a curve Glacier Rock towered ahead.

"We don't have to go up there, do we?" Jennifer asked.

111

"No. Douglas's Track goes over a saddle just to the north of the rock," Roger replied.

"Listen! A train!" Roger called.

They looked back across the narrow valley. The railway on the opposite slope could be clearly seen. The red and white carriages of a tourist train, hauled by a maroon and yellow diesel-electric locomotive crawled along it. The friends watched the train snake along through the cuttings and tunnels until it was hidden by trees. Then they resumed their upward march.

Barbara still led, but she was cautious in the long grass. A strong fear of snakes made her watch carefully where she put her boots. Their movement stayed at a slow plod as the track entered dry, open eucalyptus bush on a steep ridge. Wendy and Roger fell far behind. They called out to wait but Barbara pushed on until she came out in a clearing near a huge steel pylon carrying power lines.

Gordon dropped his pack. "Ah! That's better. What a view!"

Lofty joined him and pointed out various features. "That is the Barron Gorge down to the left. And those buildings out on the plain across the river are Smithfield. You can see Kamerunga where we started from, at those bridges past all those sheoaks."

Karen joined them and turned to look. "Oh, the sea! What a view!"

Lofty pointed. "That is the Coral Sea. Trinity Inlet there leads into Cairns. See the airport? And Mt Whitfield? Cairns city is beyond it and to the right," he explained.

"Can we see the Great Barrier Reef?" Karen asked. They stared out at the distant ocean. The water appeared grey and shiny from that angle.

"No. But that flat disk, the dark thing there on the horizon, that is Green Island, and the little spec of yellow off to the left near the horizon is a sand cay," Lofty added.

"Upolu Cay," Roger said as he puffed up to join them. "Good snorkelling."

He slumped down in the dry grass. Wendy flopped down beside him. For the next few minutes they sat and talked and had big drinks of water while they admired the scenery and recovered their breath. Barbara fidgeted. She had another drink and stood up.

"Come on. Let's push on."

"What about lunch?" Roger asked.

112

Barbara looked at her watch. It was ten past twelve. "No. Not yet. When we get to the railway."

"What a slave driver!" Roger grumbled. He felt in his pocket and extracted a jellybean which he popped into his mouth. He held the packet out. "Jellybean anyone?"

Wendy and Gordon both accepted one. Roger stood up and put out his hand. Wendy took it and he hauled her to her feet. By then Barbara was already scrambling up a section of hillside so steep she had to pull herself up from tree to tree. The track then led around a pile of boulders to a flat area under a mango tree. Here she waited for the others. The sound of the train grew suddenly louder and it appeared out of a cutting only a hundred metres further up the ridge, to clank and rattle out of sight in the direction of Kuranda.

"Keep going. The railway is just up there," she urged and led them on up through tall blady grass.

There was no breeze and it was stifling in the tall grass. She wiped sweat from her eyes, the stopped. Ahead of her was a set of steel steps that went up to a walkway over the railway. She paused to get her breath while she waited. One by one the others joined her.

The group plodded up the long series of steel steps and then crossed the footbridge high above the line. Then they plodded slowly up a zigzag foot path cut into the hillside above. Five minutes of hard walking later they came to a gravel vehicle track. This went on upwards for another hundred metres, curving around a clump of rainforest to a crest.

Barbara walked out onto a bare rise under a power pylon and looked around. Gordon puffed up to join her. "Wheh! That was hot work. Which way do we go now?" he asked.

"In the shade for lunch," Roger said as he arrived. He pointed to the trees to their left.

"And after that?" Karen asked.

Roger pointed up the track. "My guess would be along to the junction of MacDonalds Track and Douglas's and hope to find which way these people went."

Karen frowned. "Where's this MacDonalds Track? You didn't mention it earlier.

Roger indicated the electricity wires overhead. "It is the vehicle track along this power line. It goes to Kuranda."

"Shouldn't we follow the railway toward Kuranda?" Dan asked.

Barbara agreed, "Yes, but I want to follow these Smiley People first. We can go to Kuranda later. I want to follow Douglas's Track"

"That could lead us a long way from Kuranda," Lofty cautioned.

"Maybe. But I reckon they will end up at that property southwest of Kuranda. That's why I want to go up Douglas's Track," Barbara replied.

"But we don't know if they went that way. What if they went along the railway?" Lofty asked.

Barbara shook her head. "We will have to chance that. We can ask this hermit fellow. Besides, I don't think they would have walked along the railway, I mean, all dressed up in yellow robes with trains thundering past! That wouldn't be much good for meditation," she replied.

Roger agreed. "It is against the law to walk along the railway now. Besides, I didn't see any sign they had pushed through all that long grass back down there to get onto the railway."

"Let's hope we can find the hermit," Gordon added.

Dan chuckled. "Probably be able to smell him," he suggested.

This lightened the mood, and they walked a hundred metres up the vehicle track to where the jungle on top of Red Bluff provided shade. They seated themselves on the edge of a steep drop which gave them an impressive view out over the Stoney Creek valley and coastal plain. The roofs of Rainforest Estate lay just below them appearing to be no distance away at all. A cool breeze funnelled up the hillside.

"Good view," Gordon commented as he dug in his webbing for his lunch.

"Makes the walk worthwhile," Jennifer agreed, placing herself between Lofty and Roger.

As they began eating Dan asked, "What about that monk. Do you think he was for real?"

They fell to discussing the meeting with the monk while they ate. Barbara wolfed down her boiled egg sandwiches and turned over in her mind the monk's every word and gesture. To her everything in the last week had been so topsy-turvy that she had no problem accepting his existence, or in believing what he had said.

After half an hour she became impatient. The others appeared content to relax and talk. She packed away the rubbish from her lunch and stood up.

114

"It's nearly one o'clock. Let's get moving."

"Fair go Barb!" Roger groaned, but he hauled himself upright.

Gordon stood up as well. "Barbara's right. We don't know how far we have to go so the sooner we move the better."

Barbara was pleased that Roger and Gordon had supported her. Lofty got up next. "You are right. Half the day is gone and we've come hardly any distance at all."

Webbing and packs were hoisted on and they set off up the slope again. Two minutes of panting effort had them at a bare crest under another power pylon. Just beyond were two signs. One pointed north along the vehicle track and said: MACDONALDS TRACK. The other pointed into the jungle to the left and read: DOUGLAS TRACK.

Barbara walked to the track junction and stared at the dust. "Now, which way did those people go?" she muttered. To her dismay there were dozens of boot prints in the dust.

Roger knelt and studied them. "The most recent ones go left," he said.

"Douglas's Track then," Barbara said.

She straightened up and set off walking. The track was just a foot trail and but clear of undergrowth and easy to follow. It dipped into thick rain forest and then went steeply up the crest line of a narrow ridge into more open forest

As they puffed slowly up the slope Barbara noted that they had lost most of the view, the dense vegetation blocking it off.

But at least it is cooler, she observed.

After about five minutes Barbara came to a track junction. An overgrown track led off down to her left. Wiping perspiration she glanced at it. Doubt clouded her mind as clear in the soil were footprints leading down the side-track.

The others came to a puffing halt beside her. Roger pointed down the old track. "That is the original Douglas's Track. It ran across the side of the mountain from that water reservoir and went below Red Bluff and crossed the railway at a clump of bamboos to the west of Tunnel Fourteen. It zigzags up through the jungle here on our left," he explained as he pointed. "But it is all overgrown now. This track the National Parks people call Douglas's Track isn't the original one at all."

Barbara took out her map and studied it while biting her lip in

115

indecision. On her map she traced both Smiths Track and Douglas's Track.

Douglas's Track goes closer to where I think we want to go, she thought. *Besides, the monk suggested we talk to the mad hermit who lives in the jungle somewhere up the mountain here.* She suppressed a shiver of fear and pointed down the side-track.

"I wonder if this is where the mad hermit lives?" she suggested.

"Might be," Roger agreed. "Do we really want to see him?"

Barbara nodded. "Yes, I think so."

"Then we will do that," Roger agreed.

Barbara began to swing off her pack, but Roger shook his head. "Not here. Lots of people use this main track, tourists and fitness fanatics and Boy Scouts and so on."

Karen looked worried. "You've been along this track?" she asked Roger.

Roger nodded. "Both of them, several times. I used to do a hike every month and I came along both tracks with the Scouts."

The friends walked down the overgrown track for fifty paces and then, at Roger's direction, took off their packs and placed them beside it. He then led the way on down. The track led steeply down through thick tropical rainforest, descending in short zigzags. It was narrow, forcing them to walk in single file. In places it was eroded but it was easy to follow and relatively clear of obstructions other than a few fallen tree trunks which they had to clamber over.

The old track wound down through a thick belt of 'wait-a-while'. Lofty snagged his sleeve on one of the dangling tendrils. "Aaargh! Mongrel!" he cried. He backed up and eased the row of tiny barbs out of the cloth. "Watch out for wait-a-while," he cautioned.

"What's that?" Karen asked. She came from Townsville and all her bush experience was in dry savannah country.

"Wait-a-while? Look," Lofty said. He showed her the long tendrils with their thousands of tiny, hooked barbs. "It grows from these palms. It is the Lawyer Vine plant," he explained.

"Why Lawyer Vine?" Jennifer asked.

"See that vine growing out of it? That is lawyer cane. They make cane furniture out of it but in the old days schoolteachers used it to cane kids," Lofty explained.

116

Barbara carefully pulled at a tendril. "You can't cut it with a jungle knife," she explained. "It is too strong. It just rebounds and catches you. And all the other tendrils flick around and catch you too."

"Mongrel stuff!" Roger agreed. "You can't break it, even these thin ones. It will rip you before it breaks."

"How do you get through it if there is no track?" Karen asked.

"Detour around or use scissors or secateurs," Lofty answered.

"Fine if you've got them but I wasn't planning on sewing or gardening!" Karen said.

"We were," Roger replied. "I've brought my secateurs."

"Me too," Lofty said.

He extracted them from his basic pouch and demonstrated how easily they snipped off the tendrils. Barbara also had secateurs. It was part of the standard kit in their unit. They set to work snipping their way through the tangle and then continued on down.

After a few hundred paces the path skirted several large rock outcrops and huge boulders.

Lofty pointed to their right. "Looks like a bit of a cave over there," he said. Barbara looked and saw a rock overhang which could provide a small amount of shelter.

Roger indicated a faint foot trail leading towards the rocks. "Here is a side-track," he commented. Turning off the main trail he followed the faint track past a large rocky outcrop. The others followed.

Roger rounded another rock pile and stopped so abruptly that Barbara ran into his back. In a small clearing under a rock overhang squatted a bearded man. He wore filthy, tattered clothes and had bare feet. His face, arms, and legs were grimy and covered in scratches and sores. Soiled blankets lay under the overhang along with a litter of cooking utensils and personal items. The whole place stank of urine and rotting food scraps.

The Mad Hermit eyed them but made no move. Barbara forced herself to step forward beside Roger.

"Hello," she said, feeling both scared and silly. "Could you help us please?"

The Mad Hermit grunted and chewed his beard for a moment, then asked in surly tones, "Who are you and what do you want? Are you lost?"

"My name is Barbara. No, we aren't lost. We know where we are thank you. We are searching for a friend. She... er.. .she is with a group of

117

religious people who say they are seeking the true path to enlightenment and... and happiness."

"Happiness?" the Mad Hermit asked sharply.

"Yes. They are happy people," Barbara replied.

The Mad Hermit suddenly moved so fast that the group could only stand dumbfounded. He sprang up and scuttled into the forest, scattering leaves and deadfall as he scrambled on the slope. As he did, he uttered loud whimpers and several high pitched squarks.

The terrified Mad Hermit vanished behind a large tree and there was silence. The friends looked at each other in frightened astonishment. Barbara gulped and put her hand to her breast. Her heart hammered pit-a-pat very rapidly. After a moment she plucked up the courage to call out, "Hello! I'm sorry. I didn't mean to frighten you. We aren't those people. They are not our friends."

There was silence for a minute then an eye appeared around the side of a tree trunk. The man's whole face came slowly into view. He looked thoroughly scared and his mouth worked convulsively.

Barbara spoke again, softly. "It is alright. We are friends. We won't harm you. We are just looking for a friend. She has been taken by these people."

"Are you searching for the truth?" the Mad Hermit asked nervously.

"Yes."

The Mad Hermit suddenly stepped out from behind the tree as though nothing had happened and walked back down to them. Barbara had to resist the urge to step backwards. *He's mad alright,* she thought, observing the peculiar, far-off expression in the Mad Hermit's eyes.

The Mad Hermit said, "If you seek the truth you have come to the right place." He stopped a few paces from them. A waft of rancid body odour reached Barbara and she had to consciously prevent her nose from wrinkling in disgust.

The Mad Hermit suddenly leaned over and patted a tree. "God is all around you. God lives in the living things. That is why they are alive. He lives in the trees. The trees are Mother Nature's home and her living temple. This is where the truth is."

The Mad Hermit let out several chuckles which made the hairs on the back of Barbara's neck stand on end. He knelt and bowed to the tree. There was an embarrassing pause while the Mad Hermit muttered and jabbered to the tree. Then, abruptly, he stood up and faced them. A smile lit up his face and his eyes glittered, but he said nothing.

After another pause Gordon broke the silence. "Excuse me. Have you seen other people walking up the track today?"

"I often see people walking up the track," the Mad Hermit replied. "Some go up, and some go down."

"We want to know if any went up today, people dressed in yellow and singing," Gordon asked.

Again the man cried in fear and sprang behind a tree. "Leave me! Go away! Go, before the evil ones return! Go!"

The friends edged backwards in alarm. Barbara stood her ground.

"Please help us. Which way did the evil people go?"

The Mad Hermit rolled his eyes and pointed up the slope. "They go to the high place. They believe God lives in high places. They are wrong of course because God lives in the trees."

Unexpectedly he smiled and bowed to the tree, gently stroking it. Then he pointed up again. "There is a man who lives up there who talks to God. He claims he is a prophet. He might be able to help you. Mind you, I think he is mad." The Mad Hermit tapped the side of his head and gave an idiot grin which caused Barbara's skin to come out in goose bumps. "Now go! But remember, the prophet is mad, and he is wrong. God does not live in the sky. He lives in the trees. Respect the trees!" He glared at them, then pointed and shouted angrily, "Now go!"

Barbara nodded. "Thank you," she managed to say.

She turned and the others did likewise. Without a word they walked quickly back to the overgrown old track where they broke into an excited babble.

"Shh!" Barbara hissed. "Don't talk here. Further up the track."

Lofty led, then Gordon, then Barbara followed by Wendy, Jennifer and Dan. They went as quickly as they could walk, collecting their packs on the way. Then they hurried back up as fast as the steep slope and the weight of their packs would allow.

They stopped to get their breath back and a drink. Dan jerked his thumb back. "What about that joker back there?"

Lofty shook his head. "The Mad Hermit? Crazy as a cut snake," he said.

Roger nodded. "Right out of his tree."

They all laughed at that.

"At least we know the Smileys came this way," Barbara said.

Wendy looked anxious. "Wasn't he frightened of them! Did you see how he reacted when you mentioned the Happy People?"

Gordon agreed, "Yes. He was terrified. That's a worry. He called them the 'evil ones' and so did the monk. I think we'd better be very careful."

"Too right!" Lofty agreed. "We'd better be a bit more circumspect in our questioning."

"Could we say we are looking for something else and then sort of lead the conversation around to ask if they had seen any other people?" Wendy suggested.

"Good idea!" Barbara approved. "What can we say we are looking for?"

"Here in the jungle? What about researching for a Geography assignment?" Lofty suggested.

"Hmmm. Yes, maybe," Barbara replied.

Roger clicked his fingers. "I know," he cried. "Thylacines."

"Thyla... whats?" Jennifer asked.

"Thylacines."

"What are they?"

"A thing like a Tasmanian Tiger," Roger replied.

Jennifer laughed. "Tasmanian Tiger! This isn't Tasmania!" she cried.

"No, but they used to live here," Roger explained. "No-one is sure whether they are extinct or not. Silver Wolf reckons he knows a bloke who once saw one."

"Silver Wolf!" Jennifer sneered. "This isn't Canada either. Who is Silver Wolf, an Indian Chief?"

Roger blushed. "No. He is my Scout Master."

"Are you still a boy scout?" Jennifer asked in a derisory tone.

Roger faced her. He coloured with embarrassment. "Yes I am. And I think it is a wonderful organisation that does a lot of good for a lot of kids, and I thoroughly enjoy it. I've learnt a lot of jolly useful things as a scout."

Jennifer sneered. Wendy gave Roger a look of sympathy for she was also in the Rangers.

Barbara stepped forward. "Don't fight. Roger has a good idea. We

120

are looking for Thylacines. Roger, you do the talking. The rest of us will shut up. Then we can lead the conversation around."

"Why are we looking for them?" Karen asked.

"Oh! Umm. Let me see... I know. For the University. Some study of rare animals," Roger said.

Lofty indicated his watch. "It is two o'clock. We had better push on."

Barbara looked around. Already the sun had moved behind the bulk of Glacier Rock and they were in cool shadow. They resumed their upward trek, Lofty still leading and snipping off any overhanging wait-a-while tendrils. The group threaded their way through more vines dragged down by a fallen tree.

"What was this track for?" Karen asked. "Where did it go?"

"For pack animals to take supplies to the Hodgekinson Goldfield at Mt Mulligan back in the 1870s," Roger replied between breaths.

Karen gasped. "Mt Mulligan! Isn't that where you had that trouble a couple of months ago Barbara?" she asked.

Barbara nodded and pursed her lips. The darkness seemed to grow and she had trouble seeing. Her breath felt crushed. Her mind raced in a turmoil of horrible memories. She grunted and nodded again but said nothing. She noted Roger frown and shake his head at Karen.

They plodded on up the track in silence for a while till pumping hearts and weakening thigh and calf muscles called for another halt. After a drink and a short rest they went on upwards. After another hundred sweaty metres up the mountain the track came out of rainforest into open sheoak country. It curved left, slanting diagonally up the side of the mountain on a narrow bench-cut. They began to get glimpses of Cairns and the coastal plain out through gaps in the trees.

By 2:20pm they were at another track junction on the saddle north of Glacier Rock. Here the main track began to dip down into more rainforest to the west. They halted and dropped their packs and webbing.

"Wheh! That was a good stiff climb," Gordon said. "Which way now?"

"Follow the track?" Lofty suggested.

"Which track? There are three," Roger said, pointing to a faint trail in the grass going off to the right and a good track going left.

"Where do they go?" Wendy asked. "Where is this Speewah place?" she asked, as she read the National Park sign at the track junction.

121

Barbara opened her map and Lofty took out his compass. He pointed. "The one going west is Douglas's Track and it goes to Speewah."

Roger nodded. "It does. It is a nice walk, and mostly very easy to follow," he said. Barbara looked. It was true. The old pioneers track was clear and obvious. A trail going off to the left was almost as good and the sign pointing that way read: GLACIER ROCK. Only the trail going right was not obvious. It showed only crushed grass indicating recent use.

"So up to the left is Glacier Rock, and this one running along the ridge line northwards must lead to Kuranda," Barbara decided.

"Let's go to Glacier Rock. It isn't far and the view is superb," Lofty suggested.

"Good idea," Barbara agreed.

"Can't we have a rest first?" Jennifer suggested, wiping perspiration from her face.

"No. I want to find this Mad Prophet who lives on top of the mountain," Barbara said. "Come on."

122

Chapter 12

MORE SURPRISES

Barbara set off up the foot trail which led through open forest. Much of the grass had recently been burnt off and there was almost no undergrowth. The others followed in a straggling line. The going was relatively easy. The trail followed the crest of a low ridge. For fifty metres it went uphill before crossing a knoll studded with rocks. It then went down across a dip then on up a steeper slope through waist high blady grass under a canopy of open eucalypts and sheoaks.

After five minutes walking, the friends arrived puffing on the crest of Glacier Rock. The group gathered under a low, spreading tree just back from the very lip of the precipice and gazed out. 300 metres below them lay the railway line which snaked its way around the jungle clad slopes of the Stoney Creek valley. Stoney Creek Falls was clearly visible a kilometre away. Spanning Stoney Creek just below the falls was the famous curved railway bridge.

Gordon stood beside Barbara and looked around with evident approval. "It's a magnificent view. Worth the climb," he said. Barbara gazed out over the distant sugar fields to the sea and agreed.

Karen was also impressed. "It's a lovely view and a lovely day."

"We've come a fair way," Dan observed.

"No we haven't!" Jennifer sneered. She pointed down into the valley. "We only started just down there. That's only a few kilometres away. Those houses down in the valley are that 'Rainforest Estate' aren't they?"

"Yes," Lofty confirmed.

Barbara looked. The houses did seem rather close. It made her feel depressed. All that effort to get such a short distance!

Jennifer went on, "And what have we found? A monk who talked riddles and a mad hermit who stank like a blocked toilet!"

Lofty looked around. "Which reminds me. I wonder where this prophet is who..."

He fell silent so abruptly that Barbara glanced sharply at him, caught the astonished expression, and spun round to look in the same direction.

What she saw made her gasp with fright and her reactions made the others turn as well.

Standing about ten paces away was a bearded man holding a wooden staff. He wore a long caftan type garment patterned with broad vertical stripes of red, white, yellow, and green. The first thought which crossed Barbara's mind was 'Moses', to be corrected to 'Joseph and his coat of many colours'. She knew at once he was 'The Mad Prophet'.

The Mad Prophet suddenly smiled and spoke, "Greetings friends and fellow travellers in the journey of life. Welcome to my mountain top."

"Er... umm... er. Hello," Lofty stammered back. They all struggled to recover from the shock.

The Mad Prophet nodded and smiled before saying, "What good fortune has directed your steps to this place? Is it to hear the word of God?"

Gordon answered guardedly, "We have come seeking enlightenment."

"Good!" the Mad Prophet cried. His eyes lit up and he raised both arms. "You have come to the right place. Here you are close to God. He is just up there."

The Mad Prophet pointed into the sky. As he spoke his voice rose to an exultant shout and he advanced several paces closer to them. Barbara took a step back and was uncomfortably aware that the cliff edge was just behind them. While managing to smile she began to shuffle sideways away from the edge. The others moved with her.

The Mad Prophet suddenly shouted and waved his arms. "But we are lucky. HE is coming again! It will be soon! Oh praise be! The end of the world is at hand. Repent of your sins and prepare to die! Prepare to meet your God!"

The Mad Prophet's voice became an angry scream. He stepped closer to them, waving his arms and jabbing his forefinger accusingly at them. Barbara felt a wave of cold fear sweep over her and she licked her lips. Anxious lest this madman should attack them she tensed ready to jump aside. Knowing that there was a drop of several hundred metres only a few paces behind her added to her fear. Gordon stepped forward in front of her. She was simultaneously grateful and resentful that he was apparently trying to shield her.

The Mad Prophet, now only a couple of paces away, suddenly dropped his arms and lowered his voice. He shook his head sadly and said, "Yes. We must all pay for our sins. And there are many sinners. The world is full of evil people. I have seen them."

Barbara and the others continued to edge away from the top of the cliff. She tried to think of something to say. The Mad Prophet continued on, changing abruptly to a cheerful voice and smiling again, "But brothers and sisters you have come to the right place. I have had the truth revealed to me. This is the very place where God will return to earth. You may stay here with me until that happy time when God comes down from the sky and ends the wickedness in the world!"

The Mad Prophet leered at Jennifer. Barbara gave a sour grin. *Serves her right for wearing that shirt,* she thought, suspecting what sort of wickedness was on the Mad Prophet's mind at that moment.

By this time Roger had moved several metres away from the cliff edge. The Mad Prophet suddenly turned to glare at him. His eyes glittered and he hissed, "I hope there are no sinners here who have evil thoughts. They will not find the true way to God. They will not go up into the sky! (Pointing up). They will be cast down, thrown into the pit of darkness! Down! (Pointing over the cliff and shouting). Down into hell!"

The Mad Prophet's eyes blazed and spittle flecked his beard. Roger looked both embarrassed and scared. Barbara felt sick apprehension in case the man became violent.

Lofty suddenly walked over close to the Mad Prophet and asked, "These evil people you saw, did they wear yellow?"

The Mad Prophet's mouth gaped open. He took a step backward and stared at Lofty in alarm. "Yes. They claim they are true believers, but I can see they have black hearts. Are they your friends?" The Mad Prophet abruptly shifted his staff to a defensive posture.

Lofty stood apparently relaxed. "No. They are our enemies. Which way did they go? We seek them to do God's work."

The Mad Prophet stepped back and stared hard at each in turn. "Are you Crusaders on a quest against the dark forces?"

"Yes," Lofty replied.

"Praise be to God! A miracle! I knew you were good people," the Mad Prophet cried. His eyes glittered and his gaze lingered on Jennifer's breasts. He licked his lips before pointing north. "They went that way. I do not know where they went. When I heard them coming I hid, for they are bad people and have threatened to throw me over the cliff."

125

"Thank you," Lofty replied, gesturing to the others to move. "We must go now. We must follow them."

The Mad Prophet looked worried. "Are you sure? The end of the world is close. You can stay here with me and watch the sinners meet their just retribution. You will be safe with me for I am God's chosen messenger." He leered at Jennifer again.

"We are sure. We must do our duty," Gordon put in. He took Barbara firmly by the hand and walked away from the cliff.

The Mad Prophet looked sad and asked pleadingly, "Go if you must, but I would like you to stay (this directed at Jennifer). But be warned! The end of the world is close! And beware of the evil ones. If you go that way you may meet a terrible fate. I will pray for your souls."

Gordon ignored the Mad Prophet and kept walking. The others followed. Barbara glanced out of the corner of her eye, afraid lest the Mad Prophet attempt to detain them but he just stood looking sad.

The friends walked quickly down the slope. When they were fifty paces away Lofty spoke, "Strewth! I nearly crapped myself when that bugger appeared. Talk about out of his tree! The end of the world!"

Gordon chuckled. "He sussed you out Roger, you sinner with evil thoughts!"

Roger scowled then grinned. "Bloody hell, I was scared. And speaking of evil thoughts he could hardly take his eyes off you Jennifer."

Jennifer blushed and sniffed. "He's just a dirty old man."

"Serves you right for wearing that top," Wendy snapped.

Jennifer stopped and turned to face her, hands on hips. "What's your problem? Jealous?"

Wendy went red but didn't answer. Instead she kept on walking. The boys all gaped in astonishment, their eyes flicking from Jennifer to Wendy. Barbara did also, thinking that Wendy had nothing to be jealous about compared to Jennifer.

"That will do," Lofty said. "Don't start fighting amongst ourselves. I was scared too."

They kept on walking and a few minutes later were back at their packs at Douglas's Track. Here they stopped to have a drink and recover their breath.

Dan shook a water bottle. "I'm nearly out of water. When will we come to a creek?"

Barbara unfolded her map and had a look. Gordon leaned over and their arms touched. "Which way do we go?" he asked.

"That way the Mad Prophet said," Barbara replied, pointing. "North along the crestline."

Lofty picked up his webbing. "Let's move then, before the Mad Prophet follows us."

Barbara folded the map and looked at her watch. It was five past three. The day seemed to be flying past. They hoisted on their packs and set off, Gordon and Lofty leading, Barbara third with Karen behind her. A faint trail led around a clump of rocks and through a thicket of burnt suckers, then up a ridgeline through open sheoak forest. The grass had been burnt off so that underfoot was ash, bare earth and new shoots.

It was easy going at first, but the slope got steeper and steeper. The friends slowed down and soon came to a halt.

Gordon mopped sweat off his face. "Just as well this is winter. I wouldn't like to do this on a summer day."

Barbara looked up. Not a cloud in the sky. She was now feeling very drained, the exertions of the previous day having taken their toll. She was beginning to feel very sore where the pack straps chafed on her shoulders. Muscles unaccustomed to hard work were beginning to tire and ache. She noticed that Wendy looked very tired.

After a few minutes rest, they plodded on up to the crest of the hill. The ridge top was open forest, a mixture of sheoaks and eucalyptus trees with waist high blady grass beneath. The trail led north. They began to get glimpses of seemingly endless hills out to the west. The country around them appeared to be a jumble of jungle covered ridges. They walked across a low saddle and skirted several outcrops of rock.

Lofty suddenly stopped. Barbara followed his gaze and was surprised to see a lean-to shelter made of saplings and a tattered canvas tent-fly. A litter of rubbish, empty bottles and camp equipment was strewn about. Beside a log a man lay on his back. He was wearing torn jeans and a blue patterned 'lumberjack' shirt, from which tattooed arms protruded.

"Is he alright?" Barbara asked, wrinkling her nose in disgust at both the sight of the man's soiled clothing and the smell of his camp.

"Don't know," Lofty replied.

He walked over to the man and leaned over to look at him. As he did, the man opened one eye. Lofty stepped hastily back. Barbara regretted asking. She just wanted to walk away. But the man groaned and abruptly sat up. He blinked at them and rubbed his eyes. He was unshaven and looked unwell. In his right hand he clutched a large bottle.

The man groaned again and licked his lips. "Who the bloody hell are you mob?" he asked.

"Just bushwalkers," Lofty replied. "Are you alright?"

The man squinted at them, then groaned and pressed a hand to his forehead. "Aw! Yeah, I'm okay. Are you more of them God-botherin' bastards?"

"No. But we are searching for... for something," Lofty replied.

The man rolled his eyes and raised the bottle to his lips. Then he snorted angrily and hurled it against a rock where it smashed.

"Bloody thing's empty! You mob got anything ter drink?"

"No. Sorry."

"What bloody good are you!" the man snarled while trying to heave himself up onto the log. "Yer haven't got any rum, eh?"

"No."

The man spat, then burped. "Yer as bad as them happy bastards in the yellow togs, mob of sanctimonious turds they are!" He spat again.

"Did they come this way?" Gordon asked.

The man seated himself on the log with an effort and turned a bloodshot eye on Gordon. "You more of them fools lookin' fer happiness in religion, eh? Stupid idiots! There's no joy in religion, just restrictions and bloody guilt. You want freedom and happiness? Well you'll find it for sure in a bottle."

He bent behind him and picked up a large glass flagon. "Alcohol! You can depend on that for a bit of release from misery. Cripes! The bloody thing is empty. Now I'll have to go back ter drinkin' me own brew. Jungle Juice she is. Bloody powerful stuff. Yalbogie Firewater I calls it."

He laughed and dropped the flagon and nearly fell off the log. Barbara was revolted by him. He had plainly pissed his pants not long before and his hands were shaking. He kicked several bottles at his feet.

"Can't find any," he muttered. "That's bad. Gawd I need a drink! If I don't get one, I'll start seein' them Oojoombie mongrels again."

The drunk's manner abruptly changed and he looked fearfully around. He lurched to his feet and staggered to where an axe was embedded in a tree stump. After several efforts he wrenched it free, muttering and swearing the whole time.

Barbara felt a surge of fear and plucked at Gordon's sleeve. The man turned to face them, swaying on his feet and waving the axe in the air.

"Bastards!" he shouted. "Come here and annoy me! Laugh at me! Won't give a man a drink! Piss orf! This is my bloody camp. Leave me alone. Git outa hear ya hear!"

He began to walk towards them. The friends hastily backed off, Lofty and Gordon trying to placate and reassure the man. He stopped and put a hand to his head, then slumped down on the log muttering. With a loud groan he slid onto the ground.

"Come on!" Lofty said.

He led the way quickly on along the ridgeline. The others needed no urging to walk fast. Fifty metres on they came to a knoll from which they could see out through a gap in the trees. Beyond stretched a jumble of jungle-clad ridges slashed by the great gash of the Barron Gorge. The afternoon shadows accentuated the steep cliffs and sharply outlined the crestlines.

Gordon stared at the jungle covered hills. "Gee! That's pretty rough country," he observed.

Wendy pointed. "Is that Kuranda? Those buildings we can see?"

"I'll check," Barbara replied, pulling out her map.

Karen glanced back. "I wonder who that fellow back there is?" she said.

Roger also glanced anxiously back. "God knows. I wasn't game to ask," he replied.

Jennifer looked worried. "Shouldn't we check that he is alright?" she asked.

Lofty gave a grunt. "You can if you like," he replied. "I don't fancy getting too close to a drunken maniac with an axe."

Dan shook his head. "But what is he doing here? Isn't this a National Park?" he asked.

"Yes, it is," Barbara replied as she studied the map. "I doubt if he should be camped there but it's probably been a while since a Park Ranger wandered along this mountain top." She turned to Wendy. "No, that isn't Kuranda. It's a place called Dean's Lookout. It is just opposite Hydro, at the top of the Barron Falls."

"How far is Kuranda?" Roger asked.

"About six kilometres in a straight line."

"Fine!" Roger said sarcastically, gesturing at the jumble of jungle-covered ridges. "But we can't walk in a straight line."

"Probably ten or twelve kilometres then," Barbara answered.

"Where do we go now?" Wendy asked.

"Down there I reckon," Lofty pointed down the steep grassy hillside. "See where the grass is flattened? There is a bit of a track, and we know the Smileys came this way. Our alcoholic friend said so."

They set off down the hill. The trail led them through waist high grass and weeds. Barbara found going down as difficult as going up. The grass hid numerous stones and her leg muscles felt all thrown into reverse. Wendy slipped and fell heavily on her bum several times. Barbara noticed that she looked very down. She obviously wasn't enjoying the hike. Barbara wasn't either but was happy that they were on the right track.

It took fifteen minutes of slipping, stumbling and sweating with the afternoon sun on their faces before they reached a rough vehicle track. Nearby was a steel power pylon.

"Left, or right?" Lofty asked.

Roger studied the ground for tracks. "Left. Towards Kuranda."

"Let's have a break first," Barbara insisted, seeing Wendy's tired face.

"I'm out of water," Dan said, holding a water bottle upside down.

"There is a creek about half a 'K' on," Barbara said. "It might have water in it."

She had a drink herself and noted that she was on to the fourth, and last, of her own water bottles. It made her realise how thirsty she was. She felt quite worn out.

This became weariness close to exhaustion within half an hour as they toiled over three ridges following the powerline track. This ran in a cleared strip and the sun blazed down on them. Down in the hollows it was very hot with no shade and no breeze. Nor was there water in the small creeks they crossed, yet, annoyingly, the track was just damp enough to be greasy. This made walking awkward. Roger slipped over once and so did Wendy. She fell hard on her bottom. Tears came to her eyes as she struggled up. Barbara dropped back to help her.

"I'm okay," Wendy sniffled. "I'm just chafed and sore from yesterday. I'm very unfit."

"Aren't we all!" agreed Barbara. She shifted her pack on her aching shoulders.

The group paused briefly on an open hilltop under a power pylon, to get their breath more than to admire the view. Then the track curved left and downhill into a tunnel of rainforest. This was easier going and cooler but still had minor problems presented by dangling tendrils of wait-a-while to snag the unwary.

After another ten minutes of plodding down a slope which became quite steep a boulder-lined creek came into view on the left. It was flowing with crystal clear water. A small shady clearing under trees on the inside of a sharp bend looked very cool and inviting. A small steel bridge spanned the creek and the vehicle track went up a steep slope on the other side, to vanish amongst the jungle.

The friends stopped at the bridge. Lofty checked his map. "Surprise Creek," he said.

Roger swung off his pack. "Let's stop and have a good rest," he suggested.

Chapter 13

THE SWIM

Jennifer studied the deep pool upstream of the sandy flat. "Let's have a swim," she suggested.

"Good idea. But I didn't bring any bathers," Wendy replied.

Jennifer grinned, "Skinny dip. There's no-one to see us."

Roger looked anxious. "I wouldn't be so sure about no-one," he said. "This is near where Kirk had his fight with Tarzan, and think of all those odd characters we met today in a supposedly uninhabited National Park."

Jennifer replied sharply. "Shut up Roger! You are just trying to scare us. You aren't game, that's all," she teased. She dropped her pack and sat down on a water-smoothed rock.

At the thought of others seeing her nude Barbara felt mild panic. *I'm not sure I want this sort of stress,* she thought. She looked at Gordon and their eyes met.

He smiled and shook his head. "A swim is a good idea. But us boys will go down there out of sight and you girls can swim in this pool here. We don't want Dan getting all overheated."

Jennifer smirked. "Spoilsport!" she said with a giggle.

Barbara gave Gordon a grateful smile. She felt really hot and grimy and a swim was just what she needed. She dropped her pack and webbing beside Jennifer's and rubbed her sore shoulders.

The boys made their way downstream. This took them around a bend for about thirty metres. The girls went to the pool on the upstream side of the track. A small waterfall emptied into it. The pool appeared a little gloomy in the jungle shadows but was still inviting.

Wendy walked over to the creek and bent to test the water with her hand, "Brrr! It's cold!"

As she sat down on her pack to unlace her boots, Barbara was in an anxious turmoil over whether to swim nude, or to leave on her bra and panties, or to change into her bathers. Judging by the nervous chatter, she thought the others felt the same way.

Jennifer decided it for them. She tugged of her boots and then peeled off her jeans before standing up and taking off her T-shirt. "Ah! That's better," she said, arching her back and stretching, apparently oblivious to the other girl's stares.

Barbara couldn't help looking and that both troubled her and excited her. Jennifer next pulled off her undies and casually tossed them onto a rock before walking to the water and wading cautiously in.

After that example the others felt constrained to follow suit. Karen was next to undress. Barbara noted that, while Karen's breasts were quite small they were nicely shaped, and she had a slim waist and nice legs. From the back she presented a very pleasing profile. She gingerly hobbled over the rocks and gravel and into the water.

By this time Barbara felt very hot and self-conscious. She pulled off her boots then stood up and took off her shirt and trousers. Wendy did likewise, glancing nervously at Barbara as she undid her bra and took it off. Barbara did the same. Out of the corner of her eye she couldn't help noticing Wendy's breasts. They were very big and rounded. And they really did wobble! Poor Wendy!

As Wendy made her way into the water she bent forward. Barbara couldn't help staring. Then Wendy stubbed her toe on a rock and bent right over to rub it. Barbara gaped. She saw that Wendy had pale, white skin, and a big bum.

"It's freezing!" Wendy cried. She stood hesitantly on the bank, covering herself with her arms.

Barbara looked away knowing that she was interested in looking but feeling ashamed of herself for being that way. For a minute or so she hesitated, taking her time to remove her watch and to undo her bra. To overcome her own embarrassment she breathed deeply, flung off her underclothes and strode quickly to the water.

"Oh my gosh! It is cold!" she cried.

"Come on in," Jennifer laughed, splashing her and Wendy with icy water. The two girls shrieked and floundered in. To hide her body Barbara at once submerged herself.

The water was freezing but very refreshing. Barbara rubbed sweat off herself and wiped her face. Then she relaxed and allowed herself to enjoy the sensuousness of the water flowing over her bare skin. She admitted to herself that she was enjoying the thrill of being nude and the sense of freedom that came with it. But it was very cold and she also had a nagging sense of time passing quickly. She noted that the sunlight had moved off the pool and up the slope.

"I wonder what the time is?" Barbara said.

But none of the others had a waterproof watch so could not tell her. To find out she waded ashore, hotly conscious that the others could all see her. To get to her webbing she had to walk out past the trees beside the track. As she did Barbara looked down to the right to check whether any of the boys could see her. She felt very daring and her heart beat rapidly. As she bent to pick up her watch, she felt very naked.

Oh heavens, I'm naughty! she thought. But in her heart she knew she was enjoying the thrill.

Behind her there was a shrill shriek and giggles of laughter as Karen and Wendy threw handfuls of cold water over Jennifer. Barbara saw that it was 4:30.

Time we got moving, she thought.

She stood up and, as she turned, she saw Lofty's head poke up over a boulder. He gaped in delighted astonishment then bobbed down. A shout of male laughter indicated that Lofty had made some comment.

Barbara turned to face the girls. She knew that by taking a couple of steps she would be out of sight of the boys but was now enjoying the dare and stayed where they might see her. She found she was simultaneously excited and ashamed but also realised that she did not mind if the others looked at her.

She called to the girls, "Time to get out."

They all looked and nodded, and Barbara noted their eyes take in her body. A rush of excitement mingled with feelings of shame and arousal. Smiling with the sheer pleasure of it all she stood and began clipping on her watch. Wendy led the others out of the water and Barbara was again ashamed that she wanted to look. Jennifer and Karen followed, all stepping carefully on the wet stones in their bare feet.

Lest the other girls take offence at her gaze, Barbara turned to pick up her bra. Then she froze in shock. Standing not ten metres away, at the end of the small bridge, was a man.

Her gasp made Wendy look. Wendy let out a scream and tried to cover herself with her arms. Barbara instinctively did the same, stepping in front of Wendy as she did. Out of the corner of her eye she saw the boy's heads appear. Then Gordon scrambled up over the rocks. He was naked and she glimpsed his muscular, tanned limbs and his penis waggling out of its matt of pubic hair.

Part of her mind noted that she was relieved, both because he was normal and because he was hurrying to her aid. She also realised in a flash of insight that she was not the slightest bit offended by the boy's nakedness or by them seeing her nude. Instead it made her feel excited. She turned her back on the man and clasped Wendy to shield her.

Gordon scooped up his trousers and hauled them on, followed by the other boys. Lofty wrapped a towel around himself. Karen tossed trousers to Jennifer, then picked up a shirt and draped it over Barbara's shoulders.

"Grab Wendy's shirt too," Barbara called.

She was acutely aware of Wendy's flesh pressing against her own. Karen did so. Wendy took it and turned her back on the man, using Barbara as a screen. Barbara struggled to get her wet arms through the long sleeves and then hastily buttoned the shirt. As she did, she glanced down to check that it was long enough to cover her. She was hotly aware that Gordon and the other boys were getting a good side view of her as she did this.

By the time she had the shirt on the boys were there. They confronted the man, who had not moved. Barbara grabbed her trousers and dragged them on.

The man spread his hands, palms upwards and said, "I am sorry I frightened you."

He spoke with a peculiar European accent. His complexion was olive and his hair and eyes were black. He wore jeans and hiking boots, a long-sleeved shirt of mauve with lavender floral patterns and he had a red neck cloth and a large gold earring in his right ear. On his back was a rucksack and he carried a staff. While the girls struggled with their clothing, he turned to face the boys.

Lofty was quite belligerent. "Who are you? What are you doing here?"

"I did not come here to fight I assure you," the man said soothingly. "I am just a traveller. I am here because this is a public walking track and I view the scenery. I am not the peeping-tom. I did not creep up. I was just walking along the track enjoying the beauty of nature and viola! There, indeed, were nature's beauties." He then bowed low and said, "Ladies, I am sorry. I did not mean to scare you."

Barbara blushed as she buttoned up her trousers. To her surprise she saw that Jennifer was wearing trousers but had not pulled on a top and was standing with just her folded arms for modesty.

Lofty nodded, for what the man said was quite true. He asked, "Have you seen a bunch of people wearing yellow coats going this way?"

The man considered, tilting his head and placing a finger to his cheek. Barbara studied him. *A gypsy,* she decided. *That's what he looks like.* She knew that wasn't the politically correct name for such people, but could not think what it was.

The gypsy replied, "I have seen many people this day. Some wore yellow and some wore white."

"Where was that? Which way did they go?" Barbara said, facing him.

The gypsy fixed glittering black eyes on her and shrugged. "I am only on holiday but... But a man must work. I can tell you much that you want to know but you must pay for my services. I have special powers, but I only use them sparingly."

Karen stepped forward. "Are you a fortune teller?" she asked, with more than a hint of scepticism in her voice.

"I can see things that others cannot," the gypsy replied gravely.

Gordon gave a snort of incredulity. The gypsy turned to face him and said, "For example, I can see that you have come from far away. You do not come from this place."

"Anyone could work that out," Gordon scoffed. "Everyone is a tourist here."

"You do not come from Cairns, but he does. And so does she, and her," the gypsy replied, pointing first at Roger, then at Barbara and Wendy.

Barbara was surprised and doubtful. She tried to remember if she had seen the man around town. She asked, "What is your fee?"

"A gold coin each? That will buy me a good dinner," the gypsy replied. Then he smiled. "Of course I don't mean a real gold coin. A two-dollar coin each will suffice."

"Alright," Barbara agreed, feeling in her pocket.

The gypsy swung off his rucksack and seated himself cross-legged. He reached inside and pulled out a bundle of cloth.

Surely he hasn't got a crystal ball! Barbara thought.

The gypsy unrolled the cloth and spread it on the sand. Inside was a smaller ball of black velvet which he unrolled carefully to reveal a genuine crystal ball the size of an orange.

Barbara was fascinated. She knelt down to examine the object. Its interior shimmered with green and gold, then red and blue, then yellow and purple and all the hues between, but she could detect no pattern or picture. Jennifer knelt beside her to look, still covering her front with just her arms. As she leaned forward her breasts bulged over them most revealingly. Barbara felt a surge of annoyance and embarrassment. She nudged her and when their eyes met she showed her disapproval.

Jennifer frowned but she took the hint and stood up and went to get her shirt, not taking any care to hide herself as she pulled it on. Barbara noted the boy's eyes widen with interest, including Gordon's. That caused her a surge of resentment which she recognised as jealousy.

The gypsy pretended not to watch but Barbara noticed his eyes also flicker. She decided he was in his thirties and good looking in a Latin kind of way. To take everyone's attention off Jennifer, she placed a handful of coins on the velvet and said, "I am looking for a friend. Can you tell me where she is?"

The gypsy stared deep into her eyes for a long minute, then nodded and bent to peer into his crystal, murmuring quietly to himself. He focused intently on the shimmering colours, then said, "Strange men have caused you to cross the mountains."

Barbara's eyes met Gordon's. His expression plainly said, 'any fool could guess that.' She looked back, just in time to see the gypsy's expression change. The colour seemed to drain out of his face. He looked at each in turn with a mixture of horror and alarm.

"Who are you people? What have you done?" He looked nervously around and licked his lips. Beads of sweat appeared on his brow. He muttered and stared into his crystal and said, "This is terrible! I see death, much death. And worse! There is a ghost walking nearby. And I see two people, a man and a woman, a blonde woman, young, like you. The man is dead, but the woman is alive. But..."

He bent closer to the crystal, his voice sinking to a strangled whisper, "But... the dead man is walking! He is one of the walking dead!"

The gypsy snatched up the crystal and sprang to his feet. Barbara felt a thrill of fear and the hair stood up on the back of her neck. The gypsy shook his head and cried, "I don't understand this. When I first looked I thought you were seeking laughter and joy, but now all I see ahead of you is misery and death."

137

Barbara stood up. The gypsy picked up his money and snatched up the velvet cloth. He went on, "Be warned! Be on your guard! If you go that way you may meet great evil. Someone has freed the dark forces. You will be in great danger... except you."

The gypsy pointed at Gordon. Then he muttered and peered again into the crystal and his eyes appeared to glaze over. He shook his head. "I do not understand. You have some powerful protection. You must go on. It is your fate. But you others should turn back, or you may be doomed."

The gypsy knelt and bundled the crystal into his rucksack, all the while muttering in a foreign language. He appeared genuinely scared and this communicated itself to all of them. The man stood up and swung on the rucksack and made a sign with his hand. Then he picked up his staff and walked quickly off up the steep track in the direction of Glacier Rock.

The group stood in shocked silence till he was gone from sight.

"What a horrible man!" Karen cried. "He didn't have to scare us like that."

"What a load of hocus pocus," Lofty said angrily.

"But he knew about the monk and his good luck charm," Jennifer pointed out.

Gordon gave a wry grin. "He was more interested in your charms," he observed dryly.

Barbara let her fear flare into anger. "Yes Jennifer. You didn't have to flaunt yourself like that."

"I wasn't flaunting myself! I just forgot," Jennifer retorted.

"That will do! We didn't mind," Gordon said.

Gordon taking Jennifer's side seemed to drive a hot little needle into Barbara's heart. "Well I did!" she snapped.

There was a moment's tense silence. Then Lofty stepped forward. "Roger didn't. I thought his eyes would pop out. Besides, I saw you running around in the nuddy just before."

"I was just looking at my watch," Barbara replied with embarrassment.

"Forget it," Gordon said. "You can all run around naked as much as you like. The point is that fortune teller just gave us all a fright."

There was another uncomfortable silence. Then Wendy spoke, her voice a mere whisper, "Zombies! He said he could see one of the walking dead!"

Chapter 14

ROBBS MONUMENT

Barbara felt a cold wave of fear sweep over her. They all glanced nervously around. The jungle suddenly seemed gloomy and sinister.

Roger spoke first, "Nonsense! There are no such things as zombies. He was just trying to scare us."

"He succeeded then," Gordon replied with a wry smile.

Dan looked worried. "What will we do now?" he asked.

"Go on of course," Gordon answered.

Lofty snorted. "Huh! Easy for you to say," he replied with a grin. "He said you'd be okay."

"We could go back," Jennifer said. She looked very pale.

Barbara bit her lip. "You can go back if you like but I'm going on. I'm going to find Fiona."

"Let's get moving then," Karen said. "I don't like this place."

"We have to get dressed properly," Barbara said. "You boys go away for a few minutes."

"Aw! Spoilsport. We could help," Lofty said.

"Get going!" Barbara said, but she smiled.

As the boys walked off down the creek Wendy said, "What if another man comes along?"

Jennifer shrugged. "Then it's his lucky day," she replied as she stripped off her T-shirt.

The girls moved to their packs and then stood facing away from each other as they undressed again. Wendy took out a towel and rubbed herself vigorously. "Gosh I got a fright when I looked up and saw that man. Do you think he was a Gypsy?" she said.

"Yes. I think he was. I got a fright too. It serves us right for not keeping an eye open," Barbara replied, looking up into the surrounding jungle just to check he was gone.

"Was he a real fortune teller do you think?" Jennifer asked.

"No. It is all nonsense," Barbara said sharply. But deep down she had a niggling doubt. She decided not to get out her towel as she was

139

now mostly dry. So she pulled on her panties and began putting on her bra. Out of the corner of her eye she noted Wendy doing the same and she was hotly aware she wanted to watch. The self-knowledge made her bite her lip with shame.

Wendy said, "Gordon looks good, doesn't he?"

"Yes," agreed Barbara.

"Which do you prefer, circumcised or uncircumcised?" Wendy giggled.

Barbara had a series of mental images of penises she had seen, usually erect and being forced at her. She grimaced. "I don't know. I've never thought about it. I'm not sure I like any."

"Oh Barbara!" Wendy said, moving to one side to look at her. "Do you... I mean...?" she stammered, then stopped.

Barbara bit her lip and glanced to check how close Karen and Jennifer were. "I'm not sure I like men at all," she whispered.

Trembling with emotion she adjusted her bra. *Do I like men? Or do I like women? Or am I queer and like them both?* she wondered. By then she felt she was on fire with desire and shame.

Lofty called out from down the creek, "You girls dressed yet?"

"No. Wait a minute," Wendy shrieked.

"One minute, okay? Start counting, Dan," Lofty called.

The girls giggled and snatched up their clothes. Barbara hastily pulled on her clothes, then sat on a rock to dry her feet before tugging on her socks and boots. She was in an emotional turmoil over what had just happened, alternately burning with embarrassment and arousal.

The boys joined them just as Barbara finished dressing. Her whole body seemed to tingle and tremble from the overexertion and stimulation. She shivered with reaction and checked her watch. "We'd better get moving. It is nearly five o'clock. It will be dark in an hour."

Packs were reluctantly hoisted onto sore shoulders and they set off across the small bridge and up the steep slope beyond.

"Where will we spend the night?" Roger asked as they halted on the steep slope. "If we are going to camp, we'd better pick somewhere soon."

"Not here. I don't like this forest," Wendy said.

Barbara looked at the jungle beside the track and agreed. It seemed like a threatening wall. "We have to go to Kuranda remember," she said.

The track went so steeply upwards it took a real effort of will power to keep plodding on. Barbara rapidly tired and her heart began to thump painfully. She was very conscious that the light was beginning to fade, that they were now in the shadow of a ridge to the west. After a few minutes she had to stop. Looking back she saw that Jennifer and Wendy were stopped further back. Roger was with them.

After a short rest they plodded on. The track curved upward around the shoulder of a steep hillside. Thick jungle hemmed them in. After about ten minutes' walk, the slope levelled out then went downwards. Daylight appeared ahead, the jungle forming a dark tunnel over the track. They passed through a gate and came out onto a flat, open area of bitumen.

A car was parked there, and a man stood looking out over a splendid view of the Barron Gorge. He was dressed like a tourist, and when he saw them he nodded and gave them a cheerful greeting.

Wendy groaned and dropped her pack. "Oh! I'm exhausted. What is this place?"

"Wright's Lookout," Roger replied. "Come and look Gordon. You can see right down the gorge."

The cadets joined the man on the edge of a steep, scrub covered slope. "Hello," he said. "Hiking?"

Barbara nodded. "Yes," she replied. She did not really want to talk to strangers.

Wendy looked around. "I've been here before," she said. "But we came by car."

Dan laughed. "Good idea. Why didn't we?" he commented.

The man smiled at Barbara and asked, "Have you come far?"

Roger answered. "From Kamerunga. We started down there beyond the end of the gorge and came up that ridge on the right," he explained, pointing as he did. He took out his map.

The man pointed. "It's an impressive view. Is that Cairns I can see?" he asked.

"Yes, it is," Roger replied.

Barbara suddenly shivered as a cold breeze funnelled up the gorge. She saw that the sun was still on the higher peaks but where they were was in shadow. She turned to the man and asked, "Excuse me, have you seen a group of people wearing yellow cloaks."

The tourist gave her an odd look. "No, I haven't. But I saw half a dozen people dressed in white robes."

"A religious group?" Lofty asked.

The man shrugged. "Could be. I don't know who else would run around dressed like that," he agreed.

"When? Where?" Barbara asked.

"About ten minutes ago. They went down a side-track just back there," the tourist replied, pointing north along the road towards Kuranda.

Barbara at once started walking that way. Roger cried out in exasperation, "Barbara! Fair go! Give us a break."

She stopped to allow them time to have a drink and to stretch tired muscles. The tourist said goodbye, climbed into his car and drove off, leaving them standing in a group looking down the gorge.

Roger took the opportunity to take out his mobile phone and called his mother. "Seeing we have line-of-sight to Cairns," he explained.

Barbara thought this a good idea and turned her phone on and phoned her father. She told him where they were and reassured him that they were safe. "But we might be a bit late getting to Kuranda," she added. "We are still four or five kilometres south of it."

He told her he would inform the caravan park that they might be late. She thanked him and turned the phone off and put it away then looked around. "Time to go," she said.

"No, time to eat," Roger disagreed.

"We could eat here," Dan suggested.

Lofty shook his head. "There could be carloads of tourists all the time," he replied.

"We had better decide," Gordon said. "It will be dark in half an hour, and I don't want to be cooking in the dark."

"Let's look at these people in white robes first," Barbara said.

Again she set off, swinging on her pack as she went. There was some grumbling, but the others followed her. The road led down to a road junction a hundred metres on. The main road to Kuranda went off to the north. On the right a narrow bitumen road went steeply down through a belt of trees. To the left was a disused gravel pit.

As Barbara started down the bitumen road on the right Roger called to her, "If we are going to do a recon let's dump our packs."

Lofty pointed to the left. "In this gravel pit, out of sight of the road," he suggested. They trudged into the old quarry. It went further back than first appearances had suggested and was ringed by long grass, weeds and jungle. As Barbara unclipped her pack strap Gordon moved to help her. He swung the pack down and placed it out of sight in the grass.

"Thanks," she murmured.

She stretched and realised what a relief it was. There seemed to be aches and pains in every muscle of her body. Wendy rubbed her shoulders and groaned. She looked very tired.

"We'd better hurry, it's getting dark," Lofty urged.

"Do we all have to go?" Dan asked.

Lofty shook his head. "No. It is only a recon patrol. It will be better if only a couple of us go. You can stay here and guard the gear if you like," he replied. He took off his webbing and placed it next to his pack.

"I might stay too, if that's alright?" Wendy asked.

"Yes. That's okay." Barbara said. She also slid her webbing off. *We don't need it for a short recon,* she reasoned.

Leaving Dan and Wendy the others walked back to the road junction and went down the bitumen side road. As they did Roger said, "This is a dead-end. It leads down to a pump station or something beside the railway."

It was only a hundred paces. The road curved steeply down to the left and ended in a gravel car park about 25 metres across. Parked side by side facing the railway were three cars. On the left was a large concrete tunnel entrance closed off by a locked steel gate. The friends walked over and peered through the gaps. The tunnel sloped steeply down into blackness. Gurgling and swishing noises echoed up it.

Roger pointed down the tunnel. "It is a surge tank for the tunnel which takes water from the weir at Hydro down to the power station down in the gorge," he explained.

"We can read Roger," Karen added, pointing to a sign.

Barbara had been there before on a day trip and wasn't interested. She turned and walked across to a fence beside the railway line. Leaning on the fence she looked both ways along the line. There was no-one in sight. To her left, a hundred metres away, was the huge granite boulder called *Robbs Monument*. On a hunch she pointed that way.

Roger nodded. "Worth a look," he agreed.

They had to climb over a safety fence to get to the railway. Once there they walked cautiously towards the huge rock.

"Strewth! What a monolith!" Gordon exclaimed as they got closer.

The huge rock towered above them. It was perched on the very lip of the gorge between the railway and the steep drop.

"Who was Robb?" Jennifer asked.

"The engineer who built the railway back in the 1880s," Roger explained.

"It looks like something out of Stonehenge," Jennifer suggested.

"Yes, it does... Oh! There are people!" Barbara gasped.

She stopped and stared. They were about twenty metres back from the rock and six people dressed in white had suddenly risen up out of the grass. The people had their backs to them and were looking up at the rock with their arms raised.

Karen gasped. "They are praying to the rock!" she whispered.

"Druids!" Lofty added.

Barbara gestured to the long grass on their right. "They haven't seen us. Quick! Hide!" she hissed.

The only hiding place was in the long grass between the railway and the gorge. The other side was a high stone cutting. The friends made a bit of noise as they pushed into the long grass but were apparently not heard by the people, two men and four women. As the friends crouched in cover on the edge of a steep slope the six druids began to chant and dance.

The friends had trouble seeing because the grass and weeds obscured their view. This meant raising their heads to look but the six druids seemed oblivious to anything but their own activity. The druids next joined hands and skipped back and forth singing. Barbara noted that they all wore garlands of flowers in their hair and the women's clothes appeared to be a single white rode gathered at the waist by a cord.

Lofty leaned over and whispered, "It's getting dark. I reckon we should go. I don't think this bunch of loonies has anything to do with the Smiley People."

Barbara nodded. Twilight was setting in and the sun had gone from the top of Red Peak across the gorge. "I agree. Let's go."

They backed out onto the railway as quietly as they could. As they did a car's headlights appeared up on the hill.

Jennifer let out a little gasp. "A car! It's coming down here!" she whispered anxiously.

"Could be anyone," Roger said doubtfully.

"There is another car behind it," Gordon said.

"And another," Lofty added. "I think we'd better hide for a minute."

Barbara agreed. They followed her back into the weeds. They were still only about thirty metres from Robbs Monument. Even as the friends hid in the bushes more cars could be seen arriving. Motors were switched off, doors slammed, and voices called in greeting.

"Not just tourists," Roger observed.

"Not at this time of day," Gordon agreed, indicating the swiftly gathering gloom.

Barbara crouched down beside a clump of lantana. Gordon joined her. She was comforted by his presence and didn't mind that their arms touched. He whispered and pointed back towards the rock, "Look, they've lit a fire."

Flames flickered up from a bonfire beside the railway. The druids in white flitted around it throwing on more dead branches. Voices from the direction of the car park drew Barbara's attention. She cautiously raised her head and saw people walking towards them in the twilight. Some were wearing white druid robes, but she could not make out what the others were wearing until they got closer and the firelight provided enough illumination.

She was so surprised at what she saw that she let out an astonished gasp. Many of the people wore nothing at all, or only girdles and garlands of flowers. She stared in disbelief until Gordon gripped her arm and pulled her down into the grass. Scared, she sank down, heart beating rapidly as the people came closer.

Barbara could just see through the lantana and grass and although she thought she shouldn't look her eyes seemed to take control. She stared with prurient interest as about a dozen naked men and women went past, all laughing and chattering. A couple of druids followed.

Barbara was very conscious of her pounding heart. She also became aware that she was gripping Gordon's arm and was pressing against him. He put his arm around her shoulders and gave her a reassuring hug. The closeness made her illogically worry that she might smell after sweating all day.

She glanced around and saw that Jennifer had pressed up against Lofty, gripping his arm. From the looks on her friend's faces Barbara guessed they were as astonished and as interested as she was.

145

More cars arrived and more naked people went past. The friends cautiously raised their heads to watch. The druids all greeted each other before one raised his voice in command. At this all the nudes formed up in a semi-circle on the railway facing the fire. The robed druids grouped themselves at the base of the huge rock opposite them.

A male druid stepped close to the fire and began to chant at the top of his voice. The nudes all chanted back and began to sing.

Roger leaned over to whisper, "They will look bloody silly if a train comes along now!"

Gordon and Lofty both chuckled.

A naked woman next stepped forward and began a slow dance, the firelight accentuating every curve of her body. Barbara glanced at the boys and saw they were all watching intently. It made her feel both annoyed and jealous.

"I think it is time we went," she murmured.

Gordon grinned. "Fair go! The show's just getting interesting," he whispered back.

Barbara pursed her lips but found her own eyes drawn back to the dancer's curves. She was a very attractive and shapely woman and Barbara found her sensuous movements very arousing and disturbing to watch. She could only guess at the effect she was having on the boys. But her effect on the watching male nudes was very obvious as most of them became visibly aroused.

Karen touched her and whispered, "Don't druids make human sacrifices on the full moon or something?"

Lofty grunted and replied, "Dunno. But from the look of this mob all they'll be sacrificing will be a virgin or too, if they've got any."

"Don't be crude," Barbara hissed. "Come on. Let's go."

She began carefully edging out of the dry grass, all the while watching the dancing woman. The others followed. She noted Gordon and Roger both licking their lips and that their eyes were also focused on the naked woman's every movement.

A couple of minutes slow crawling had them all out on the railway.

"Walk on the rails, not on the ballast," Gordon whispered. He stepped up on one rail and took Barbara's hand. "Hold on to me. That way we can balance each other."

They began walking slowly along the line. There was just light enough to see. Their rubber soled boots made no sound. Barbara looked over her shoulder and saw that the others were doing the same thing, Jennifer holding Lofty's hand and Karen holding Roger's.

When they reached the car park Barbara let go, wondering if Gordon wanted to keep holding her hand. After a check to ensure there was no-one at the cars she relaxed and looked back. She could just see the people in the glow of the fire.

"We could have stayed a little longer," Lofty grumbled. "It was just getting interesting."

"Yes, we could have studied the finer points of their theology," Roger agreed.

The boys all laughed quietly and Barbara snorted although she wasn't really disgusted. "We are lucky they didn't see us," she said.

Lofty chuckled, then said, "With that woman prancing around in the nuddy we could have marched past in three ranks and they wouldn't have noticed us!"

Karen shook her head. "I hate to think what they would have done if they had seen us. I was scared."

"We would have been the sacrifice," Gordon suggested.

Karen shivered. "Let's get out of here before more of them come," she said.

"Wait a minute. Who's got a torch? I want to note their car numbers," Barbara said.

"Here," Gordon pulled out a small pocket torch. He and Barbara went quickly from car to car noting the registration plates by the light of the shielded torch.

"Look at this," Gordon said. He pointed the torch beam at a card stuck on the dashboard of the white car they had first seen. It read:

TROPICAL DRUIDS
New members welcome
for information phone Ruth
(09) 99 468606

Barbara began scribbling the details into her notebook. A sudden shout by the druids made her stop in fright but it was just the start of some sort of ritual chant. The whole group began to dance and sing.

Karen looked anxiously back towards the druids. "Hurry up," she hissed.

"We are coming," Barbara said. They walked quickly up the bitumen road. As they did, they looked back repeatedly at the distant fire and the tiny prancing figures. Then they rounded the bend and it was all darkness and gloom. Only the faint greyness of the gravel road led them into the gravel pit.

The glow of another fire at once attracted their attention. Barbara felt her heart stop in fright before she realised it was only Dan and Wendy cooking on a hexamine stove. As the group crunched towards them over the gravel, Dan called out, "You lot took long enough. What were all the cars?"

"Put the fire out. Grab your gear. We are getting out of here. We will tell you why as we go," Barbara ordered.

Dan grumbled but did as he was told. They retrieved their packs and webbing. Barbara realised she was sweating and shaking from the exertion and emotion and was glad it was dark. She had a big drink and pulled on her pack.

"All ready? Okay, let's go. Now, if a car comes along take to the jungle and stand still," she commanded.

Then she led the way out onto the road and turned left towards Kuranda.

Chapter 15

KURANDA BY NIGHT

Wendy was annoyed. "What's the matter Barbara? Why can't we eat there?" she asked, tiredness evident in her voice.

Barbara described what they had just seen, then said, "Besides, I promised dad we would spend the night at the caravan park. It's only a few kilometres to Kuranda."

"You don't think these druids might be the people Fiona is with?" Wendy asked.

"No, not a chance. They are a different group altogether," Barbara replied.

She could not imagine Fiona or her father being amongst the naked people dancing around the fire. That set her imagination working. The images had aroused her uncomfortably and she tried to picture Fiona there.

The thought of the druids, added to the pitch blackness of the surrounding jungle, infected them with concern and hastened their footsteps. They marched along the bitumen road in a straggling line of ones and twos. Under the overhanging jungle canopy it was so dark they could barely distinguish the grey blur of the road, but Barbara would not allow torches.

The road led downhill for half a kilometre, then uphill and to the left. Most of the time the group trudged along in silence except for occasional grumbles or curses. It was a warm night and they sweated freely. The road dipped to cross a small creek then curved right and uphill. A narrow side road went off to the right. The road then curved down to the left again.

By the time they had crossed another creek and climbed the slope beyond it they had strung out over fifty metres and were feeling the strain. When Barbara reached the bitumen side road which led to the Barron Falls Lookout she stopped and waited for the others to catch up. Wendy was last and Gordon was with her and was carrying her pack. This surprised Barbara as she hadn't noticed him drop back.

When Wendy arrived, she asked, "How much further is it Barbara? I'm had it. I still haven't recovered from yesterday's climb."

"Two or three kilometres," Barbara replied. She felt very tired herself and her emotions seemed to be going up and down by the minute.

"A car!" Karen cried.

Headlights glowed on the jungle at the next bend.

"It's okay. It's coming from Kuranda," Roger said. The car came round the bend and for a moment its headlights shone full on them. It swept past on the road they had just come along.

"More druids?" Dan suggested.

"They are a bit late. They'll have missed all the action," Lofty said.

"What if they tell the others they saw us?" Jennifer asked.

"So what? The druids didn't see us. We could have just come from Kuranda for all they know," Roger replied. "Let's not get paranoid. Come on. I'm hungry. Let's get to Kuranda."

They resumed their march. Walking on the bitumen was easier and the first part went downhill. It was still very dark, with jungle on both sides. Barbara knew she was so tired she was starting to get dizzy. She found it a real ordeal to keep pushing herself along. After about fifteen minutes she glimpsed the first lights from houses set back in the jungle and that boosted her spirits.

"Houses. Not far now," she called.

The first houses were scattered and isolated and there were patches of dark jungle. Then a streetlight appeared, as welcome as a lighthouse to a storm-tossed ship. It cast a cheerful glow over an intersection which led off to a whole street of houses. A car went past towards the town centre. By then the friends were walking along a concrete footpath.

They halted for a short rest before continuing. Road and footpath plunged into a black mass of jungle which Barbara found spooky, and she was glad Gordon was walking beside her. He still carried Wendy's pack.

Another streetlight and more scattered houses boosted her hopes that they would soon arrive as she was now worrying about Wendy. It seemed much further than she remembered.

But then, I've only ever travelled this way in a car, and it never seems as far then, she told herself.

They trudged painfully on. After what seemed like an age, they rounded the curve and went down the steep slope to the bridge over

Jumrum Creek. The last half-kilometre was uphill and that felt like the hardest part of the whole march.

It was 8pm when they reached the brightly lit main street and came to a sweating standstill. Packs were dropped and they stood on trembling legs for a minute. Barbara looked up and down the street. Few shops appeared open and there was not a soul to be seen. Not a single car could be heard moving. Only the sound of laughter and singing from the hotel across the street indicated human activity.

"Kuranda on a Saturday night, eh?" Gordon asked with a chuckle.

"It has its moments," Roger said. "I've had some good times here."

"Aaah! Smell those hamburgers!" Dan said. "I'm going to buy one."

"I'm going to buy two," Roger added.

That raised a laugh. They walked across to a cafe and piled their gear on the footpath. Barbara took out her mobile phone.

"Buy me a hamburger please. I will phone dad again in case he is starting to worry," she said to Gordon. She turned the phone on and moved away a few paces to make the call. She was instantly glad that she had done so. The relief in her father's voice was obvious. He asked how the day had gone and she talked about the steepness of the mountains and how unfit she was and said nothing about the strange characters they had encountered.

After assuring him they would spend the next day in and around Kuranda, and that she would phone again that evening, she phoned Capt Conkey and passed on the same information.

Feeling much happier Barbara turned off her phone and joined the others sitting around two tables. They were the only customers in the cafe. Gordon had also bought her a cup of coffee which she drank gratefully. For twenty minutes they relaxed and consumed milkshakes, hamburgers, and hot chips, all the while discussing the events of the day and what to do next.

"We still have to find this caravan park," Lofty said.

"It is on the other side of the highway, off the Myola Road," Roger said. "It must be a kilometre or more."

That brought groans from all of them. Wendy looked as though she was on the edge of tears. Barbara checked her watch.

"It is getting late. We had better move."

"I wonder can we get a lift?" Jennifer suggested.

They paid for their food and left the cafe, the proprietor already wiping down the tables and putting up the chairs. Webbing and packs were hauled on with groans and curses and the friends trudged off along the main street following Roger.

The distance was more than two kilometres and they found it a real trial. Much of it was uphill. Two cars passed them but there was clearly no chance of hitching a ride, so they slogged on. By the time they reached the blaze of orange streetlights and traffic lights at the junction with the Kennedy Highway they were all sweating and puffing and Wendy had begun to cry. Lofty took her pack this time and Roger her webbing.

After crossing the highway they went up a steep bitumen road and turned right down a narrow secondary road which was swallowed up by a wall of dark jungle. This road was also bitumen and wound through an inky tunnel of rainforest for half a kilometre, before emerging on a hilltop with open fields on the right.

It was just on 9:30pm when they reached the caravan park. A sign directed them along a concrete path lined with ferns and plants to the office. Lofty rang a bell on the counter and a cheerful elderly man appeared. Barbara said who she was and the man nodded, and said, "Yeah, been expecting you. Your dad rang up twice to check if you'd arrived yet. You'd better phone him straight away," he said.

"I already have, thank you, half an hour ago," Barbara replied.

The man pointed to where they could put up their shelters and where the amenities were. Roger purchased a soft drink and a packet of Jaffas from the shop which took up half the office. That made Barbara realise just how thirsty she was, so she purchased a fruit juice.

The tired group then plodded down a grassy slope to a line of trees along a fence at the bottom of the lawn. There was enough light from several distant streetlights, from a hut and from a caravan about fifty paces away, for them to see by. With sighs of relief they dropped their gear. Into Barbara's tired brain leapt another worry: who was to sleep beside whom? For a moment she thought Gordon was going to suggest that they share a 'hutchie', but then he turned to Dan.

"Come on Dan, we will use these two trees," he said.

"All us girls should sleep in one big hutchie," Karen suggested.

Jennifer nodded. "Okay. It's not going to rain, and we can tie one side up to the fence," she agreed.

Barbara was too tired to argue. She and Wendy pulled out their plastic 'Shelters Individual' and clipped them together. These always had nylon cord tied to the corners because they used them at least once a month, so it was the work of moments to tie two corners between two trees and to fasten the other two corners to the fence to form a 'veranda' roof. The other hutchie was clipped to the side between the trees and then pegged down to the lawn with thin wire pegs.

The boys put up a similar hutchie between the next two trees so that they almost formed one long shelter. When it came time to move their gear in Barbara was a bit nervous about who she wanted to be next to but this was solved by her hesitation. Karen rushed in and claimed the end beside the boys. Jennifer took next place, so Barbara went third, leaving Wendy on the end.

In the boy's shelter Lofty went closest to the girls, then Roger, Gordon and Dan. Barbara thought she detected a few undercurrents of tension over this. She knew, by the looks he gave her that Gordon wished her to be beside him. She also thought that Wendy was annoyed and jealous of Karen. Jennifer looked sharply at her as well.

Karen seemed unaware of this. "Hot shower for me," she said as she rummaged in her gear.

This was unanimously voted on. Even though they had had a swim earlier they had done a lot of sweating since then. There was a general movement to the shower block.

There were only three showers in the female ablutions, each in a cubicle. Barbara was last to arrive, so she had to wait. She sat on a bench and slowly removed boots and socks and massaged her sore feet. From the male showers next door came sounds of laughter and jokes. Steam billowed. Morale leapt up.

After a few minutes Jennifer turned off her shower and opened the door of her cubicle. She was still drying herself with a towel.

"Here you are Barbara. You can use this shower. I'm finished."

Jennifer turned side on and began towelling her back. Barbara was given a clear side view of her. The sight made her simultaneously embarrassed and aroused. She would have preferred to wait till Jennifer was dressed and gone but it seemed bad manners, so she moved into the cubicle beside her.

She undressed slowly, taking her time to undo buttons. But Jennifer

153

stayed chatting and seemed to take forever to get dressed and appeared quite unaware she was embarrassing Barbara. Barbara could not help seeing, or being seen. She realised her heart was beating fast and that she felt quite flushed. In the end she quickly peeled off her underwear and stepped into the shower recess and pulled the plastic curtain across.

As she adjusted the shower Barbara bit her lip and shook her head. She shivered and ran her hands over her body.

Am I like that? she asked herself.

Again she shook her head and looked down at herself. Strong memories of various sexual encounters filled her mind. She was still a virgin, a fact which sometimes surprised her, considering what she had experienced. For her age she knew a lot about sex. When she had been in Year 9, she had been well on the way to becoming a real little tart.

I certainly liked boys then! she remembered. That was when her family was breaking up and she had been in desperate emotional upheaval, on top of being a normal teenage rebel.

She was sure she would have allowed boys to go 'all the way' if she had not been so brutally treated. Much of the love play she remembered as being very enjoyable.

It had been Cadets who had saved her: Gwen Copeland, her first section commander, plus Graham Kirk, Roger and Lofty, and, most of all, Fiona. At that critical moment Fiona had given her a sympathetic ear and a shoulder to cry on. She had provided friendship, care and a good role model. Barbara shook her head sadly as she remembered those tormented days and nights.

"Good old Captain Conkey," Barbara murmured.

He had known about her behaviour, yet he had taken her under his wing and given her a second chance. And his 'Promise', that had helped when temptation had reared its ugly head. Capt Conkey made all the cadets promise to him personally that they would behave on cadet activities. Many kids sneered at it, but Barbara knew that, on several occasions, it had been her unwillingness to betray that trust which had saved her from misbehaviour.

Not that she had been a saint! She smiled. There had been a few sharp rebukes and the odd dressing down, but always with understanding and helpful counselling. She knew she had changed a lot, and mostly for the better.

154

And as for sex, there hadn't been a boy who had touched her in two years now, except for Gordon at the Promotion Course, and that was only a hug and a kiss.

That, she thought wryly, *is probably why the rumours about me being a 'lemon' have been going around.*

Did she prefer women? Or was it just that she had been subjected to such appalling and brutal experiences by men? She shuddered at the memories: the escaped convicts at Home Hill, the teacher who had harassed her the previous year, the Pig Hunters at Bunyip River, then that madman Berzinski at Mt Mulligan only two months ago.

She tried to answer the question honestly. *I do prefer men, I think. Yes, I know I do. Deep down I crave a normal loving relationship. But is Gordon the right man?*

Still pondering this she dried herself. Because she was going to bed she did not put on a bra or panties but just slipped on trousers and shirt. *It will be alright. It is too dark for anyone to see,* she told herself. But lurking on the edge of her consciousness was an impish desire to let Gordon get a glimpse.

Feeling much refreshed but still quite sore she walked slowly back to the hutchie, the speed dictated as much by her sore muscles as by her thoughts.

The others were preparing for bed with much laughter and rummaging through gear. It was a pleasant night, not cold at all, and Barbara stood alone for a moment and looked up at the stars. She sighed then shivered. *If only!* But she wasn't quite sure what she hoped for. A tear suddenly trickled down. She brushed it away and walked over to the others.

Groundsheets and sleeping bags were unrolled and packs arranged as pillows. The others were in high spirits, but Barbara was very quiet and did not join in the banter. She arranged her bed and lay down. Once in her sleeping bag she slipped off her trousers and lay back to relax. A small, tingling thrill of being almost naked swept through her. But then dejection gripped her. She felt torn up inside. She felt she did not know what she was or what she wanted, and they had failed to locate Fiona.

Unconsciously she sighed. That made Wendy lean over and pat her shoulder. "It'll be okay, Barbara. We will find her tomorrow."

"I hope so. The miserable clues we collected today don't add up to much," Barbara replied.

"They brought us here. That's a start," Wendy said. "We will pick up the trail in the morning, don't you worry."

She squeezed Barbara's shoulder then lay back. For Barbara, it was like an electric bolt had just shot through her. Her heart hammered so that it was like a pounding in her ears, and she knew that she was suddenly aflame with desire. But in the heat of her surprising passion the truth came to her.

I am a real woman. I love women, but I love men more, and I need a man.

But what was really exciting her was the self-knowledge that now came to her in a flash of revelation that it was really Gordon she wanted to be with. *Or a man, the right man,* she told herself.

The wave of Barbara's passion broke as suddenly as it had appeared, replaced by the heat of shame. Sobs and tears of frustration and shame came welling up. As Barbara groped for her sleeping bag, Wendy sat up and reached over and put her left arm around her.

Barbara began to cry. She just could not stop herself. Wendy moved and cradled her head on her shoulder and put both arms around her and began to hush and comfort her.

"What's going on? What's wrong?" Wendy asked.

Barbara said nothing, just sobbing in Wendy's embrace for a long time. The waves of passion and lust subsided, to be replaced by ever stronger flushes of hot shame.

What a wanton creature I am! she thought miserably. *The other girls will despise me. And the poor boys! I am nothing but a tease! Oh! If only my life wasn't such an emotional storm!*

At last she calmed down. Wendy's embrace, from being warm and comforting became embarrassing and uncomfortable. Now Barbara felt humiliated and despised herself for giving in to temptation and for losing control. Gently she disengaged herself. With a whispered thanks she moved away. Unsure if the others were awake or asleep, she quietly dressed, shivering the whole time.

She slid into her sleeping bag, her mind still puzzling over what sort of person she was. Exhaustion drew her into a deep sleep.

Chapter 16

KURANDA BY DAY

Barbara opened her eyes and stretched. She felt stiff and sore but rested. The air was cool and moist. By the brightness of the light she guessed it was just after sunup. She looked beside her and saw Wendy, still asleep, her tousled hair half covering her face. Seeing her made Barbara blush with shame and she worried about how her behaviour the previous night would affect the group.

After a few minutes of silent dejection, she pulled on her boots and tramped stiffly across the dewy lawn to the toilet. When she returned ten minutes later the others were awake. Gordon crawled out of the hutchie and stretched himself. For a moment he looked at her quizzically (or so she thought). Then he smiled.

"Lovely morning, Barbara. How are you?" he asked.

"A bit tired and a few sore muscles," she replied, trying to act normal.

"You and me both," Gordon agreed. He started to chat casually about the weather and Roger's snoring, as though nothing unusual had occurred the previous night.

Roger snorted and said, "It wasn't me. It was Dan. And I couldn't sleep for the smell of your socks. What a pong!"

Barbara was afraid to look at Jennifer and Wendy, but both just said hello and seemed cheerful and normal. Barbara still felt ashamed of herself but relaxed a little. She rolled up her bedding and packed it, then pulled out her hexamine stove and mess gear and began cooking breakfast.

Gordon dumped his pack next to her and sat on it. He also lit a hexamine stove.

"What is the plan today?" he asked, as he poured water into a mess tin and put it over the flame to heat.

"I'd like to look at this other Smiley property to the southwest of town," Barbara replied.

"Didn't you promise not to?" Gordon asked.

"No. I promised to try to stay out of trouble," Barbara replied. "It

157

was the commune I promised not to go near. It is the other way." She pointed north.

Barbara made herself a cup of sweet coffee and drank it. It tasted good and lifted her spirits. She then munched on a muesli bar while heating a can of 'Ham and Egg'. She watched with interest as Gordon prepared his breakfast.

He is very controlled and methodical, she thought. *I wish I was. He is different from what I remember, quieter, more intense.*

Gordon turned his head and his eyes looked full into hers. "What are you thinking?" he asked.

"That I don't know much about you," she replied. She realised that Wendy, who was beside her, was 'all ears' by the way she pretended to be busy.

Gordon smiled. *What a nice smile,* Barbara thought. *He is handsome. Those dimples...*

He began to spoon Pork and Beans into his mouth. Between mouthfuls he shrugged and said, "Not much to know. There aren't many mysteries about me. What you see is what you get."

"What do you want to be when you leave school?" Barbara asked.

"An engineer, civil. You know, dams and bridges and so on. That means four years at Uni," Gordon replied. "What about you?"

Barbara shook her head. "I don't know. I can't decide."

But she had sudden desire to go to university too. *I hope my marks are good enough!* she worried. They talked school then, about the subjects each studied. The meal proceeded pleasantly for another fifteen minutes. By then the sun was above the trees and shining on them.

After cleaning his mess gear Gordon picked up his towel and toilet bag. "I'm for a shower and shave. What do we wear today? Are we doing any scrub bashing?"

"No. Look like a tourist. Casual, so we can blend into the crowd," Barbara said.

Later she walked to the shower to clean her teeth. After a quick shower she brushed her hair and changed into baggy blue shorts, a loose white cotton blouse and gym boots. There was a laundry at the caravan park, so she washed her dirty clothes.

Still feeling confused and anxious about her mixed emotions, she picked up her wet clothes and walked slowly back to the camp. To make a clothesline, Barbara tied some nylon cord between two trees. After hanging her wet clothes on it, she tidied up before sitting on her pack to study the map.

Dan came to her. "Will we leave our gear here?" he asked.

"May as well. Just take your money. The rest should be safe enough," Barbara said.

"What money!" Roger cried.

Gordon sat down beside her. "Well, what's the plan?"

"Wait for the other girls to come back," Barbara replied.

When all were seated a few minutes later Barbara looked at her watch. It was 8:45 am. She said, "This morning I think we should just wander around Kuranda pretending to be tourists. We can ask about the Smileys and see what clues we might pick up. Then, after lunch, I would like to go to look at this other property."

She looked them over to see they were appropriately dressed. Gordon wore a casual shirt and jeans. So did Lofty and Dan. Roger wore shorts and a flannel 'Lumberjack' shirt. Wendy wore white shorts which didn't exactly go with her white legs, and a red pullover. Her hair was down and she looked very pretty. Karen wore jeans and a blue shirt while Jennifer wore jeans and another too-tight T-shirt.

Before they left, they checked with the manager at the office. They were allowed to store their packs and webbing there. He advised them of a short cut to town along the railway. To reach this, they strolled through the pleasant park-like grounds of the caravan park and down a grassy path to the railway.

Turning right, they walked along the line. On their left was a belt of trees and a steep drop down to the Barron River. They got glimpses of the water through gaps in the foliage. The day was clear and sunny and quite warm, especially in the railway cuttings where there was no breeze. They passed under the highway bridge, a high concrete structure which crossed both the river and the railway, then turned right up a short flight of steps to the township.

This brought them to the bottom of the car park at the Kuranda Markets, an untidy collection of booths and stalls with a feeling of Bombay or Chiang Mai about them. Even though it was only just after 10 o'clock the place was already crowded with tourists of all nationalities.

Once among the throng in the markets the group rapidly split up.

Barbara and Gordon walked side by side. Gordon appeared relaxed and seemed interested in all kinds of things: ceramics, paintings, jewellery, printed cloths, hand-woven rugs, woodcarvings. He purchased a T-shirt and a bundle of postcards.

"Let's find the Post Office," he said. "I want to send these today."

The pair strolled out of the front gate of the markets and along a footpath thronged by hundreds of Japanese who poured past them like a human tide. By the time the pair reached the main street, this had ebbed to a mere busy crowd.

Barbara wasn't really enjoying herself. Many previous visits to Kuranda robbed the lovely little town of any novelty for her. She felt very tense and defensive, but she did notice that many of the girls they passed gave Gordon admiring glances. That made her feel better. At the corner cafe he left her for a moment and re-appeared with two milkshakes.

"For you," he said, offering her one. "I hope you like strawberry. Let's sit here for a minute while I write these postcards."

He steered her to a chair and seated her, then sat opposite and gave her a smile. She smiled back and accepted the milkshake. It had malt in it and she didn't like malt, but she said nothing. So while Gordon wrote she sat sipping slowly and watched the passing people.

They sat there for twenty minutes before continuing their stroll. Gordon was plainly very happy but also nervous. This made Barbara feel guilty. He had come all that way to be with her and they had hardly spoken.

"Thanks for the milkshake," she said as they stopped to look in a shop window.

"My pleasure. Anything else you want just name it," Gordon replied.

He tried to make it sound light-hearted banter but there was a tense edge to his voice which hinted at it being very important to him.

"No malt next time," Barbara said.

For a moment Gordon stood stock still. Then he turned to face her, his eyes very grave. "I'm sorry. You should have said. You must tell me things like that. And at least there will be a next time."

Barbara looked into his eyes and felt her chest tighten. She wanted to speak but her throat seemed constricted. After swallowing to clear it she said, "If you like. But please don't get a crush on me. You will only get hurt."

"Get a crush! Barbara! I've loved you ever since I first laid eyes on you!" Gordon replied.

Barbara blushed. She wasn't sure what the emotion was: pleasure, vanity, pride, conceit, or fear? "Oh Gordon don't! I'm not worth it. I am just trouble," she answered.

"That's for me to decide," he replied, a distinct catch in his voice.

Barbara shook her head. "But you will find I am a horrible person really. You won't like me when you get to know me," she replied. She could feel her emotions rising and tears began to prickle her eyes.

Gordon took both her hands. "First I've got to get to know you. I came all this way just to do that. There has been nobody else in my thoughts but you for six months now. I have to know if we are suited for each other, one way or the other. Please give me that chance."

In part of her mind Barbara wanted to turn and run. Yet another part told her that the decent thing was to give this boy... this young man... a fair chance to get to know her... and a third part then burst into flame and engulfed her so that she stepped forward and hugged him.

Their lips met. Barbara seemed to reel and spin. His arms felt so strong, so comforting. His body was firm and fit and pressed against hers in a way that seemed just right. Barbara realised she needed to breathe. She opened her eyes and he was smiling at her, wonder on his face.

Then she became conscious of the fact that they were standing in the middle of a busy footpath. Passers-by grinned and gave them knowing looks. She blushed and eased herself free, but let him keep possession of her hand.

"You can have your chance," she murmured. "But I warn you, I'm a bit difficult. I'm not just the girl-next-door," she said. Then she smiled and added. "You might regret it."

"I might," Gordon replied. "But not as much as living the rest of my life wondering."

Barbara studied his eyes and face. "Don't get too serious, please. We are a bit young for that. Come on. Let's find the Post Office."

They began walking slowly along hand in hand. To Barbara the sun suddenly seemed brighter, the sky bluer, the lush vegetation even greener. She knew she was very happy.

At the corner of Fongon Street they met Roger and Dan. Roger was staring down the street and looked very down in the mouth.

"What's the matter Roger?" Barbara asked.

"Nothing," he replied, trying to pretend he was cheerful.

"There is so. What is it?" Barbara persisted. She knew him far too well to be deceived. She glanced quizzically at Dan, who shrugged and pointed.

"Lofty. He's got three girls trailing after him, one on each arm."

Gordon chuckled. "He's only got two arms," he pointed out.

Barbara felt a surge of sympathy. Poor Roger! He was in love with Wendy, and she was in love with Lofty. And Lofty... she was shocked. How could she have forgotten! Lofty was in love with Fiona. Fiona! She had completely forgotten about her. A sudden surge of guilt stung her emotions.

While I've been having a happy romance Fiona is still missing.

"Fiona!" she cried. They all looked startled. "We aren't here on holiday. We are supposed to be looking for Fiona. Start asking people about the Smileys," she ordered.

"Gosh yes. Oh! I say. There's a Smiley bus!" Roger exclaimed.

A cream mini-bus with golden 'smiley face' logos on the doors was driving past. The name of a travel company was printed underneath.

"I don't think so," Dan replied. "Come on Roger. We will ask along the other side of the street."

Barbara felt angry now, angry with herself for being so frivolous and selfish as to forget Fiona while she fell in love, angry with Lofty for flirting, angry with Wendy for hurting Roger.

She walked into the nearest shop and said to the man behind the counter, "We are looking for a religious group called the Happy People. They wear Smiley badges. Do you know where we might find them?"

The man's reaction was so startling that, in other circumstances, they might have laughed. One moment he was giving his best shopkeeper's smile, the next he was staring at them aghast and clutching the counter. He quickly recovered and, with a blank expression which didn't hide the worry lines at the corners of his eyes, replied, "Never heard of them. Sorry."

Barbara was amazed. The man turned away and she was about to ask again when Gordon tugged at her hand. She followed him outside.

"Did you see that!" she cried. "He knows alright."

"And he won't tell you a thing. He's scared stiff," Gordon added. He shook his head and looked at Barbara. "Talk about taking the bull by the horns! Can't you be more subtle?"

"I could be, but I'm not going to be. Come on. Let's try the next shop," Barbara replied.

Gordon protested but it was no use. Barbara was determined. She walked in and asked the lady there, and got a similar response. That made her repeat the process until they ran out of shops.

They walked on past some houses and came to the police station. It was set amongst trees and ferns and was perched on top of a steep grassy field in which two horses grazed. As she and her friends walked past Barbara felt a twinge of guilt, and annoyance. Police! Fiona had been missing for a whole week and what have they found?

The group followed the palm-lined footpath down to the railway station. Another flood of tourists was coming the other way from a recently arrived train. Huge motor coaches growled up the hill spewing dirty diesel fumes. The place was like a disturbed ant's nest.

Barbara led Gordon all the way down onto the platform. She then asked one of the railwaymen about the Smileys. He was a middle-aged man in blue Q-Rail shirt and hat. He frowned, pushed his hat back on his head and scratched his forehead.

"If I were you I wouldn't go around asking those sorts of questions," he replied gravely. Then he spun on his heel and walked off.

"Heavens!" Barbara exclaimed. "Everyone we speak to is scared of these Smiley People."

"Maybe we should be too," Gordon replied seriously.

"Oh! There are Lofty and the girls," Barbara cried. She pointed up to where their friends stood on the pedestrian overpass. Barbara noted that Jennifer was pressed up against Lofty on one side and Karen on the other. Wendy stood a little to one side looking dejected.

Barbara ran up the steps to join them. "Have you found out anything about the Smileys?" she asked.

They looked at her blankly for a moment.

"No... No, we haven't," Lofty replied. He gave a guilty frown.

"We've just been seeing the sights so far," Jennifer said, snuggling against Lofty's arm.

"It's a pretty place,' Karen added. "We've just been down on the river bank. We were going to watch the train leave."

"No time. We must go and ask more people about the Smileys. Someone must be game to say something," Barbara replied.

"No!" Gordon said. "I don't think that is a good idea. It's too obvious, and everyone we have spoken to so far has been terrified. We will try another way."

For a moment Barbara resented Gordon's opposition. She met his eyes and noted the firm line of his mouth. Then she felt foolish. Maybe he was right. She nodded. "What, then?"

"Just look and listen this morning," Gordon said. "Then we do your recce this afternoon."

The hoot of a diesel locomotive's air horn distracted them. They turned to lean on the railing and watch as the tourist train pulled out on its run back down to Cairns.

As the last carriage vanished around the distant bend, the friends turned and walked back up the footpath towards the main street. Gordon reached out and gently took her hand as they walked along. Barbara felt a simultaneous thrill of fear and pleasure. She also admired Gordon for having the courage to risk a rebuff in front of the others. She gave his hand a squeeze and smiled.

Barbara felt a nudge from behind and looked to see Wendy smiling and obviously delighted that Gordon was holding her hand. It made her feel embarrassed but pleased.

Poor Wendy! she thought. *She's the one who needs the love!*

Chapter 17

ANOTHER LEAD

"Look! Smiley Badges!" Karen called.

She pointed to a man stepping off a tour coach. He looked like a tour guide but had a bright green smiley badge pinned to his shirt pocket. The man turned and waited as about forty Japanese, obviously 'Honeymooners', and all wearing green smiley badges, filed off the coach.

Lofty shook his head. "I don't think these are the happy people we are looking for," he observed dryly.

They all laughed and continued walking. Barbara was annoyed with Lofty. He was ahead of her with Jennifer on his right and Karen on his left. He was holding Karen's hand and had his other arm around Jennifer's waist.

Oooh! The two-timing cad! Barbara steamed. *Poor Fiona!*

They crossed over the intersection of Fongon Street and met Roger and Dan. Roger pointed to a shop across the street. "See that bloke there, Barbara? He was just pointing you out to another bloke."

Barbara looked and recognised the shopkeeper she had first asked about the Smileys. "Was he now! That's interesting. What did the man look like?"

"Chubby, red-faced guy driving a white four-wheel drive. Here he is now."

A passing vehicle slowed and the driver looked towards them. Barbara had an impression of a man in his late thirties or early forties with a round, cheerful face and thinning, sandy hair. For an instant their eyes met before the man looked away. The vehicle accelerated off along the street.

Dan said, "That is the man Pat and I saw talking to the guard at the gate into the commune."

"Quick! Note the registration number," Gordon called.

But it was too late. The vehicle was too far away. They watched it turn left at the end of the main street.

165

Barbara felt a rush of excitement. "He must be a Smiley. If only we can find out who he is and where he lives."

"I didn't like the way he looked at us," Gordon said.

Roger agreed, "You are right there. He was giving us the old 'once-over' then."

"What can we do now?" Barbara asked.

She wanted to jig in frustration. She bit her lip. What if the man had nothing to do with the Smileys? What if the Smileys had nothing to do with Fiona's disappearance? What if they were just on a wild goose chase? She wracked her brains but could not come up with an immediate plan, other than walking to the second Smiley property. She suggested this.

Gordon nodded. "That is probably all we can do," he agreed. "Let's have an early lunch and then set off."

"I'll second that," Roger agreed.

They trooped over to the same cafe where they had eaten the night before and sat around two tables. Hamburgers and milkshakes were ordered. While they ate they talked. Barbara sat next to Gordon. Wendy and Dan sat with them. Roger ended up with Lofty and the other two girls.

Barbara noted Roger's face. *He's only pretending to be happy. He wants to be here with Wendy,* she thought.

Then she noted Lofty's expression. He was laughing and flirting with the two girls as though he didn't have a care in the world. Karen had a hand on his thigh and Jennifer kept rubbing against him. It made her boil.

Doesn't he care about Fiona at all?

It was only 11:30am when they finished lunch. Barbara took her map out of her shoulder bag and unfolded it. The others crowded round to look. Roger leaned forward to study the map. "Which way do we go?"

"That way," Barbara pointed. "Back along the road towards Barron Falls, then down this side road."

"I need to go to the toilet first," Dan said.

"So do I," Karen added. "Where is the nearest?"

Roger pointed along the street. "Just along there in the park at the end of the block," he said. "I'll come with you. We won't be long."

They paid their bills and moved out onto the footpath. Another flood of tourists: Germans and Scandinavians this time, was ebbing like the tide towards the railway station. Roger, Dan, Jennifer and Karen all headed off towards the toilet. To escape the human flow the others retreated into a Newsagent. That reminded Gordon about his post cards. He purchased some stamps and went off in search of a post box. Wendy went to browse among the novels. Barbara wandered idly around. She came upon Lofty flicking over the pages of a girlie magazine. He was looking at glossy photos of naked women. Women, Barbara noted, with breasts on them like ripe watermelons. She wrinkled her nose in distaste, but couldn't stop herself glancing at some of the other magazines.

In the past she had surreptitiously looked at similar magazines, firstly out of curiosity, then to compare them with herself. Later she had done it because she liked what she saw. It was partly this that made her worry whether she was normal or not. But deep down the magazines disturbed her. She disliked the way boys leered and sniggered at them, and the thought of them getting aroused at the pictures made her feel somehow unclean.

To find Lofty looking at one at this time made her unease flare into anger. Lofty unwittingly threw petrol on the fire by holding it up for her to see.

"What about them, Barbara?" he said, trying to hide his embarrassment with bravado.

Barbara glanced at the photo and sneered. "They are gross. She looks like a freak. Besides, I wouldn't have thought you'd have needed to look at any pictures of them the way Jennifer has been flaunting herself."

Lofty went red and closed the magazine. "Sorry. I didn't mean to offend you. And leave Jennifer alone. She's alright."

Barbara felt hot anger sweep over her from head to toe. "But what about Fiona? Here you are flirting with Jennifer and letting Karen massage you as though you don't care about Fiona at all!"

Lofty's face darkened with anger as well as embarrassment. He tossed the magazine down and turned to face her. "What if I do flirt with them? What's it to you? And why should it affect Fiona? I care about her a lot, but she's not my girlfriend."

"But... but she will be hurt," Barbara replied. She was suddenly unsure. "I thought... well... I thought you were in love with her. I know she loves you."

Lofty stared at her in surprise. "Loves me! I knew she liked me as a friend. And I like her a lot. But I've never taken her out, well, only as part of a group. Never on a date, just the two of us. I want to find her because I care about her, and because I care about you. But don't tell me who I can and can't talk to."

"I wasn't!" Barbara snapped angrily. "But I don't want to see her hurt. So don't you just dump her like that."

"I'm not dumping her! She isn't mine to dump!" Lofty cried. "I thought she was your girlfriend."

Barbara went cold with shock. "Just what do you mean by that?" she hissed between clenched teeth. She became aware of Wendy beside her.

"It's what everyone thinks. That she loves you and that you are her girlfriend," Lofty replied angrily.

"Do you mean we're lesbians? Is that what you think?" Barbara said.

"That's what people say," Lofty replied.

Barbara was stunned. She boiled with anger and tears of hurt and humiliation prickled, yet she felt ice-cold. She noticed Gordon was standing beside Lofty, his face a mixture of disbelief and shock.

Wendy stepped between them. "Don't fight please. We've got enough problems as it is."

Barbara looked at her, her mind trying to form a rebuttal to Lofty's accusations, but the thoughts strangled in her own doubts. Tears misted her eyes and she felt the urge to run and hide.

At that moment, Roger and Dan appeared. "Quick! Quick!" Roger cried excitedly. "We've just seen some Smileys!"

"Where?" Wendy asked.

"At the park. Five or six of them. They walked past singing, and are all wearing yellow cloaks like monks," Roger replied.

Barbara wiped her eyes. "Come on!"

She pushed past Lofty and Gordon. The group spilled out onto the footpath. She was shaking with emotion and her mind was in turmoil, but she clung to the idea of the Smileys.

"Which way did they go?" she asked.

"Along the road that way," said Dan, pointing to the left.

Lofty glanced that way. "That is toward the highway crossroads."

"Quick!" Roger urged. They began to make their way through the crowd as fast as they could. Jennifer and Karen joined them.

Lofty pointed to the left. "Cross the street. There are fewer people there," he said.

They ran across, dodging cars as they went, and raced along the footpath to the petrol station on the corner.

"There they go!" Dan cried.

Barbara caught a glimpse of two or three bright yellow cloaks flitting through the dappled sunlight under the tunnel of rainforest about two hundred metres away.

"They've gone into the jungle," Roger said. "Run, or we'll lose them."

The friends ran along the side of the road past the service station and shop. Barbara was aware that Gordon was running beside her. She glanced at him, and he met her eyes. A stab of hurt went through her at the look on his face: clenched jaw, worried frown. Did he think she was a lesbian? Was she? She wanted to scream to release the pain.

They crossed an intersection and ran along the footpath into the tunnel of rainforest where the main access road curved up to the right towards the highway. Within a minute they reached a side-track which led steeply down into the jungle. It was just a dirt walking trail.

By then Roger, Wendy and Jennifer had fallen behind. Lofty stopped and held up his hand. "Hang on. We don't actually want to catch them. We just want to follow them."

"I'd like to see their faces," Barbara said. She was puffing and perspiring by this.

"We will have to get in front of them to do that," Gordon pointed out. "We don't want them to become suspicious."

Lofty nodded. "We will just catch up enough to keep them in sight and see where they go," he said.

As soon as the others caught up they walked quickly down the track. It went along the side of the slope through jungle then went down several short flights of steps to emerge beside a creek full of murky looking grey-green water.

The track led across a small concrete weir and up more steps into the jungle on the other side. Barbara had a fleeting glimpse of yellow among the trees halfway up the other slope.

"Jumrum Creek," Roger said. "This track leads to the road to Barron Falls."

"Are you sure?" Karen asked.

169

"Positive. We took some Cubs through here on a nature ramble last year. We are still in the middle of town," Roger replied.

Barbara led the way across the small weir and up the steep slope on the other side. A narrow dirt foot track wound up through the rainforest and she went up this as fast as she could walk. It ended abruptly a hundred metres on at the side of a bitumen road on a ridgetop.

By then she was panting hard and sweating. The group had strung out. Gordon, Lofty, and Dan were with her, but Jennifer, Roger, and Wendy were well behind. Barbara stopped just inside the rainforest and looked up the road. It was the road to Barron Falls and at this point it curved left into a clearing with houses on both sides. About a hundred metres away, six people in yellow cloaks were walking along the side of the road away from them.

"Wait till they are out of sight," Gordon cautioned.

"I was going to," Barbara replied. She looked around as Roger and Wendy puffed up to join them.

As the group of Smileys vanished over the crest where the road entered more rainforest Barbara started walking. They moved in single file beside the road along the grassy verge. Several cars went past in both directions. Barbara took no notice of them.

When the friends were in the middle of the clearing another vehicle came up behind them from the direction of the town centre. It slowed down as it passed and Barbara glanced at it. She found herself staring into two tiny, bright blue eyes in a round, red, cheerful face. The off-white 4WD then accelerated. In the back sat two men dressed in khaki work clothes who stared at them.

"Mr Smiley!" Barbara gasped.

"Yes. And he had a good look at us," Gordon added. "I'm not sure if this is a good idea now. We had better be careful or we could walk into trouble."

"Trouble! Who? Me?" Barbara quipped, but she felt a tightening in her gut and knew she was scared as well as upset.

They reached the crest at the road junction just in time to glimpse the last yellow cloak go around the next bend in the road. There was no sign of Mr Smiley's vehicle.

"Faster!" Barbara urged. "The road to their other property turns off to the right somewhere along here."

She strode along as fast as she could. There were so many cars using the road they were forced to keep on the grass verge.

"Bloody tourists!" Lofty grumbled. "Polluting the mountain air! They should walk and enjoy it."

At the next bend Barbara again glimpsed the yellow figures. "They've gone left. I thought they would have turned right. That road they just passed should be the one."

Mystified by this Barbara pulled out her map and checked it. On either side of the roadhouses were tucked away in the jungle at the end of narrow driveways. Some were expensive modern structures. Others were shacks which looked as though they belonged in a South East Asian slum. The jungle looked very green. Through gaps in the trees she could see jungle clad ridges ahead.

The group marched downhill past the road junction and on along the Barron Falls Road. At the bottom the road curved right and went up a long hill through more jungle. The houses ended. The yellow figures were nearly at the top of the next hill.

"I remember this hill from last night," Karen said. "I was ready to drop."

"I'm ready to drop now," Jennifer groaned.

Barbara glanced back and saw that the group had spread out over 50 metres, but she did not slow down. The hill taxed her legs and lungs and by the time she reached the top she was starting to feel genuine distress.

This forced her to slow down, which worried her as she was only getting occasional glimpses of the yellow figures as the road went around several curves. She passed a turn-off leading to a house, then a bitumen road which went off on the left to the Hydro Weir. For a moment Barbara hesitated, unsure which way to go. Then she spotted a flash of yellow at the next curve. She went on along the Barron Falls Road.

This curved left and the figures were lost to sight. Then the road curved right and she glimpsed them again before another curve left hid them from view. Another road went off on the left, a half-overgrown vehicle track which led along a ridgetop through thick jungle towards the river. She glanced along it then abruptly stopped. She strained her eyes and wiped perspiration from them.

Was that someone moving along the side-track? She wasn't sure. It might just have been shadows as the trees moved in the wind.

171

Gordon stopped beside her. "What's wrong?"

"I thought I saw something yellow moving along this track, just where it goes out of sight in the jungle."

"Couldn't be. Look. There they are." Gordon pointed as three yellow clad figures went out of sight around the next bend in the main road.

Barbara looked down. "Someone has just been along this track. Look. There is a boot print in the dust and that grass is freshly trampled."

"Maybe. But those yellow buggers went this way," Gordon said.

Barbara shrugged and resumed walking. She was tiring now and her brisk walk was slowing. She forced herself to step it out, ignoring sore muscles and the start of a stitch. As she walked, she pondered and began to worry. Had the yellow group split up?

She glanced at the jungle on either side and suddenly felt afraid. They were now well out of town. Then a very worrying thought came to her.

What if we are being led into a trap?

Chapter 18

BARRON FALLS

At the next bend in the road Barbara got a glimpse of yellow. Lofty pointed. "They've gone towards Barron Falls Lookout," Lofty observed.

"Good. I was worried they might take the track back to Wrights Lookout," Barbara said.

Dan snorted. "Huh! We will look bloody silly if they lead us all the way back down to Kamerunga!" he said.

Roger laughed aloud at this but it did bother Barbara. *We are on the trail,* she told herself.

A minute later they were at the turn-off where the road forked. The one to the right went to Wrights Lookout. The left fork went to the Barron Falls. Twenty metres along it this again forked.

"Which way?" Gordon asked.

Lofty shook his head. "Doesn't matter. It is a loop. Some of us go each way. We will meet at the car park at the bottom end," he said.

Barbara and Gordon went right. The others went left. Two hundred sweaty paces down the slope they met up again where five cars were parked. Concrete steps led down to a small lookout platform on the hillside. They stopped on this and leaned on the railings. Barbara ignored the view. She had seen it a dozen times. Her eyes swept left along the railway below them to where it curved out of sight at the top of the Barron Falls. No sign of people in yellow.

She started along the elevated timber walkway which led to the railway, but Gordon protested.

"Hang on a sec. Wait for the others. And let me have a look at the view."

Barbara stopped but made no attempt to hide her impatience. Gordon read the sign and looked out.

"Falls? Where is the water?" he asked, eyeing the 300 metres of jagged black rock which dropped almost sheer to the bottom of the gorge.

Lofty pointed to the top of the falls one kilometre away. "All dammed up behind a weir," he explained. "It all goes through a tunnel to a hydro-electric power station down in the gorge. Remember that tunnel entrance at Robbs Monument? You only see water going over the falls when the river floods during the wet season."

"Oh come on!" Barbara cried. "They will get away."

At that moment, Wendy and Roger came into view. Wendy was limping and Roger looked fed up. As soon as they arrived Barbara went on down the walkway. This led into the jungle. It was a zigzag of about 300 hundred paces of walkways, bridges and a walking track cut into the hillside, and it brought her out onto a footbridge across the railway. As she strode across this, she looked both ways but saw no sign of the yellow people. That got her all anxious that they had lost the Smileys.

She went quickly down a flight of steps onto the railway platform which, with its attendant safety fence, extended for 300 metres along the lip of the gorge. There were a few tourists at the small shelter shed at the bottom of the steps. Without hesitation she strode over to them.

"Excuse me," she asked. "Have you seen any people wearing yellow cloaks walking along here?"

A young man in his twenties with the look of a honeymooner lowered his camera. "Yes. Three of them. Just a few minutes ago. They went that way." He pointed down the line.

Barbara hurried south along the platform, passing under the footbridge as she did. At the end of the platform she was confronted by several signs warning her in no uncertain terms that it was illegal to walk along the railway line and of the possible harsh penalties for doing so. This caused her to pause but then she shook her head and stepped down off the platform onto the sandy track beside the line.

From behind her Roger called, "Barbara, did you see these signs?"

"Yes, never mind them. Hurry," she replied.

"But we could get into trouble," Roger said.

Barbara shook her head impatiently. "Fiona's already in trouble," she called over her shoulder as she stepped down off the platform.

Gordon stepped down past Roger and said, "Anyway, it's a Sunday. Surely there won't be any railway people to catch us?"

"Only on the trains," Roger answered, still troubled.

Barbara snorted and snapped, "Huh! I can't see a train driver stopping his train and getting down to chase us. Come on!"

At that Roger shrugged and followed, the others on his heels. Barbara broke into a trot, hurrying along the narrow sandy footpath beside the railway line. She felt an irrational sense of urgency.

"If we lose them after all this!" she muttered fiercely. She heard the others groan and complain but a glance showed them following so she ran on.

Lofty jogged along close behind. "Did that tourist say three?"

"Yes."

"Where did the other three go?"

"Don't know. Down that side road possibly," Barbara replied.

"Why would they split up?"

A horrible thought came to her. "To trick us? To decoy us?"

At that they slowed but kept walking along the railway. Barbara studied the lie of the ground. On her left was the massive gorge, a very steep drop for hundreds of metres close beside them to the left and steep cuttings and thick undergrowth on the right.

Good spot for an ambush. They could toss our bodies over the cliff. No-one would ever even think to look there, she thought.

"Surely they didn't know we were following them?" she asked.

"They could know. Don't forget Mr Smiley drove past us, and he also drove past them. He could have given them orders," Gordon said.

"But why?" Lofty asked.

"I don't know," Gordon replied.

"He could be worried that we are onto something," Barbara suggested.

They rounded a curve. Still no sign of anyone. Roger called out so they stopped for a minute to allow him to catch up. Karen and Dan joined them. Wendy and Jennifer came into view well back. Barbara looked over the side and could see all the way to the bottom of the gorge far below: black, jagged rocks and pools of green water.

Gordon looked down and said, "Well, it is an impressive view anyway."

Roger puffed up to them. "What's going on? Where are they?"

Barbara told him. Roger pulled a face and said, "I don't like this. And I don't like this place. Just along here is the old lookout where Kirk had his fight to the death with that maniac Tarzan."

Barbara felt a thrill of fear. Gordon was just curious. "Where? Tell us about it."

175

They continued walking in a group while Roger recounted the story. They rounded another curve. A rumbling vibration came to them, then the blast of a diesel's air-horn.

"Train! Off the track. Hide!" Roger cried.

They scrambled into the blady grass on a mound on the lip of the gorge. The other side was a steep rock cutting, and crouched behind bushes. A diesel locomotive rumbled around the bend. A dozen carriages followed, each crammed with smiling Japanese tourists.

When the train was gone the friends resumed their walk. The line curved again.

"Look!" Barbara gasped.

They had entered a long cutting with a low, wooded knoll on the left. About fifty paces further along was a bridge over a jungle creek. Just near the bridge two men in yellow cloaks, the hoods thrown back to expose their heads, were fighting with a third man in yellow.

Even as they watched a blow felled the third man. He crumpled beside the railway and one of the men kicked viciously into his ribs. The other grabbed the fallen man and began dragging him towards the cliff top.

"They're trying to throw him over!" gasped Karen as both men grabbed the prostrate figure and lifted him. The man clawed at the grass and shrieked in terror. He was punched and kicked again.

Barbara grabbed Dan. "Dan, use your mobile phone and call the police, quick!"

Dan nodded and stopped to do so. Barbara did not wait. She began running towards the men. As she got closer, she saw one of the two thugs pulled down by the desperate struggles of the third man. She had no doubt he was in fear of his life. The other thug, a solid, middle-aged man with a square face, pulled an object out from under his cloak and lashed at the third man's head knocking him senseless. Only then did Barbara see that what the thug was holding was a gun.

At that moment, the thugs heard them and looked around. The thug with the gun looked alarmed but recovered instantly.

"Stop!" he shouted, pointing the pistol at them. "That is far enough."

Barbara skidded to a halt about ten paces from the men. To her relief her friends crunched to a standstill beside her.

"What are you doing?" she cried.

176

"Just a little disagreement. Mind your own business," the man snarled.

He licked his lips nervously and looked from one to the other. Barbara noted that under his yellow cloak the man wore a khaki shirt and long trousers, brown leather boots, and had an orange Smiley Badge on his left shirt pocket. The other thug was dressed the same. He was a thin weasel of a creature with untidy black hair.

He is not just worried, Barbara thought. *He is very frightened, and he doesn't know what to do next.*

Lofty spoke first, "Why are you hitting that man?"

"He broke the rules," the weasel said.

"Shut up!" the older thug snapped at him. He turned to face the group. "We are police, undercover drug squad. Now clear out."

"I don't believe you," Barbara replied. "Show us your ID."

The man scowled. "We don't carry it on this sort of job. Now get out of here," he snarled.

"No."

The thug's eyes narrowed and he aimed the pistol at Barbara, confirming her suspicions that he was a liar. She cast around for some way to prevent the situation getting out of hand as she was sure that, if they went away, the third man would be murdered.

The thug snarled at them, "This is none of your business. Now clear out before you get hurt."

At that moment, the man on the ground raised his head and cried out, "Help! They are going to kill me. Help!"

The solid thug lashed out with his boot. It cracked into the man's temple and bowled him over into the long grass.

Barbara gasped in horror. Gordon took a step forward, calling, "That's enough of that! Leave him alone!"

The solid thug glared at Gordon and pointed the pistol first at him, then at the man on the ground. "Keep back! Clear out!" he shouted. "Who the bloody hell are you anyway?"

Jennifer tugged at Barbara's sleeve. "Let's go before he decides to take hostages or shoots someone," she whispered.

The thought had occurred to Barbara, but she did not feel she could just back out and let someone be killed, but equally she could see a worse tragedy looming if the man lost control. She was very frightened but also determined.

Roger murmured to Lofty, "We can take this guy. That automatic's not cocked."

"No. Not yet. Too risky," Lofty muttered back. On hearing that Barbara's blood ran cold with fear, and she wanted to say don't but she also thought it was a possible plan so stood silent.

The man glared at them. "Stop whispering! Bugger off or I will shoot you as well."

Nobody moved. The thug aimed the pistol at Lofty. "Go away before you get hurt."

Lofty laughed. "What are you going to do? Murder all of us?"

That made weasel look really worried. He licked his lips and said, "Come on, Kurt. Let's get outa here."

"Shut your ignorant trap and get your gun out, you bozo!" the older thug snapped.

The weasel pulled out an automatic pistol as well. Barbara's mind raced. She was very scared, but so were the thugs. But she knew she couldn't just leave the man to be murdered in cold blood.

Besides, this is a real clue. If these men are prepared to murder someone, they would not hesitate to kidnap a girl, she thought. *Or of murdering her,* her reluctant mind added.

Barbara went ice-cold at that thought. She stood and glared at the men, ignoring their threats. She thought the man would give up and leave before he would start shooting at them, but realised it was a fearful risk.

He is bluffing, she reasoned. *If he was going to shoot, he would have by now.*

But what to do next? It was a stand-off, and the thugs were getting more and more agitated. The injured man moaned.

The solid thug cocked his pistol and aimed it at the head of the man in the grass. The group tensed.

Suddenly a voice called out from up on the slope behind them, "This is the police. Drop the guns and put your hands up!"

Barbara glanced up. A policeman in a bullet-proof vest and armed with an automatic rifle was kneeling on top of the cutting. There was rustling in the grass and another policeman appeared and went into a crouching fire position amongst the ferns, his rifle aimed at the weasel. A third policeman appeared and started talking on a hand radio.

The two thugs gaped in astonishment. The weasel dropped his gun at once and stuck his hands up. Reluctantly the older man did the same. The policeman with the radio called out, "Now move away from the guns, backwards. Move! You kids stay where you are."

The two thugs moved to the base of the small knoll ten metres away. The policeman with the radio slithered down the grassy bank, checked the two pistols and placed them beside the railway, then crouched over the injured man. After checking his pulse the policeman started talking on the radio.

Barbara was so relieved it took her a moment to realise that the police must have been very quick. Then she reasoned that it wasn't possible.

For them to get Dan's phone call and then get here from Kuranda would take at least half an hour, not a few minutes, she thought. *So how...?*

Before she could puzzle it out there were running footsteps and voices on the railway behind them. They turned to look, and got another surprise. Running along the track were two plain-clothed policemen (so she assumed by their appearance), Dan, and Captain Conkey! Captain Conkey was in casual clothes, not in uniform.

The detectives drew pistols and covered the two thugs while the police up on the bank climbed down. The thugs were then searched, handcuffed, and seated in the grass beside the railway. Capt Conkey wiped perspiration from his ruddy face and looked at them. He glared at Barbara. She found it hard to meet his eye.

"Yes sir!" he mimicked. "We promise to keep out of trouble!"

Barbara blushed and bit her lip. She straightened up and met his gaze. "We didn't plan this sir. It just sort of happened," she replied.

The two detectives, both middle-aged men, one portly and one spare, came over to them. Roger let out a low groan. "Oh no!" he murmured. "Not again."

"Hello Roger, remember me?" the thin, hatchet-faced, plain clothes policeman with the moustache asked.

"Yes sir, I do," Roger replied.

"Up to your usual tricks I see," the detective growled. Then he smiled. "Well, introduce me to these people."

"Yes sir... er.. people this is Inspector Sharpe. Sir, this is Barbara and this is..." Roger introduced his friends.

Inspector Sharpe shook hands with each, then said, "Glad to meet you all. Roger will tell you later how we know each other." He turned to the bulkier policeman with short cropped, grey hair. "This is Superintendent Blunt. He is in charge of this investigation."

Lofty sniggered and nudged Gordon. "Sharpe and Blunt! They've got both ends covered," he whispered.

Inspector Sharpe heard him and raised an eyebrow. However he said nothing and holstered his pistol under his grey suit coat.

The superintendent glared at them. "You kids may well have wrecked this whole investigation, blundering in like bloody elephants! Months of dangerous undercover work wasted!"

Barbara was embarrassed as the implications sank in, but she was stung by the Superintendent's manner. She said, "We didn't mean to. They were going to kill that man."

Superintendent Blunt raised his eyebrows and turned to glance at the injured man who still lay unconscious in the grass.

"Tell me what happened."

They recounted the incident. This led to questions on what they were doing there. Both detectives frowned and so did Capt Conkey as Barbara mentioned how they had been tailing the people in yellow. It made her feel guilty and foolish.

The superintendent snapped angrily at her, "You mean you kids were deliberately following these people!"

"Yes sir."

"Damn and blast! Now you may have ruined everything! We had them under surveillance the whole time. How do you think we got here so fast, you silly girl!"

Barbara blushed but being belittled stung. Her mind raced and she snapped back angrily, "So how come that man wasn't saved earlier?"

She saw two of the uniformed police exchange uncomfortable glances and the Superintendent's eyes flickered and narrowed. She saw her advantage and took it. "I am right, aren't I? If we hadn't arrived that man would have been murdered! You only arrived at the end!"

At that moment, two paramedics came into sight carrying a stretcher along the railway. Superintendent Blunt grunted but Barbara could see she had scored her point. He fixed her with a steely eye then turned and said, "You kids wait here. Sergeant Smith, a word."

He and Inspector Sharpe walked out of hearing with the sergeant. The paramedics began to administer First Aid to the injured man.

Barbara shuddered and sighed with relief. Roger met her eye and gave her a thumbs-up and grinned. She smiled and relaxed, suddenly feeling drained.

After a few minutes the superintendent issued orders and the two thugs were escorted away. He walked over to the friends. "You lot can help carry this stretcher. Let's go." He said it in such frosty and uncompromising tones that none of them even considered not obeying.

They grouped around the stretcher. One of the paramedics began to give instructions but Roger cut him short. "We are army cadets. We know the drill. Just give the orders."

On command they picked the stretcher up and moved off. Lofty grouped them into two teams of four and they changed every hundred paces. As they panted along Barbara turned to Dan.

"The cops were quick. What happened?"

Dan nodded. "Gave me a fright. I made the phone call and went to follow and there they were. They came down a track in the jungle. I didn't know who they were and was about to bolt when I saw the OC."

"So they were watching and closing in," Gordon observed.

That comment made Barbara bite her lip. She still felt that they had done the right thing and was sure they had saved the man's life but now the worry surfaced: What if they had now made it harder to find Fiona?

It was awkward carrying the stretcher along the railway, but they did not pause. By the time Barbara was on her third relief they had reached the shelter shed at Barron Falls. At that moment, a train sounded its horn from up the line.

Inspector Sharpe swore. "Blast! Just what we don't want. Put the stretcher down here at the end of the platform. Hide that yellow cloak and cover this bloke up. Say he is a tourist who tripped and hit his head on the railway line."

As they placed the stretcher down, the train drew to a stop with a metallic clatter and hissing of air. They were close to the locomotive and the throbbing of the diesel motor made it hard to talk. Tourists swarmed off to stand at the safety rail to look at the falls. A few came over to look but were easily turned away by a grim-faced Inspector Sharpe.

After five minutes the train driver sounded his horn and the passengers climbed back aboard. The train resumed its journey down the mountain. Barbara had an image of hundreds of curious faces, people staring and pointing. Then the train was gone leaving only two tourists who must have come by car and who were doing the tourist thing of having their photo taken by each other with the falls in the background.

The group carried the stretcher up the footpath to the car park. An ambulance and two cars were parked there. As soon as the stretcher was eased into the ambulance Superintendent Blunt said to Inspector Sharpe, "Travel with this character. I want him guarded every moment. He is not to be alone even for a second, and I mean armed guards."

The seriousness of that made Barbara go cold with fear for Fiona. What had she gotten mixed up in? The superintendent then turned to them. "I will see you kids at the police station. Make sure they get there, Captain."

Barbara noted the hard lines around the Superintendent's mouth and knew deep down that when this man said 'do it', he meant it. This impression was confirmed by Lofty after the Superintendent had walked over to a grey car nearby. He murmured, "I wouldn't want to make an enemy of that man!"

That didn't help Barbara feel any better when she remembered arguing with him.

"How do we get back to Kuranda?" Jennifer asked.

Inspector Sharpe grunted. "Humpf! Same way you got here, walk," he snapped.

Roger groaned and Dan snorted. "Bloody hell! You could do give us a lift, sir."

Inspector Sharpe shook his head. "No vehicle available. By the time there is you could be there. So get going. It isn't far." he said with a grin. "Be good exercise anyway."

"Is it safe?" Karen asked.

Inspector Sharpe frowned and said, "Why not? Just keep together."

Barbara had a mental image of the road winding through the jungle. "What will we do if we meet the other three Smileys sir?" she asked.

The Inspector had turned to climb into the ambulance. He spun round to face her. "What other three?"

Barbara described how they had been following six people. Inspector Sharpe swore under his breath. "Where is this other road you thought they went along?"

"Back that way," Barbara answered.

She described the turn-off. Inspector Sharpe took out his radio and gave instructions to have the overgrown side road searched. "Now, back to Kuranda. If you see these Smiley People ignore them and just keep walking. Tell our people if you meet them."

He climbed into the ambulance and it drove off after the superintendent's car.

"Come on. Let's move," Capt Conkey ordered. He set off up the road.

Roger called after him. "Do we have to go along the road sir?"

"Why? How else could we get there?"

"Along the railway," Roger replied.

"Why? They both go to Kuranda."

"Yes sir, but the railway is shorter, and it hasn't got any hills." Roger said.

Capt Conkey shook his head. "No, it is against the law. The road it is."

That eased the tension and they all laughed. As they started walking Barbara said to Capt Conkey, "We are sorry sir. We didn't mean to cause trouble."

Roger agreed. "We didn't know you were in Kuranda sir."

Capt Conkey compressed his lips. "I wasn't. I was at home enjoying my holiday. Then I got a phone call from Inspector Sharpe saying you were interrogating every shopkeeper in Kuranda about the Smiley People, and could I please come and call you off before you jeopardised the whole undercover operation."

Barbara bit her lip and looked at her boots. Capt Conkey went on, "By the time I had driven up here they told me you were last seen pursuing a group of suspects along the Barron Falls Road. We set off after you. And I'd have to say you are damned lucky we did!"

They all hung their heads. Capt Conkey snorted. "Come on, step it out! My car is back at the police station."

He walked briskly up the hill towards Kuranda.

Chapter 19

AWKWARD QUESTIONS

For the first hundred metres they walked in silence, all feeling thoroughly chastened. Barbara walked beside Gordon. She met his eyes and he gave her one of his wry smiles.

"It'll be okay," he assured her. He reached over and took her hand. Her impulse was to snatch it away but then she felt comforted and allowed him to hold it. He went on, "You certainly are full of surprises. Tell me about yourself. Tell me about your childhood."

Barbara didn't really want to, but she began. By then they were at the junction of the road to Wrights Lookout. The group turned right and headed for Kuranda. Because of the traffic Capt Conkey insisted they walk in single file on the right-hand side. This effectively ended the conversation until they were around the next bend and came to where the side road went off along the flat ridge top. A police car was parked there and two police were visible in the edge of the jungle as they slowly searched.

Barbara badly wanted to join them to help track the three Smileys but could only make a face and keep walking. It was hot by then and she found she was sweating and thirsty. The road wound around and down and then past another turn-off, the bitumen road to the weir and inlet station. Then it went left into jungle and uphill until they came to the first houses in the jungle. As they passed the bitumen road going off to the west Barbara bit her lip and wondered if they would be able to get away to search the Smiley property that was along that road.

Probably not, she thought gloomily.

By now they were all puffing and perspiring, and Wendy and Karen were both grumbling and looking unhappy. But Capt Conkey was not in a good mood and insisted they keep walking.

As the group walked up over a long crest with houses down among the jungle on the right and more open allotments on the left Gordon suddenly let out a gasp and pointed. "Look, the other three Smileys," he hissed.

Barbara looked and saw three figures in yellow cloaks walking on the same side of the road as them and in the same direction. "Is that them? How did they get there?" she replied.

Roger answered from behind her, "They could have gone down to the river along that dirt road and come back along the bitumen one from the inlet."

"They may not be the same three," Lofty suggested. By now the group had come to a standstill and were watching as the three Smileys vanished over the crest a hundred metres ahead.

Barbara thought hard. "They may not be, but we should follow them anyway," she said. She set off at a brisk walk.

Capt Conkey hurried after her. "Now steady on young lady! You are not following them."

"Then you phone the police sir, and we will stop following them when we know the police are watching them," she replied.

Much as she respected Capt Conkey she was also determined to find Fiona and the three people in yellow were her only clue at that moment.

To her relief Capt Conkey agreed so she kept walking. He strode along behind her and took out his mobile phone and called the police. By the time he had made the call the group were at the next side street where the houses were in a clearing. The three Smileys were just visible going on down the other side of the hill. They were now walking along the concrete footpath that paralleled the road and were entering a patch of jungle that formed a tunnel over the road and footpath.

Capt Conkey frowned and said, "Inspector Sharpe has asked us to keep an eye on them until he can get a plain clothes team back to take over. He says it should only be five minutes."

"Good!" Barbara muttered. She glanced back and saw that her friends were hurrying to keep up with them.

Roger was close behind. As the friends crossed the sunlit clearing he pointed across the road to the left. "That is where we came up out of the jungle."

"They are heading towards Kuranda at least," Capt Conkey said. Then he shook his head and muttered, "Oh no! Damn and blast!"

Barbara saw why. The three Smileys had suddenly turned right and vanished into the jungle. The friends kept walking until they came to that point and Barbara saw that a concrete walking path went downhill into the jungle. A sign showed that it went all the way to the riverbank near the mouth of Jumrum Creek. She turned to follow but Capt Conkey told her to stop.

Barbara shook her head. "Oh sir! We are a big group. We can just pretend to be tourists. You call the police and tell them where we are going."

Capt Conkey rubbed his chin and said, "I don't like it. I think we should just go back to town."

"Please sir! We will be alright in a group," Barbara insisted. "It's just a tourist walking track."

Reluctantly Capt Conkey agreed. Once again, he took out his mobile phone and began calling. Barbara did not wait but hurried on along the track. Her friends followed. The track was narrow and wound through the jungle so that visibility was at best only about 25 metres, but she did not care.

If we meet the Smileys, we just pretend we are tourists on a nature ramble, she thought.

The track was longer than she expected. It went steadily downhill for about 500m but emerged beside the railway line about two hundred metres from the rail bridge over Jumrum Creek. She crossed the railway and came to a junction with a path that led left along the top of the riverbank, just in the trees. Through the screen of thick jungle Barbara got glimpses of the river. The others joined her and she looked around. By then all were sweating heavily and Barbara was feeling thirsty and footsore.

To her dismay there was no sign of the Smileys. She carefully studied the sand beside the rail line, hoping to see boot prints. But there were none. The path that went left was concrete, so no prints were visible. Lofty said, "Which way did they go?"

Barbara shook her head. "I don't know."

Capt Conkey put his phone to his ear and said, "Doesn't matter. We are going to Kuranda so go left. I will tell Inspector Sharpe what has happened."

Reluctantly Barbara obeyed. She walked along the footpath with Gordon beside her He saw her disappointment and took her hand. "It will be alright," he said to comfort her.

At that moment, they heard loud laughter down on the riverbank. A

186

woman let out a loud shriek and could be heard giggling as she ran up the bank. She suddenly burst out of head-high grass onto the railway line just in front of Lofty, Jennifer and Karen, who were leading. The woman was totally nude, and by the tan of her body, usually went that way.

She stopped when she saw them. She cried out something in a foreign language and bounded back down the path through the grass. Barbara felt Gordon's hand tighten on hers. She glimpsed the upper half of a bearded man who laughed and grabbed the woman. Both ran giggling back out of sight.

Capt Conkey gave a wry smile, and said, "They sound happy, but I don't think they are the Happy People we are looking for." Then he turned and called back, "Keep walking Dan, don't stop to look."

They laughed and continued on. Talking and laughter from more than two people floated up from the riverbank. Barbara pictured a group of naked people and what they might be doing, then felt uneasy and wished the incident had not occurred. She pondered again if she was odd.

My brain seems to be nothing but a maggoty mass of evil thoughts at times, she told herself. She shook her head with dismay and thought, *That little scene has affected me more than the confrontation with the two thugs!*

She forced herself to resume talking to Gordon. They walked on, side-by-side, and Roger called to them, "That bridge ahead should be the one over Jumrum Creek. We have less than a kilometre to go after that."

"Thank God!" Wendy added. "I'm exhausted, and I'm getting chafed... Oooh! Look! Two men."

Out of the belt of thick jungle along the riverbank on their right two men had appeared. The first one saw them and stopped so suddenly the second man bumped into him. They both visibly hesitated before the first man turned left and marched quickly back towards the friends. He wore jeans and a khaki shirt and looked about thirty. Over his arm was a bundle of yellow cloth!

The second man also carried a roll of yellow cloth. He had tattooed arms protruding from a green shirt with the sleeves rolled above his biceps.

He looks guilty about something, Barbara thought. *Furtive anyway. I wonder what they have been doing?*

The two groups passed each other on the pathway, so close that the friends had to step aside. As they did Barbara studied the men closely while trying to pretend not to. After they had passed in the opposite direction Barbara glanced back over her shoulder.

"Keep walking," Capt Conkey muttered.

He urged them to keep moving but took out his phone again and started using it. It was not till they reached the end of the Jumrum Creek bridge that he stopped and looked back. The two men could be seen hurrying across the railway line. They vanished back up the walking track. Capt Conkey rubbed his chin thoughtfully and frowned, then turned and walked down onto a short foot bridge beside the rail bridge.

"Sir, I think those two men are Smileys," Dan called from the back.

"I am sure they are," Capt Conkey replied. "Now keep walking."

Barbara stared hard at the two dwindling figures. "But sir, if we follow them we might find their hideout."

"No," Capt Conkey replied flatly. "Our instructions are to keep walking and that is what we will do. We will leave them to the police. They will have someone watching the top end of that track by this time. Now come on."

They crossed the footbridge and followed a vehicle track to the right out onto the riverbank. Here the bank was a nicely kept park lined with trees and the path was easy to follow. Several families and groups of tourists gave it a sense of safety and normality. The path ran west below the railway yard. Five minutes easy walk had them at the steps that led up to the railway station and the footbridge overpass. Capt Conkey led them up this and on to the car park beside the station. Five minutes later they were seated in the police station and Capt Conkey again reported the sighting of the two Smileys to Superintendent Blunt. He answered that he had two undercover officers tailing the two men.

"They picked them up as they came out onto the Barron Falls Road," he explained.

"But there were three," Barbara said. "We followed three down to the riverbank."

"They may not have been the same men," Capt Conkey answered.

Lofty spoke in reply, very emotionally. "I'll bet they were. I reckon they murdered the third man and chucked his body into the river. That was what the other ones we followed were going to do, murder that man and toss his body into the gorge."

Superintendent Blunt looked thoughtful and muttered, "You might be right. Where did you see these men on the riverbank?"

They described the location and Roger even drew a sketch map. They were then seated in a waiting room. The next two hours were not enjoyable for Barbara. She realised that her accusations about the police not caring and not doing anything had been both hasty and unjust. She wondered if she should apologise. She also worried about whether their interference might have made it harder to find Fiona, and whether their hike might be cut short. Parents were phoned one by one. Capt Conkey and the superintendent did the talking. The parents were assured they were safe and not in trouble. Capt Conkey asked each if they wished to be present while their children were interviewed and, in each case, obtained their approval for him to be present in their place.

The parents were naturally alarmed that the children should be in a police station but Capt Conkey's reassurances that they were not in trouble, that they had saved a man's life and were only being questioned as witnesses calmed them. Most wished to speak to their son or daughter.

When it was her turn Barbara was reluctant to speak to her dad. She felt too guilty for comfort. His first words gave this a sharp twist. "Hello Bubs. Keeping out of trouble as usual I hear."

"Aw Dad! It wasn't like that. We just followed these people and it sort of happened."

"Didn't you promise Captain Conkey not to go off prying into other people's affairs?"

Barbara flushed. She licked dry lips. "Yes dad," she replied hoarsely. "But I wanted to find Fiona."

"I know. Now promise me you will stop looking for her or I will drive up and collect you right now."

"No Dad, I won't, promise. But now that I know the police are on the job I promise that I won't go deliberately searching. But if we find something we will tell the police," Barbara replied.

"Put Captain Conkey back on please," her father asked. Barbara did so. She went and sat with the others, feeling thwarted and depressed.

Roger said gloomily, "I suppose this will be the end of our trip. My mum was not amused and she is a real worrier."

"That will be a shame," Jennifer said. "We were just getting to know each other."

189

She glanced at Lofty as she said this. Barbara noted both Karen and Wendy purse their lips slightly.

"Perhaps we could go somewhere else?" Gordon suggested. "There must be other places."

"Good idea," Karen agreed. "I'm sick of this Smiley nonsense. I don't like being scared."

At that point a detective they had never seen before arrived and called for Barbara and Capt Conkey. They were taken into another room and Barbara was asked to tell the whole story. She only covered what they had done that day. She wasn't going to get the others into trouble by admitting the other things they had done. The detective typed the story onto a computer as she talked, adding details as he asked her questions.

Being questioned by the police was no new experience for Barbara so she answered easily. It took half an hour before the detective had the computer printer run off a copy of her statement for her to sign. She was then sent to sit on her own in a room overlooking the river.

After about twenty minutes, during which she brooded and fed her black thoughts, she was joined by Lofty. A few minutes later Roger came in. The others did not take as long and by 5:30pm all were seated in the room. Capt Conkey and Superintendent Blunt joined them.

The superintendent hitched up his trousers and scowled at them. "Thank you all for your co-operation and assistance," he growled. "But next time have a bit more faith in us. Don't try to be amateur detectives. You will do more harm than good. Next time someone might get killed."

The superintendent fixed a steely glare on Barbara. She had been rehearsing her apology but now she stiffened her upper lip and stared back defiantly. He went on, "Now, the question is: What are we going to do with you? Are your parents coming to collect you?"

Barbara again felt a sharp stab of frustration and defeat. She turned to Capt Conkey. "Sir, can we go on with our hike if we go somewhere else? I do know we have caused you a lot of trouble and wasted a day of your holidays, but we would like to."

Capt Conkey looked at the superintendent who asked, "Where did you have in mind?"

Roger spoke up, "West sir. Along the railway to Mareeba. That would take us two days. It is a good hike. I've done it before."

"Hmm. I'll have to think about it," Superintendent Blunt replied, rubbing his chin. Barbara tried not to show her dislike of the man. He even had long grey hairs growing out of his nose! Secretly she wished there was still some way she could go on looking for Fiona.

"What should we do now sir?" Lofty asked.

"Go and have tea," Roger interjected. "I'm starving."

That eased the tension. Capt Conkey nodded. "Yes. Go back to the caravan park and eat. Stay in a group and wait there till I come. I will discuss this with your parents."

"And don't mention a word of this to anyone. Is that clear?" Superintendent Blunt added.

"Yes sir," they chorused meekly.

The group filed out onto the footpath.

"Which way?" Gordon asked.

"Along the railway," Roger said. They walked down the hill to the station. The sun was already behind the trees and darkness was only half an hour away. The railway station was deserted and they saw no-one till they reached the highway bridge. Three scruffy looking men were sitting around a small fire under the bridge and Barbara felt concern that there might be an unpleasant incident as the men were drinking. The friends walked past in silence as quickly as they could. Ten minutes later, just on dusk, they arrived back at the caravan park. They collected their gear and walked down to their camp.

By then Barbara was very depressed. *Another day of emotional ups and downs and still no sign of Fiona!* she sighed.

When they reached their hutchie, she just wanted to flop down and cry. With an effort she pretended she was fine. Wendy looked exhausted. She lay down at once.

Barbara stood and spoke to her. "Come and have a shower, Wendy. You will feel much better," she urged.

The others agreed and Wendy was chivvied to her feet. They dug out soap, towels and a change of clothes and walked to the shower block. This time Barbara was first in. She stayed under for ten minutes, luxuriating in the flow of warm water as it eased her tired muscles.

Slowly, she towelled herself dry and dressed. Then she returned to the hutchie. All the while her mind turned over the events of the day. The result was an uncomfortable jumble. They had certainly learnt something about the Smileys, but there was no clue about Fiona.

Chapter 20

THE OUTLINE OF EVIL

Near the showers was a covered barbeque area with electric lights and two tables. Gordon and Lofty were there cooking their tea so Barbara took her food and went to join them. A family was using one of the tables and their proximity rather limited the conversation to begin with.

Barbara placed her cooking gear on the table and asked, "Aren't you grubs going to have a bath?"

"No, we aren't," Gordon replied.

Barbara wrinkled her nose in mock distaste. Gordon laughed and added, "We are going to have a shower instead."

He walked around the table and put his arms around her shoulders and hugged her. "Cheer up old girl. We will find her."

Barbara nodded and forced a smile. Gordon released her and she sat on the bench and began preparing a meal. As she did she mulled over her reactions to the hug and decided she had not resented his comforting touch.

In ones and twos the others joined them. Barbara instantly noted that Jennifer wore a loose white shirt, and no bra. She wished she wouldn't dress like that as she found it unsettling, and she resented it when the boy's eyes, and particularly Gordon's, kept straying there.

Barbara made herself a cup of coffee then began heating a can of 'Beef Stroganoff'. As she did the family packed up and left. Soon after that, two men walked in out of the darkness: Capt Conkey and Inspector Sharpe.

Lofty greeted them, "Hello sir. What's the news?"

"Let us have a feed first please, then we will tell you," Capt Conkey replied. Both men had purchased hamburgers and they sat down and began to eat. Roger, who was a strong admirer of Inspector Sharpe, the result of a desperate adventure near Atherton two years before, provided him with a cup of coffee. Barbara did likewise for Capt Conkey.

Twenty minutes later, when all had eaten, Inspector Sharpe looked

192

around to check that they were out of earshot of anyone else, then said to them, "First I want a promise from each of you. Some of what I am going to say is strictly confidential. I am only telling you because I think it might jog your memories and help us. You must promise me not to breathe a word to anyone, and I mean anyone, brother, mother, lover, I don't care. Not to anyone until I say you can, which may be never."

They each promised in turn. Inspector Sharpe nodded and went on, "We have been investigating complaints about the Oojoombies or Smiley People for several years now. Recently there has been a sharp increase in the number of complaints, and of suspicious disappearances. So we began a major investigation. This was well under way before the disappearance of your friend Fiona."

Inspector Sharpe looked hard at Barbara as he said this, making her feel quite guilty. He then went on, "It is an undercover job mostly, but progress has been very slow. The Smiley People are a world-wide organisation so our investigation is linked in with Interpol. The event which sparked it off finally was the case of Jeremiah Cranberry. Two weeks ago he sailed a small yacht into Townsville harbour. He was arrested on arrival because the yacht had been stolen two days earlier from Casuarina Beach."

The mention of Casuarina Beach made the friends sit up and look at each other. Inspector Sharpe went on, "Now Mr Jeremiah Cranberry had an interesting tale to tell. He admitted stealing the yacht, but it was the reason he gave for doing it that was fascinating. He said that he was a wealthy man, which used to be true, and that a year ago his life was a mess. He had developed a drug habit and fallen in with the wrong crowd. His wife left him, and he was contemplating suicide when he was befriended by a man calling himself the 'Reverend' Norris Pomfrey. Reverend Pomfrey 'saved' Jeremiah and took him to live at a 'Happy House' in Sydney."

"After a few weeks Jeremiah was persuaded by a missionary, the Reverend Carter Billings, an American, to come to their commune. Jeremiah agreed to this because, from their descriptions, life on the commune sounded wonderful. He was driven to Bankstown Airport and put in a twin engine light plane along with half a dozen other people.

"The plane took off and flew for hours, most of it over the ocean. It landed after dark on what Jeremiah was told was the island of Santa

Monica, which is way out in the South Pacific near Vanuatu. The airstrip was in some sort of jungle clearing although Jeremiah couldn't be sure as it was dark. He was positive there were no buildings anywhere near it.

"The group were met by a number of men and split up. Jeremiah went with a Hispanic American named Pedro. He was placed in the back of a closed van and driven along a very rough road up a mountain. At the top he was grabbed by two men in khaki uniforms and tossed into a concrete cell."

On hearing that it seemed to Barbara that her worst fears were being confirmed. *Poor Fiona!* she thought unhappily.

Inspector Sharpe went on, "For the next three weeks he was kept a prisoner. He saw no-one except the two guards who brought him meals. He says there were other prisoners in adjacent cells but he never saw them and was unable to communicate with them. The guards never spoke to him except to give orders. He thinks one is a German and the other a South African. From his account the place is cold and wet with lots of fog and rain.

"One day Jeremiah was visited by two Americans. The senior was a fat, middle-aged man with glasses named Cushing. The other is thin, with a black moustache and is called Caleb Buckman. They asked him to sign certain legal documents transferring his money to the Happy People. He refused and was tortured."

Barbara winced at this. *Poor Fiona! Is she being tortured?* she wondered. Then her stomach turned over with revulsion and fear as 'or worse' crossed her mind. She remembered seeing movies on TV where girls were kidnapped and sold as slaves into the sex trade. *Oh I hope not!* she thought.

Inspector Sharpe consulted a notebook and went on, "After a week of being tortured Jeremiah gave in and signed the papers, on the promise he would then be freed and taken to the commune. He was dragged out of the cell and tossed into the back of a Land Rover. That was his first glimpse of the place in daylight, and he said it was a concrete building in the jungle on a mountain top. He could see the sea and other mountains in the distance.

"The Land Rover was driven by our friend Pedro. The South African came as guard. They drove down the mountain through thick jungle. At the bottom the vehicle got bogged in a muddy creek crossing. While the guard was attaching a tow rope to a tree and the driver sitting in the driver's seat Jeremiah took his chance and broke free.

"Jeremiah ran into the jungle. It was his belief that the men were going to murder him, and certainly they chased him and shot at him. But he managed to escape and hid in thick jungle. He says he then wandered in the jungle for days. He is not sure how long as he was weak and sick. His appearance when we spoke to him bears that out. He was covered in bites and scratches and his clothes were in tatters.

"At last Jeremiah got a glimpse of the sea so he made his way down a steep mountainside to the beach. Believing that the only people on the island were the Smiley People he hid until dark, then swam out and stole the yacht. He at least knew how to sail that. He went straight out to sea, almost due east, to be out of sight of land by daylight.

"At dawn he found himself surrounded by coral reefs. He threaded through them using the engine, heading south to get around the end of the island. You see he thought he was a thousand nautical miles to the Northeast of Australia, and he wanted to get clear of the island. He sailed Southeast for two days skirting the inside of a massive chain of reefs, just keeping the land in sight. By then he was out of food and water, and he had become suspicious that things weren't right. The only island that big that he knew of is French New Caledonia. So he headed inshore to investigate and to collect water.

"Imagine his surprise on closing the land to recognise Magnetic Island and Castle Hill at Townsville. So he sailed in and called the police."

"Poor bugger!" Lofty chuckled. "He would have had to sail a long way to get around the southern end of this island!"

Gordon laughed. "The icebergs and penguins would have given him a hint that all was not well."

They all chuckled at this image. Inspector Sharpe continued, "That was when I got involved. I interviewed friend Jeremiah in Townsville Hospital and, I must confess, I found the tale a bit far-fetched. There were, are, two problems with his story. The first is that he had a long history of mental illness and had been undergoing psychiatric treatment for years. He was said to live in a fantasy world and often made-up stories."

Roger rolled his eyes and they all laughed.

"Yes," Inspector Sharpe agreed. "But the other problem is that he is now dead. Within 48 hours of me speaking to him he was found dead in his hospital room. There was no obvious cause of death, and the post-mortem could not determine one."

There was a moment of shocked silence while they absorbed that.

"Voodoo!" Roger gasped.

Barbara felt all the hairs on her scalp stand up and she shivered. Inspector Sharpe made a wry face, "That was one theory, given the little we know about this religion. But there is no medical evidence to support it," he said.

They discussed this for several minutes before the Inspector ended the speculation and went on, "For some time the government had been concerned about these Smiley People and Superintendent Blunt was put on the case, with myself as his assistant. He was already working on a case which involved the mysterious disappearance of Henry Mosman. Do you remember him?"

"Of course we do!" Jennifer cried. "He is just about the most famous sportsman in the country."

"That's right," Dan agreed. "He won five gold medals at the Olympics, was 'Ironman' of the year, won the Marathon at Perth."

Inspector Sharpe nodded, "That's him. Well, the link is that, just before he vanished, Henry Mosman had been frequently in the company of the Reverend Pomfrey. When Henry went missing his father began to make waves. In case you don't know it Henry's father is the notorious 'Moneybags' Mosman who owns half of Sydney's North Shore. He is one of the wealthiest men in the country and has a fair amount of pull in official circles, hence the 'Super' being put on this job."

Gordon frowned. "What happened to Henry sir?" he asked.

"We don't know. Last year, after he was beaten in the Commonwealth Games, he underwent some sort of personality change, severe bouts of depression and too much alcohol. It seems he was then befriended by the Smileys and 'saved'. Then he vanished. We are hoping he is still alive," Inspector Sharpe answered.

"A prisoner on the mountain," Roger suggested.

"Why would the Smileys keep him a prisoner?" Karen asked.

Inspector Sharpe explained, "Well, if these people operate the same way with him that they did with poor old Jerry then at some time legal moves will take place to transfer some of his money. So far nothing has happened, so we are hoping he is still alive."

"Do you know where he might be sir?" Lofty asked.

"We are not sure. We are trying to find out. But we do think it is somewhere in the Kuranda area here because the yacht poor Jeremiah stole was reported as having been taken from Casuarina Beach. Do you know where that is?"

Barbara answered. "Yes sir. We were there last Friday." As she said this, she saw Capt Conkey raise an eyebrow and she felt a spurt of guilt. "We went to the beach sir," she said defensively.

Capt Conkey nodded. "I did note that you were not at school."

Roger now spoke. He said, "This Henry Mosman bloke might be at their commune."

"No," Barbara replied, shaking her head. Before she realised what she was doing she added, "The only concrete buildings there are two small store sheds."

Capt Conkey looked at her then laughed. "Oh is that so? How do you know that?"

Barbara mentally kicked herself. She blushed and met her friend's eyes. Then she faced him. "We had a look on Friday sir."

"Aha! So that is why you promised not to go there without any argument. You had already been there! I thought you said you went to Casuarina Beach?" Capt Conkey snorted.

Barbara blushed and bit her lip then nodded. "We did sir. But we climbed up over the mountains to do a recce of the commune."

"Taking a risk, weren't you?" Capt Conkey queried.

Barbara looked him in the eye and said, "Maybe, but it was for Fiona. Besides, Cadets gave us the skills to do it, and we did it properly. We even mapped the place."

Inspector Sharpe pursed his lips and narrowed his eyes. "Tell me about it," he ordered.

Barbara described the reconnaissance trip on Friday. She detailed the layout of the commune and described the people she had seen.

Inspector Sharpe nodded, "Yes, that fits with what we know. We have looked at the place too, both uniformed people and a team posing as council road workers. Nothing suspicious has been found, just smiling people gardening and singing hymns."

"Then this Mosman fellow must be at their other property over towards Speewah," Barbara said.

Inspector Sharpe raised an eyebrow. "You have been busy! Is that where you were going next?"

Barbara nodded. "We were on our way there today when we saw the Smileys and followed them instead. We won't go there now."

"Don't. We have people watching the place. It seems to be their local HQ. A chap named Pastor Smith lives there. If you had tried to sneak in they would have caught you. It is surrounded by a high barbed wire fence and set in wide lawns. There are at least two armed security guards, those chaps in the khaki uniforms with the orange Smiley badges, plus savage dogs and an assortment of electronic surveillance devices. We are bringing in a team of experts from the SAS to penetrate the place."

Barbara bit her lip again as the realisation of just how much danger she might have led her friends into hit her.

Gordon spoke next, "There seem to be a lot of these people sir. Are they a big organisation?"

Inspector Sharpe nodded. "Yes, worldwide. They certainly have people in America and in Canada as well as the West Indies and South America, in Guyana and Paraguay in particular. They have communes in both of those countries. They also have branches in the UK and Europe."

"Do you know how they are organised?" Capt Conkey asked.

"Not really," Inspector Sharpe replied. "We have lots of disconnected fragments, but they don't form much of a picture yet. We don't even know who their leader, the Grand Oojoombie, is. Nobody has been able to give us a name, a physical description or anything. We don't even know if the Grand Oojoombie is a man or a woman. For a time we thought it might be a woman. But we don't know. We have nothing, not even a nationality."

"But someone must have seen him!" Karen cried. "How could you build a whole religion on somebody no-one has ever seen?"

"Have you ever seen Jesus?" Roger asked with a dry grin.

"No, but... that's silly Roger. The Apostles saw him," Karen replied. "That was a long time ago."

"That is enough theology," Inspector Sharpe interrupted. "I can tell you a bit more. And it is because of you people that we found it out. It was told to me by the man you rescued this afternoon."

Barbara felt a twinge of guilt, mollified by the tacit admission that the police would have been too late. She had quite forgotten the man. So it seemed had the others, for Jennifer asked, "Oh yes! How is he?"

198

"He is in hospital with mild concussion. He came round while I was there, and he provided some interesting information. He is a Frenchman named Alain le Plaisterer and he is the Second Cook for the Third Oojoombie."

"The third!" Lofty cried. "How many are there?"

"We aren't sure. We think possibly four or five. They appear to rank one below the Grand Oojoombie. The Third Oojoombie is a woman named Patna Kandami. She is an Indian. India type, not Red Indian. She seems to be the head of the branch that runs the communes. Here, I'll explain."

The Inspector turned to a blank page in his notebook. He drew a diagram of five circles. "The top circle is the Grand O. Then there appears to be a First Oojoombie who is some sort of Grand Vizier type who controls the G.O.'s personal staff. There is a Second Oojoombie who apparently has charge of the finances. Money in, money out, legal aspects, that sort of thing. He is possibly an American living in Florida named Hiram Goldstick."

"Goldstick?" Capt Conkey asked. "Is he a Jew?"

"Possibly."

"They are certainly ecumenical these Smiley People," Roger observed.

"International anyway," Inspector Sharpe agreed. "Now, the Third Oojoombie is this woman Kandami. She has just flown in from America with a staff of fifteen."

"Fifteen!" Wendy gasped.

"Yes. And all legal: cooks, drivers, a butler, a valet, secretaries and so on," Inspector Sharpe said. "We have a full list from Immigration. They arrived on Friday on a business trip in their own executive jet. It is sitting down at Cairns Airport now with their own pilot twiddling his thumbs while he waits."

Barbara shuddered. *Poor Fiona! And silly me! Blundering into this spider's web of an organisation and risking my friend's lives.*

To her the Smiley People now sounded like a monstrous hidden octopus with tentacles everywhere. The whole business loomed even more like a dark nightmare. The thought made her glance uneasily into the surrounding darkness. Then another awful thought crossed her mind: If the Smileys had their own jet, if they could fly in from America, or fly

Jeremiah what's-his-name from Sydney, they could have flown Fiona and her father out of the country!

For the first time she began to doubt they would find Fiona. She shivered violently. Gordon sensed her mood and took hold of her hand and squeezed it. She was grateful for that and gave an answering squeeze.

Lofty asked, "You said a fourth and possibly a fifth Oojoombie sir?"

Inspector Sharpe nodded. "Yes, I did. They definitely have a branch which looks after recruiting new members, and they also have their own security department. That is obviously where your two friends in the khaki uniforms come from."

"Have they said anything sir?" Jennifer asked.

"Not a word. They deny everything and have just demanded to get lawyers. They are both locked up at the moment, but I have to say I am not too hopeful of getting much out of them. I think they are too scared to talk."

"What about the cook, sir? Did he tell you more?" Lofty asked.

"A little. He only recovered consciousness for a while then the doctors whisked him away. He is under guard in Cairns Base Hospital. What he did say was that he flew in with the Third Oojoombie the other day. He did not know the two security guards, had never seen them before. He explained that the domestic staff are kept isolated, but, given the usual degree of servant's gossip I am hopeful he will be able to tell us much more when he recovers."

"Why were they going to kill him?" Barbara asked.

"He says he inadvertently broke a religious taboo. He included some pork in a mixed dish."

"Pork!" Karen gasped. "You mean they were going to murder him because he put the wrong thing in the food! That's ridiculous. I don't believe it."

Inspector Sharpe shrugged. "Maybe you don't but the poor old cook does. He is a thoroughly frightened man. He is sure they will try to kill him once they find out he is still alive."

Barbara shivered again. What horrible people! If they could murder someone for such a trivial thing, what chance did Fiona have? And why had they taken her? Her father was well off by local standards, but he wasn't really wealthy. So why? Had Fiona or her father learned something about the Smiley People they shouldn't have, and been murdered to silence them? Were their bodies rotting somewhere in the Barron Gorge? She felt tears prickle and sobbed.

She managed to hold back from crying but was too choked up to speak for a while. Gordon looked at her with a worried frown and squeezed her hand again. "Okay?" he asked.

Barbara bit her lip and nodded but a tear did escape. It trickled down her cheek.

Roger gave her a sympathetic look. He asked, "What about this druid mob sir?"

Inspector Sharpe put his head back and laughed. "Oh, the druids! We aren't worried about them. They are a harmless bunch of middle-class trendies. They just sing and dance, and I must say their religious services look a lot more fun than most."

"My word yes!" Roger agreed. They all laughed at that, even Barbara, but she blushed at the memory.

Lofty then asked the question that had been at the front of all their minds. "So what about us sir? What do you want us to do? Do we have to go home?"

The two adults looked at each other. Inspector Sharpe spoke first. "No. You can go on with your hike as long as we know where you are, and as long as you don't go looking for more trouble."

"We won't," Lofty assured him.

Barbara wasn't sure whether she wanted to go on with the hike or whether she wouldn't rather go home. It had all been physically and emotionally exhausting. She looked up at Gordon and he smiled. That made her feel guilty.

I must be fair to the others, she decided. She unfolded her map.

Roger explained his plan, "We thought we might walk along the railway to Mareeba sir. It should only take us two days. We could be at Koah tomorrow night and Mareeba the day after."

The two adults studied the map. Inspector Sharpe turned to Capt Conkey. "Well Captain, what do you think?"

"Seems okay. I've walked it myself several times. So have most of these people, except they walked it from the other direction and mostly at night, from Mareeba to Oak Forest."

Barbara winced at the memory. It had been during a week-long 'Senior Exercise' two years before. It had included testing for the

Adventure Training Award and had been one of the most interesting cadet activities she had ever been on.

"We have too," she said. "It was a real challenge, and the exercise had a great story line."

Roger nodded and agreed and both Lofty and Wendy exchanged what looked to Barbara like guilty glances. At the time Lofty had been Wendy's section commander and Barbara had suspected, along with most of the company, that they were boyfriend and girlfriend and had possibly done things that were against the Code of Conduct.

Capt Conkey smiled and said, "It was a great exercise. So the others will enjoy the walk. There isn't much at Koah Inspector, but they will find a phone." He turned to Barbara. "What will you do when you reach Mareeba?"

"Phone our parents to come and get us," Barbara replied.

"Alright then. Do that. And be sure to phone me both nights," Capt Conkey said.

"And stay together as a group tonight," Inspector Sharpe added. "Don't wander around on your own, even to go to the toilet. Do not leave the caravan park. I don't want you wandering that road through the jungle in the dark."

Barbara felt a real stab of fear. Did he think they might be in danger?

Obviously, or he would not have given such a clear warning, she decided, and shivered again.

Chapter 21

A FRESH START

After Capt Conkey and Inspector Sharpe had gone, Barbara made herself another cup of coffee. Gordon and Lofty went off to have a shower. Roger produced a chocolate and offered them all squares. He and Dan sat and talked quietly over all that they had learned. Barbara did not feel like joining in. She certainly thought about it but felt she had discussed it enough for the time being.

Roger asked, "Anyone want some Milo? Wendy?"

Wendy said yes but Barbara sensed she was just being polite and did it so as not to hurt Roger's feelings. She looked very tired and down at the mouth.

"You should go to bed Wendy," Barbara said.

"I know," Wendy replied. "I just...I just don't want to walk down to the tent on my own."

Barbara nodded. She felt a bit scared too. Loud laughter came from the male showers. Barbara made a face. Judging by that the boys weren't.

Stupid great louts! she thought in annoyance. *It isn't fair!*

For the millionth time she resented the impositions life placed on females. She resented their male confidence, their male ignorance, their bloody male arrogance! But she also conceded that deep down she was glad the boys were there.

Roger handed Wendy a hot Milo and sat opposite her. Lofty and Gordon appeared from the showers, both glowing with good health, flicking each other with towels and playing the fool.

"Bed for me," Lofty said as he passed.

Dan got up and followed. So did Jennifer and Karen. Wendy looked bleakly after them and seemed to be on the edge of tears. Roger pretended not to notice but Barbara could see he was only putting on a brave face. Poor Roger! Poor Wendy!

Gordon came into the shelter and made himself a hot chocolate. "Nearly bedtime," he observed as he sat down.

"What time is it?" Wendy asked.

203

"Nine thirty," Gordon replied.

"Yes, bed for me," Wendy said, draining the cup. She thanked Roger, stood up and rinsed the cup. "Come along Roger, walk me down to the tent please," she asked. As she did, she flicked her eyes towards Gordon and Barbara.

"But... Oh! Oh yes! okay," Roger said.

He stood up and went with her. Barbara was both annoyed and amused by Wendy's unsubtle tactics, clearly designed to get her and Gordon together alone.

Then Gordon stood up as well and Barbara wondered what to do. She wanted to go to bed. She was very tired, but she also wanted to give Gordon a chance. He looked down at her quizzically and said, "You can go to bed if you like, Barbara."

She shook her head. "No. I wouldn't sleep. I'd worry too much. Besides, you want to talk to me."

He sat down opposite her. "Is it that obvious?"

She smiled. "It is to everyone else."

"You aren't in love with me are you," he stated rather flatly.

"No, I'm not. I like you Gordon, but at the moment I am too emotionally mixed up to know what I want," Barbara replied.

Gordon looked wretched for a moment, then recovered. "I wish you hadn't kissed me. I am in love with you."

Barbara felt a peculiar sensation of simultaneous pain and pleasure. "Thank you," she whispered. She looked into his eyes. "I don't want to hurt you. You are too nice," she added.

Gordon shrugged, "Just tell me if I am wasting my time and I will stop bothering you. I will get over it," he said, his voice a hoarse croak.

The look on his face made Barbara's heart tighten up. She reached across and took his hand. "I'm sorry. I've hurt you already. You must think I am an awful person."

"You are certainly full of surprises," Gordon agreed. "But I expected that. I knew you weren't just a milk-and-water nonentity. I knew there was fire and passion in there. I've seen it."

Barbara gave a wry grin. "I seem to live in a state of constant turmoil. I'm always in some sort of trouble. I get so mixed up at times that I don't know whether I'm Arthur or Martha!"

"Or whether you like men or not," Gordon added.

It took a moment for what he had said to register. Then it swept over her like a wave of ice water which left her trembling slightly. For a second or two she was speechless, unable to decide if she was outraged or relieved. Then she looked up and met his gaze, her eyes searching his.

Gordon's face was calm and concerned. There was just a faint flutter in the eye lids and a tremor in his lips to indicate that, for him at least, it was a moment of decision.

Barbara searched his face while the passion mounted within her. Admiration surfaced first. *He has had the guts to confront me with it,* she thought. *And he knows it is all or nothing, that our relationship could end this minute.*

She withdrew her hand and stood up, trembling slightly as strong emotions warred within her. He continued to look her full in the face. With an effort she kept control of her voice. She said, "Some men I don't like. Others I hate. But I like you. Whether I prefer women more than men I am not sure. It is a battle I have to fight."

Gordon stood up as well. "It is not a battle you have to fight alone. You can't. You will only find out from experience, and it is a battle you must fight. And I need to know too."

"And what if I prefer women?" Barbara managed to croak, her eyes misting over.

"Love has a physical dimension so I suppose that, inevitably, my love will wither," Gordon said. It was obvious he was forcing himself to speak the truth.

Barbara slowly nodded her head. "Just give me a little time. Don't force things. Let it develop naturally. I am certainly not ready for a full relationship at this time."

"If you mean sex, I am not asking you for that. If we are both in love that will just happen naturally. I certainly won't press you," Gordon replied. Then he grinned. "Not that I don't dream about it and hope."

Barbara smiled at his boyish confusion. "You wouldn't be normal if you didn't."

"Barbara, I think you are wonderful. You are the most beautiful and remarkable girl I have ever met," Gordon replied. He reached forward and she gave him her hand. Adoration shone from his eyes.

"Oh Gordon, don't worship me. I'm far from perfect. I'm a flesh and blood woman, not a marble idol." she said. Then, sensing it was the moment for candour, she went on, "I know a lot about boys, and men. But I'm still a virgin, which is a bit of a miracle really. When I was in Year 9, I was well on the way to becoming a real little trollop. Some horrible things have been done to me by men over the last two years. That is why I have such a strong reaction at times."

It hurt, she could see. He struggled manfully to hide it and to accept what she said. He said, "Well I am no saint either so let's leave the past. It is the future I am interested in." He stopped and looked earnestly into her eyes.

Barbara could see the strong emotions at work. She moved to keep things from going too far too quickly. "Let's stop before we say something we might regret. There will be time later. Walk me down to the tent please."

Gordon nodded and smiled. His eyes glistened. Without conscious thought Barbara stepped forward and put her arms around his neck and pressed herself against his chest. She put her head on his shoulder so he could not kiss her. He hugged her, sighed and kissed her gently on the top of her head.

Without another word they walked arm in arm down to join the others. As they got close, they separated and went to their beds. The others were lying down talking quietly and Barbara was very conscious they must all have seen. Feeling very aware of Wendy's curiosity and delight Barbara crawled into her sleeping bag. Once she was comfortable, she lay back, intending to listen to the others, and to think things over, but instead she dropped instantly into a deep sleep.

When Barbara opened her eyes, it was daylight. The sun's first rays were just lighting the treetops. The sky was clear blue, the air cool. Birds twittered. She stretched and fell fit and well. Beside her Wendy sat brushing her hair. She smiled but Barbara could see she wasn't happy. Her eyes gave her away.

Barbara sat up and looked around. *It must be Lofty. It has to be,* she thought.

It was. Lofty lay on his back. Karen lay on his side of the tree and half on him. Her head was snuggled onto his chest and her left arm was over him. Both were sound asleep, Lofty with a smile on his lips.

The little minx! Barbara thought. *Oh, poor Wendy.*

At that moment, Jennifer woke up and she was even less amused.

To Barbara it seemed that it was Jennifer's pride that was hurt, rather than her heart. She let this be known by pushing Karen roughly to wake her. Lofty also awoke and, by the blush which mottled his face, Barbara guessed that her supposition was correct.

Then Barbara saw Gordon smiling at her. She forgot the others and smiled back. That set the tone for her morning. Gordon went to have a shower and shave then sat beside her while they cooked breakfast. Barbara observed closely his every movement. If it hadn't been for her worry over Fiona's possible fate, she knew she would have been deliriously happy.

Which was more than could be said for most of the others. Roger had a long face because Wendy was mooning over Lofty. Wendy had the dejections because Lofty was ignoring her and flirting with Karen. Jennifer and Karen were both quietly picking on each other over Lofty. Lofty didn't look happy.

Who does he have on his mind? Barbara wondered. Only Dan seemed unaffected by all of it. *Another day of this and we won't be a group at all,* Barbara decided. *We will split into jealous factions.*

After breakfast they cleaned up and packed. The hutchies were taken down and unclipped. Barbara changed into a green cotton shirt and jeans, plus her army boots. The others wore an assortment of clothing. Jennifer wore her loose cotton shirt, still without a bra. Then Barbara noted that Wendy also had no bra under her shirt! Barbara was surprised because Wendy was usually very self-conscious about her 'wobbles'. In fact her shirt buttons strained to stay done up, allowing tantalizing glimpses.

Is she doing that deliberately to compete? Barbara wondered.

Just before 8 o'clock a white car pulled up on the driveway near them. Inspector Sharpe got out and walked across the lawn. He looked very smart in suit and tie and appeared relaxed and fresh.

"Morning all. Sleep okay?" he asked cheerfully. "I am just checking that you are all safe and that there are no problems."

"We have one major problem sir," Roger said seriously. Barbara looked at him in surprise.

"Yes?"

"Lofty snores. And his socks need washing," Roger replied, just managing to keep his face deadpan.

Lofty snorted and threw his sleeping bag at him and they all laughed.

207

Barbara smiled and relaxed. "We will be on our way as soon as the clowns can get the circus on the road," she said to the Inspector.

"Good! Are you following the road or the railway?"

"Railway sir, it is flatter, and there will be less traffic," Barbara replied.

Inspector Sharpe nodded. "Fine. Don't forget to phone Capt Conkey tonight. He will keep me informed. I am off to Cairns now to speak to your mate the French cook."

"Dunno about a French cook," Lofty said. "I think I'd rather have a French maid."

"Hmm. You are a bit young for that sort of thing I should think," Inspector Sharpe replied, giving him a doubtful glance. The girls all sniffed. Jennifer said cuttingly, "I doubt if you could afford that sort of luxury."

Lofty reddened. Inspector Sharpe looked at them all and took his leave. As he drove off Gordon stepped forward. "Stop sniping at each other. Now, give me the money and I will go and pay the bill."

"I'll come with you," Roger offered. "I need some more lollies."

In the end the whole group lugged their gear up to the office. More food was purchased and packed. Roger took the opportunity to purchase a soft drink, which he drank then and there, and two Mars Bars and a Cherry Ripe.

"Emergency supplies," he explained.

They hoisted on packs and webbing and walked through the grounds and down to the railway. By the time they reached it they had begun to perspire.

Roger looked up. "Not a cloud in the sky!" he grumbled. "So much for winter."

They turned left and started walking. It was easiest to walk in single file along the narrow sandy track between the ballast and the long grass. Dan led the way, followed by Roger. Gordon and Barbara came next then Wendy, Lofty, Jennifer and a sulky faced Karen last.

For the first half hour or so the walking hurt. Stiff muscles had to warm up and loosen. Chafing from belts and pack straps had to be dealt with. Slowly they settled into the rhythm of marching. There was very little talking.

The first two kilometres of the railway led through rain forest and deep cuttings, with an occasional glimpse of the Barron River through the trees to their right. A mildewed signpost indicated the site of 'Fairyland', an abandoned railway halt in a small clearing surrounded by jungle and many ferns. After that the railway curved around to the left until they were heading generally west.

At 9:15 they came out into open country: rolling green pastures dotted with horses and dairy cattle up on their left, and a line of jungle hiding the river on their right. They passed below the Kuranda State High School on its open ridge. The dark, jungle-covered mass of Rainy Mountain appeared on their right-front. Barbara studied her map as they trudged along and noted the mountain's name. She also noted the Black Mountain Road.

It is only two kilometres away across the river, she calculated. *And there is a side road to it which crosses the river at Myola, just ahead of us.*

But she sighed. It was no good. She had tried to find Fiona and had failed. Now she tried to re-assure herself that she had done her best, but the defeat and loss still hurt.

There was a brief commotion at the front. Dan had nearly trodden on a snake which had been sunning itself just beside the track. "Big brown bastard!" he called.

"Taipan?" Lofty asked.

Dan shrugged and continued walking. "Dunno. I didn't try to count his belly scales," he replied. Barbara knew that the only accurate way to identify most snakes was by counting their scales. But poisonous snakes were so much a part of the normal hazards of hiking in North Queensland that the cadets simply kept on marching and kept a wary eye out for them. Fear of the repulsive reptiles provided Barbara with a welcome distraction from her brooding thoughts.

They came to a bridge and had to walk on the two planks bolted between the rails. Barbara found it a bit scary as it was a fair drop underneath and there were no railings. After that came half a kilometre of straight track and an even higher, longer bridge.

Beyond it was the siding of Myola. At this place there was a second track for trains to pass, a small wooden shelter shed which needed paint, and a loading platform on the left which was piled with logs. The place had a disused and overgrown look about it. As she went to cross the bridge Barbara noted that a man was sitting in the shade of a mango tree back from the platform edge. She had to concentrate on where she put her feet till she was across, and when she looked up she was surprised to see that it was Superintendent Blunt. He wasn't wearing his suit jacket, his tie was loose and his paunch bulged over his belt. His clothes looked as though he had slept in them. He raised a small, brimmed hat as they approached.

The thought that he was checking up on them made Barbara angry. As they reached him and opened his mouth to speak, she snapped, "You don't have to keep watching us all the time. We have given our word. We can be trusted you know!"

Superintendent Blunt appeared quite unruffled by her attack. He raised a placating hand, and said, "I'm sure you can be. Captain Conkey speaks very highly of you, even though you did not keep him fully informed. However, that is not why I am here. Yes, I am watching you, but only because I am worried about your safety. Drop your packs in the shade for a minute."

They did as they were told. Barbara felt a stab of shame at the rebuke she had just been tactfully given. While they did this Superintendent Blunt spoke on a hand-held radio for a minute, and Barbara noted a police 4WD parked behind the logs in the overgrown station yard. A policeman sat in it. Superintendent Blunt put the radio down on the concrete platform and hauled his baggy trousers up over his beer gut. Barbara eyed him with distaste.

He said, "The reason I am worried about you is that there have been two developments which are both bad news. The first is that, at 8:30 this morning, we fished a body out of the Barron River just downstream from Jumrum Creek."

Barbara gasped. "The two Smileys we saw!"

Superintendent Blunt nodded. "Quite probably. Whoever it was, they put a bullet into the back of the man's skull. Well, you gave us a good description and we are on the lookout for them. But you realise that makes you people possible witnesses and that is why I am keeping an eye on you."

"Surely these people wouldn't know about us or where we are?" Lofty said.

"I wouldn't bet on it," Inspector Blunt grunted. "You were pretty conspicuous in town yesterday. We don't know who is in this Smiley organisation, or how big it is, or where its tentacles reach. But we are certain they are very dangerous."

Barbara felt as though a cold hand had suddenly gripped her stomach. "Sir, do you think the dead man might have been one of the six we saw? They split into two groups of three and the ones we followed were going to kill the cook."

"It is a strong possibility," Superintendent Blunt agreed.

"The dead man," Lofty asked. "Do you know who he is?"

"No. Early twenties. Blue T-shirt, jeans, joggers, and a .22 bullet in the back of the head. No identification on him."

"You said two bits of bad news," Roger prompted.

"Yes. Only twenty minutes ago Inspector Sharpe phoned me. He had just reached the Cairns Base Hospital. The man you saved, the cook, he is dead."

Barbara felt the cold hand move up to grip her heart.

Wendy gasped and cried, "That is awful. How did he die?"

Inspector Blunt shook his head. "We don't know. The injuries he got in the fight don't account for it. And he had an armed constable next to his bed all the time. We are investigating."

No-one said it, but from the way their eyes met, and the goose bumps came out, Barbara was sure they all thought it: Voodoo!

Don't be ridiculous, Barbara told herself. *That is just primitive superstition.* But she couldn't shake a nagging doubt.

Gordon asked, "What about the two thugs you captured?"

"They haven't said anything. They are both obviously terrified, and not of us. We are moving them right now to a safer location," Superintendent Blunt said.

"Should we go home?" Wendy asked. She looked quite scared.

"I thought of that but I'm not sure it would make you any safer. In fact it would make it harder for us to protect you. Here you are in a group and your movements aren't as predictable. You can keep an eye on each other. But if there is any more trouble I shall have you moved to safety," Superintendent Blunt explained.

"What happens now sir?" Lofty asked.

"You go on with your hike but keep your eyes and ears open and be on your guard. We are organizing a big raid on this estate near Speewah in a couple of hours' time, and also on their commune. Now, I've got a lot to do, so take care."

Superintendent Blunt hitched up his baggy trousers and walked over to his radio. He picked it up and, after a farewell wave to the cadets, walked up to the waiting vehicle. As he did, Barbara noted that he wore a pistol in a holster on the back of his belt. The sight of it really brought it home to her just how deadly dangerous the situation was.

The friends broke into excited discussion as the vehicle drove off.

"This is awful!" Wendy cried. "It gets worse and worse. I'm scared."

"So am I," Roger agreed taking her hand.

Lofty pursed his lips. "These Smileys are certainly a ruthless pack of mongrels," he observed.

Dan nodded. "Nothing to smile about, that's for sure," he agreed.

"This is not time for jokes!" Jennifer snapped, betraying how frightened she was as well.

Barbara had a big drink then chewed her bottom lip. Poor Fiona! What chance did she have against such terrible people?

Chapter 22

THE RAILWAY

It was a very subdued group that continued walking ten minutes later. The going was easy but hot. At times they had to walk on the sleepers as the weeds encroached on the path. Barbara found that awkward and irritating as the sleepers were not evenly spaced and their upper surfaces varied. Some were flat and some had curved upper sides. She also began to view the wall of long grass and jungle on her right with a new and worried eye.

To her the green tangle wasn't just a pretty backdrop anymore. The word 'Ambush' drifted around her consciousness, and she tried to use her minimal tactical knowledge to try to pick where one might happen. That was a depressing experience as she could not think of any effective counter-action other than the survivors making a run for it.

For long stretches she could not see a single house and she felt very isolated, although her map told her there were houses along the road not a hundred metres up the slope on their left.

They may as well be on the moon, she thought. *We are quite invisible to them down in these cuttings.*

At 10:30 they came out of a cutting and crossed another high bridge. From it they could see open, rolling pastures away up a valley to the left. They also got glimpses of the bitumen road which ran roughly parallel to the railway. Half a kilometre further along another deep cutting blocked them in, followed by another bridge, and then they had a steep grassy hill on the left, topped by houses. Thick jungle still lined their right-hand side. The map informed Barbara that this was growing along the banks of the Barron River.

In front of one of the houses at the top of the slope Barbara saw a police car parked beside the road and felt real relief. The Inspector's men were keeping an eye on them! This time she did not resent it. The railway curved left and gave them good views down a steep embankment to beautiful stretches of the river. It was flowing slowly between banks covered with jungle and lined with sandy beaches. There were many rocks and small islands and the water was crystal clear. It looked very inviting.

The group passed behind more houses inhabited by Aborigines. Groups of small black kids ran down to their back fences to stare at them curiously as they passed. The effort of walking and the passage of time both helped them to relax their fears a bit. Barbara noted that Roger was now behind her, with Wendy behind him. Lofty had moved up to second place behind Dan.

The bulk of Rainy Mountain was now on their right. They came around the side of a steep hillside and crossed the highest bridge yet.

'Mantaka' read a place name. The line curved left with another steep hill on their left. The vegetation changed to part jungle, part dry bush. There was no breeze as they passed behind the shoulder of the hill. The sun blazed down and sparkled on the river. The clear pools and rippling murmur of rapids sounded very appealing. *A swim would be nice,* she thought.

They trudged on, crossed another high bridge with the road close beside it. Barbara looked for the police car but saw no sign of it. She shrugged. *They can't waste all day just keeping an eye on us,* she told herself.

But it caused her to worry again, and to tense up. She tried to imagine the police raids on the commune and the other property. They must now be under way. Would they find Fiona? Or her corpse?

The railway curved right. Roger pointed down. "Nearly trod on a bloody big Taipan here on a hike with Kirk a few years ago," he said.

"I hate these bridges," Wendy said as they approached another. "What do we do if a train comes while we are on it?"

"You run, jump, or stand on these little platforms sticking out," Roger said. "We had to do that on the big bridge at Blackwater Creek once."

Gordon laughed. "Judging by the number of trains we have seen today the risk is pretty low."

Lofty looked back over his shoulder as he stepped out onto the bridge. "These creeks are bloody deep. You wouldn't want to get dizzy and lose your balance. It's a bloody long drop. I... aargh!"

Barbara saw Lofty stumble and cried out. Instinctively she grabbed at his pack. Lofty fell heavily and she also started to fall. Gordon grabbed her arm. They all fell in a heap on the rails. By then Lofty was half over the edge and so was Barbara's head.

It WAS a long drop!

Barbara clung on and felt strong hands haul at her arm and webbing. She was dragged back into the centre of the bridge, still gripping Lofty's pack.

He screamed in pain, "Aaah! My leg! Stop pulling!"

Dan had turned and grabbed hold of Lofty as well. "Let go Barbara. I've got him. Don't pull. His leg is through the sleepers," he cried.

Barbara let go. She tried to struggle to her feet, but Gordon pushed her down. "Take off your pack first or you might overbalance," he ordered.

With trembling fingers she unclipped her pack and shrugged it off. Gordon lifted it to one side then helped her to her knees and then to her feet. They crowded round Lofty.

Gordon took command. "Dan, carry the packs across. Take Lofty's too, and his webbing," he ordered.

"I'm stuck," Lofty gasped, struggling to get up. His face looked very pale and he was in obvious pain. Beads of sweat broke out on his brow. "I can't move my leg!"

"Is it broken?" Karen asked.

"Don't know. I can't get it out. It hurts," Lofty replied. He shuddered and wiped his face.

"Now is just the time for a train to come along," Roger commented while helping Dan to collect more packs.

"Shut up Roger!" Lofty cried, glancing nervously along the line. "Just get me out and save your silly comments!"

Barbara knelt to help free Lofty's leg. It was jammed hard down between the two sleepers as far as his thigh. Gordon stood behind him and hauled on Lofty's webbing. Jennifer and Wendy held them to help them keep their balance.

After a few anxious minutes they eased the leg free. It wasn't broken, or at least not snapped across. It plainly hurt though, and it was a difficult and dangerous job supporting him from both sides while he hobbled to the end of the bridge.

Once off the bridge Lofty was lowered onto the grass in the shade of a lone mango tree that was growing beside the track. Karen at once knelt beside him and began gently feeling along his leg. Jennifer bent over beside her and tried to help. Barbara couldn't help noticing that, in all the struggling, several buttons on Jennifer's shirt had come undone, giving the boys a clear view. Even in his obvious pain Lofty couldn't help looking.

Barbara wondered how she could tactfully draw Jennifer's attention to it. She looked up at Wendy who stood beside her, and got a bigger shock. More than half of the buttons on Wendy's shirt had come undone or burst and she was all but fully exposed.

Barbara stood up and started moving to draw this to Wendy's attention when Roger noticed. He reached over, seized Wendy's shoulders, and spun her around, then looked away, his face a bright red.

He then said firmly, "You too Jennifer. Lofty's heart has had one bad shock already. We don't want him getting too excited."

Jennifer looked up, then appeared to be shocked and hastily covered herself. Dan chuckled and added, "Karen had better stop playing with Lofty's leg then."

Karen darted a glare at him and went on gently testing the kneecap. By this time Wendy had buttoned up what she could of her front, but one button was missing which left quite a gap. She was bright red with embarrassment, and this obviously fuelled her jealous anger.

"She had enough practice playing with Lofty's leg last night!" she snapped.

Roger laughed and said, "I don't think it was that leg she was playing with."

"Shut up, Roger! Don't be gross!" Wendy cried, turning on him.

Karen had stopped and was glaring up at her. "You watch your mouth, you cow!" she spat.

Barbara stepped forward. "That will do! Stop bickering!"

Karen stood up, shaking with rage. "She's saying things about me!"

"They're true," Jennifer retorted.

Karen turned and slapped her. There was a moment of shocked silence then Gordon stepped between them and seized Karen's wrists.

Lofty let out a sniff. "Don't mind me," he said. "I'm only the patient."

"You are the cause of this," Wendy snapped. "Flirting all the time!"

Gordon spoke sharply, "Stop fighting the lot of you. Sit down and cool down."

The angry girls eyed each other for a minute but did as he said.

Wendy suddenly burst into tears and turned to Barbara. She wrapped her arms around Wendy and hugged her. Gordon led Karen over to the shade of another tree. Jennifer sat down on her pack and sulked.

Barbara led Wendy a few paces aside and comforted her. "Things will be alright. Take out another shirt and get changed while we look after Lofty."

Wendy nodded and wiped her eyes. She bent to her pack and dug out another shirt and a bra. Then she walked off into the bushes. Barbara turned to Gordon, who had walked back to where Dan was tending Lofty.

"Thanks for that," she said.

He smiled, stepped closer, and before she realised what he was doing he took hold of the front of her shirt. She glanced down and saw that he was doing up a button to cover her own bulging cleavage.

"They weren't the only ones with button problems," Gordon murmured.

He then put his arms around her and hugged her. To her own surprise she didn't resist. Instead she responded by putting her arms around him. She pressed against him. It felt very comforting, and it was only after a minute that she realised that Gordon had been well and truly aroused by what he had seen.

For a moment the discovery made her freeze, and her emotions went into turmoil. Ugly memories battled with natural instincts. She uttered a low groan in his ear and closed her eyes. Then she relaxed and knew it was normal, so she hugged him tighter.

Lofty saved them from becoming a public spectacle. He called out in a loud and disgusted voice, "Oi! What about me?"

"Bugger you mate," Roger replied in a bantering tone. "We will leave you as the rear-guard to hold up the pursuit while we get clear. March or die!" But he knelt down and asked, "Now, where is this bloody leg broken?"

Dan joined him. Barbara stepped back from Gordon and knelt with them. They soon had his webbing off and stripped his trousers down, so he lay in his underpants, just decently covered by his shirt. It was apparent that his leg wasn't broken but it was certainly badly bruised and some of the muscles were clearly wrenched. Already the skin was going dark blue or black in some places, and a sort of sickly greeny-yellow in others.

"Not broken anyway," Roger said. "Do you think you can walk?"

"Dunno. I'll give it a try," Lofty replied. "Get me a good strong walking stick and I'll have a go."

Dan went off to chop a sapling down with his clasp knife. Wendy returned from changing her shirt. Karen came to stand and look.

Lofty self-consciously hauled his trousers up. "Help me up," he said.

Gordon and Roger hoisted him up and Dan gave him the walking stick. Lofty took a cautious step. It clearly hurt but he took several more, wincing as he did.

"It'll be okay," he reassured them.

"Do we go on with the hike or would you rather we got a lift back to Kuranda to have a doctor look at it?" Barbara asked.

"Go on with the hike," Lofty replied. "I'll be fine. Help me on with my pack."

"No. I'll carry it for a bit," Gordon said. He looked doubtful and also tried to persuade Lofty to go back to Kuranda. Lofty refused. "When I break down, not before. I want to go on." he insisted.

Barbara still had doubts, but he insisted and began to hobble slowly along the line. She shrugged and pulled on her gear. The others did likewise and slowly set off after Lofty. He led, followed by Dan and Wendy, then Barbara and Gordon, Karen, Roger and Jennifer, who still had a sour expression on her face.

Barbara sensed the open hostility of the other girls and shook her head sadly. What a disaster of a holiday! What an awful week!

Lofty slowly increased pace although he was limping badly and was plainly hurting. He refused to stop and insisted that exercise was the best thing for it. The unhappy group trudged slowly on. After a kilometre Roger took Lofty's pack off Gordon and Wendy took his webbing.

They passed Kowrowa Halt and slogged along a long, boring straight for two kilometres. 11:30 passed. Barbara found it very discouraging to walk along a seemingly endless straight railway. Ahead of her she could see a heat haze shimmering above the two shiny steel rails which snaked off to apparent infinity. From an interesting trip the hike became a real trudge. The only good thing was that Lofty's leg seemed to be improving. After a while he was limping rather than hobbling.

At last they reached the end of the straight and came to another high bridge. Lofty hesitated momentarily before carefully walking across.

After that there were more uneven sleepers and crunching of gravel for half a kilometre, then another bridge. While crossing this bridge Barbara held Lofty's arm to help him keep his balance. She noticed that he looked very pale and that he was sweating profusely.

On the other side, Gordon took Lofty's pack again and Barbara relieved Wendy of his webbing. The heat now seemed all-enveloping.

Like a summer day! Barbara thought.

They were moving out into dry, savannah country although a thick belt of trees still lined the river. There was no breeze. The cool shade and clear pools in the river looked even more inviting.

Another high bridge loomed ahead. When they reached the end of it, they halted. It was the highest yet, about 20 or 30 metres of drop into a gully choked with lantana and weeds.

"I think we should stop soon," Barbara said.

"Didn't we decide on 'Silky Oak' as the place to stop for lunch?" Lofty asked.

"Yes, we did, but that was before you hurt yourself," Barbara answered.

"What is this place?" Dan asked, indicating a road bridge which crossed the river down to their right.

On a steep, grassy bluff on the far bank stood a lovely old farmhouse which looked as though it dated right back to the early days of white settlement. Barbara went to open her map, but Roger answered before she had time.

"Oak Forest."

Lofty nodded and set his jaw. "Then we push on. It is only a few more kilometres."

Gamely he stepped up onto the bridge and led the way across. As he was reaching the middle Dan made a loud train whistle noise. Lofty laughed and waved his arm. That eased the tension and they all followed. On the other side he asked for his webbing and pack, but Gordon said no and passed the pack to Dan instead. Karen took the webbing from Barbara. They resumed the march in silence.

After a hundred metres, they crossed a gravel road and came to a siding with a house up to the left. Then for a time they walked through open bush with no sign of settlement or farms. The railway ran along the side of a steep drop, giving them glorious views along the rock-studded bed of the river. Several bends, two small bridges and few kilometres on they came to another high bridge.

A couple of hundred metres beyond it another gravel road went down to a bridge across the river. Further along the line was another railway siding.

"Silky Oak," Barbara said after consulting her map.

Roger pointed down to the right. "Don't cross this rail bridge. Go down this foot track beside it. That leads to the river."

He led the way down a dusty maintenance track. This emerged onto a dry part of the riverbed, a hundred metre wide area of pebbles and sand dotted with clumps of small trees. The small trees were all bent over and twisted by the wet season floods.

The track led them to the gravel road where it joined a low, concrete causeway. This in turn gave way to a short and narrow wooden bridge. The river constricted at that point to a narrow channel about 25 metres wide. The water looked deep and was flowing swiftly. The far bank was a wall of jungle through which the dirt road climbed in a deep and gloomy cutting.

Just as they reached the end of the causeway at the bridge Roger growled with disgust. "I was going to suggest stopping here for lunch, but the place is a pigsty." He indicated a litter of papers, food scraps, drink cans, and worse.

Barbara looked around and gasped in shock. An old man, with a face like a wrinkled walnut, dressed in faded and torn clothing, sat in the shade on the end of the bridge. He was holding a fishing line. She started to turn away as she was tired and dejected and in no mood to be social to strangers, when the fisherman spoke.

"It was all them religious weirdos yesterday what left all that rubbish. I hope youse ain't more of them," he said.

"No. No we aren't," Gordon hastily assured him.

"Scared away all the bloody fish," the fisherman grumbled. "What with all their singin' and bloody splashin' in the water. One of them mass baptism affairs it were."

"These religious people," Gordon asked. "How were they dressed?"

"Mostly dressed in funny yella togs, like a sort of a dress most of 'em," the fisherman replied.

"Most of them? What were the others wearing?" Barbara asked.

"Oh, just ordinary sort of working clothes. Only a few of them there were. They sat off on one side and didn't do any of the singin' or prayin'. Unfriendly lookin' mob they were. The only thing they had in common was they all wore a little orange Smiley badge on their shirt pocket," the fisherman explained.

Smileys! Barbara thought.

"That was yesterday?" Roger asked.

"Yep. All bloody afternoon," the fisherman replied. He pointed across the river and said, "They camped just up along there among them trees last night."

"Where did they go?" Barbara asked, her interest now fully aroused.

"Off that way. North along that road," The fisherman replied, pointing up the gloomy tunnel in the jungle.

"Do you know where that road leads?" Barbara asked. She pulled out her map again.

"Yep. It joins up with the Black Mountain Road eventually, but a long way up. I ain't bin along it meself. Heard a few bad stories about what happens to folks what do," the fisherman said.

"What sort of stories?" Karen asked.

"Folks what have gone along it ain't never come back, is what I heard. Anyway, yer can't go that way. There's a locked gate just up there," the fisherman explained.

Barbara studied the map. The road was marked on it. She lifted her head and looked along the road. To her it appeared simultaneously beckoning and forbidding.

The fisherman followed her gaze. He shook his head and grunted. "Nah! I wouldn't advise going that way. Ye'd be trespassin' anyway. All private property, eh? Take my advice and don't cross the river or yer could get inter real deep trouble."

"How did these religious people travel? Were they in cars, or a bus or something?" Roger asked.

The fisherman shook his head. "Nah. They was walking. Except them fellas with the orange badges, they had a little truck, a Land Cruiser."

"Which way did they come from?" Lofty asked.

"Same way as you fellas, along the railway."

They asked a few more questions but the fisherman could add little and after a while became surly. Barbara was intensely interested. She

221

studied the map intently and traced various roads and tracks to try to find the most likely route to the commune, but the connecting roads seemed to go well to the west and north of it.

"Let's have lunch," Lofty suggested. "I need a break."

They turned and moved upstream along the sandy riverbed to get away from the litter and filth. Fifty metres further up the riverbed they found an area of clean sand under the shade of several small trees right beside a tiny beach. They dumped their packs and gear and sat down. Barbara stood looking at the river, her mind in turmoil.

Gordon nudged her. "You okay? You look worried."

"I am, about those Smileys. I wish we hadn't just met that fisherman. He's opened a real can of worms in my brain. We must tell Superintendent Blunt at once."

"At once? Can't we have lunch first?" Roger asked with a smile, but his eyes were serious.

"Well, as soon as we can. If these Smileys were here yesterday, he may not know about them," Barbara replied. She took out her mobile phone and turned it on. "Drat! No service."

Lofty agreed. "They are a long way from either Kuranda or the commune. What are they doing here?"

"Mass baptism," Dan replied. "Maybe it is a sacred spot for them."

"Walking," Roger said. "It might have been the 'Pilgrimage of Penance' mob that we were trailing at Kamerunga."

They all agreed this was a possibility. A horrible thought occurred to Barbara. She voiced it, "If it is the Pilgrimage of Penance then Cyril might be with them."

She found the idea of anyone she knew falling into the clutches of these terrible people appalling. The boys weren't as sympathetic.

"Serves the silly bugger right," Lofty said.

"We must warn the police," Barbara insisted.

Lofty nodded. "We will, but another hour won't matter," he replied. "Anyway, I need a rest." He sat down on his pack and massaged his leg.

"We will tell them as soon as we reach the next farmhouse," Roger said. "Now let's eat."

Reluctantly Barbara sat and started preparations for lunch.

Chapter 23

HOT ON THE TRAIL

The group sat beside the river for nearly an hour. Barbara fretted about getting to a phone, but the map showed that the nearest was probably at a farmhouse a few kilometres further along in the Blackwater Creek area, a place called 'Corwa'. So she made herself rest and eat. When she had finished her lunch Barbara cleaned her teeth and rinsed her face. She realised she felt hot and sore, and the water felt cool and refreshing.

Jennifer obviously thought the same as she said, "Let's find somewhere nicer and have a swim."

"Good idea," Roger agreed.

Barbara wasn't happy with that idea, for several reasons. "We should get to a phone quickly," she said.

"A few more minutes won't matter," Lofty argued. "Besides, I feel like a swim."

There was a general chorus of approval. Barbara still wasn't happy, and Jennifer snapped at her, "Then you go to the phone while we have a quick swim."

Barbara considered that for a moment, but Gordon shook his head. "No. You are not going on your own, and I would like a swim too."

"Oh alright!" Barbara conceded. "But I don't feel like digging out my bathers."

That caused general ribaldry and comments of 'who cares?' but Wendy did and said firmly, "The boys can swim in one pool and us girls in another, but we will go upstream a bit, where that old fisherman can't see us."

This was agreed to so boots were pulled on, then webbing and packs. Lofty cried out in pain when he went to stand up and had to be helped up by Roger and Gordon.

"It's okay," Lofty reassured them. "I'm only bruised, I think, and m muscles have gone stiff. I'll be fine once I warm up."

Led by Jennifer they made their way upstream. Some of the time th walked on the sand beside the water and at other times they clambe

over rocks or threaded through the trees. Beside them the river widened to a hundred metres in width but became so shallow it was barely knee deep at its deepest point. Then it narrowed to a jumble of rocks and shallow rapids. After about a hundred metres, when she was sure they were out of sight of the old fisherman, or anyone else at the bridge, Barbara stopped.

The river at this point was only ten or fifteen metres wide. Their side was sandy and studded with outcrops of rocks and numerous clumps of bushes and trees. The other bank was covered in jungle and dropped steeply into deep water.

"This will do," Barbara declared. "Boys here and girls upstream past that next lot of trees."

"Spoilsport," Gordon said.

"You will have to wait," Barbara replied, then realised what she had implied. Lofty and Roger both grinned.

Lofty chuckled. "Wait for what Gordon?" he asked with mock innocence.

Roger smiled. "Is that a promise?" he asked. "Start running now Gordon, before she sinks the claws in."

Gordon snorted. He met Barbara's eye with a delighted gaze which made her smile even in her embarrassment. *Yes,* she thought. *I do want him to see me nude.*

But she poked her tongue at Roger and Lofty and shook her head at her own wicked thoughts. Wendy grinned.

The girls walked another fifty paces and found a pleasant little beach shelving into clear, waist-deep water with a sandy bottom. It wasn't completely hidden from the boys, but the other girls agreed it was just the place. They dropped their gear and began undressing.

Barbara felt a bit anxious about taking her clothes off in case other people saw them. To avoid embarrassing her friends she studiously avoided looking at the other girls. The others undressed in silence until Jennifer looked up from hauling off her boots, and said, "Wendy, I'm sorry I called you names earlier."

"That's alright. We all had a bad fright when Lofty nearly fell off the bridge," Wendy replied.

"It was because of Lofty," Jennifer observed. "But we may as well not have bothered. He isn't interested in us, or only in so far as we are girls and he is a boy."

"Why is that?" Wendy asked.

"Because I think he is in love with Fiona. He told me he was feeling guilty for flirting with us," Jennifer replied. She looked directly at Karen.

"I know," Karen replied. "He told me last night, and we weren't doing anything either!"

Barbara noted that Wendy hung her head and pretended to concentrate on unlacing her boots. Poor Wendy! So, it was as she had suspected: Lofty loved Fiona. The knowledge cheered her up, till she remembered that Fiona was still missing. The thought made her glance at the rainforest across the river. Was she somewhere over there?

If only! No. I promised. We must tell the police what we have heard as soon as we reach the next farm, she told herself.

She pulled off her socks and stood up to take off her clothes, quite forgetting to worry about what the other girls might be thinking. Thankfully she shrugged off the last of her underwear and stretched.

Jennifer shook her head in admiration. "Barbara, you look gorgeous," she said. "Gordon would go crazy if he could see you now."

"Sorry. I didn't mean to make an exhibition of myself," Barbara replied. But she did enjoy the titillation as the others looked at her, more than a gleam of envy showing amongst the curiosity.

Jennifer shrugged. "I don't mind," she answered. "I think naked women are nicer and more interesting to look at than naked men."

"Not me," Wendy spoke up. "I think naked men are really fascinating."

"When have you been with naked men, you naughty girl?" Barbara teased. Wendy blushed and laughed and did not answer. Barbara waded slowly in, the cold-water causing waves of goose bumps to sweep up her body. Wendy stood up and cast off the rest of her clothes. She turned to Jennifer who was also standing.

"Let's be friends please."

Jennifer finished peeling off her panties and stood facing Wendy. Then she smiled and stepped forward and put out her hands.

"Yes."

The two girls hugged each other. Barbara was very glad. Jennifer then released Wendy, and said, "Come on, we will scrub each other's backs and give each other a massage."

The two girls splashed into the water and cried out how cold it was. Barbara lowered herself in till only her head was out. It felt delightful.

She suddenly felt happy and had the urge to embrace them all, even Karen, who was somewhat self-consciously wading in.

For the next ten minutes they chattered, giggled, paddled, and swam happily. Barbara enjoyed every moment of it; the sensual pleasure of the cold water rippling over her bare skin, the mild thrill of being nude with others looking at her, the physical pleasure of massaging each other's sore shoulders, the sheer pleasure of touching and seeing.

I like girls, she decided. *But I'm normal. I am a woman and I like men. I wish we were swimming with the boys.* She knew this would be quite unfair to the boys as it would fire their lust. She imagined this for a few minutes and found herself getting aroused. *Yes. I do like men. And I need a man to love me.* That led her into thoughts of whether she was ready emotionally, and of the old dilemma of virginity. *Not just any man though,* she told herself. *He must be the right man.* But was Gordon the Right Man? That was something she wasn't sure of. *If I am not sure, then perhaps he isn't,* she mused.

Wendy interrupted her contemplation. "Come with me Barbara. I want to go to the toilet, and I don't want to go into the bush alone."

"Where?"

Wendy indicated the thick jungle and weeds on the other bank. "What about just over there?"

Barbara looked around and saw that the other choice was to cross a hundred metres of rocky outcrops, pebbles and open sand to the trees lining the south bank. She nodded. The two girls swam across the narrow stream in a few strokes, the last few metres being too deep for wading. There was a tiny beach where they climbed out and made their dripping way up into the forest.

A few metres in was an animal pad that ran along the bank through weeds and deadfall. Wendy looked nervously around, trying unsuccessfully to cover her bosom with her arms. Satisfied they were alone she turned left and they walked along the trail until they were out of sight of the other two girls.

"I'll just go here," Wendy said.

Barbara felt the urge to go herself. "I'll go too. I will be just over there," she said. She pointed to the next bush. "And don't use the wrong leaf. Remember when Kate used some stinging tree."

Wendy giggled. "Don't get bitten on the bum by a snake."

226

"More likely to be leeches in here," Barbara replied. Wendy's smile vanished and she looked around in horror. Barbara walked on another ten paces past the bush and into the shadow of several large trees. She felt very daring walking naked in the forest and her heart beat rapidly. After a careful check to ensure there were no centipedes, snakes, leeches, or scorpions that might attack her while she was at her most vulnerable, she squatted down.

When she was finished she stood up, wondering if Wendy was finished. She didn't want to go back and embarrass her. As she stood there, she heard crashing and crunching noises in the undergrowth.

Pig? she thought in alarm, remembering that other occasion when she had been chased by a pig while naked. *Well not quite naked. I did have my boots on,* she thought. *Which is more than I've got on now!* With her heart beating fast she peered through the jungle and tensed ready to run.

Then a man's harsh voice made her go cold with fright.

Wendy called out, "Barbara! Someone is coming."

"Sssh!" Barbara hissed. She had just glimpsed movement up in the forest: a flash of yellow in a patch of sunlight.

Barbara's heart leapt. As silently as she could she scuttled quickly back to where Wendy was crouching behind a tree.

"Smileys!" she hissed. "Quick! Go back and tell the others. Tell them to be quiet and to hide. Tell the boys too. Quick!"

"What are you going to do?" Wendy asked, her face a study in consternation.

"I'm going to hide and watch."

"Barbara! They might see you!"

"So? I'll run and they'll get a thrill. I'll be alright. Go! Quickly!" This last emphasised by the sound of Jennifer giggling and a distant shout from the boys. Barbara pushed her. "Don't forget to tell the boys. Run!"

Wendy scampered off along the animal pad, her buttocks and thighs very white and wobbly. Barbara turned and began walking cautiously the other way. The men's voices were much closer, and she again caught glimpses of movement through the trees. She tried to work out how many people there were. At least four or five she decided. They were walking down the gentle slope towards the river in a tight group and were about thirty or forty metres away.

As the men got closer they went out of sight into a dip. But as they did, they crossed a narrow, sunlit gap and she was able to see them clearly and count them: six. And one of them wore a khaki shirt and carried a gun. At that Barbara's heart seemed to stop and she swallowed.

Fear and curiosity warred within her. *I want to see what they are doing,* Barbara decided. The men stopped at the riverbank and she could hear the murmur of their voices but could not see them. *I wish I had some clothes on,* she thought, very conscious of her nakedness. Then she smiled. *No I don't! If they see me they will act like stupid men: all goggle-eyed and leering. I will just run and dive in the river. They won't catch me. And they won't suspect that I was deliberately spying on them. Spies don't sneak around in the nude!* she reasoned.

She suppressed a giggle and that told her it was real fear she was trying to hide. For just a moment she considered what might happen if the men caught her: rape, or worse? She shivered and shook her head to clear the ugly thoughts.

Besides, the others are just near. If I scream, they will come and save me.

She began cautiously moving from tree to tree, careful not to step on dead twigs and leaves. From behind a tree she looked down into the shallow depression. What she saw amazed her. There were six men. Five of them wore yellow tunics or clothing of various shades from washed out cream to bright lemon: and they were all chained together! A long chain was fastened to them by padlocks around their waists. The sixth man was an ordinary looking fellow of middle-age. He wore boots, grey trousers, and a khaki shirt, on the pocket of which was pinned a round orange 'Smiley' badge. He was cradling a pump-action shotgun and was most obviously a guard.

Slaves! Barbara thought.

She observed the group more carefully, ignoring her thumping heart and the spiky plants which prickled her tender skin. She noted that the 'slaves' were working to uncouple a large motor-driven pump from a hose connection. One of the slaves wore little more than a tattered loin cloth and old sandshoes with no laces. Others wore only a loose yellow tunic. One wore a new tunic which still had a hood sewn to its collar and new shoes. All looked thin, tired, unwashed, and anything but happy.

The discovery set Barbara's mind racing. *If the Smiley People keep prisoners to work as slaves, then they don't kill everyone they kidnap,* she reasoned. *Fiona might still be alive!*

At a word of command four of the slaves picked up the pump by its tubular steel frame. The fifth collected the tools and the whole group set off back the way it had come, the guard keeping well away from them. He followed at a distance which kept him safe from surprise attack by his charges. Not once did any of them even glance in Barbara's direction. The guard, in particular, kept his eyes on the slaves.

She saw there was a rough foot track leading up through the jungle. Beside it was a black plastic water pipe.

Oh! What should I do? I don't want to lose sight of them, Barbara muttered to herself.

She bit her lip in indecision. Common sense said to go back and tell the others, and get dressed.

"I'll just follow them a short way," Barbara told herself, knowing in her heart that, with her quarry in view, she did not want to lose sight of them for an instant.

I'm being foolish! she told herself as she began to cautiously follow the group.

As the last person vanished from sight she flitted across the small clearing and onto the track. It made her very conscious she was naked and she held her breasts protectively.

They will be more likely to do things to me than shoot me! she thought, then had to suppress a near hysterical giggle. Her mouth was dry, her hands sweaty, and she knew she was very scared. But to save Fiona she was willing to even risk rape.

By just keeping close enough for occasional glimpses of the group through the trees Barbara managed to safely follow them. At any moment she expected to find more of them, was anticipating a camp of some sort. Navigation was easy, they just followed the track up a gentle slope away from the river. Her real fear was stumbling unexpectedly into more Smileys so she stopped frequently behind trees to scout ahead.

Several times the group halted to rest for a minute or so. Barbara crouched in cover and waited and watched. It was hot and dry and she perspired freely.

I wish I'd had more to drink, she thought.

The group moved on. The rainforest gave way to more open scrub after about 300 metres. This comprised waist-high grass and a moderately dense growth of paperbarks and stunted eucalypts. The change in vegetation forced Barbara to follow at a much greater distance, between 50 and 100 metres.

After about ten minutes more she paused. *I should be heading back. The others will be getting worried,* she thought. She bit her lip. *I wonder where these Smileys are going? They must have a camp somewhere. I will just go a bit further.*

Barbara continued on, moving at a crouch from tree to tree. The Smileys crossed a wide flat area. A range of hills loomed up through the trees and the slope began to steepen. Barbara paused behind a large tree to get a better look.

And got another shock. "Gosh! I must be blind! There are more of them, and a vehicle. There must be a road," she muttered.

The vehicle was a dull brown Land Cruiser with an open tray. Another man with a gun slung over his shoulder stood leaning on it. Nearby sat a row of seven more slaves in torn and dirty yellow clothing. When the first group reached the vehicle, the pump was loaded aboard and the seated slaves were ordered to stand up. Barbara saw that several were women.

"That girl with the fair hair, she looks like Fiona!" Barbara gasped.

She blinked and wiped sweat from her eyes. But that made things worse as she rubbed dry salt from her perspiration into her eyes and they stung and watered. She swore as her vision went blurry. To help clear them she tried to make tears come. While she did so she crouched behind the tree.

As clear vision returned Barbara looked around for a way to get closer. Only then did it dawn on her how lucky she was that she had not been seen by the waiting Smileys. She decided she must stay where she was.

At that moment, the thud of running boots sounded behind her. She looked over her shoulder in alarm.

It was Gordon. He was clad only in shorts and boots and looked very agitated. Barbara stood up next to the tree and made frantic hand signals for him to stop and to be quiet.

His face, when he saw her, was (in retrospect) comical. Relief, concern, delight, puzzlement, and interest all tried to show at once. He stopped twenty metres away and held out a bundle of clothes. As he opened his mouth to speak Barbara frowned and put her finger to her lips. She pointed towards the Smileys and motioned him to get down. Only then did she remember she was nude. She gave a mental shrug and realised she didn't care.

She turned her back on him and slid down behind the tree again. A check revealed that Gordon's arrival had not been noticed. The Smileys had all the slaves chained into a single line by this time. The fair-haired girl was hidden by the vehicle. One guard climbed into the Land Cruiser, started it up and drove off.

Barbara stared hard at the girl. Was it Fiona? But she couldn't be sure as the girl was a hundred paces away and half-turned from her. Barbara rose to a stooping crouch to get a better view as the line of slaves was ordered to start walking. Then Barbara looked over her shoulder. Gordon was now crouched behind a tree and had obviously seen the Smileys. He pretended not to be looking at her, but their eyes met and he looked embarrassed. Barbara could not suppress a smile.

Poor boy! Well, he wanted to get to know me. And for sure he has dreamed of seeing me naked. I hope he likes what he sees, she thought.

She turned back to watch the slaves. They were heading away from her around a curve which led upslope towards the hills. After half a minute they were hidden from view. Barbara sighed and stood up.

With no attempt to cover herself she walked back to Gordon. As she did, he also stood up, wonder, disbelief and embarrassment all clear on his face. He looked away.

Barbara smiled again and said, "You can look Gordon. I don't mind."

In fact I want you to look, she told herself as the self-revelation came to her. *Heavens I'm shameless! I hope he isn't put off.*

Gordon did look, but only briefly. Then he held her eyes with his until they met. "I brought you some clothes," he said, holding out the bundle.

Barbara could see that he was being stormed by strong emotions. She took the clothes from him.

He sighed and looked her up and down. "God, you are beautiful!" he said in a strangled voice.

Barbara dropped the clothes on the grass, stepped forward and put her arms around his neck. She pressed against him, her eyes holding his.

He groaned. "Oh my God!" he gasped, his voice choking with emotion. Then he seized her and kissed her.

Barbara forgot everything: the Smileys, Fiona, the heat, the others. She closed her eyes and allowed a wave of passion to engulf her. She pressed hard against him, bare breasts to bare chest, bare arms on bare shoulders. He held her firmly and stroked her.

After a minute or so they stopped kissing and she put her head on his shoulder, smelt his male sweat and didn't mind. To her own surprise she licked it and he sighed.

"I love you!" he cried.

Then he kissed her again, more urgently this time. She surrendered to him, allowing her own urges and desires to surge. She could feel that he was very aroused and was pleased.

An embarrassed cough penetrated her consciousness, then voices.

Chapter 24

THE SLAVE CAMP

Barbara opened her eyes and looked. At the bend in the track was an embarrassed looking Roger with his back to them, holding out his arms to stop the others from looking as they arrived. She glimpsed Wendy's face, suffused with shocked delight.

Gordon cleared his throat and murmured, "I think we'd better stop for the moment."

"I don't want to," Barbara said, with deliberate ambiguity.

Gordon drew his head back to look at her quizzically. Then he kissed her again and gave her another hug. She responded. "Oh! I feel as though my body is on fire," she murmured.

"Sunburn," Gordon said. "Or the beginning of heat exhaustion." He released her and gave her a gentle slap on the rump. "You'd better get dressed."

Reluctantly Barbara bent to the clothes scattered beside the track. She glanced along it and saw all the others standing with their backs turned. She thought it did look funny, but she was a bit appalled with herself when she realised she wouldn't have minded if they'd been watching. Gordon also turned his back as well and she was not daring enough to tell him she wouldn't mind if he watched.

As quickly as she could she dressed. When she was finished, she called softly, "It's okay. I'm decent now."

Her friends turned and walked towards them, their faces varying degrees of embarrassment and curiosity. Wendy was grinning from ear to ear. Lofty came hobbling into view as she began to describe what she had seen.

"Too late Lofty," Roger cried. "The show's over."

Wendy nudged him and frowned. Lofty looked mystified. "What did I miss?"

"Me being shameless," Barbara said, forestalling Gordon. "You can tell him later."

It was only then that it really hit her how stupid she had just been.

233

There we were in a passionate embrace and oblivious to the world! Those Smileys could have just walked up and captured us. She looked around. *If any more came along that road they would have seen us, can see us!*

"Get down!" she ordered. They crouched in the long grass and Barbara quickly recounted what she had seen.

Wendy looked aghast. "Slaves!" she cried. "Poor Fiona!"

"What will we do?" Jennifer asked.

"Follow them," Barbara said decisively. "We need to know where they are going." She looked at her watch. Five past three. "It can't be far because they are walking."

"Barbara! That could be dangerous. What if they see us?" Karen asked.

Barbara shook her head. "I don't think it is too dangerous. The guards are too busy watching the slaves to keep a good lookout. Anyway, we can just run off into the bush and hide."

"What about the police?" Roger asked.

"Yes. We must inform them at once. Two of us must run to the nearest farm and telephone them," Barbara agreed.

"I'll go," Jennifer offered.

"And me," Roger added.

"Okay. Good. Hang on! Let's think this out sensibly," Barbara said, biting her lip as she tried to sort out a plan of action. "I wish I had my map."

"Here, use mine," Dan offered.

He pulled it out and orientated it. After a minute's thought Barbara stabbed her finger down.

"We are about here. This road must be the one they went along."

The map showed a road junction about a kilometre to the north. Barbara thought, then shook her head. "No. We can't tell which way they will go."

"There will be footprints," Roger suggested.

"You are right," Barbara agreed. She looked at the others, aware of mounting excitement. "Now, here is my idea. Gordon and I will go on ahead. At this road junction we will mark whether we went left or right so you can follow. The rest of you go back to our gear. Roger, you and Jennifer then go to the nearest farmhouse and phone the police. The rest of you collect our webbing and follow. Don't forget to fill all the water bottles. And walk in the bush, not on the road so you don't leave boot prints or get seen. Oh, and dig out my camouflage uniform for me please."

"Back across the river!" Roger said, indicating his wet clothes.

"Take them off if you want to keep them dry," Wendy said. "We promise not to laugh."

They all did laugh and looked at Wendy who blushed. Barbara looked at her quizzically, and at Roger's red face.

Lofty answered, "Wendy came rushing back starkers to tell us to be quiet and to tell us what you were doing."

Wendy flamed crimson. "There wasn't time to get dressed," she said.

"It's okay Wendy," Gordon said. "We didn't mind."

The boys all laughed again, except Roger. Barbara again raised an eyebrow. Lofty answered.

"We didn't have any clothes on either, so Wendy got a good eyeful too, especially of Roger."

Roger blushed beetroot red. Wendy giggled and covered her mouth. "I'm sorry Roger."

Barbara smiled then said, "We promised Capt Conkey to behave ourselves."

"We also promised him and Inspector Sharpe we wouldn't go looking for trouble," Lofty reminded.

Barbara felt a prick of conscience and tried to rationalize what she was going to do, knowing in her heart she was being a hypocrite. "We didn't go looking," she said. "It came to us. And I did say that if we found something we would investigate."

"Did we?" Gordon asked.

Barbara felt uncomfortable. She wasn't sure. Gordon then put his arm around her shoulders and squeezed.

"It's okay. We are with you. Let's get moving. They've already had twenty minutes start."

"What about our packs?" Roger asked as they stood up.

Barbara thought hard for a few seconds then shook her head. "We need to go fast. Leave them," she said.

"What if we need them? It's only about three hours to dark. We will need food," Roger persisted.

Karen added, "It might get cold. If the police aren't here before dark, we might need our pullovers."

"And if we rescue Fiona she might need First Aid, or food or warm clothing," Lofty suggested.

Barbara reconsidered and nodded her head. "Okay. Bring the packs. We will meet you as soon as possible. Dan, we will keep your map for the moment if that's okay? Good, let's move," Barbara ordered.

Lofty grinned at Gordon. "You two keep your mind on the Smileys this time," he called as they parted.

Barbara snorted at him, smiled at Gordon and started walking. Within a minute she was on the vehicle track, which was just two wheel ruts in the long grass. The road curved from North to Northeast and climbed the lower slopes of the hills. After ten minutes of careful walking Barbara and Gordon came to a road junction. The other road was a roughly graded gravel track.

Gordon studied the map and said, "This must be the road which goes back to the bridge where we met that old fisherman." They looked cautiously both ways along it.

"It is, and the Smileys went left," Barbara said, pointing to the boot prints in the dust.

"We had better walk on the grass, so we don't leave any tracks ourselves," Gordon suggested.

"You aren't just a pretty face after all," Barbara answered. "I'll just make a mark to show the others which way to go." She did this then dusted her hands and smiled at Gordon. He reached out and squeezed her hand. She was happy and excited, satisfaction at finding a clue to follow overriding her fear.

The gravel road wound its way up the right-hand side of a scrub-covered ridge. It turned northwest, then west, then abruptly north to cross a low saddle amidst long grass, grass trees and scattered iron barks. Barbara and Gordon walked in the bush a few metres from the road. Just as they crossed the low crest to where the road curved left again around the side of another hill Barbara heard a vehicle coming from in front of them.

"Quick! Hide!" she cried, pointing right.

She bounded over behind some small trees. Here she crouched and turned to peer back through the leaves. Gordon joined her.

A brown Toyota Land Cruiser came into sight from the north. Barbara noted it was a different vehicle from the one they had seen earlier. This one had several steel mesh cages of the type used by pig hunters on the back. The sight caused her mind to flood with ugly memories which, for a moment, almost paralysed her with fear.

The vehicle was driven by a thin-faced, sandy-haired man she had never seen before. It vanished downhill in the direction of the river. Barbara did not delay. She wanted to catch up with the slaves and see where they were going. As soon as the vehicle was out of sight she hurried on, keeping in the long grass and ignoring the danger of snakes.

It's supposed to winter and the snakes should be hibernating, she told herself, but she was still afraid.

The road curved left, then right, then left again and headed Northwest up over a low ridge. Abruptly the open forest gave way to a vast bulldozed wasteland. Barbara stopped just inside the trees and stared at it in dismay.

"This isn't shown on the map!" she cried, biting her lip.

"Only been recently cleared," Gordon observed.

"It's going to be hard to cross without being seen," Barbara added.

The road ran out across a bare, dusty flat ridge for half a kilometre before dipping into a small creek line marked by a straggle of sheoaks and paperbarks. The road then curved up over another undulating ridge beyond.

"This way," Barbara indicated, heading off to the right to skirt along the edge of the remaining forest.

"I wonder why it has been cleared?" Gordon speculated.

"Farming I suppose," Barbara said. "They must irrigate it because this is where that plastic pipe leads to."

"Stop!" Gordon gasped. "Get down! Quick!"

Barbara didn't hesitate. She threw herself flat in the grass. "What is it?" she hissed.

"More slaves. Behind us on the left," Gordon replied.

Barbara cautiously raised her head behind a tree and looked. A dirt vehicle track ran along the open ridge top to join the gravel road a couple of hundred metres away. A straggling line of yellow clad figures, eight in number, was walking along it, followed by a man dressed in dark blue work clothes who was carrying a rifle.

I must be blind! Barbara thought. *Those people must have been walking along there while we were standing talking.* She shook her head in amazement.

Gordon studied the group. "I don't think they saw us," he said.

Barbara agreed, "No. They are just walking along."

The pair lay in cover and watched as the Smileys reached the road junction and turned left along the gravel road. Barbara noted that the slaves included both men and women. All wore the same mixture of torn and soiled yellow tunics. They carried hand tools and were linked by a chain around their waists. Their walk was a tired shuffle and their heads were bowed.

Barbara waited till the group went out of sight into the creek line, then, after a careful look around, set off at a run. She went along just inside the edge of the forest. This took them away from the road at right angles, but she did not dare risk crossing such a large open area. She reasoned that it would be very difficult for her and Gordon to come up with a plausible excuse for their being there.

It won't help Fiona if we get captured! she thought.

After 300 metres the clearing ended so they could turn left and head north, almost parallel to the gravel road. By then they were both panting and perspiring so they slowed to a fast walk. They kept well inside the timber which was open enough to allow them to walk as fast as they could, but still provided cover.

As they went over the top of the gentle ridge Barbara got a glimpse of the slaves as they went up the ridge beyond that. By then they were well over half a kilometre away.

A clump of tall trees then hid the slaves from their sight, so the pair hurried on. Barbara began to fret that she would lose them so she pushed on as fast as she could walk, ignoring her dry throat and pumping heart. Sweat stung her eyes and her leg muscles began to complain. Gordon made no comment but kept up with her.

Five minutes fast walking took them down into the creek line. This was only a dry runnel a couple of paces wide and lined with trees. A fold in the next ridge gave them some cover so Barbara went straight up it and through the edge of the clump of tall trees.

Beyond the next crest was another long, gentle down slope to yet another small creek. All the ground on the left was still completely bare, not even a blade of grass on most of it. Barbara noted that it was furrowed by evenly spaced small ditches which contoured the slopes. In places the green leaves of some crop showed in the ditches.

The slaves were nowhere to be seen. Barbara looked anxiously around then ran down the next slope through the open savannah woodland. She had to slow down for lack of breath long before she reached the creek, but now she was gripped by anxiety lest she lose track of where the slaves had gone.

Beyond the second creek was another bare, open ridge which extended for 200 metres up to her right, climbing gently towards a jungle covered mountain about a kilometre away. She uttered a few angry words as that meant detouring further away from the road but there was nothing for it so she strode up the hill beside the creek line until they reached the tree line where it traversed the ridge.

The vegetation was still open forest, so they were able to walk quickly through it. Barbara was surprised how high they had climbed and how far she could see. She saw that they were in a broad valley two- or three-kilometre's wide which had a rough north-south alignment. Off to the west was a rugged range of dry looking hills clothed in open forest. Her map told her that they were in the lower valley of Blacksnake Creek.

At the crest of the ridge Barbara paused. Her eyes at once detected movement away off to her left. She raised her hand to halt Gordon and crept forward to a good OP behind a windrow of bulldozed trees. The open ridge sloped down to another small creek. The gravel road cut across the lower slopes and through this third creek and on across another bare field. Just beyond this third creek a vehicle track led due west up a gentle, open slope for a couple of hundred metres to a flattish hilltop crowned by a straggle of fences, buildings and a residual clump of forest which had survived the bulldozers.

"It is their camp!" Barbara cried excitedly.

No doubt about it. The open-tray Land Cruiser was parked there, and the line of slaves was just entering a gate in a solid timber fence.

"Looks like a set of old cattle yards," Gordon said.

Barbara nodded, "Turned into a makeshift prison camp," she agreed. She set to work to memorize the layout.

Gordon pointed. "We could get closer if we go back to that second creek and follow it down past the road," he suggested.

"Yes, let's do that," Barbara agreed.

They quickly made their way back into the forest and back to the second creek. They followed this down to the road. As they neared it, they kept a good lookout, both for more Smileys and for their own friends. They were careful not to leave any boot prints as they crossed the road.

Ten minutes of movement brought them to a junction with the third creek. Barbara noted their position on the map. *Thank God Capt Conkey is so thorough in his navigation training,* she thought. She found it very comforting to know exactly where she was.

A few minutes stalking gave them a good view from the dry bed of the third creek up the open hillside to the Smiley camp. This was now revealed quite clearly to be old cattle yards. Barbara saw that barbed wire and wire netting had been added to the heavy timber rails. She could see glimpses of yellow clad slaves inside. A guard sat on a platform built on what had been the loading ramp at the far corner.

On the side nearest the gravel road were two open sided shelters. Another guard sat there. Two female slaves were visible, apparently cooking as smoke rose from the second shelter. One of the female slaves had very fair hair. When she walked into the afternoon sunlight it shone like gold.

"That looks like Fiona!" Barbara cried softly, gripping Gordon's arm.

"Are you sure?" he asked doubtfully.

Barbara stared hard. "I think so. It certainly looks like her."

"I hope so," Gordon said. Then he continued. "Hey! I've just had an awful thought."

"What?"

"There is no-one to stop the others when they come walking along the road with the packs. We aren't near the road."

Barbara felt her heart leap in guilt. *How stupid I am! How can I be so forgetful and careless as to risk my friends!* she berated herself.

She bit her lip and looked at her watch. It was 4:30pm.

"We'd better get back and meet them," she said. "The police should be along soon, and we need to be ready to brief them."

"Which way will we go?"

"Back the way we came, but keep a close watch on the road. Let's go."

Chapter 25

ANOTHER SHOCK

Half an hour later Barbara and Gordon were back near the point where the gravel road came out of the forest into the open country. From a hiding place in the dry savannah woodland they watched the road from behind some lantana bushes.

Barbara looked at her watch and said, "I'm worried. We should have met the others by now."

"We could keep walking till we meet them," Gordon suggested.

"Only a little way. We will have to come back here," Barbara agreed.

Hoping that being on higher ground would make a difference she turned on her mobile phone but there was still no service. That was a disappointment but she had been expecting it.

We are a very long way from any towns, and there are a lot of hills in the way, she reasoned.

She led Gordon back the way they had come, walking in the bush on the left side of the road. They had only gone 200 metres to where the road curved left around the side of the grassy hill covered in sheoaks when they met the others. They were walking in single file in the bush beside the road.

Dan was leading the way and carrying two packs. When he spotted them he dropped flat instantly. They walked over to join him. As they did, he stood up and indicated Lofty limping along about a hundred paces back. Dan wiped sweat from his face and muttered, "Am I glad to see you two!"

Wendy and Karen arrived next, also each with two packs. One was Lofty's.

Barbara looked at the packs and saw her own. "Where are Roger and Jennifer's packs?" she asked.

"They have them," Dan replied.

Barbara looked at her watch again. It was after 5pm. The afternoon sun was throwing long shadows. She said, "The police should be here soon. I hope they aren't too long. It will be dark in an hour."

"What did you find?" Wendy asked.

"Tell you when Lofty gets here. Is that my webbing?"

Barbara bent and picked up her basic webbing and put it on, then took out a water bottle and drank nearly half in one go. Lofty hobbled up to join them. He opened his mouth to speak then looked quickly over his shoulder. "Vehicle coming!" he cried.

"Hide!" Barbara snapped, pointing into the grass on the lower slope.

"It might be the police," Dan reminded.

"In that case I will jump up and stop them. Quick! Get under cover!" Barbara ordered.

She grabbed her pack and tossed it into the long grass. There was a rush and much rustling as they took cover. As they did, the sound of the vehicle came rapidly closer.

It is coming from the river so it could be the police, Barbara reasoned.

She dashed over behind a bush and crouched down, ready to spring out. Once there she peered hopefully along the road.

As soon as the vehicle came into view, she saw it was not the police. It was the brown Land Cruiser with the pig cages.

Thank God we took cover! she thought.

As the vehicle rattled past, she stared at it in disbelief. Locked inside the cages on the back were Roger and Jennifer!

Barbara was thunderstruck. As soon as the vehicle had gone, she stood up. So did the others, all their faces registering disbelief and shock.

"Roger and Jennifer!" Dan cried.

"Prisoners!" Gordon added.

"Oh what will we do?" Wendy wailed.

Barbara bit her lip. "I wonder if they managed to contact the police?"

"How did they get caught?" Karen asked.

Wendy repeated her cry, "What will we do?"

"Give me a moment to think," Barbara ordered. She stood for a moment and forced her racing thoughts into an ordered pattern. Then she faced the others. "First we will get out of sight. Up that hill will do. We will eat and get organised before it gets dark. Then we will discuss what to do."

"But that might be too late!" Karen cried.

"Can't be helped," Barbara replied firmly. "We need time to think and to work out a sensible plan. It won't do us any good just blundering in. Besides, we should eat now. We don't want any fires after dark now that we are in enemy territory." That last comment expressed a belief she had held for several hours.

"What if the police come?" Lofty asked.

"We can leave a sentry here beside the road," Barbara replied.

Lofty nodded. "Okay. I'll do that. Dan, you come and relieve me in half an hour," he said.

"You can relieve yourself while I'm away thanks. I will come back and take over as sentry in thirty minutes," Dan quipped. There was a moments silence then both laughed.

"Idiot!" Lofty replied, punching Dan's arm playfully.

"Stop playing the fool!" Karen snapped. "This is deadly serious!"

The boys exchanged glances. Barbara knew what they were thinking: *This is better. This is action. This is excitement!* She was sure their crude clowning was just a way of releasing the tension. She grabbed her pack, "Come on!"

She led the way up to the hilltop. It was only fifty metres and was as she expected. There was a small grassy dip and the place was well hidden by trees. When she was sure they could not be seen from the road she dropped her gear and sat on her pack.

Then she did something she had never done before, saying, "Wendy, will you make me a coffee and heat a tin of something for me while I do some thinking?"

Wendy nodded. "Sure. But don't keep us in suspense. What did you see?" she replied.

"You tell them Gordon," Barbara answered while digging out her notebook and pencil.

For the first time she fully understood why an army platoon commander needed an orderly to do the minor housekeeping. While Gordon described what they had discovered she drew a sketch of the 'Yards' and their surrounding area. Then she made an enlargement of what she had been able to determine of the layout of the yards themselves. She also drew a field sketch as she remembered seeing the place from the third creek.

Gordon leaned over to study the sketch. He pointed, "There was a fence running down here towards the main road."

"Are you sure?" Barbara asked.

"Positive. Three-strand, barbed-wire cattle fence."

"I didn't notice it. I must have been concentrating on the people," Barbara replied. She added the fence to the sketch and to the map.

Wendy looked up from stirring her cooking. "Are you sure it was Fiona you saw?"

"No I'm not. It looked like her but she was a fair distance away," Barbara replied.

Dan stood up, an opened can in his hand. "I'll take over from Lofty so he can cook before it gets dark," he said.

Barbara looked up and noticed that the sun had already sunk below the hills to the west. Twilight was setting in and there was a distinct chill in the air. The flames from the hexamine stoves glowed brightly in the gathering gloom. She bit her lip in anxiety and tried to work out a sensible plan of action, very aware that minutes were slipping rapidly by. It took a conscious effort of willpower to stop herself biting her nails.

What to do? she thought, feeling a rising sense of panic and dread. *Don't let fear make you indecisive,* she told herself. *Use your training. Treat it like a military problem. Do an "Appreciation". Now, that is better. You can think logically,* she told herself. Then she deliberately paused to calm herself.

First, remember what Capt Conkey is always saying, "What is the Aim?".... To rescue Fiona. Or is it to rescue Roger and Jennifer? okay, it is "To rescue my friends." Now, Limitations. Is there a time restriction?

Reasoning thus she sat and puzzled away at the problem solving. The others talked quietly but did not disturb her. Wendy passed her a mess tin of Spaghetti and Meatballs and she spooned it down and barely noticed. The cup of coffee she appreciated more.

"Aah! I needed that. Thanks Wendy. Could I have another please?"

Lofty limped up to join them and started cooking. Gordon explained the situation to him. The only part of the conversation which Barbara registered was Lofty asking, "So it might be Fiona?" The quiet desperation in Lofty's voice made her shiver with emotion.

Darkness set in by 6pm. Gordon interrupted her. "Will I go and take over from Dan?"

Barbara shook her head. "No. If a car comes you wouldn't be able to tell if they were friend or foe until too late. Ask Dan to come back up here. If the police arrive, we will just have to follow and hope. But somehow I don't think that Roger and Jennifer managed to contact them before they were caught."

Gordon made his way down slope and returned a few minutes later with Dan. They all sat in a circle in the darkness. Barbara pulled out her field jacket and put it on.

"Well," Lofty asked. "What is the plan?"

"We rescue them," Barbara stated flatly.

There were a few moments of silence. Dan spoke first, "Do you think that is a good idea? Don't you think we should wait for the police?"

"I don't believe that the police know," Barbara replied. "And yes, it is risky. Those men are armed and I am sure they will shoot if they get the chance."

"This is stupid!" Karen burst out. "They have guns and we haven't. Someone could get killed."

"I am very aware of that," Barbara replied, restraining her emotions with an effort. "That is what is chewing me up inside. But I keep asking myself what might be happening to Roger and Jennifer? What do you think the Smileys will do to them?"

"Try to make them talk," Lofty replied.

There was an uneasy silence for a moment. Barbara could not see their faces in the dark and was glad, especially when Wendy sobbed, "Torture! Oh poor Roger!"

"And Jennifer," Lofty added.

Barbara agreed. "That is probably what is being done to them at this very moment. If those Smileys were raided by the police earlier in the day, and now they find two people sneaking around in their land, they are liable to be very worried and are likely to be very rough."

"But can't we go to contact the police?" Karen asked.

Barbara thought she detected an edge of hysteria in her voice. She replied, "Yes, we can. That is part of my plan."

"What is your plan?" Gordon asked quietly.

Barbara spread her map on the ground and placed her notebook on it, then shone her pencil torch down on them, holding it low to the ground to hide the glow.

"I propose that we split into two groups. Two volunteers will try to contact the police. The remainder will move closer to the Yards, to the third creek near where the gravel road crosses it. We will do another recon and wait. If the police haven't arrived by midnight, we mount a rescue mission."

"Barbara that is crazy! How can we hope to take on four armed men?" Karen cried.

Both Lofty and Dan chuckled. "You'd be surprised," Lofty said. "We've faced these sorts of mongrels before!"

Dan agreed, "There won't be four. They have to sleep some time and I'll bet there won't be more than one or two awake."

Barbara added, "And, if they've been there any length of time, like a week or more, they will be bored and slack."

"But they will know we are around!" Karen cried. "Roger or Jennifer will talk, especially if they are tortured. These men will be expecting us! We will walk into a trap! Oh! This is awful!" She began sobbing.

"Don't you believe it!" Wendy retorted. "Roger won't talk. And I don't think Jennifer will either."

"So, who goes back to get the police?" Gordon asked.

"Two people who are fit and are good navigators," Barbara replied. "We don't know what went wrong for Roger and Jennifer, why they got caught, so we need a quite different tactic."

"The fisherman!" interjected Wendy.

"Maybe, or a gate guard," Barbara went on. "So, whoever goes back must go a completely different way. They must go cross-country in the dark on a compass bearing, not follow any roads or tracks this side of the river. They must swim the river in the dark and make their way in the opposite direction, not to Silky Oak or the Blackwater but to Koah."

"How far is that?" Lofty asked.

"Five or six kilometres, that is once you reach the railway. Probably be nine or ten all up," Barbara answered.

"Hmmm. Two Ks per hour at the very best in this stuff," Dan said. "And it will be slower going down these hills in the dark. Then maybe an hour to get through that belt of jungle along the riverbank and across the river. Then two or three 'Ks' per hour along the railway. That makes it five or six hours minimum just to reach Koah."

Lofty agreed. "That's right. And then it will take an hour or two for the cops to react. Midnight is too soon. The earliest possible time will be about 0200."

"Okay. 0200," Barbara agreed.

"So who goes?" Gordon asked again.

"I'll go," Lofty offered.

"No," Barbara decided. "Not with your sore leg. It took you hours to get here and that was along a track."

"I could go," Gordon offered. He did not sound very keen.

"No," Dan said. "This is a job for a local. I've been to Koah. Karen, you come with me."

"Okay," Karen agreed. Barbara was relieved at that. She did not think Karen would be much good on the night raid and she wanted Gordon with her. She said, "Will you be alright Dan?"

"Ma'am!" Dan replied indignantly. "I'm your platoon sergeant. I can navigate. Have you no faith!"

"Sorry," Barbara replied with a soft laugh.

They settled to discussing the details. Lofty asked, "What is this place?"

"Blacksnake Valley. North of Silky Oak," Barbara replied.

"How come these Smileys are here? We didn't know they owned it," Wendy asked.

"I suppose it's not listed in their name," Dan replied. "It is probably owned by some individual who is a member."

"Enough talk. Time to move," Barbara said.

"We will leave our packs here, but I am going to change into my uniform," Dan said.

"Good idea. We all should," Barbara agreed. "It just might bluff these characters."

They pulled out the camouflage cadet uniforms and changed in the darkness. The other clothes were re-packed then webbing and packs were hoisted on. Barbara still felt deep anxiety, but this was being overlain by growing excitement. She led the way back down to the gravel road.

Once on the road they wished Dan and Karen good luck and the two groups went different ways. Barbara walked along the verge of the road with Gordon close behind. Wendy and Lofty followed. Barbara followed the road until she reached the open area. There she detoured left, away from the road for about fifty paces, then turned and walked slowly parallel to it.

The bulldozed land was uneven and the numerous small ditches ploughed around the slope made them go very slowly. Even so there

247

was a lot of stumbling and muttering. Lofty let out an occasional soft groan but managed to keep up. It was a cold night. The sky was cloudless and looked inky black, studded with millions of stars. Apart from a faint breeze and the muffled thud of their boots in the dust there wasn't a sound. Not a single light was visible anywhere. Barbara had the awful feeling that they were a very long way from any help.

In silence they crossed the first creek and went up over the next open ridge. As they crested the rise a single bright light appeared ahead.

"That's their camp," Gordon murmured.

Keeping the light in view they went down a long, undulating slope to the second dry creek. Here Barbara turned right and followed the dark fringe of the trees along until she could see the faint gleam of the gravel road ahead. Once she was sure of her location she turned left and crossed the creek, then led them across the triangle formed by the road and two creeks to the third creek.

Here Barbara halted them. The light could just be seen through the trees. It was about two hundred metres away. When she was down in the shallow ditch that was the bed of the dry creek she stopped.

"We will wait here. We can lie down and get some sleep," she explained. "But we will keep a sentry. One hour on each. We will lie side by side in a line. That way you can just wake the next person in the line when it is their turn. No noise. No lights or walking about. If anything happens then wake everyone up. We will all get up and get ready at 0200. Meanwhile I am just going on a bit of a recce."

"Not on your own," hissed Gordon.

"Okay,"

"You be bloody careful," Lofty warned.

They quietly took off their packs and webbing and lowered them to the ground. Barbara and Gordon then made preparations, mainly by applying some camouflage cream to darken their faces and hands.

"One hour," Barbara whispered. She led Gordon quietly to the edge of the third creek and crossed it, 'ghost walking' as she had been trained.

She stayed upright and walked slowly up the hill directly towards the light. Every ten paces she stopped and crouched down to listen. She detected a murmur of voices from the yards area but no other sound.

Ten minutes of careful movement brought them to within fifty paces of the light. Barbara began edging closer, but Gordon seized her arm.

"The cattle fence," he whispered.

Barbara berated herself for forgetting. She had almost walked into it. *That's all we need!* she thought. *Stumblebum me making the wires go twang!*

She lay down in the dust and short stubble and peered at the light. It was a pressure lantern on a table under the right-hand shelter. Two men sat either side talking. They were the men she had seen that afternoon down near the river. Boxes and stretchers nearby indicated they slept there. A rifle was visible leaning against one of the corner posts.

A second shelter roof closer to them had a pile of darker shapes under it. A dull, red glow in the interior indicated a stove or fireplace.

That is the cookhouse, she decided. Beyond it to the left was the black pattern of the cattle yards with its thick, horizontal timber railings. Barbara rose and slowly ghosted to her left. *There are four men,* she reasoned. *At least one must be a sentry on guard to watch the slaves. So where is he? And where are the slaves?*

She kept moving slowly left until she could see the back of the cattle yards. A bare, sandy area about twenty metres across extended from there to the clump of trees beyond. Several fuel drums littered the area.

Still no sign of a guard, or of the fourth man. Barbara continued carefully on, ghosting around in a hundred metre circle to the trees at the rear. With her heart in her mouth she moved cautiously through them, several times crunching dead leaves or twigs as she did. Gordon followed a few paces behind. From within the trees she subjected the rear of the yards to a lengthy scrutiny.

There was no sign of a guard, so Barbara went on circling to her left, out of the trees, across a sandy vehicle track which led west, and out on her hands and knees onto the bare, open slope again. From here she could see the far side of the yards. As she crawled slowly along, she was very aware of being frightened. But she was also very confident that she had the training and experience from cadets to do the job.

At last a movement caught her eye. She froze and lowered herself onto the dusty soil, her heart beating fast. The man was walking along some sort of walkway on top of the railings. He shone a torch briefly down inside the yards. This made Barbara flatten herself into a furrow. The torchlight did not help to sort out the pattern of the interior of the yards, but it did indicate where at least some of the slaves were.

The guard moved back and sat on the cap of a thick corner post near the loading ramp. A Land Cruiser was parked there. Barbara stared at it in the starlight.

Only one vehicle? Where is the other? The one with the cages on? she wondered.

For about twenty minutes Barbara lay and watched. Gordon lay quietly nearby and made no comment. Then she then began crawling slowly down the slope away from the guard. She was worried because she hadn't been able to locate the fourth man. She tried to puzzle it out.

Was he driving the other vehicle? Where has he gone? Are Roger and Jennifer with him or at the yards?

When she was a hundred metres from the yards and sure she could not be seen against the black backdrop of a line of trees in a creek line to the north Barbara stood up. Gordon did likewise.

"Where to now?" he whispered.

"Back to the others," Barbara replied. She walked east close beside the line of trees until she saw the gravel road, then turned right and walked parallel to it. This led her across the entrance track to the yards.

"Don't leave any boot prints," she whispered to Gordon.

They crossed carefully and walked on to the third creek, reaching it just near where the cattle fence apparently ended.

Chapter 26

MOONRISE

"You've done this sort of thing before," Gordon whispered as they reached the trees along the creek line.

"A few times," Barbara replied with a smile. "After all, I am the commander of the senior rifle platoon in our unit. On most weekend bivouacs we act as the opposing force for the 'First Years'."

"I wish we did more field work like that. We do too much drill and classroom stuff," Gordon grumbled.

The pair pushed their way quietly through a thicket of young sheoaks then slid down into the dry creek bed and re-joined Lofty and Wendy. They were still awake, sitting on their sleeping bags.

"One of you should be asleep," Barbara scolded.

"Fair go!" Lofty replied. "We couldn't sleep while you were out there. Anyway, it's only 9:30. Bit early for bed."

"What did you see?" Wendy asked.

They crowded together and Barbara gave a whispered description of the reconnaissance. Wendy asked, "So Roger and Jennifer may not be there?"

"That's right."

"Where could they be?" Wendy wondered.

"At the Smiley's commune," Barbara replied. "Or perhaps near it. This road goes through to connect with the Black Mountain Road north of the commune."

"Weren't the police going to raid the commune today?" Lofty asked.

"Yes, they were. But I suspect these Smiley buggers might have more hidey-holes like this one," Barbara said.

"What will we do now?" Wendy asked.

"Carry on with our plan. If the police don't arrive then we raid this place sometime after midnight. If our friends aren't there we will rethink the plan," Barbara answered.

Lofty shook his head. "I don't like it. How will we raid the place without anyone getting hurt?" Lofty asked.

251

Barbara clenched her teeth for a moment. She was determined to try to rescue Fiona. She said, "I've got an idea. I need to think it out. You lot go to sleep and I will be on sentry first."

The others agreed to this. By 10pm the others were settled into their sleeping bags: Gordon next to Barbara (Wendy made sure of that), then Wendy, with Lofty on the other end. Barbara sat and pondered the problem of attacking the Yards. She was deeply conscious of the moral responsibility. She did not want any of her friends hurt, or killed (she admitted the possibility), nor any of the slaves. Nor did she want her friends in trouble with the police.

If we take the law into our own hands we could end up in jail, she thought.

That made her hope that the police would arrive, and she strained her ears for the sound of approaching vehicles. Every minute or two her eyes scanned the darkness to the south, hoping to see the glow of approaching cars. She also turned her mobile phone on to test it but with no luck.

After more than an hour of solid reasoning she evolved what she thought was a workable plan which did not include too much risk. By then it was close to midnight and the air temperature had plummeted to what felt like freezing point.

Having decided what to do Barbara felt very excited and impatient. She knelt over Gordon to wake him. On an impulse she bent down and kissed him. He stirred and for a moment did not know what was happening.

"Hmmm. Mmm. Uh! Ugh! What?" he muttered.

Barbara put her lips on his and kissed him again. She could just see his eyes blink in the starlight. She sighed softly then murmured, "Mmm! You feel lovely and warm."

"You feel lovely but cold," Gordon whispered.

"Warm me up," Barbara replied.

"I thought I was dreaming," Gordon said. "Now I know I am!"

He partly unzipped his sleeping bag to get his arms out then drew Barbara down on top of him. He kissed her long and passionately then nuzzled her ear.

"Stop that," she giggled. She pressed her cold nose against his neck. Gordon gave a low yelp.

"Sssh!" Barbara whispered.

"That's right," Wendy said. "We are trying to sleep."

Lofty chuckled softly. "And one of you is supposed to be on sentry," he added.

Barbara smiled and snuggled down, her cheek against Gordon's. Lofty grunted and changed position.

"Aaargh!" he cried in muffled pain.

"What's wrong?" Wendy whispered anxiously.

"Cramp," Lofty replied in a stifled gasp.

"Is it your injured leg?" Wendy asked.

"Yes."

Barbara looked at Wendy. "Massage it for him, Wendy," she suggested.

"Would you like that, Lofty?" Wendy asked.

"Mmm. Aargh! Yes, alright," Lofty replied a little doubtfully.

Wendy got to her knees. Lofty wriggled out of his sleeping bag with more muffled groans.

"Sssh! Don't forget the Smileys," Wendy hissed.

Barbara knew she should not be listening, but she was curious. She knew that Wendy and Lofty had been friends for years, and off and on had been boyfriend and girlfriend so they knew each other well.

And there had often been suspicions and rumours in Cadets that they have been a bit more than that, she reminisced.

She gave Gordon another long kiss and stroked his neck and face. He did the same to her and pulled her down for another passionate kiss. In the midst of her own rising excitement Barbara was aware of Lofty saying softly, "Wendy! What are you doing?" but it was several minutes before she could tactfully free herself from Gordon's embrace so as to peek. She ascertained that Wendy was massaging his left thigh.

"Ooo! Aargh! Oh! That's nice! Ooo! Ouch!" Lofty murmured.

"Roll on your back," Wendy instructed.

Lofty did so, but with a groan of pain. Wendy resumed the leg massage. Barbara became aware that Gordon was looking at her.

"You shouldn't be watching," he whispered.

"Poo to you!" Barbara replied with a giggle. "You just get on with being the sentry."

In reply Gordon kissed her again. It was delicious, Barbara decided. *I feel warm now,* she thought.

253

Lofty moaned again, "Aaaah! Ow! Strewth my leg is stiff."

There was a muffled movement and Barbara was surprised and delighted to see that Lofty had put his arms around Wendy and was kissing her.

"Stop looking at them," Gordon said. "Don't forget I'm here."

He kissed Barbara again. She responded but kept one eye on what Wendy and Lofty were doing.

For the next few minutes they kissed and stroked each other. Midnight came and went. Barbara noticed that Wendy and Lofty seemed to have merged into one shapeless bundle which moved from time to time and which emitted occasional whispers and murmurs.

They are only petting, she decided. *Otherwise there would be more movement. I'll bet Wendy is as happy as can be.* Then another thought struck Barbara. *Oh dear! Poor Fiona! Oh, and poor Roger!*

She sighed and lay back, suddenly troubled. Why was life so complicated? Gordon continued to kiss and stroke her but, although she enjoyed it, she had lost interest and was not aroused.

"Bedtime," she said. "I'm tired. Your turn on sentry. Wake Wendy in an hour," she told him.

"If she's asleep," Gordon chuckled.

He released her and sat up. Barbara snuggled down into her sleeping bag, her mind and body both in a whirl.

Surprisingly she was asleep within minutes, deep and sound. Wendy roused her. "Hmm! Wh...What is it?" Barbara asked, awake at once.

"It is two o'clock," Wendy whispered.

"Oh good! Thanks," Barbara answered. She sat up and looked around in the darkness. "Did you get any sleep?"

Wendy giggled softly. "No, but I didn't mind."

Barbara patted her arm and was glad for her. Carefully she stood up and stretched herself. She had slept fully dressed, boots and all. The air was very cold, and she shivered as she flexed her arm muscles. As she did, she looked carefully in all directions.

What is that glow? she wondered idly, staring at the black silhouette of the jungle clad mountain to the east. *Is it the loom of the lights of Cairns? No. Wrong direction. Heavens! It is the moon!*

When making her plan she hadn't considered the moon. For an instant she mentally scourged herself for being so negligent.

Capt Conkey always includes "Phase of the moon" and "Time of moonrise or moonset" in his orders for every night exercise we do at cadets. How could I be so stupid as to forget it! It will be nearly a full moon and will light the place up like day. That could ruin everything!

For a few seconds she considered what to do. Then she knew and she bent down to grab at sleeping bags.

"Get up quickly! And no noise," she hissed urgently, shaking Gordon and Lofty. She knelt and rolled up her bedding and was ready to march by the time the others were awake and sitting up. "Pack up fast," she urged. "The moon will rise soon."

With some grumbles the others did as they were told. While they did this Barbara had a drink, the icy water making her shiver. In a couple of minutes all sat on their packs with their webbing beside them.

"Have the police arrived?" Lofty asked, more as a statement than a question.

"No," Barbara replied.

"Are you proposing we go ahead with this attack?" Gordon asked.

"Yes."

"We could wait until just before daylight," Gordon suggested.

"No. Once the moon is up it will be very difficult to approach those yards without being seen," Barbara replied. Her mind was made up.

"What is the plan?" Lofty asked.

"Very simple," Barbara explained. "We move along this creek to the end of the cattle fence, drop our packs, then form up in extended line and just walk quietly up the slope to the shelters where the men are sleeping. We pick up their guns and use them to disarm the sentry."

Lofty shook his head. "But what if the sentry sees us?"

That was Barbara's main concern, but she replied, "I doubt if he will. He will be watching the slaves and we will keep the cattle yards and buildings between us and him as long as we can."

"I still don't like it. Someone could get shot," Lofty said.

Barbara shrugged. "You don't have to come. But I am going."

"I will come," Lofty replied.

"What if the sentry won't do what you say?" Gordon asked in a worried tone.

"Then I will shoot him," Barbara replied.

Gordon gasped. "You don't mean that!" he said in dismay.

255

"I do. I've shot a man before," Barbara replied grimly, her mind swirling with terrible images of when she had fired at Lenny the Pig Hunter the previous year.

Lofty said, "Only in the leg."

"So? I'll do it again. I don't plan to kill anyone," Barbara replied.

Gordon shook his head. "But you could go to jail. It could ruin your whole life," he said, his voice pleading.

"I don't care. I am going to save Fiona," Barbara replied. She then detailed tasks for each, talking quickly, her eye on the increasing glow behind the mountain. As soon as she finished, she hissed, "Grab your packs. Let's go."

They hoisted on their gear and followed her. Lofty moaned softly as his bruised muscles came into use and he quickly fell behind. Wendy stayed with him, and Barbara slowed down. It took Lofty an obvious effort to climb out of the small dry creek and he hobbled as he walked along the bank.

When they reached the end of the barbed wire fence Barbara swung off her pack and placed it down. The others did likewise.

"Take out your torches," she ordered.

To her relief they obeyed, and she motioned them to form in extended line. They did so: Lofty on the right, then Barbara, Gordon and Wendy. They spaced out to a ten-pace interval. As they did, Barbara glanced to her right. The rim of the rising moon was just peeking over the mountain top. To her worried mind there already appeared to be an appreciable increase in visibility.

Fearing she had left it too late, Barbara signalled 'advance'. The cadets started walking quickly up the long, open slope, stumbling occasionally on clods and in furrows. Barbara noticed that Lofty was limping badly, but he gamely kept up.

Ahead, all was in darkness. The whole world seemed silent and deserted except for them. Barbara was gripped by intense excitement. She marched up the slope at a normal walking pace with no attempt at concealment. The soft soil muffled their footsteps and to her mind they appeared like a line of ghosts.

The friends drew rapidly closer to the black jumble of shelter sheds, yards and trees. Barbara was able to distinguish the vehicle parked near the loading ramp to her right. Her eyes searched earnestly for some sign of the sentry, but she could not detect him. The shelter where the men were sleeping was directly in front of her.

Without pausing she walked into it and her questing eyes found what she sought, the rifle. It was still leaning against the corner post. In an instant she had picked it up.

Bolt action .308, she told herself. *Safety catch is on.* She clicked it off and brought the weapon to her hip ready to use. *I wonder if it is loaded?* she worried. With her right hand she felt the back of the bolt then nodded. *Yes. It is cocked. Now, there must be more guns. Yes, Lofty has found one.*

Lofty picked up a pump-action shotgun. Barbara looked to her left. Gordon had stopped against a corner post. Wendy was just visible in the cook house.

How many men are there? Barbara thought. She peered around, thankful now for a beam of moonlight shafting in. *Four stretchers. Only two with people in them. So, are there two guards or only one?*

She signalled to Gordon. He moved to her. She bent close to his ear and whispered, "Watch these two. If they try to get up bluff them that you are armed. Lofty and I will deal with the sentries."

"Be careful," Gordon said, intense worry evident in his hoarse voice.

Barbara didn't answer. In her own mind it was the guards who were in trouble. She walked over to Lofty and whispered quick instructions, then led the way to the right and out of the shelter. She walked the ten paces to the corner of the yards where the loading ramp was and peeked around. The vehicle was there. And so was her quarry. The sentry was seated on top of the fence post with his back to them. He was just visible as a silhouette against the stars.

Barbara nudged Lofty and he nodded and aimed the shotgun. Barbara had a more careful look. *Where is the fourth Smiley?* she worried. Then she shrugged. *If he is on guard logic says he should be over at the other side of the yards. We can deal with him in a minute.*

Having decided that, she raised the rifle to her shoulder and walked five paces out, away from the railings. As she did, she called out quietly but distinctly, "Hands up! We have got you covered. One false move and you are dead."

The sentry up on the fence jerked his head around. Barbara saw his eyes widen in disbelief. She also saw he had a gun resting across his lap.

"Hands up I said!" Barbara snapped. "There is a shotgun pointing at you as well."

Lofty spoke then, "You'd better believe that, buster. Now get your hands up!"

The man reluctantly did as he was told. Barbara felt a wave of relief, looked quickly around in case the fourth man had appeared, then said, "Okay. Use one hand to lower the gun. Hold it by the barrel and drop it to the ground. Do it slowly. Move!"

The man did so. The rifle fell with a thud in the grass and dust at the bottom of the fence.

"Good. Now climb down," she ordered.

The man rose, walked to a ladder and climbed slowly down. Barbara stepped back, keeping well clear of the man. She motioned with the rifle barrel. "Now, turn around, spread your legs and lean forward till your hands are on the ground. Lofty, you search. I will cover him."

She moved to one side and aimed at the man's head. Once she had his attention she snarled softly, with hard certainty in her tone, "No tricks mister because I will shoot if I have to, depend on it."

The man eyed her nervously and did as he was told. Lofty came up behind him and searched him as they had been taught to do in cadets, one boot between the man's legs and with his instep hooked around the other man's foot, ready to knock him flat in an instant. Barbara fretted that the fourth man might catch them in the act, but she could not afford to take her eyes off the man.

After patting the man down, Lofty stepped back. Barbara stayed well away from him and ordered, "Now lie down on your stomach."

The man did so. Barbara kept him covered while Lofty tied his hands behind his back with nylon cord. He then lashed the man's ankles together.

As Lofty stood up, Barbara gave a sigh of relief. "Get the gun Lofty and give it to Gordon, then cover those two Smileys who are asleep."

She then knelt facing the man. He arched his back to look at her, fear showing plainly on his face in the moonlight.

"Where is the fourth man?" she asked.

"Gone. Not here," the man replied. "Who are you?"

Barbara ignored the question. She left him lying in the dust and strode into the shelter. The moon was now fully up she noted.

"Lofty, cover this one. Gordon, that one. Wendy, watch the bloke out on the track," she ordered.

She pulled out her torch and shone it on the sleeping man. With her boot she spurned him awake. He looked up, goggling stupidly in the beam of light. It was the middle-aged man she had seen on the riverbank.

"Wake up! Get up! Put your hands up! You are under arrest!" she snapped.

259

Chapter 27

A HORRIFIC TALE

The man struggled out of his sleeping bag in fuddled disbelief. He wore only a dirty singlet and baggy, soiled underpants. Barbara wrinkled her nose in disgust.

"Lie down!" she ordered. "Tie him up Lofty."

She turned to the second man, recognizing him as the man who had driven the Land Cruiser with the pump on it. He was thin, appeared to be in his twenties, had black hair and wore only a pair of jeans. He blinked in the torchlight and for a moment Barbara feared he was going to resist. With obvious reluctance he also lay face down in the dust.

Wendy was called over to tie him up. Barbara covered the man while she did. When both men were securely trussed Barbara ordered them to be hoisted against a post.

"And drag that other Smiley in here as well," she instructed.

Lofty and Gordon moved to obey. While they did Barbara shone her torch around to check that there was no-one else. She noted that on the table stood a pressure lantern, glasses, empty beer bottles, 'girlie' magazines, a dirty plate, some cards, a set of keys, and a 'Base Station' type Radio.

As Lofty and Gordon dumped the third Smiley beside the others, Barbara said, "Lofty, go and find the prisoners. Gordon, light that lantern."

Lofty and Wendy both went into the darkness with their torches. Gordon turned his attention to the lantern.

The middle-aged Smiley shouted at her as the lantern was lit, "Who the bloody hell are you? What's going on?"

"Shut up! I'll ask the questions," Barbara snapped.

Wendy came running back. "We've found them. The slaves are in two sheds in there, men in one and women in the other but they are locked in and chained together. We need keys."

"Try those," Barbara said, pointing at a set of keys on the table. "Then bring the slaves out here and sit them over near the kitchen."

Wendy scooped up the keys and ran off. Gordon pumped at the

pressure lamp and it began to hiss and glow brightly. Using its light Barbara began a more systematic search. She emptied shirt and trouser pockets, laying the items out on the stretchers. Both men protested vigorously but she ignored them.

As she found documents and credit cards, Barbara noted the details in her notebook and placed the items on the table which she cleared of its rubbish, leaving only the lantern and radio. Several orange Smiley badges which were pinned to the shirts were added to the other items. A small booklet of pages stapled together caught her eye. She leafed through it and saw that it was some sort of code book: groupings of three letters with meanings next to them. She studied it more carefully and saw that it was similar to the codes that her cadet unit used on exercises. It was added to the pile.

At that moment, Wendy came back leading the freed slaves.

"Fiona's not here," she called. "Nor are Roger or Jennifer."

"What about the blonde girl I saw?" Barbara asked, aware of sharp disappointment.

"Not her," Wendy replied.

"Keep them out of here," Barbara called. "Get that fire going and sit them near that Wendy," she added, aware how cold it was, the chill breeze bringing tears to her eyes.

The captured Smileys obviously thought so too as the black-haired man called, "Can we get dressed? It's bloody cold."

Barbara had been looking at the slaves and saw that most were clutching tattered rags around themselves and were shivering. She turned to the man and looked at him with disdain.

"No. Gordon, guard them while we look after these people," she said. She took off her hat and rubbed her eyes.

The man who had been the sentry spoke to the other Smileys, "That's her. She's that red-headed bitch Mr Smiley told us to watch out for."

"Shut up, Wart," the middle-aged man ordered.

Lofty jeered. "'Wart' eh? Good name. I would have called you 'Fart' myself," he called.

The man scowled but did not reply. Barbara walked over to the middle-aged man.

"Where are the two people you captured this afternoon? A boy and a girl our age."

The man made no answer, but a glint of malice showed in his eye. For a fleeting second Barbara was tempted to kick the man. With an effort of will she restrained herself.

That would be wrong, morally wrong as well as illegal, she told herself. She turned to the other two prisoners and put the same question to them but they did not respond either.

Leaving Gordon to guard the prisoners, Barbara walked over to the cookhouse. Wendy had lit a hurricane lantern and Lofty was fanning the fire into life. The slaves sat in two huddled rows. She counted them. There were 22, 12 women and 10 men. All were dressed in rags and looked dirty, bewildered and frightened. They clutched filthy blankets around themselves to cover their nakedness and for warmth.

Barbara faced them. "You are safe now. We have rescued you."

"Who are you? Are you the army?" a man asked.

"No, army cadets," Barbara replied.

"Cadets!" several voices cried in disbelief. A babble of talk broke out.

"Quiet!" Barbara thundered, in the voice she used to use when she was the Company Sergeant Major. "One person only talk. Tell us what is going on here."

A thin-faced, elderly looking man answered, "We are being used as slave labour, held against our will."

As he spoke Barbara saw the blonde girl. *No, not Fiona,* she thought sadly. She asked, "Why?"

"We are planting crops. Food some of it, but drugs mostly," the man replied.

Drugs, that figures, Barbara thought. "Are you people Smileys or were you just kidnapped?"

There was an outburst of bitter laughter and talking. Barbara looked at the pinched and dirty faces which the leaping flames illuminated.

The same man answered, "We used to be followers of the Grand Oojoombie, God rot his evil soul!"

"If he even exists!" cried another.

The man went on, "There are 'Smileys' and there are the 'Happy People'. We are the 'Happy People'."

Barbara shivered at the harsh irony in his voice. She asked, "Who are you? What is your story?"

"My name is Barnaby Biddle," the man replied. He went on to recount how he came to be there. "I'm a punter, from Bundambah. That's in Brisbane. Race horses, you know! Anyway, about a year and a half ago I had a big win. Suddenly I had lots of friends. One of them was a character named the Reverend Simon Ditchburn."

Barbara nodded. "I have met the good 'Reverend'," she said. "Go on."

"Well, he converted me to the 'One true religion'. Once I was 'saved' I willingly gave money to the Smiley People. Then I was persuaded to come to the commune of Joy. Some joy! They put pressure on me to sign over all my money. When they found out it was nearly all gone, they did this to me. Made me a slave!" He shook the chain in anger.

Barbara saw that he was thin from starvation and his skin was covered with sores. "Have you been here for a year?"

"Not here. We've only been here a few weeks. I was in a group growing drugs in the jungle somewhere," Mr Biddle replied.

"Do you know where you are?" Lofty asked.

"No. Australia somewhere, I think. They told us we were on an island out in the middle of the Pacific, but we've seen things like kangaroos and kookaburras," Mr Biddle answered.

Barbara pointed to the blonde girl. "Who are you? What is your story?"

The girl stood up, gripping a filthy blanket around herself. "I am Helga Kristensen," she said in a distinct foreign accent. "I am der Svedish tourist. I from Stockholm kom. In Sveden, you know."

Barbara noted that she was a rather thin girl and not very attractive close up.

Helga continued with mounting emotion, "My friend Anna and I, ve ver kidnapped vone day. Anna zey took avay and I haf not her seen since. Zat vos six months ago. All zat time I haf been slave in dis group. Zese men," she gestured angrily towards the trussed Smileys. "Zey rape me and ze ozer women all ze time, venefer zey please. Zey make us do horrible things. Zey treat us like animals! Zey..." She broke down sobbing.

Another woman stood up and comforted the girl. Barbara was aghast. She quickly questioned more of the slaves: Bruce Brown, 19, from Sydney, recruited by the Rev. Pomfrey, Abigail Leslie, 24, from Mt

Isa, recruited by an American, Carter Brown, Keith Thrumm, a 26-year-old Canadian recruited by the Rev. Fergus McKenzie, Blundell Parry, 38, from Mississippi, USA, a 30 year old plumber from Lower Hutt in New Zealand, a 19 year old waitress from French New Caledonia, a 27-year-old accountant from England.

By the time Barbara had spoken to all of them, she was truly amazed at the size of the 'Smiley' organisation. She was also angered and outraged at the terrible things that had been done to these people.

"Why didn't you try to escape?" she asked.

"We did!" Mr Biddle cried passionately. "But they kept us chained up all the time and there were always guards watching, day and night. We've had no privacy at all, even when we went to the toilet, or when one of those scum was doing something to one of the women!"

A man named Calder took up the theme., "They told us that if we tried to escape they would hunt us down with dogs. They showed us the dogs. Big, savage mongrels: Dobermans and Pit-Bull Terriers. They threatened to torture and kill anyone who tried to get away. And, if we managed to get away, they said the voodoo would catch up with us and cause an agonising death. They also threatened to murder members of our families."

"Did you believe them?" Lofty asked.

"Did we believe them!" the man shouted in outrage. He shook with emotion, both fear and anger. "Of course we did! I've seen two people executed by those bastards there. A bloke named Dan Adcock, a brickie from Newcastle. He was whipped one day for answering back. He tried to strangle that Wart mongrel with the chain. Martin, that's the filth with the black hair, he just walked over and shot him." The man trembled violently and shut his eyes.

After a moment the man collected himself and went on, "They made us bury Dan in the jungle in an unmarked grave. The second case was a nice young bloke named Michael. He got free one day, ran off into the jungle. But they got him. Next afternoon they dragged his body in and hung it up all the next day as a warning to us all. They told us that they used a zombie to sniff him out."

Wendy gasped. "Zombie! I don't believe you."

"Nor did we," Mr Biddle replied bitterly. "But the Oojoombies are big on voodoo and they let us see a zombie once. He was chained up and looked and smelled horrible. The guards claimed he was better than a dog at following a scent."

Barbara felt the hair on the back of her neck prickle up and she shivered and tried to tell herself that there were no such things as zombies. She also saw that her friends were looking very anxious and scared.

"What else did they do?" she asked.

"They are just animals those three!" Biddle screamed, pointing accusingly. "They whipped us, starved us, kicked us, and worse. And what they did to these poor girls beggars the mind. They used to force them to have sex whenever the mood took them, with the poor girl chained up in the gang and all of us there. They did it deliberately to humiliate us as well as for their own sadistic gratification."

Barbara shook her head, unwilling to believe people could be so revolting, so evil. Wendy looked appalled. Lofty clenched his teeth hard, a stony look on his face.

He's thinking of Fiona being raped, Barbara realised. *Poor Lofty! Poor Fiona! Oh my God! We must act. We must rescue them!* she thought.

Fuelled by a deep anger she turned to Mr Biddle. "Did a vehicle come here this afternoon with two prisoners in a cage on the back?"

"Yes, it did. A boy and a girl. Al Hunter was driving it. We didn't know what had happened. We were too far away to hear. At first we thought they were just more slaves arriving, but it quickly became obvious they weren't. The Smileys were real worried, and after a bit of a confab Hunter drove off that way." He gestured northwards.

Barbara nodded, "And you say there are other groups of slaves? Do you know where they are?"

"No, we don't. They keep the groups away from each other. Each gang is kept together, until we get sick and die. We've lost four that way."

He started to go into details, but Barbara stopped him. "Tell me about the other groups."

"We can't tell you much. We have only overheard the guards refer to them from time to time. There is a ration and supply truck driven by a bloke named 'Stretch' which comes around every few days."

An older woman, in her forties, interrupted, "What are you going to do with us?"

Barbara thought fast. "We are going to get you out of here to safety. Just wait a few minutes while we get organised. Stay here."

Barbara led Lofty and Wendy back to where Gordon watched the three captured guards. Now she viewed the three with a very different eye. The Smileys refused to answer any questions, so Barbara motioned her friends to follow. She led them out of earshot.

Standing out in the open away from the lantern light, she realised how bright the moon was, and how cold the air was.

She said, "I don't know why the police aren't here, but I don't want to wait. From what those slaves have said I am afraid that Roger and Jennifer are in terrible danger."

"What can we do?" Lofty asked.

"Try to find them."

"What about your promise?" Gordon asked.

"I think it has been overtaken by events. I'll apologise to Capt Conkey later," Barbara replied.

"So what do you propose we do?" Lofty asked.

"That we search this place thoroughly for any clues to where other Smileys or slaves might be. Then some of us take the slaves back to safety while the others go to look for Roger and Jennifer." Barbara said.

"Who goes back?" Wendy asked.

"Lofty," Barbara replied without hesitation.

"Why me?" Lofty asked.

"Because we must do a forced march and with your injured leg you couldn't do it."

Lofty conceded this reluctantly. He thought for a moment then pointed to the Land Cruiser and said, "I could drive you in that, then return to take the slaves back."

"You could," Barbara agreed. For a minute she reconsidered, then shook her head and said, "No. You take these people to safety first. Use the vehicle to ferry them at least part of the way. Get the police as quickly as possible and come to help us."

"What about these characters?" Lofty asked, indicating the three Smileys.

"We can't take prisoners with us," Barbara said. "So we will tie them up and hide them down in the creek there. That way, when their slimy mates come looking for them, they won't find them. We can come back with the police to get them later in the day."

Gordon met her eye. "So three of us are going to march on along

266

this road to look for Roger and Jennifer while Lofty takes these slaves to safety and gets the police?"

"Yes."

"I don't like it," Lofty replied.

Gordon nodded. "Nor do I," he added. "We are getting fewer and fewer. First, we sent off Roger and Jennifer and they got captured. Then we sent Dan and Karen and there is no sign of them. Now you are proposing to send Lofty off on his own."

"We can't send Wendy on her own. You can go if you prefer," Barbara replied. She felt mounting impatience. She wanted to move.

"What if Lofty walks into the same trouble that Roger and Jennifer did?" Gordon asked.

"He shouldn't, because now we know there is danger and he will be alert. He'll go a different way from the others, that's why," Barbara said.

"There is a gate," Lofty said. "The fisherman said so. If they guard the gate leading off the Black Mountain Road to the commune, then the odds are that they will guard this one. I will just avoid it."

"With twenty slaves?" Wendy put in anxiously, gripping Lofty's arm.

"Well what else do you suggest?" Barbara asked. She was getting irritated.

"Wait for the police," Gordon repeated.

Barbara shook her head. "What if they don't come? Or what if more Smileys turn up first? What do we do then, have a shootout?" she replied.

"Alright. Then we could all go back with the slaves and get them to safety, then return with the police," Gordon persisted.

Barbara rebelled at this. "No. That will waste too much time. Roger and Jennifer are in great danger. We must save them. I am going to find them."

Lofty shook his head, exasperation showing on his face. "Barbara don't be so stubborn!" he cried.

"I am not being stubborn! I am just determined."

"Stubborn!"

"Determined!"

Gordon stepped forward. "That will do!" he snapped.

"Yes," Barbara agreed. "I am going anyway. The only way you can stop me is to chain me up with those slaves. Now let's settle the details and get moving."

Chapter 28

SUNRISE ON MILDEW MOUNTAIN

"Timings," Barbara said. "It's about five or six kilometres back to Silky Oak. You could go that way, or you could go the same way that Dan and Karen went. That would be safer."

"I'll think about it," Lofty answered, studying the map intently in the light of the lantern. "Sssh! Don't let those Smiley mongrels overhear us." He jerked a thumb at the three guards. "With these slaves it will take at least five or six hours. Then I have to contact the cops."

Lofty looked at his watch. "Strewth! It's nearly four o'clock already. I wonder what the hell is keeping Dan and Karen?"

Barbara also did some sums. "It's about 24 or 25 kilometres from here to the commune. If we step it out, say 4 kilometres per hour consistently, and that's not even normal marching speed, we should get there by 10am, or by 11. Say midday to be on the safe side. It's a bit hard to tell as this road doesn't seem to be marked the whole way."

"It can't all be Smiley land surely?" Wendy asked as she studied the map.

Barbara frowned and then shook her head. "No, I don't think so. There is a lot of State Forest and I remember seeing plenty of private properties marked on the Land's Department map," she replied. "Now, Wendy, give all these slaves some food and a hot drink if you can, while we deal with these three. We will be twenty minutes or so. Lofty, find one of the chains the slaves were locked up on."

When Lofty returned with a long chain and a collection of padlocks Barbara told him to fasten them to the guards. Lofty did this in the same way that they had found the slaves, the chain looped around their waist so tight it could not be pulled down over the hips, then padlocked in place. Two metres further along the next Smiley was secured.

When this was done Barbara said to Gordon, "Okay, untie their legs."

When all were untied, she motioned for the Smileys to get up. The younger men looked at their leader who lay motionless and glared defiance.

268

"Fine! If you won't get up, we will drag you!" Barbara flared. She walked over and grabbed the end of the chain from a surprised Gordon and began hauling.

The older man cried out in pain and dismay. Barbara stopped dragging and snapped at him, "Okay, if you don't like it then co-operate. Get up and walk!"

Sullenly they did as they were told. Wart asked, "What are ya gunna do with us?"

"You'll see."

"Can we get dressed?" the older man asked. Barbara looked at him in disgust. He was shivering with cold. She saw that they all were. She replied, "No. You can have what the slaves had. Lofty, bring something to gag them with. Now walk!"

Barbara led the way out into the darkness, the end of the chain in her left hand and the rifle in her right. Gordon and Lofty followed. Some of the slaves called out in threatening tones but they made no attempt to interfere.

In her anger Barbara forgot the cattle fence. She saw a post just in time and swerved to follow the fence downhill. The three Smileys stumbled along behind, their obvious anxiety growing by the minute.

"What ya gunna do?" asked Black-hair. Barbara made no reply which increased his fear. He whined, "Don't shoot us!"

"Why not? You murdered people," Barbara replied. She could not remember a time when she had been so implacably angry.

"We can pay!" the older man pleaded.

"No. Give us information."

This got no answer. The man was obviously more frightened of the Smileys. At the end of the fence Barbara swung right and followed the third creek along to its junction with the second.

Here she halted and said, "Okay Gordon, padlock each end of the chain to a big, thick tree. Lofty, gag them all."

"Ya can't do that!" wailed Wart. "What ya gunna do to us?"

"Leave you here till the police can collect you," Barbara replied.

"But it's cold. And we need food and water," the older man cried.

"Tough! I couldn't give a bugger. It's more than you deserve," Barbara replied stonily.

Gordon finished fastening the chain to two trees. Lofty gagged the men. As soon as he was finished, Barbara turned on her heel and set off back to the yards. Lofty and Gordon followed. There was silence till they reached their packs.

"Barbara, they could be there for hours," Gordon protested.

"So what? Serves them right. We can't let them go."

"I know that. I was thinking of their hands being tied all that time. The circulation will be cut off. They could lose their hands from gangrene."

"But if their hands are untied, they can remove the gags and yell out if more Smileys come," Barbara replied.

"Barbara! Be reasonable," Gordon persisted.

They argued for several minutes. Barbara became distinctly peeved. In the end she snapped, "Oh well, if you must! Go and cut their hands loose. But leave the gun here so they can't grab it, and be quick."

Gordon hurried away. He returned a few minutes later. Lofty asked, "Do we take our packs?"

"Yes. You never know," Barbara replied.

She swung on her own pack, then picked up the rifle and Wendy's pack and set off up the slope to the yards.

When Barbara got there, she found slaves milling everywhere. "Sit down!" she shouted.

They resented it but obeyed. When they were silent, she told them that Lofty would be taking them to safety and that they should obey him.

"What if we don't agree?" a man called in a shrill voice.

"Then you can go to hell for all I care," Barbara flared. "If you don't like it, then make your own way to safety, but don't interfere with our plans, or get caught again."

Her uncompromising tone silenced them. She went on, "You can collect any personal gear if it is here."

That caused a derisive laugh from most of the slaves. Barbara nodded. "Okay Lofty, load them on and good luck."

While Lofty squeezed as many slaves as would fit onto the Land Cruiser Barbara had the others search the whole yards using the lanterns and their torches. Barbara collected all the ID items and placed them in a plastic bag in her webbing. Knowing from experience that she would be sweating as she marched, she took off her jacket and packed that as well.

Gordon found a box of .308 ammunition. "Twenty-five rounds," he said.

That reminded Barbara. She eased the bolt of the rifle open and checked. Yes, it was loaded. And there were five rounds in the magazine. She re-cocked the rifle and slid on the safety catch, then placed the box of bullets in her left basic pouch.

Gordon had a .22 automatic rifle. A search uncovered two boxes of ammunition for it. He pocketed them.

Lofty re-joined them. "Okay. I'm ready to go. See you at the commune at midday."

Wendy went over to him and placed her hands on his chest. "Take care," she said, looking anxiously up into his face. Lofty looked troubled, and a little embarrassed.

"I will," he answered.

He gave her a quick hug and kissed her forehead, then turned and climbed into the Land Cruiser. The vehicle was almost hidden by the dark mass of people clinging to it, some even sitting on its bonnet. Lofty started up and the vehicle set off slowly in first gear. Lofty did not turn on the headlights as there was sufficient starlight for him to see by.

The friends watched the vehicle and its straggle of walkers till it turned right on the gravel road. Then Barbara looked at her watch and said, "It's 4:30. Let's get moving. Gordon, put out the lanterns. Packs on!"

Within a minute they were striding down the slope. By then the sound of the Land Cruiser's engine had faded and only the chilling whisper of the wind in the trees disturbed the silence.

As they turned left onto the main gravel road, Wendy stared the other way and said, "I hope Lofty will be alright."

"He will be. He's no fool. Anyway, with a bit of luck he should meet the police coming the other way," Barbara replied.

She adjusted her gear and cradled the rifle across her basic pouches. She was relieved to be moving, to be up and doing. Now she felt driven by an urge to rush to the aid of her friends.

They walked three abreast along the road. Another dry creek was crossed. Gordon said, "Well, that was interesting. You certainly are full of surprises, Barbara."

"I told you that you might not like me once you got to know me," Barbara replied.

That caused an uncomfortable silence, which made Barbara

consider that maybe he was having a hard re-think about her. She didn't care. *There are more important things than romance at the moment,* she told herself.

Wendy spoke to relieve the strain, "At least it is warmer walking. I was freezing back there."

They trudged on, their boots crunching on the coarse sand and gravel. The road was easy to follow in the moonlight. It wound up and down gentle, rolling ridges, partly through open, cleared fields, and partly through savannah woodland.

"What do we do if a vehicle comes along?" Gordon asked.

"If it comes from the front we hide. If it comes from behind, we stop it," Barbara answered.

"What if they are Smileys?"

"We stick them up," replied Barbara grimly.

"Very risky!" Gordon said.

"You think the whole plan is, don't you?" Barbara asked.

Gordon nodded. "Yes. I think we should have all gone back to get the police," he replied.

"You didn't have to come. You can turn around if you want to," Barbara answered, vaguely aware that she was a bit disappointed in his reaction.

"I'm not a coward. I wouldn't leave you and Wendy. I care about you," he answered stiffly.

Only care? Barbara thought, then shrugged.

The exertion was causing perspiration under her armpits. She hoisted her pack to a more comfortable position. The friends settled into the rhythm of marching.

At each creek line Barbara halted and crouched down in the dip to use her carefully shielded torch to check the map. She ticked each creek with a pencil.

"Keep your eyes and ears open," she said. "We don't know what else is along this road and we don't want to blunder into trouble, like a guard at a gate."

An hour of solid marching went by.

"Daylight soon," Wendy said, indicating a paleness in the eastern sky beyond the mountain there.

The trio tramped up another long, open slope. A line of large trees

272

stood clear against the sky on the crest line. As they got closer Barbara cautioned the others to silence and slowed down. She peered into the gloom, then shifted the rifle ready to use.

Acting on an instinct, she waved them into extended line on the right of the road. They walked cautiously forward through open scrub until they reached the trees. Just beyond these were a barbed wire fence and another gravel road running at right angles to the one they had been following. This road went up a long ridgeline to their right. Barbara slid off her pack and rolled it under the fence, then followed. On the other side she looked cautiously around in the moonlight.

The gravel road they had been following went through a gate twenty metres to their left and continued on northwards. There was a sign on the gate and no hint of any guards so Barbara walked down to it. She noted that the gate was padlocked. The sign was on her side of the fence, and read:

O. J. PASTORAL Co
KEEP OUT
TRESPASSERS PROSECUTED

"Well, we are out, so they can't prosecute us now," she said. The idea made her smile.

Wendy peered at the sign. "So who owns this land?" she asked.

"Don't know. Private property possibly."

Barbara spread her map on the ground, and they crouched to study it by torchlight.

"We are here. This road going off to the Northeast isn't marked on the map, but it goes up this ridge. Then I reckon it must link up with this road in the State Forest," Barbara said.

"Do we follow it, or go straight on?" Wendy asked.

That was what Barbara had been worrying about. She studied the map and bit her lip, then said, "I think we should follow it. It goes across towards the commune. I think this other road will end at those mountains ahead of us. Let's have a look and see which way most of the traffic goes."

They walked over to the road junction. Barbara shone her torch on the road. Tyre tracks showed plainly in the dust.

"Definitely up the ridge," Barbara said. She looked that way, noted the increasing pink glow in the sky, and shivered as a cold breeze sprang up. "Come on, rub out our boot prints and let's keep walking. It's too cold to stop. We will have a break on top of the mountain."

Her watch read 05:50. That spurred her on. "We have come nearly five kilometres, which is good going," she said.

They swung on their packs and set off up the slope. This turned out to be much longer and steeper than Barbara had expected, and they were soon panting and perspiring. The sky seemed to get lighter by the minute and by the time they had climbed the first steep pinch everything was suffused with a peach-pink glow.

They slogged on upwards. The vegetation was all open eucalypt forest. A cattle grid on the next crest gave them pause. Barbara looked back, chest heaving. Sunlight was shining on the upper slopes of the mountain across the valley behind them. It looked very pretty.

"What a lovely morning!" she said, as Wendy puffed up to her.

Wendy grunted and stopped. "Be another hot day," she said, indicating the cloudless sky. She looked flushed and tired but managed to return Barbara's smile.

"Come on. Breakfast on top," Barbara urged. They trudged on. The road levelled out and followed the top of the ridge line. Out to their left they were treated to a magnificent vista of rolling hills, forest and distant mountains, all dominated by one massive, pyramid shaped peak clothed in jungle.

"What mountain is that?" Gordon asked, as Barbara consulted her map.

"Black Mountain, I think. It is off this map," she replied.

They went down slightly with a steep drop on the left and a patch of rainforest in the re-entrant on their right. The road then went up a pinch even steeper than the previous one. This went on for several hundred metres and really tested their heart and lungs. They passed a large gravel pit on the right and came out on a crestline bathed in sunlight.

"Stop here. This is the top," Barbara gasped.

She led them off the road amongst some trees and dropped her pack. From there she could see that the road wound down the other side of the mountain to vanish into a vast forest of dark pine trees. Beyond the pines loomed another large jungle-covered mountain. She studied the map.

"If we are here, then that is Mildew Mountain and the commune is on the other side of it," she said.

Wendy eyed Mildew Mountain with dismay, "Do we have to go over it?"

"No. The road goes around the northern end," Barbara replied.

"Why Mildew Mountain I wonder?" Gordon asked.

"Probably pretty wet," Barbara answered. "There's another further south called Rainy Mountain."

They dropped their gear and settled down to breakfast and their morning toilet. Barbara lit her hexamine stove and put a mess tin of water on to heat. She took out a muesli bar and began munching. All the while she was conscious that she was trembling slightly and wanted to get up and keep marching.

We have only come six or seven kilometres. That means we have about eighteen to go, she mused. Then another thought crossed her mind.

"How are you feeling Wendy?" she asked.

"Okay, why?"

"Because we just walked as far from the Yards to here as we did on the first day from Kamerunga to Wright's Lookout."

"Not as steep," Gordon observed.

"Just as high though. We climbed 250 metres to get to the top of this ridge," Barbara replied. She smiled with satisfaction, took another bite of her muesli bar and hummed while she chewed.

After coffee Barbara heated a can of 'Ham and Egg'. She idly watched Wendy take off her boots to check for blisters. Gordon peeled off his shirt and lathered his face using warm water from his mess tin. He began to shave. It was such an essentially masculine act that Barbara sat and watched in fascination.

He is handsome, she thought. *Good skin, firm muscles, and no fat.*

A sound attracted her attention. A vehicle engine! She swung her head around. *Coming from the Northeast.*

"A car. Put out the stoves. Hide the gear. Quick!" she cried.

As they moved hurriedly further into the trees and long grass the vehicle appeared out of the pine trees at the bottom of the hill and began winding its way up. A white 4WD Barbara noted from behind a tree. She saw it had a radio aerial on it.

Is it police? Or Forestry Department? she wondered.

275

The vehicle went out of sight behind a spur, re-appeared and went out of view again. The three friends crouched under cover. Barbara tensed ready to spring out and flag it down. The vehicle roared into view at the next bend and she glimpsed a round, red face.

Mr Smiley!

And he wasn't alone. A tanned, nuggety looking man in his thirties was driving and another man sat in the back. He was holding a rifle upright between his knees.

The friends lay flat in the grass as the vehicle growled over the crest in low gear. With a roar and grating of gears it raced on down the other side.

Gordon shook his head. "I don't like the look of that," he said.

Barbara bit her lip. "No. That was Mr Smiley himself. That is bad news. They will know something is wrong at the Yards within ten minutes," she replied.

"If they don't already know, or suspect," Gordon said grimly.

"How could they?" Wendy asked.

"That radio that was on the table. Maybe they called and got no answer, or maybe the guards had to make routine calls," Gordon suggested.

"Oh dear!" Wendy said as she pulled on a boot. "I hope Lofty doesn't meet them."

"He should be well clear by now," Barbara answered. "Let's get packed and move."

Chapter 29

A TEST OF CHARACTER

The three cadets hurriedly completed their breakfast and packed. Barbara stuffed her cooking gear away and hauled on her webbing.

"Let's get moving," she urged.

"Hang on!" Gordon protested. "I need a nature call first!"

"Me too," Wendy agreed.

Barbara had to agree to the necessity of this, particularly as the mention of it made her aware of her own body's insistent needs. They separated into the bush. Ten minutes later they were on the march.

During the half hour they had been halted all their muscles had stiffened up and there was some moaning and groaning until they warmed up and the muscles loosened. As usual they found going downhill nearly as hard as going up. The rough road surface didn't help. There were frequent slips on loose sand and pebbles and Wendy fell heavily on her bum. Tears came to her eyes, and she limped for a while, but she kept on walking.

Five minutes of rapid descent had them down on the edge of the pine forest. Wendy pointed to a sign. "This is a State Forest. What are the Smileys doing here?"

"Probably just passing through like us," Gordon suggested.

"Or, like all crooks, not telling the Forestry people what they are up to," Barbara added. As she walked, she kept sliding her thumb along the road on her map, trying to estimate where they were. "We are now back on a road which is marked on the map I think," she said. She found that a comfort.

The gravel road was now well graded and in good condition. It wound its way northwards along the crest of a wide, flat ridge, detouring around the occasional rocky outcrop or steep re-entrant. The trees appeared to be fully grown: endless rows of dark green conifers.

"Pinus Radiata," Wendy said as they discussed them.

"Wendy! I didn't know you were a botanist," Barbara said in surprise.

"I'm not," Wendy giggled. "There was a sign back there."

The sun was still so low that they were walking in the shadows of the trees. Bars of sunlight shone through here and there to make the dew on the grass sparkle. Barbara breathed deeply, savouring the coolness and tang of the pine resin. She noted that under the pines was a tangle of waist high blady grass, ferns, and weeds.

For a time they walked in silence, Barbara setting the pace. The road seemed to go on and on. Each bend revealed another half kilometre or so of road and more pine trees. The monotony of it began to irritate. As they rounded another bend, Barbara hitched her pack up. The sun shone full in her face, and she unfolded her map to check if there was a section of the road which ran east.

"Vehicle!" Wendy cried.

It was coming from behind them. Barbara made an instant decision and pointed. They bolted into the long grass and ferns to crouch behind trees with hearts thumping.

It was the white 4WD but only the driver was in it. The vehicle raced past at high speed and vanished.

"I wonder where he is off to in such a hurry?" Gordon asked.

"Back to the commune to get reinforcements perhaps," Wendy said.

Barbara bit her lip. "There may be more Smileys closer than that. We had better be a bit more careful, especially at bends."

They pushed through the weeds back to the road and resumed their march. From then on they slowed down as they approached bends and Barbara scouted forward to carefully scrutinise the terrain ahead of them before they exposed themselves on the next straight. It slowed them down a lot and added nervous tension to the physical strain, but she insisted and the others agreed to its necessity.

At 0750hrs Barbara called a halt. She led them into the forest about twenty paces and they trampled a small clearing in the long grass before sitting on their packs.

"Five minutes," Barbara said, unscrewing her water bottle cap.

"Getting hot fast," Wendy commented. She wiped perspiration from her face. Barbara noted that there was not a cloud in the sky.

"How far have we come?" Wendy asked.

"Another four or five k's I reckon. That makes ten or eleven. We should come to a place called 'Pony Pocket' soon," Barbara replied.

"Ponies don't have pockets!" Wendy said.

Gordon smiled. "Silly, a pocket is a natural clearing in a forest."

"I know that," Wendy replied. "I was only joking. If I don't I'll cry. I'm so worried about the others that I feel sick."

Tears watered in her eyes. Barbara swallowed a swig from her water bottle and gave Wendy a reassuring pat. "Eight o'clock. Let's move."

They marched on as fast as they could go. Barbara felt sore feet starting to develop. Her shoulder and leg muscles began to ache, and she was aware of chafing from her pack and webbing on her shoulders, around her hips, and from her trousers between her thighs. The rifle seemed to get heavier and heavier. From time to time she glanced at Wendy to see how she was coping but she appeared to be managing.

"Vehicle!" Gordon cried.

They scuttled into the forest. As she did, Barbara ran through a huge spider web and had to stifle a shriek. She also had to push the thought of snakes to the back of her mind. It was the same 4WD, heading back towards the Yards. Another man, wearing sunglasses and cradling a shotgun, was sitting beside the driver.

Wendy shook her head as the dust of its passing settled. "Oh! I hope the police arrive soon."

"They should. They'll be looking for us by now," Barbara said.

"How can you be sure? Lofty may not have reached safety yet," Wendy said.

"Because we did not phone in from Koah last night. They will know something is wrong," Barbara replied.

"Yes," Gordon agreed. "But they won't be looking for us twenty kilometres north of the river."

"Maybe not. But surely Dan and Karen have reached a phone by now," Wendy said. She looked at Barbara for reassurance.

Barbara nodded. "Hope so. Come on, let's move."

Around the next bend the road dipped down into a fairly large creek line. The trees changed abruptly from a plantation of exotic pines to natural eucalypts and paper barks.

"We might get some water here," Gordon said hopefully. They looked in the creek but there was only a slimy trickle with a dead toad lying in it. They made faces and walked on up the opposite slope. At the top they reached the edge of a large open area at least two kilometres across. It was lush grassland dotted with a few tall trees and many horses and cattle.

"Pony Pocket for sure," Barbara said

"Do we cross it or go round it?" Gordon asked.

"Take too big to go around," Barbara replied shaking her head.

"What if the Smileys come along when we are in the middle?" Wendy asked anxiously.

"According to the map it is private property. This fence beside us is the State Forest boundary, I think. Yes, there is the sign. So we are on a public road. They can't do anything to us," Barbara replied.

Gordon looked serious. "They can of course. I doubt if the Smileys respect the law," he said.

Barbara studied the clearing. The road ran straight across the middle. There was no sign of any habitation and she felt very isolated.

She shrugged. "We will just pretend we are on a cadet exercise and take things as they come. Come on. The sooner we start the sooner we get across."

She began marching as fast as she could. The others followed. As she strode along her eyes searched the distant wall of jungle surrounding the pocket while her mind tried to do the sums to calculate whether they would be across before the 4WD could drive to the Yards and back. She knew they were taking a calculated risk and the thought made her feel very anxious. Several times she wondered if they should not opt for the safer course and skirt around the clearing.

The road was fenced on both sides and the grass had been cropped short. That made her even more anxious. *We will have trouble hiding in the grass,* she thought.

In the middle of the clearing there was a T-junction. Another gravel road ran roughly east-west. They paused for a moment while they consulted the map.

"This is the road shown on the map alright," Barbara said. "We are here. We are about half way to the commune."

Barbara turned right and continued marching. It was hot out in the open grassland, and they were soon sweating freely. Barbara kept looking over her shoulder to check on Wendy and to watch for the 4WD. They crossed a small wooden bridge over a creek choked with guinea grass. No water was visible, so they went on. On the other side the road had tall trees on both sides and Barbara was able to relax slightly. For 300 metres they stepped it out through the tall timber which not only gave some cover but also some shade. Grazing horses looked up to watch them as they passed.

Barbara noted with satisfaction that the jungle covered bulk of Mildew Mountain was now on their right. That meant they were passing its northern end.

"We should reach the Black Mountain Road soon," she said, mainly in an attempt to boost Wendy than for information.

Thankfully they reached the far side of the clearing. The road entered rainforest, but this gave little relief from the heat as the trees did not meet overhead, allowing the sun to stream down on them. After a few more minutes walking they crossed another small bridge. This creek had a shallow trickle of reddish looking water which did not appeal to them so they went on, although Barbara knew they must refill their water bottles soon.

They puffed and sweated up over a low hill with jungle on the left and a field of open pasture on the right and at 0845hrs reached another T-junction. This was with a well-graded gravel road which ran North-South. A signpost confirmed Barbara's map reading.

"Black Mountain Road!" she cried. "Only about nine kilometres to go."

"Will we make it by midday?" Wendy asked.

"We should, if we push on. It depends," Barbara replied.

"What about a blow? I'm ready to drop," Wendy replied. She was flushed and sweating profusely.

Reluctantly Barbara agreed. "Okay. Not here. In the jungle," she said. She led the way off the road.

As they pushed their way into the rainforest Gordon asked, "What does it depend on?"

"On whether... Ouch! Ow! Bloody 'Wait-a-while'," Barbara cried.

She backed up to disengage herself from it then used the rifle to fend off other tendrils. After ten more metres she stopped, satisfied they could not be seen from either road. Packs and webbing were dropped.

Barbara had a drink before finishing her answer to Gordon. "It depends on whether we have to do any creeping and crawling through this stuff."

"Why should we?" Gordon asked.

Barbara picked up a stick and drew in the leaf mould. "The Black Mountain Road runs roughly south from here till it gets to the Christmas Pocket area. About four kilometres south from here a side road goes off to the east. This side road wriggles its way down between the Black Mountain Road and the coastal mountains till it re-joins the Black Mountain Road again just north of McKenzies Pocket. The commune is on that side road."

"So?"

"Well, on the road into the commune from the southern end we know there is a gate with a guard. Dan and our CSM saw it on their recon on Friday. It stands to reason that there will be another gate with a guard on the northern entrance," Barbara explained.

"Hmm. Yes. I see," Gordon said. He drained a water bottle. "I'm out of water. We'd better find some soon."

"Vehicle coming!" Wendy called.

They crouched to peer through the undergrowth. The vehicle came from the south. It roared past the intersection and on along the Black Mountain Road.

"Aborigines," Barbara observed. "There is an Aboriginal community further along the road."

"Why don't we go there and phone the police," Gordon asked.

Barbara thought hard about it and studied the map. The community was about twenty kilometres away. But she shook her head.

"No. Too far, and I don't feel like trusting anyone at the moment. We gave the commune as our RV and if we aren't there Lofty will get worried."

The others accepted this. They relaxed for a few more minutes before Barbara urged them into motion again. Out on the road they turned south. The Black Mountain Road wound around a small hill covered with bushes and a few large trees. Then, to Barbara's dismay, it led across another large open clearing.

Barbara stopped under cover at the edge of the clearing and studied the lie of the ground for a minute then said, "This time we detour. If there are guards then that point where the road re-enters the rain forest is the best place for them to be. We don't want to get caught out in the open like raw recruits."

She pointed to the far side of the clearing where the road vanished into a tunnel of rainforest. "That is the perfect spot for guards to hide in ambush."

She led them into the jungle on the left. Several horses were grazing in the paddock, but they just lifted their heads to look before continuing to eat. Keeping just inside the edge of the jungle Barbara led her friends across to the far side of the paddock, about 200 metres from the road. Once there she turned right and began walking along the edge of the thick wall of jungle that marked the eastern side of the field.

After walking for a few hundred paces, Barbara stopped and pointed to her right. The roof of a house showed just over the crest of another grassy hill on their right.

Gordon said, "There is a house. Should we go and see if they have a phone?"

Barbara shook her head. "No. They might be Smileys for all we know. I don't trust anyone. Besides, if there is going to be trouble it will be soon." She gestured ahead to where the road vanished into the dark tunnel in the rainforest. "If there is anyone there, they have probably seen us."

After that statement it took a conscious act of courage to keep walking forward. Barbara hefted the rifle into position ready to use and realised her palms were slippery with perspiration. But she kept determinedly walking. After another two hundred paces she reached the far end of the field and turned right. At that point she took off her pack and crawled under a fence. The others followed.

Barbara now walked slowly along just inside the edge of the jungle, every nerve alert for signs of trouble. The rifle was held ready in hands she found sweaty. But nothing happened and they reached the gravel road.

"I can see a sign," Wendy said in a hoarse voice as they crouched in the edge of the jungle.

But it was only a boundary marker to indicate that they were re-entering the State Forest. Barbara noted that a dirt road led off to the house which still tempted them from about half a kilometre away. After listening and looking in all directions she breathed out and realised she had been holding her breath. She took several deep gulps of air and walked out onto the road in the shadow of the trees.

This is silly, she told herself. *I shouldn't be risking my friends like this.*

Inside the rainforest it was moist and cool. Wendy sighed with relief. "That's better," she sighed.

"Yes, it is certainly cooler," Gordon agreed.

"I meant we now have somewhere to hide," Wendy replied.

Barbara looked at her watch. 0920hrs. *How time seems to fly!* she thought. With an effort of will she forced herself to go on marching. *Only eight more kilometres to go,* she consoled herself, hoping she could make the distance.

She was painfully aware that she had the beginnings of blisters on both feet, little toe on the right, heel on the left, and that her feet felt squashed and on fire. The muscles of her back and shoulders were numb. The chafing was starting to develop from irritation to agony. Worse still she was getting very thirsty and hot.

We will have heat exhaustion soon, she thought. *And poor old Wendy is limping and wilting.*

The road ran almost straight for a kilometre, climbing slowly. Barbara found that very taxing, both mentally and physically. As she walked, she kept glancing anxiously at her friends and noted that they were suffering but looking grimly determined.

They are really hurting too, she thought.

Then there were a series of curves around the ends of low spurs. On both sides was thick rainforest. The friends plodded on, but Barbara could see that they were all tiring fast. It had become an endurance test, a test of character.

"Vehicle!" Wendy cried.

Barbara turned right, but even as she ran for cover she realised she had made a mistake as she was confronted by a low bank. She had to leap to get up onto it and it took a frantic scrabble for her to haul herself up. As she grasped a tree to pull herself upright, she glanced sideways and saw Wendy slip back, unable to clamber up. She tried again and Gordon raced along, grabbed her pack and hauled her up. They stumbled and scrambled behind trees just as the vehicle rattled around the corner from behind them.

It was an old red truck driven by an old man who clearly needed dentures. The truck vanished in the direction of Kuranda.

"I don't think he was a Smiley," Wendy said as she dusted dead leaves and dirt off her knees.

"He looked more like a 'Gummy' to me," Gordon said. It was a feeble joke, but they all laughed at it.

"Better to be safe than sorry," Barbara said, but she had a nagging doubt that they should have risked it and flagged a lift to Kuranda to reach the police. She was now having serious second thoughts about the wisdom of her plan.

They resumed their march. The road wound left, then right, then went up another long straight for several hundred metres.

"Vehicle!"

Again it came from behind and they just had time to scramble into cover. It was the white 4WD, and Mr Smiley was in it, along with two other men, all grim faced.

"Our friend Mr Smiley," Gordon observed. "And from the sour face he has discovered the breakout from Stalag 13."

"Yes. I hope Lofty got those slaves to safety before he arrived," Wendy answered.

"I think he must have," Barbara said. "I doubt if Mr Smiley would be back so soon if he had caught up with them. He didn't look happy."

"Not a good example from the leader of the 'Happy People'," Gordon observed dryly.

Wendy smiled but sighed, "Oh! I hope Lofty is safe."

"What about Roger?" Barbara asked. "What about Fiona? And Jennifer? Stop worrying about Lofty. He can look after himself."

They moved back onto the road feeling hot and tired and not a little out of temper. Barbara checked the time as she started marching. 0945hrs.

Nearly time for another rest. We should have only about six kilometres to go.

At that moment, they crested a small rise. Barbara stopped in astonishment and signalled the other two to halt and hide, but she was not quick enough.

They were seen.

Two people stood on the road about fifty paces ahead staring at them in obvious alarm. The people were dressed in long cheesecloth shirts over some sort of wrap-around 'lap lap' or sarong and had garlands of flowers about their foreheads. A man and a woman. Long hair and bare

285

feet Barbara noted as the two people cried out in dismay and seemed to dance in agitation before rushing into the jungle.

"Strike me pink!" Gordon cried. "What was that?"

"I don't think they are Smileys," Barbara replied.

She was more mystified than afraid. Instinctively she had levelled the rifle. *Maybe that is why they ran?* she wondered.

"They were scared of us," Wendy said.

"Certainly scared of something," Gordon agreed.

Barbara frowned. "Why should they be scared of us? We must just look like soldiers. Why should people run away from their own country's uniform?" she asked. It both puzzled and irked her. "I'm going to ask them," she decided.

"How? Do you reckon you can find them in there?" Gordon asked as they walked along to where the two people had taken to the jungle.

Barbara nodded. "Yes, I do. They aren't dressed for scrub-bashing. They won't get far. Wendy, you note our compass bearing."

Barbara stepped up over a drainage ditch and pushed her way into the jungle. Once out of sight of the road she unclipped her pack and dropped it. The others did likewise. Then she advanced slowly, listening and looking, rifle ready but not held in a threatening way. She didn't have far to go. About forty paces in she found the pair huddled behind a big tree. Both were shaking with fright.

Close up they were a sorry sight. Their ages appeared to be middle or late twenties. They were very dirty and their hair was stringy and unkempt. They wore beads and bangles and earrings. Both looked half-starved and had numerous cuts and scratches on their arms and legs. The man had a huge tropical ulcer on his leg which had eaten out a suppurating hole which looked so revolting Barbara had to look away.

She asked, "Who are you people?"

The two cowered and clutched at each other. For a moment there was no reply, but when Barbara repeated her question the woman answered, "We are the Children of the Forest," as though that explained all.

Gordon and Wendy joined Barbara and the two eyed them fearfully. "What are Children of the Forest?" Barbara asked.

The woman did not answer, but instead started pleading, "Do not hurt us please. We mean no harm." She stared at the rifle with eyes dilated by fear.

"Why should we want to hurt you?" Barbara asked in astonishment. The 'Forest Children' made no answer but moaned and shivered in obvious terror. Barbara tried another question, "Have you seen any of the 'Smiley People' along this road?"

At this the two gibbered in terror and began crying.

"You obviously have," Barbara said with a wry smile. She asked, "Why are you afraid of them?"

The woman rolled her eyes. Barbara's nostrils twitched at the odours of unwashed bodies, incense and marijuana. The woman looked up at her. "They are evil people. They hunt us. We do them no harm. We do no-one any harm. But they hunt us when they see us."

"Hunt you? What do they do if they catch you?" Barbara asked.

"Sometimes they rape us. Sometimes they kill us. Sometimes they keep us as slaves to work in their gardens of ecstasy," the woman explained.

"Do you know where any of these slave groups are?" Barbara asked.

The woman nodded her head. Barbara was both annoyed and exasperated. She thought the Forest Children were rather pathetic. "Can you take us there?" she asked.

"No!" cried the woman. "No!"

"Alright. Calm down. Can you show me on a map?"

The woman shook her head. Barbara looked at the others and shrugged. Then she asked, "Can you tell us anything about the Smileys?"

The mention of the name made both Forest Children whimper again. The woman spoke, her eyes darting fearfully around. "They are evil. We have heard they are summoning up the dark forces from beyond the grave. It will be a bad time when night falls."

Wendy gasped. Barbara felt herself break out in goose bumps and her scalp 'crawled' and tingled. She bit her lip and wondered what else to ask, and what to do with them.

We can't take them with us, she reasoned. She said, "If you see any Smileys do not tell them you have seen us."

Neither Forest Child replied. They squatted hunched over with their heads down, clasping their legs and trembling. They appeared to be in a trance. Barbara spoke to them several more times but got no response. She shook her head in disbelief then motioned her friends to move back to the road.

287

Chapter 30

DEEP IN EVIL TERRITORY

Wendy looked anxiously around.

"Zombies!" she whispered. "They said the Smileys were summoning up the dead tonight."

Barbara felt a prickle of fear but frowned. "Rubbish! There are no such things as zombies," she snapped.

"How do you know?" Wendy asked, still obviously very anxious.

Barbara shook her head in exasperation. "Because if they existed we would have a live one in a zoo or a dead one in a museum!" she snapped. She was irritated because her own superstitious fears had been aroused. "And you would be taught in primary school how to deal with them."

"What will we do with the Flower Children?" Gordon asked.

Barbara shrugged and said, "Nothing. We will just leave them and keep going. They obviously live around here somewhere. It is ten o'clock. We will push on for another kilometre then have a break. We should be at the turnoff by then."

Wendy sighed at this, but she resumed walking without complaint. As they walked, they quietly discussed the incident.

"Environmental nut-cases," Gordon concluded.

They rounded another bend. More jungle. The road seemed to go on for ever. Another bend. Barbara halted abruptly and motioned them back. She then crept forwards a few paces and crouched to peer through the fringe of the jungle.

"The turnoff," she explained. "We will move inside the jungle till we get there."

"Can we have a break?" Wendy asked.

Barbara nodded. "Yes. Come on, let's get off the road."

They pushed their way into the jungle on their left for about fifty paces, their secateurs busy on small vines and 'wait-a-while'. Gordon swung off his pack and dropped it. As he did, Barbara frowned and hissed, "Don't drop your pack, Gordon. That makes a noise."

Gordon gave her a hurt look and frowned. "Sorry, I didn't think."

288

Barbara and Wendy both lowered their packs and the trio sat quietly on them for ten minutes. Barbara shared the last of her water. Then she studied her map. "There should be a creek about 200 metres in along the Smiley's road," she said. "Sandy Creek. With any luck it will have water in it."

At 1030hrs she got them moving again. They pushed forward through the jungle using the road as a guide. They found progress slow, as well as hot and frustrating. They were continually getting snagged on vines and saplings or having to detour around clumps of wait-a-while. It took fifteen minutes to reach the road junction which was a mere hundred metres from the bend.

Barbara scouted carefully for any indication of Smileys but saw none. At the junction was a sign which warned them that they were entering private property and that trespassers would be prosecuted. The trio moved along in the edge of the jungle beside the side road. About a hundred metres further along they saw a wire gate and another sign.

Moving even more cautiously Barbara worked her way along in the jungle parallel to the road. The others followed in single file.

Voices!

Barbara looked back and met Gordon's eyes. He nodded. Barbara crept forward until she could see the gate. At this point the road ran along a low embankment covered with weeds. She crawled up this and carefully looked along the road in both directions.

She froze. Two men had walked up out of a side-track about fifty paces further along. They stood on the road talking. One was Mr Smiley. The other she had never seen before, but he wore a jungle green jacket and what looked like a US Army camouflage cap and carried an automatic rifle.

Mr Smiley spoke to the man and pointed. Barbara followed his finger and saw that they were at the end of a small concrete bridge.

Must be Sandy Creek, she decided. *And he is posting a sentry, or setting an ambush!*

She watched as the armed man went down into the jungle beside the end of the bridge. From there he could fire along the road without being seen. Barbara realised with a shock that anyone opening the gate or walking along the road would have no idea the man was there, until too late. She felt real fear grip her bowels.

With even greater caution she eased herself back down on her stomach until she was back in the jungle. She described to the others what she had just seen.

Gordon frowned and said, "It sounds as though the Smileys are very worried about us."

Barbara nodded. "This must be their other guard post. There is a side-track just along there. I'm going to have another look. Wait here."

She took off her pack and webbing and cautiously made her way forward. As luck would have it, she met what seemed to be the thickest clump of wait-a-while she had ever seen, and it took her ten sweaty and anxious minutes to creep forward to a position from which she could observe.

There was a sandy clearing in a hollow formed by an old flood channel where two creeks met. In it were a tent, campfire, litter of rubbish, two vehicles and four men: Mr Smiley, his driver, the third man from the 4WD, a thin, leathery man in his late forties or early fifties with a hard face, and a tall, dopey looking man in his late teens or early twenties with black hair. He wore a camouflage jacket and jeans.

As Barbara lay watching them, Mr Smiley gave orders. When he finished, he and his driver and the thin, hard man climbed into the white 4WD. It started up, drove up the track onto the road, turned left and accelerated away in the direction of the commune. The dopey character muttered to himself and settled down beside the fire to do some cooking.

Barbara looked at her watch. *Ten past eleven! We will be late at the commune unless we hurry,* she thought. Then another awful thought occurred to her. *We must get there in time to warn the police. They could drive into an ambush!*

As carefully as she could, she backed off till she was well clear of the camp. Then she retraced her steps back to the others. After a quick explanation she studied the map. "We have to detour around these characters," she explained. She saw that the road curved left just past the bridge, so she penciled a course and worked out the magnetic bearings. It would mean a jungle traverse of about 500 metres.

Too bad, she shrugged.

They set off, angling away to the left of the camp. Within a hundred metres they came to a creek with very steep banks. The water was clear and shallow, running over a sandy bottom. Barbara checked her map.

"Sandy Creek. We will fill our water bottles."

They slithered down from tree to tree and dropped their gear on the bank. The water was cool and tasted good. Water bottles were filled and they drank as much as they could. Almost at once they started to perspire again. This caused salt to sting their eyes and the numerous small cuts and scratches they had accumulated.

Within a few minutes Barbara pushed them on. They waded across in knee deep water which wet their trousers and socks. Then they went up the other bank and on through the jungle. She led the way with her compass in her left hand and secateurs in her right, the rifle slung vertically against her side. After a hundred metres of slow progress she stopped worrying about noise and just crashed her way through unless a vine or wait-a-while stopped her.

"Those Smileys will just think it is wild pigs," she explained.

That made Wendy and Gordon both look nervously around in case there really were wild pigs. Barbara didn't care. She was now consumed with anxiety. They would be late at the commune which she estimated was still at least three kilometres away, almost an hour's walk, even along the road.

It took twenty minutes of irritating, sweaty work to crash their way through the jungle back to the road. After a short halt for a drink, and to check both ways along the road, Barbara led them out onto it.

"It is nearly midday now," she said. "Five to twelve. If we are going to reach the commune on time, then we need to move fast. We will have to risk walking along the road. They shouldn't have any more guard posts."

The friends continued their painful march, Wendy now visibly lagging and slowing down. The road ran straight for several hundred metres, then curved sharp left, then right, then left again.

"Can we stop for a rest please," Wendy called.

Barbara slowed, unwillingly, and allowed her to catch up. "The commune is only half a kilometre past the next bend," she said.

Wendy clenched her jaw, put her head down and kept walking. Gordon gave Barbara a worried and slightly disapproving glance but said nothing.

At the next bend they slowed down and looked cautiously round. The next section of road was straight and ran through a tunnel of trees until a distant patch of sunlight indicated the clearing of the commune.

"We had better take to the scrub again," Barbara said. "It doesn't look too bad." She led them off the road on the right and up a gentle slope, then turned left to move parallel to the road.

It was the easiest bit of jungle they had yet moved through: plenty of waist high ferns but almost no vines or wait-a-while. They moved at a slow walk until they reached a small creek. This had a trickle of water in it and some small pools of clear water.

"We must be about halfway," Barbara said. Taking off her pack she looked both ways along the creek. "I'll bet this is the creek they get their water from. I remember seeing a track leading down to it," she said. She had a drink and crouched to refill the water bottle. "This is what we will do. You two stop here to have a rest and some lunch while I do a quick scout forward to the edge of the clearing. I won't be long." She looked at her watch. It was 1230. "I will be back by 1300."

"Barbara, be careful," Wendy cautioned.

"I'll come with you," Gordon offered.

Barbara shook her head. "No. Don't leave Wendy on her own. I have been here before. I know the layout of the place."

"I will be alright," Wendy insisted.

Barbara knew it was foolish to go alone so she relented. "Alright, leave Wendy the rifle Gordon."

Gordon handed Wendy the automatic .22 and followed Barbara. Within fifty paces Barbara was sure of where she was as the sunlight of the clearing showed through the trees ahead. She crept from tree to tree, eyes searching everywhere before she moved forward again.

After five minutes of this she reached the edge of the clearing. Here she crouched among some ferns and peered through them. Directly in front of her was the front lawn of the commune. Across in the middle of this were two wooden buildings: an office and another hut with a veranda along the side facing her. Two vehicles were parked on the access road near a concrete footpath which led to the office: a white utility and a silver-grey Mercedes. Just beyond the second building a blue van was parked with its bonnet up. Next to it was a truck.

There was not a soul in sight. Barbara moved slightly to look for people like the gardener she had nearly blundered into last time, but she could see no-one. At that moment, she heard voices. A solid man in blue overalls came out of a door in the second building, walked down the four steps and across to the blue van. A second man came out onto the veranda after him. It was the thin man with the hard face. He was holding a bottle of something and took swigs from it while he talked. He leaned on the veranda railings while the man in blue overalls leaned into the front of the van to work on its motor.

All very peaceful and homely, Barbara thought. *Now, where are Roger and Jennifer? And where is Fiona? And where are Lofty and the police?*

She decided she would have to scout along to the right past the store sheds and the big shelter to the living huts.

Just as she began to move, she heard more voices, off to her left. She crouched to watch. Out of the jungle on the other side of the gravel road came a line of slaves. They emerged from the overgrown timber track which Barbara knew was there, crossed the road and trudged up the access track to halt in front of the office. Barbara did a quick count: 15 slaves and two guards.

The slaves had the same tattered appearance as the ones they had already rescued, clad only in yellow rags. As before they were chained together. One of the guards proceeded to padlock the end of the chain to an orange tree growing in the lawn if front of the second building. The slaves were then seated in a huddle.

The other guard now drew Barbara's attention. *He looks a real brute,* she thought.

The man wore a camouflage cap, brown Battledress jacket, Austcam trousers and army boots. He had a walkie-talkie slung over his left shoulder and a wicked looking sub-machine gun over his right. In his hand he held a whip.

The other guard, in nondescript grey work clothes and carrying a sporting rifle and a vicious looking stock whip, walked over to the office and went in. Barbara turned her head and met Gordon's eye. She gave a slight jerk of the head and they crept backwards through the ferns for twenty metres.

"Go and get Wendy, quick!" she whispered. "Leave the packs."

Gordon nodded and headed off. Barbara crouched behind a tree and continued to observe. There was no activity for the next few minutes. The man in overalls worked on the motor of the van and chatted to the man drinking on the veranda. Both ignored the slaves whom they presumably

293

saw all the time. The guard with the sub-machine gun stood on the lawn facing the seated slaves, a scowl on his face.

He's been a soldier that fellow, Barbara decided. *We had better mark him down to be especially wary of.*

A rustle of ferns preceded the cautious arrival of Gordon and Wendy. Barbara quickly pointed out the main features. Wendy nodded and asked, "What are we going to do?"

"I don't know. Wait I suppose."

"Wait for what?" Gordon asked.

"The police. I don't want to start a gun battle. I'd have to shoot one of those men," Barbara replied.

Gordon looked at his watch. "Yes. It's nearly one o'clock. The police should be here by now. I wonder what is keeping them?"

As if in answer to her question there were loud voices in the office. A person appeared in the doorway and stumbled down the stairs.

It was Karen!

Her hands were tied behind her back, her shirt was torn, and there were bruises on her face.

Behind her came Dan. He was kicked down the stairs by the man in grey so that he went sprawling on the concrete path. As he tried to get up the guard kicked him again. This brought hoots and jeers from the man on the veranda who waved his bottle in the air and had another drink.

Dan's face was covered in blood. He had no shirt and his upper body and arms were covered with bruises and red dots. A middle-aged Indian woman in a sari appeared in the doorway behind the guard and began pointing and giving orders. Barbara trembled with shock and anger. She bit her lip and tried to decide what to do. She glanced at Gordon and Wendy and saw horror and dismay on their faces.

The man in grey picked up another chain from the veranda. He padlocked this around Karen's waist and then around Dan's. They were then pushed and kicked until they were seated with the other slaves. The man in grey then walked off across the lawn to the right to the concrete block store sheds.

What can we do? Barbara wondered.

She felt a compelling urge to act but could not think of a sensible plan. She could feel a rage building up which she knew she must control. She turned and signalled Gordon and Wendy to move up level with her in 'extended line' on her right. She wasn't sure what she intended doing but her instinct was to be ready. They began moving to comply.

Over at the small store sheds near the banana trees there was the rattle of a bolt and a harsh command, "Out! Now!"

Into view came Roger and Jennifer. Barbara gasped in shock. Roger was shirtless and covered in bruises and red weals and dots. He had dried blood on his chin and a black eye.

Roger has been tortured too! Oooh! The bastards! Barbara thought. She shook with rage and gripped the rifle tightly.

Jennifer had a torn shirt and looked bruised and battered. She walked with head bowed and looked utterly miserable. Both had their hands tied behind their backs. The guard in grey walked behind them snarling threats and waving the stock whip.

What can we do? Barbara's mind screamed.

When Roger and Jennifer reached the group of slaves Roger spoke to Dan.

The guard in the brown jacket immediately snarled, "No talking!"

Then, to Barbara's horror, he lashed at Roger with the whip. It struck him across the neck and shoulders and left a raw mark. Barbara pushed off the safety catch of the rifle and half rose.

The guard in grey pushed Jennifer roughly down on the lawn. He knelt and placed his rifle on the lawn then picked up the chain and fastened it around her waist. When he was finished fastening the chain, he knelt behind her and deliberately fondled her. Jennifer cried out in protest and tears ran down her face.

This brought a shout of laughter from the drunk, who staggered down off the veranda waving his bottle, and a reaction from Roger which earned him another vicious slash by the whip. That made Roger cry out and turn to face the guard in brown. During this, the Indian woman just stood in the doorway and smirked.

The man in grey bent and picked up the chain and ordered Roger to move closer. At that moment, the drunk, who had staggered over to near Jennifer, grabbed at her shirt. He jerked at it to tear it open and partially succeeded amidst more jeers and laughter.

Roger reacted. He kicked at the drunk but was instantly whipped and knocked flat by the guard in brown. The guard lashed at Roger with his boot, striking him hard in the ribs. Roger squirmed to avoid more kicks and tried to get to his feet. He was knocked down again. The Indian woman screamed at the guard.

"Shoot him! Teach the others a lesson!"

The guard in brown backed off and unslung his sub-machine gun. *Bang!*

The guard in brown suddenly collapsed in a screaming heap.

Barbara ejected the spent cartridge, re-cocked the rifle and sprang to her feet.

"Charge!" she shouted.

As she raced out onto the lawn, she was aware of goggling eyes as all heads turned to look at her. She saw the guard in grey scrabble for his gun. Dan tripped him and he went sprawling.

"Leave the gun or you are dead!" Barbara threatened as she ran up to the man. She glanced right. Gordon and Wendy were running forward ten paces apart. "Gordon! Grab his rifle! Hands up the lot of you!"

Roger rolled over from under the wounded guard who was screaming in pain. He snatched at the man's sub-machine gun and wrenched it free. Because his hands were tied behind his back, he could not use it but he moved away, out of the man's reach.

As Gordon scooped up the rifle, the drunk recovered himself. To Barbara he was a truly disgusting sight and she had to restrain the urge to kill him on the spot. The man had obviously lost control of himself as the front of his trousers was now wet. Barbara levelled the rifle at him. She shook with emotion and breathed great gulps of air. Her finger actually did itch on the trigger, and she had to make a conscious effort to control herself.

She screamed, "Don't try anything, you revolting pig! Put your hands up and lie down on your front. Gordon, guard him."

She remembered the man in overalls. He had straightened up so quickly in alarm that he had struck his head on the bonnet of the van. This had fallen down on him and he had just managed to struggle free. Now he was standing dumbfounded rubbing his head. By then Wendy was crouched against the petrol storage shed aiming her rifle at him. Barbara waited till Gordon had the drunk covered on the lawn then ran forward to the office.

The Indian woman had turned and run inside and was reaching into a briefcase.

Barbara bounded up the stairs and aimed her rifle at the woman. "Hands up!" she shouted. "Put them up slowly! Or I will shoot."

She levelled the rifle to aim at the woman's chest. In her fury Barbara meant it and saw that the woman sensed this. Slowly she raised her hands. Barbara glanced around the room, and saw no-one else.

"Outside!"

Barbara backed out, followed by the woman.

"Lie down. Don't move!"

Reluctantly, her face a mask of hate, the woman did so.

Wendy suddenly yelled. Barbara looked. Wendy was now aiming at a chubby, middle-aged man in dirty white clothes: the cook. He had come out of the big shed and had a pistol in his hand.

"Drop the gun! Hands up!" Wendy called. She was still crouched under cover with her rifle aimed directly at him.

Good girl! Barbara thought.

The man looked at her. For a moment Barbara feared he would try to shoot but he must have decided Wendy was too hard a target to hit. Reluctantly he dropped the pistol and came forward with his hands up to stand near the mechanic.

Barbara looked around. "Wendy, check in the cookhouse," she ordered.

Wendy ran to the door and looked in. Then she stood back and gave all clear. Barbara shook her head. She was amazed.

We've captured the commune!

Chapter 31

RAPID DECISIONS

For a moment Barbara stood with her mind and emotions in a whirl. Then she took a grip on herself.

Come on! You are a Cadet Under-Officer. You have been trained to take command. So take control, she told herself. *Remember what Capt Conkey says, "Be decisive. Any order is better than disorder." So act!*

With her resolve stiffened Barbara turned and said, "Gordon, get all these Smileys lying in one line on the lawn over there. Wendy, find the keys and unlock Dan, Karen and Jennifer."

"What about us?" a slave asked querulously.

"Shut up! I'll get to you," Barbara snapped. She moved to look down at the wounded Smiley who was still rolling on the lawn, moaning and whimpering. There was blood all over the grass and his trouser leg was soaked in it. He gripped his leg and sobbed for someone to help him.

Good shot! Barbara thought. *I've broken his leg. He won't give us any more trouble.*

But she knew he would. Dimly she understood that there would be very serious legal repercussions which would flow from her actions. Having shot a man before and then having endured the court cases that followed she knew more or less what to expect. That, combined with a squeamish reaction to the brutal act of shooting someone made her feel nauseous. She felt like vomiting and collapsing but instead she took a grip on her emotions.

No time for that now! We must act, she told herself.

Gordon stood beside her, "We must do something about him."

"Bugger him! We will worry about him in a minute. Just guard the others," Barbara snapped. She turned to the wounded man, "Shut up you or I will choke you with your own bloody whip!"

The Smiley's eyes goggled in pain and fear, but he subsided back to moans and groans. Barbara knelt beside Roger and took out her pocketknife. As she cut the nylon cord binding his wrists, she realised that the red spots on him were blisters.

298

Roger rolled over and sat up. He began rubbing his wrists and flexing his cramped hands. "Thanks Barb. You arrived just in time." Their eyes met and she smiled. She felt a surge of affection.

Good old Roger! He is as brave as a lion.

To hide her emotions she pointed to the red blisters. "What caused those?"

"Cigarette burns. But I didn't talk."

"Oh Roger!" Barbara gasped. She felt all choked up. Poor Roger! She patted his shoulder.

Roger shrugged. "It'll be okay." For a moment he gripped her hand and strong emotion made him tremble. Then he smiled and stood up. He picked up the sub-machine gun and checked it. "I'll guard these mongrels. But there are more of them around. We had better have a sentry."

"Good idea. Get Gordon to act as sentry and you guard the captured Smileys. Are you up to it?" Barbara agreed.

"Too right," Roger answered with a grim smile. He called to Gordon, "Hey Gordon! Come over here and watch the entrance road just in case Mr Smiley or any of his slimy mates turn up."

By this time Wendy had freed all the others, including the slaves. They began to mill around. Barbara faced them and shouted for them to sit down and shut up. The last thing she wanted at that moment was to lose control or waste time arguing, there was still half the commune to search, and more Smileys to worry about, including Mr Smiley himself.

"Where is Fiona?" she asked as Jennifer and Karen joined her.

Jennifer shook her head. "Haven't seen her," she answered. She suddenly burst into tears and wrapped her arms around Barbara and began to thank her. "Oh Barbara! It is a miracle. How did you find us? I've been so scared. Oh thank you!" She gushed on and broke down into sobbing.

"We'd better find you a new shirt," Barbara said.

Karen spoke and pointed. "Our packs are just in that office," she said.

"Good. Get changed into uniform."

Jennifer nodded and wiped her tears with the back of her hand. She covered her front with her arms and walked over to the office.

Barbara said, "Karen, help me with this turd."

She jerked her thumb at the wounded Smiley. They walked over and

Barbara pointed the rifle at his head. His eyes dilated in terror and he began to plead and blubber.

Barbara curled her lip. "Shut up! Lie still or I will shoot."

Karen used Barbara's knife to slit open the leg of the man's trousers. There was an ugly big hole oozing blood just above his left knee. The exit wound was even worse. Karen shuddered as she bound it tightly with two field dressings Barbara extracted from her webbing. The man gasped in agony and passed out. The two legs were then splinted together.

"He should be taken to hospital," Karen said.

"So should you be, from the look of your face," Barbara answered. "Did... did they do anything to you?"

"Other than hitting us and using cigarettes? No. I think that was next," Karen answered.

Her lip trembled and she began to cry. Barbara patted her shoulder while her mind turned over the problem.

"There must be a telephone or radio here."

"There is," Karen replied through her sniffles. "In that office."

Barbara walked over to the office. At the door she paused. "Dan, take that chain and lock all these prisoners to that tree. Then go and get the cook's pistol and watch that no-one comes from the other part of the commune and surprises us."

Barbara went up the steps and into the office, to halt in astonishment. Jennifer was standing there with her hands held high above her head. Crouched behind a table in the corner and pointing a pistol at her was a Smiley. She recognised him as the man with the sandy hair and moustache who she had seen in Mr Smiley's 4WD. He looked very frightened, and the pistol wavered between her and Jennifer.

The Smiley croaked, then swallowed and managed to speak, "Don't move or call out. She is my hostage. If you do anything I will shoot her."

For a moment Barbara stood transfixed as she took in the scene. Her mind raced as she weighed up the situation. Then she snorted, "Crap! Drop the gun or I will drop you. I can shoot straighter with this rifle than you will be able to with that pistol."

She raised the rifle to her shoulder and sighted it at the man's head. His pistol again wavered and he stared at her. She met his eye as she sighted on his right eyeball and she could sense that something in her attitude was transmitting to him the fact that she was deadly serious.

I can kill him before he can pull the trigger, Barbara thought. Her finger took the 'First pressure' on the trigger and the man saw this and dropped his gun.

"Don't shoot! I give up!" he cried.

He stood up and put his hands up. Barbara looked around to check there were no more hiding in the room. In doing so she noted that the telephone had been ripped off the wall and the radio had been smashed. Rage flared for an instant and she shook her head and again aimed the rifle. The man cowered in terror and called for mercy.

"Stop whining!" Barbara called, her lip curling in contempt. She said to Jennifer, "Pick up the pistol. Don't step in front of me! Now step back here and keep him covered."

As soon as Jennifer was safe beside her, Barbara questioned the Smiley. "Did you warn Mr Smiley or anyone?" she grated.

The man's eyes flickered towards the smashed radio and he licked his lips. At that moment, Barbara heard a vehicle coming. She looked through the side window and saw the white 4WD race into view from the right. Her gaze took in Gordon standing beside a large hoop pine in the front lawn.

"Gordon!" she yelled.

The vehicle skidded to a stop at the turnoff. Dust billowed and there was loud swearing. With a roar of its engine the vehicle swung round.

Bang! Tat-a-tat-a-tat.

Several weapons blazed from the vehicle. Barbara ran to the door. She saw that Gordon had leapt behind the tree. The vehicle was already accelerating away.

Thwack! Thud!

Bullets smacked into the building near her. As it was only constructed of timber planks they smashed right through. Several cracked close past her head. She threw herself flat on the lawn, aimed and fired.

Too fast! Aim you silly girl! Use your training! she berated herself.

She re-cocked the rifle but it was too late. The vehicle had moved out of sight. Annoyed with herself she scrambled to her feet.

"Gordon, are you alright?"

Gordon stood behind the tree holding his rifle. He nodded and licked his lips.

"You didn't shoot?" Barbara stated in surprise.

He shook his head. "No."

Barbara shook her head. "Watch out they don't come back on foot and snipe us from the jungle. Go over to the edge of the jungle there."

Roger and Wendy both raced up, weapons ready. Barbara put on her safety catch. "They've gone. It was Mr Smiley. I saw him," she explained. "There is another prisoner in there. He warned Mr Smiley, then destroyed the radio and telephone."

They walked over to the hut and looked in. Jennifer stood there, shivering and crying but still gripping the pistol with both hands and pointing it at the man. He was shaking with fright, his eyes flicking from her eyes to the gun and back.

Barbara snapped at the Smiley, "Come out here you! Jennifer, you get dressed. Roger, go back and guard the prisoners."

The man was taken over to be chained up with the others. Barbara stood for a moment fretting over options: What to do next? How to contact the police? How to get the wounded man to hospital?

There were several vehicles they could use. *But whichever way we go there are armed Smileys,* she thought. Quickly she reached a decision.

"Let's search this place and get out of here," she said.

"Why?" Jennifer asked as she dug out a camouflage shirt from her pack and pulled it on. "Why not wait for the police? Ow!" that last as she winced when the material rubbed on her bruised back.

"Because here we are a sitting target, and I'm not so sure about the police arriving."

"What about Lofty?" Karen asked.

"He has had nearly twelve hours now. And he may also be in trouble. I mean, what happened to you and Dan?"

"We were doing fine," Karen answered. "Till we were near Koah. There was a man sitting under a rail bridge watching it and the dirt track next to it, like he was expecting us. He had a gun and put us in that van and brought us here."

"Well, I want to get somewhere safer," Barbara said. "And I also want to find Fiona. I am worried that now we have hit them the Smileys might get desperate."

She thought for a moment, deciding on a course of action and mentally marshalling her troops. Then she went to the door and called, "Roger, you get changed. Then go with Dan and quickly search the rest of the commune, but for heavens sake be careful. Arrest anyone you see and bring them here. Wendy, can you and Karen go and find our gear and bring it here? Jenn, you guard those prisoners."

They moved to obey. Roger came into the office and took his pack. Barbara began a thorough search of the place. She was deeply worried now, about the legal consequences of what she had done, and she wanted some proof for when they ended up in court.

No good capturing this lot if we have no evidence to have them locked up and to justify our actions, she thought.

But her search was fruitless. Everything in the office referred to the normal running of the commune and there was no hint or mention of prisoners or slaves or other groups of Smileys. Even the woman's briefcase was no help. All it yielded was a small automatic pistol. Barbara checked it was loaded but not cocked and on 'safe' before putting it in her right basic pouch.

By then Wendy and Karen were back. Barbara went out and said, "Search all the vehicles and this other hut."

She went over to the wounded man and checked his condition. He was semi-conscious and obviously in great pain. For the first time she felt a twinge of remorse.

I hope he doesn't die, she thought, her worry deepening.

Roger and Dan returned, both shaking their heads. "Not a soul," Roger reported. "We went right to the last hut and down a couple of foot tracks into the jungle."

Barbara nodded. "Okay, Dan, you find your gear and get dressed. Roger, can you bring me the prisoners one at a time please?"

Roger did so, the Indian woman first. Barbara interviewed her in the office, seating herself at one of the tables. The woman was shrill and indignant. Her name was Wanda Wandami and she was the commune secretary and she knew her rights. She demanded to see her lawyer and refused to answer any questions.

Barbara listened for a minute then said, "Roger, lock her in that shed you were locked in."

Then the cook, nothing, the mechanic, all innocence, the drunk, surly and unco-operative. Barbara spent only a couple of minutes on each, very aware that time was passing. Roger marched the last one in, the sandy haired man she had found in the office. He was frightened but would not talk either. She told Roger to chain them all up and to lock them in the other shed.

Then she questioned the slaves but after the first three she gave it up. They all had similar stories and wanted to talk and talk and gush gratitude. All they knew was that they were part of group C2 and that they had been tending plots of marijuana in the jungle up the track opposite the commune. They believed there were other groups of slaves but had never seen them. None of them had met Fiona or heard of her.

Barbara went out and faced the group on the lawn and told them to collect food, bedding and clothing, then turned to see what the others had found. Dan held up a Chinese semi-automatic military rifle and a bandolier of ammo. "In the next hut," he explained.

Roger produced some ID Cards, a grubby notebook ("In the drunk's pocket.") and a map ("Behind the seat in the truck.") and a hand radio. Barbara flicked through the notebook.

"This is some sort of Roll Book. Look, names and dates with ticks and so on," she said.

Quickly she scanned it and noted: HQ: 4 with their names: Colonel Smiley (Colonel eh?), Master Sergeant Kowalski, Signaller Bragg and Driver Crane. Then five 'Squads' or 'sections': C1 with 5 in it, C2 with 4 men, C3 with 4 men, C4 with 4 men, and C5 with 6 men. She added them up and whistled. 27 men!

That is a lot of armed crooks! she thought anxiously. It reinforced her belief that they should move quickly to a safer place. *If we stay here, we will just get trapped and hit.*

Then she studied the captured map. "Ah! This is what we want," she cried. She spread it on the concrete path and the others crowded round to look. She pointed. "Here is the commune. Up that track was Group C2. That is these people. The wounded bloke is 'Knife' Costigan and the man in grey is Stevens, both from Section C2."

"So where are Broke and Benson?" Roger asked as he read down the roll book.

"Broke is the drunk," Dan said.

"And Benson is the man with the moustache," Jennifer added.

Barbara said, "Group C4 were the people at the 'Silky Oak' yards."

"We only got three," Wendy commented, reading over Roger's shoulder.

Barbara nodded. "Yes. So Krinkle is still on the loose," she agreed.

Roger studied the map and frowned. "There are only four lots of slaves shown on the map. Why are there five groups of guards?" Roger asked.

"Gate guards possibly," Dan suggested.

"Could be. How many were there at 'Silky Oak'?" Barbara asked.

"Not sure," Roger answered.

"What happened to you there? How did you get caught?" Wendy asked.

"We swam the river and walked to the nearest farmhouse. We asked the bloke there if we could use the phone to ring the police. He seemed suspicious and asked why so we told him. He said 'Sure, come in,' and the next thing we know he is pointing a shotgun at us and calling on a walkie talkie."

"One of those," Jennifer added, pointing to the radio lying on the lawn.

Roger went on, "Next thing a man with a pig truck turns up and we were locked in the cages on the back." He sounded increasingly indignant as he described their treatment.

"We know, we saw you," Wendy added.

Dan looked thoughtful. "I know what happened," he said. "Even though Roger and Jenn wouldn't talk Mr Smiley would have recognised you when he questioned you. He would have warned his gang to be on the lookout and spread out his guards to catch us, and he did!"

Karen nodded. "He was a very worried man," she said. She shuddered at the memory of being interrogated. "I hate these people!" she cried and started to sob.

"That's enough ancient history," Barbara interrupted. "We can talk about it later. We have to get moving."

"What is the plan?" Roger asked.

Barbara pointed at the map and said, "Group C3 is about two kilometres further along this road. I think we should try to rescue them."

"Be bloody risky," Roger said. "They will be alert now. We could walk into an ambush."

"Fiona might be there," Barbara replied stubbornly. "Besides, we are at risk here, and we need to get these people to safety. We can scout as we go."

"Why not drive?" Dan asked.

"Because we would drive into a roadblock for sure," Barbara replied. She described how the men were watching the gate at Sandy Creek. The others reluctantly conceded it was too risky. Barbara said, "Get everyone together and collect our gear. Call Gordon in."

In a few minutes they had all the slaves seated on the lawn. Barbara addressed them, "We are leaving. You can come with us, or you can go where you like. There are armed Smileys back that way, and more along the road the other way." She pointed. "If you go due east you will come to the sea near Casuarina Beach. That is on the Cook Highway north of Cairns."

"Which way are you going?" a man asked.

Barbara did not answer. She continued, "If you decide to come with us you do as we say, and don't argue or grumble."

"What about the prisoners?" Gordon asked.

"We leave them locked up here."

"What about the wounded Smiley?" Karen asked.

That gave Barbara pause for thought. She bit her lip. "Put him with his friends. They can look after him. As soon as we are gone, they will break out anyway. They can drive him to hospital in one of these vehicles."

"But they will escape!" Dan objected.

"Doesn't matter. We have their ID and credit cards. The police can round them up. You can stay and guard them if you like but I am going," Barbara replied.

"Why can't we drive in the truck?" a man asked.

Barbara again explained her fear of ambush. "You can take one if you want and good luck to you. Now, anyone who is coming with us get your packs on and let's get moving."

She looked at her watch as the group dissolved in movement and talk. Nearly 2 pm. Gordon came over to her: Barbara, this is silly," he cautioned. "Why don't we just sneak away through the jungle?"

"That is more or less what I intend, but if we find other groups of slaves I'd like to free them. We still haven't found Fiona," Barbara answered.

"Fiona! Don't be crazy. This is obsessive. Someone will get killed!" Gordon exploded.

"People have already been killed," Barbara replied coolly. "You don't have to come."

Gordon pursed his lips but hauled on his pack and followed her.

Barbara pointed to the radio and ID cards. "Grab all that stuff Wendy," she instructed. She picked up the captured map and folded it.

Roger sucked in his breath as he hoisted in his pack.

Barbara saw him wince and asked, "You okay? Do you want someone to carry your pack?" she asked with concern.

Roger shook his head and settled the pack gently. "I'll be fine in a minute," he answered. "Dan and I will scout." He checked the sub-machine gun.

"You go first," Dan said with a grin.

Barbara frowned. "You take care," she said. Impulsively she reached out to gently squeeze Roger's sleeve. He grunted, gave her a smile and gestured to Dan to start moving.

"We'll be alright," Roger assured her, giving the sub-machine gun a pat. "We've both got a score to settle with these Smiley turds."

The pair moved off twenty paces apart down to the edge of the jungle and along it. Barbara gave rapid instructions to the main body. It appeared that all the slaves were coming with them.

We make a fair-sized mob, she thought.

Seven cadets, all armed and in uniform, plus the straggle of slaves in a motley variety of clothing taken from the Smiley's hut. She posted Karen and Jennifer as rear-guard. Satisfied they were as ready as she could get them in a few minutes she turned and followed Roger and Dan. Gordon followed her, then Wendy. They spread out to 10 to 15 paces apart as though on patrol. After a few sharp rebukes the slaves stopped chattering and walked in silence.

Now to find Fiona, Barbara thought.

Chapter 32

SCRUB TURKEY

Barbara was acutely aware that they were now embarking on what was potentially a much more deadly undertaking. Now the enemy was real. And the enemy was alert to their presence. Shots had been fired and blood spilt. She tried not to think about the wounded Smiley lying in the hut behind her but inside she felt sick with remorse and dread.

There was a brittle tension in the air as they walked. Roger and Dan scouted along the edge of the rainforest about 50 paces ahead, weapons at the ready. At Barbara's insistence all of the others walked on the right-hand side of the road clearing, right against the edge of the jungle. She was very conscious that it would be much safer walking through the jungle on a compass course but felt driven by the need to move fast to rescue Fiona. The tactical compromise was that they walked right on the edge of the jungle, or inside it if there was no wait-a-while.

They passed the vegetable patch and came to the pine forest they had passed through on Friday. At the turnoff into the pines Roger stopped and waited for her.

"We could go that way, over Mt Burton and down to the sea," he suggested.

Barbara shook her head. She knew she was being wilfully stubborn, but she felt sure that Fiona was in one of the two groups of slaves further along the road. Ever since seeing that first group of slaves back at the Barron River her hopes of finding Fiona had increased strongly.

"If the police come it will be along this road. But we can put it to these people again and some of you could lead them out," she replied.

They crossed the main gravel road and moved fifty paces up the side road away from the road junction. Once the slaves were grouped in hiding in the weeds Barbara explained the situation. As she talked, she pointed to the jungle covered mass of Mt Burton off to the east.

A man asked, "How high is this mountain?"

"About 300 metres from this side, then a thousand or so down to Casuarina Beach," Barbara answered.

"And you have been that way already?"

"Yes, on Friday."

"Are you going that way?"

"No," Barbara replied. "We are going to look for our friend."

"Where does this road lead to?" another man asked, pointing south along the main gravel road.

"It joins up with the Black Mountain Road which goes to Kuranda, but, as I explained, the Smileys have a guard post and gate before then," Barbara said.

"And you think the police are coming?"

Barbara nodded. "We hope so." She explained about Lofty and the other slaves. In fact she was now very worried that Lofty had also run into some sort of problem, but it did not affect her resolve.

A woman asked, "What will you do if the Smileys come along?"

"Hide in the forest."

"We could get lost and die!" the woman cried. She had obviously had her fill of rainforest, judging by the pallor of her skin and the numerous scratches and rashes on her arms and legs.

Barbara smiled dryly. "Not us. We can navigate," she replied.

"What if the Smileys find us?" another man asked.

Roger answered that, holding up the SMG for emphasis. "Then we will fight the bastards!"

"But someone could get killed!" a man cried.

Another man spoke up, "Those who live by the sword die by the sword," he quoted.

"A better way to go than most," Roger answered shortly. "Besides, old soldiers never die, they only fade away," he quoted back.

Dan grinned. "Or if my dad is anything to go by, they drink themselves away in the RSL," he added.

The man began to wax indignant at this. "Blasphemy!" he spluttered.

Barbara cut him short, "That's enough! You don't have to come with us. If you do then keep your mouth shut and do what I say. So, who wants to come with us?"

To Barbara's surprise they all did. Not one wanted to leave them to try walking over the mountain. This was not what she really wanted but she accepted the responsibility with a shrug and bite of the bottom lip, then said, "Okay Roger, let's move. Stay in the pine trees."

Roger and Dan moved on, this time moving parallel to the main gravel road, keeping it just in sight on their right. They followed a course that kept just inside the edge of the pine forest. Barbara followed them. She didn't really care what the slaves did with themselves as long as they didn't interfere, and she felt a bit guilty about that.

I'm a selfish bitch! she thought.

As they walked along, she shrugged and looked back to see if any had changed their mind. But it appeared that they all had followed.

Progress was slow, both because of the need for caution, and because many of the slaves were sick and kept stopping to rest. It was also hard and unpleasant pushing through the waist high weeds and ferns and under the lower branches of pine trees, but Barbara did not want to risk being caught out in the open by an ambush or by a vehicle full of armed Smileys. Fear of snakes also slowed progress as it was impossible to see where they were putting their feet.

It took them nearly an hour to reach the vicinity of the next possible slave group. Barbara kept careful check of their position as they moved. The pine trees gave way to more rainforest. At a sharp bend she signalled to turn left into the jungle. Barbara led them on a compass course into the jungle for about a hundred metres before she was satisfied they were safe. She had them all crowd in close.

"According to the map we are only about 200 metres from a track junction where a road or vehicle track leads off to a place called Scrub Turkey. There is supposed to be another group of slaves somewhere along that track, Group C3. We are going to do a reconnaissance. While we are gone there is to be no talking, no wandering around. Just sit here in silence and you will be safe."

"Will some of you stay here to protect us?" a man asked.

Barbara nodded. "Yes. Two. Karen and Jennifer, you will be their guards. Make sure you keep them all here and silent. Remember you people, if you stay still and quiet you will be quite safe," she answered. She could see that the people didn't like it much, but she did not care. "You agreed to come with us, now obey orders," she said.

Then she briefed the others. "We will move on a compass course. On the way we should find Blacksnake Creek and we can refill our water bottles. Have them all drunk dry before we move."

While the slaves drank Barbara sat and worked out her compass bearings and paces. When they were ready, she said to Karen and Jennifer, "We should be back in about an hour, two at the most. If we don't come back by dark then tomorrow morning backtrack to the pine forest and go east over the mountain to the sea."

The recon patrol set off. Dan and Roger again went as scouts. Barbara navigated and Wendy and Gordon followed. They went straight through the rainforest (or at least as straight as it was humanly possible). Barbara got occasional glimpses of the road up to her right till it curved away. They reached a small creek which had clear water flowing down it and they stopped to drink and to refill all the water bottles. Then they continued. It was slow and nerve wracking. The jungle was very quiet and only a few bird sounds disturbed the stillness.

Suddenly a vehicle motor roared into life down in the jungle to their left. They heard loud voices and slammed doors and the vehicle came driving up the slope towards them. The cadets moved quickly into cover behind trees and ferns.

Mr Smiley's 4WD appeared through the jungle about 25 metres ahead. It roared up a track to the main road then turned left and accelerated away.

"Four men in it," Roger whispered, holding up four fingers. Barbara nodded. She wondered what to do next.

Shouted commands to move and the crack of a whip down in the jungle to their left decided her. Slave Group C3! It had to be!

Urgently she signalled the others to close in and then whispered quick instructions, "Gordon, you and Wendy stay here as a cut-off watching the road junction. Be very careful in case they have a sentry somewhere here. We will go and have a look."

Gordon looked very worried. "Barbara! Please! Don't start a gun battle. Be careful."

Barbara barely heard. She was too excited. Her adrenalin was pumping. Fiona might be there. And anyway, there were slaves to rescue and Smileys to hunt!

I'll wipe the smiles off their ugly faces! she thought with savage satisfaction.

She led Roger and Dan downhill, keeping well to the left of the vehicle track. From time to time she glanced behind to check on the others.

Good old Roger! Good old Dan! she thought. She knew she could depend on them.

It was slow going as the wait-a-while was very thick and she had to continually use her secateurs. Barbara got snagged and scratched a dozen times, but she mostly ignored this and pushed on, sweating and puffing from the exertion. After about 200 metres she got glimpses of movement through the trees. She moved even more cautiously and found herself behind a rough 'lean-to' shelter of made of plastic sheeting tied between two trees and covered with leaves. Underneath were bundles of gear and bedding on stretchers. Beyond it, parked on the track, was a Land Rover. A Smiley was standing there supervising two slaves who were busy loading the vehicle.

About to bug out? Barbara conjectured.

Voices came from further to the left, so she moved back and in a semi-circle in that direction. Fifty metres further on she reached a fair-sized creek with pools of knee-deep water and steep banks.

Blacksnake Creek again, she thought.

The voices came from beyond it so she found a place where she could cross without wetting her boots. It was a hard scramble up the other bank, and she got snagged by wait-a-while but after freeing herself she pulled herself up using tree roots and vines. The others followed with weapons at the ready.

The ground levelled out and sunlight ahead indicated a clearing. That was where the voices were, so she headed for it. When she arrived closer, she saw it was an old timber track.

Must be the Scrub Turkey track, Barbara decided.

She edged through a thicket of wild ginger plant which grew head high along both sides and took a look. The vehicle track was now overgrown and only a footpad through the weeds remained.

Barbara at once ducked back and made frantic signals to Roger, who had become ensnared by a vine ten metres back, to stop moving and to take cover. A line of slaves was coming along the track from the left. They were chained together and carrying heavy Hessian bags. Barbara was only a couple of metres from the track, but she judged it safer not to move. With her heart pounding and mouth dry with apprehension she crouched down and pushed off the safety catch.

The first slave went past, head bowed with exhaustion. Then a second and a third trudged past her. Barbara started counting: Four, five, six, seven, eight...

The line suddenly halted. The ninth slave had stumbled and fallen not five paces from Barbara. She could just see him through the weeds, a bald, middle-aged man. He groaned and attempted to rise. The harsh voice of a Smiley sounded, and she heard the man push his way forward. He stopped only three paces away. She could see his boots and jungle green trousers. Then she saw the barrel of a shotgun pointing at the bald slave's head.

"Get up!" the Smiley snarled. "If you don't get up, I will shoot you like the useless dog you are!"

Barbara glimpsed the slave's terrified face as he struggled to rise. "I can't!" the slave quavered.

The Smiley shrugged, "Then the pigs can have your carcass."

From the expression on the slave's face, and from what she had heard, Barbara believed the Smiley would carry out his threat.

I can't let him be murdered in cold blood! she thought.

Without further thought she rose and took a pace forward. As she did, she brought her rifle up to the hip and aimed it at the Smiley's stomach.

"Drop the gun or I will drop you!" she ordered.

The Smiley turned to gape at her in amazement. Fear flitted across his face. She saw his gun start to swing in her direction and her mind said, *Pull the trigger!* but her mind also warned her of the possible consequences of such an appalling act, so she hesitated.

One of the slaves did not. He tossed the heavy sack he was carrying at the Smiley, pushing his gun aside and making him lose his balance. The shotgun went off with a shattering *bang!* Barbara and most of the slaves cried out in fright.

"Drop the gun! Hands up!" Barbara shouted in desperation.

She wasn't sure if the Smiley was going to obey or not. In any case he didn't get the time. The same slave flicked the chain connecting him to the fallen slave over the Smiley's head and jerked it viciously back. The Smiley let out a strangled cry as he was seized by another slave. A third wrenched the shotgun from his grasp and brought the butt smashing down on his head.

There was more shouting and crashing in the undergrowth. Slaves tried to run or dive for cover but were held by the chain. Barbara whirled around and saw another Smiley in khaki. He had just come around the bend of the track from Blacksnake Creek. He stared in horrified amazement then yelled and fired a shot from a rifle. As he did, Barbara had the chilling experience of meeting his eyes and knowing he was trying to kill her. The bullet tore through the broad leaves with an audible *Th... th... th... uk!*

As the man re-cocked the bolt action rifle, Barbara snapped a shot in return, nearly hitting Roger as he burst out of the weeds.

"Shit!" Roger shouted in fright. He jumped aside.

The guard turned and ran before Barbara could raise her rifle to the shoulder and aim properly.

"Stop him!" Barbara yelled. She started running along the track in pursuit, brushing past Roger. "Dan, guard this lot!"

Barbara pounded down the overgrown track with Roger close behind. Ahead, at the creek, she heard shouted warnings and cries of alarm.

A voice shouted, "Bloody soldiers! Get that Rover going!"

Barbara rounded the bend. The track dipped steeply down to the remnants of an old timber bridge, then up into the clearing where the camp was. Barbara glimpsed tents, a fireplace and a litter of camp gear but was focused on the running man. Two slaves in yellow dived flat in long grass behind the fireplace. The Smiley in khaki raced up the other bank.

Barbara skidded to a halt and crouched against a tree in case of other Smileys. "Stop or I will shoot!" she yelled.

She tried to steady the rifle, aimed at the man's back, and then could not pull the trigger. Her whole being seemed to freeze at the idea of shooting him in the back. So she moved the point of aim down to his legs.

Bang!

"Missed!" she snarled.

She swore loudly as she re-cocked the rifle. The running man vanished around the bend in the track, and she heard the Land Rover start up.

"Gordon! Wendy! Stop them getting away!" Barbara yelled at the top of her lungs.

Roger ran past her down the slope. Panting for breath and gripped by fierce excitement Barbara bounded down the bank after him. They took the jumble of old logs forming a rough bridge at a flat run, were barely conscious of doing so, and raced up the slope through the clearing. As they did, the Land Rover started moving and went roaring up the track towards the road. At the bend Barbara got a fleeting glimpse of its back, the man in khaki half in and half out.

"Gordon! Stop them!" Barbara yelled again and resumed running.

She and Roger went pounding up the track. They heard a single shot. The Land Rover changed gears and accelerated away. The noise diminished as it drove off along the main road southwards. Fearing the worst Barbara pushed herself to keep running, ignoring the flapping webbing and laboured pounding of her heart. She was gasping hot breaths by then and her eyes stung.

As they rounded another curve, she saw Gordon and Wendy standing on the track. Barbara came to a panting standstill beside them.

"Gordon... puff... you... didn't stop them," she cried.

Gordon looked at her and shook his head, "No, we couldn't"

A gasping Roger arrived. "Who fired that shot?" he asked.

"The driver fired a pistol at us," Wendy replied. She looked very pale and was trembling.

"You could have fired back!" Barbara said.

"We could have," Gordon replied. "But it would have been cold-blooded murder, and I couldn't do that."

Barbara felt a twinge of guilt at that. "Yes. I suppose so. But you could have shot the tyres or engine or something," she said.

Wendy answered her. "We couldn't. We didn't know who they were, and there were two slaves in the back. It would have been too risky."

Roger turned to Barbara and put his hand on her shoulder. "Calm down old girl. You just had a bad fright. I think we have done very well. We have hit the bastards again and saved another bunch of slaves, and nobody's been killed."

"Oh dear!" Barbara cried. "Unless those slaves pounded that Smiley's brains to pulp! I hope Dan stopped them."

"Aren't there supposed to be four guards in Group C3?" Roger went on. "If so, we have missed one. Let's go back and be a bit more careful this time." He looked at her reprovingly. "I nearly had kittens when I saw you go pelting off down the track like that. You are damned lucky you didn't run into a bullet coming the other way."

Barbara had calmed down a bit by then. She quivered with excitement but agreed she had been foolish. Then she trembled as a wave of hot realisation of the risks she had just run sank in. Shuddering with released emotion she breathed deeply.

"Sorry," she said. "When that Smiley was going to shoot that poor fellow, I just had to act."

"I know," Roger agreed. He patted her arm again. "You are a real tiger, aren't you?"

Barbara nodded and forced a smile. She saw that Gordon was looking at her but he was not smiling. She thought, *I told you that you wouldn't like me once you got to know me,* but she didn't say it.

Instead, she said, "Wendy, you stay here as sentry in case the Smileys come back. If they do yell out to warn us and then hide in the jungle. Gordon, would you go back and bring Karen and Jenny here with that other bunch of slaves? Bring our packs please."

Wendy nodded. She looked intently into Barbara's eyes and said, "Barbara, your eyes are a brilliant green."

Roger grunted. "Mark of the tigress," he said. "Come on, let's get back and help Dan."

Barbara blinked and for a moment had a sharp insight into what her true personality might be like. She trembled and breathed deeply, then started walking back down the track behind Roger. They searched as they went. On arrival at the clearing beside the creek they found that Dan had brought the slaves and the unconscious Smiley to there.

"Where is the fourth Smiley?" Roger asked.

One of the slaves answered, "That will be 'Mincer' Markham. Mr Smiley took him away early this morning."

"Why 'Mincer'? Does he cut people up?" Roger asked.

The slave gave a short laugh. "Nah! He's called that because that's how he walks. He's a poof. They all are in Three Section. No women in this group," he added bitterly. "Sorry Miss." He kicked the unconscious Smiley. "This is 'Prissy' Pringle. He's the section leader."

Roger sat the slaves in a line and did a head count. "Fifteen of you. Is that the lot?"

"No. Should be seventeen," the slave answered.

"Two went in the Land Rover," Barbara added.

"That'll be Pederson and Bruce. They are their favourites," the slave said. He spat.

Barbara shook her head in disgust. Then she said, "Where are the keys? Unlock them Dan." While this was being done she said, "Listen you slaves, you can come with us, or go where you like." She repeated her speech about what she expected. "If you are coming with us then grab any personal gear, have a big drink and we will get moving. Roger, help me search the camp."

Barbara was now feeling the reaction and a sharp disappointment. Still no Fiona! She and Roger ransacked the Smiley's tents and bundled all Identification and likely evidence together. These she quickly studied then stuffed into Roger's pack. The slaves were freed and stood talking in an excited group.

Roger pointed to the unconscious Smiley. "What about him?" he asked.

Barbara knelt and examined the man. She saw that he was blue around the lips and had a snoring type of breathing.

"Concussion?" she asked Dan who knelt with her.

"Reckon so."

Barbara bit her lip. "We can't leave him here in the jungle. He might not be found in time. We will have to take him with us. Dan, make us a stretcher," she instructed.

This decision caused an angry growl of disapproval from the slaves. Barbara silenced it, "Shut up! If you come with us you do what I say. If not, clear out and look after yourself."

Dan soon had a functional bush stretcher rigged, it being one of the skills they often practiced in the cadets. Roger detailed the four largest slaves to carry it and indicated four more who were to be the relief.

As soon as the Smiley was lifted on Barbara said, "All had a drink? okay, let's march."

At the main road they met Gordon, Karen, and Jenny with the other slaves. They wanted to know all the details.

Barbara shook her head. "Not now. I want to get away from this area before they counter-attack or something," she said.

"Where to?" Karen asked.

"Kuranda if we have to," Barbara replied. Wendy groaned but hoisted on her pack. Barbara took hers from Gordon and pulled it on. But now Barbara was faced by a cruel choice. With a stretcher to carry there was no possibility of moving in safety through the jungle. Barbara knew this from her experience on several cadet exercises in rain forest. Reluctantly she gave the order to walk along the road, even though she knew it was a terrible risk.

They began walking south along the side of the road, Roger and Dan again acting as scouts.

This time Barbara had more trouble keeping the slaves quiet. They made quite a sizeable gaggle and were an amazing sight.

Like a mob of refugees, she thought. They also straggled a lot. As well no-one wanted to carry the stretcher with the injured Smiley on it.

She dropped back to speak to them, "We need him!" she snapped. "He is evidence. Now do as you are told or bugger off!"

She took the shotgun off the slave who was carrying it and checked it, then handed it to Karen. As she did, she did a mental check which surprised her. All of them now had a firearm, either a rifle or shotgun, except Roger, who had the SMG. And they had two pistols as well. She tallied them up and grinned.

Satisfied that they were prepared for trouble, including from the rear, Barbara stepped it out to regain the lead of the main body. When she got there, she said cheerfully to Gordon and Wendy, "In the last twelve hours we have disarmed nine Smileys. That is nearly a third of their force."

"That means two thirds of them still have guns," Gordon replied gloomily.

"Oh cheer up Gordon!" Barbara said. "We've got them on the run. And I'm going to keep them that way."

"Barbara, leave it to the police. We will all end up in jail, or dead!" Gordon replied.

Barbara didn't want to argue. She changed the subject. "I don't think Lofty has made it," she said soberly, then instantly regretted saying it because of the look of distress which crossed Wendy's face.

Luckily Roger and Dan had halted to talk to her. Both were crouched under cover among the last trees of the rainforest. Beyond was a large area of pine forest. Barbara signalled halt and checked her map.

"Macalistairs Pocket," she said. "Let's get off this road so we aren't so easy to find or to ambush."

The slaves had all flopped down beside the road and it took some effort to get them up and moving. Barbara took over as point. She led them straight into the jungle with instructions for Karen and Jennifer to obliterate their tracks. Fifty paces in from the road she turned right and took them out of the jungle into a stand of mature pine trees on a compass course. She didn't work out and exact bearing but just went due south.

That will be near enough, she reasoned.

In among the pines they had to duck and crouch a lot to get under the overhanging branches. Pine needles and dirt fell down the back of her shirt to irritate her. Barbara walked through several spider webs, and as she pushed through the waist high weeds and grass she had to thrust the fear of snakes out of her mind, but they crept insidiously back. The whole place was gloomy and unpleasant but certainly much safer.

After a hundred metres or so they crossed one of the firebreak tracks, which was all overgrown with grass, and plunged into another plot of fully grown pine trees. By then they were all sweating and cursing as it was hot and stifling. She had to keep the pace slow to allow the slaves with the stretcher to keep up. The tail of the long single-file column became a problem as the people at the back began calling out to "Slow down".

Barbara told Roger to take over as point and stood and waited till the end passed her. Then she moved with the stretcher, helping to carry it while scolding the slaves for making too much noise. She also encouraged the sick and weak. Jennifer took over from her on the stretcher after a hundred paces and she paused to get her breath. She kept looking at her watch.

Nearly 4pm, she thought. *I'm ready to drop.* It was then that she realised that she, Gordon and Wendy had been on the go almost non-stop since 2am, 14 hours without a proper break!

They reached a swampy little creek where the slaves all had a drink and then entered a stand of much smaller pines, crossed another fire trail and went through more pines of about ten metres in height. Another small swampy creek was crossed. Beyond the paperbarks which lined its course was a large belt of baby pines only shoulder high. The line halted, the slaves collapsing where they stood. Barbara made her way up to the front.

"Will we cross this open area?" Roger asked.

Barbara studied it, and her map. It appeared to be about half a kilometre across to another stand of fully grown pines. The whole area was a wide, gentle ridge and was 2 kilometres long.

"Yes," she decided.

It would take too long to detour around it. Roger nodded and signalled to Dan, then walked out into the baby pines. Dan waited till he was twenty metres ahead and followed. Barbara did the same, aware of grumbles and pleas for a longer rest from the slaves.

"We will stop in those trees over there," she told them. "Now walk as fast as you can."

As soon as she was out in the open Barbara looked around and was able to check her bearings. She noted Mt Burton and Mildew Mountain and was satisfied her navigation was accurate.

And that mountain in the distance ahead of us is Rainy Mountain. Kuranda is just beyond that.

She resumed walking, moving as quickly as she could and feeling very conspicuous as she realised that the main road was visible only a few hundred metres to their right. On the very crest of the ridge it got worse. The down slope for several hundred metres was newly ploughed ground with tiny pine seedlings only knee high. She urged everyone to move faster and even swore a few times as slaves slowed or stumbled.

Thankfully they reached the cover of the fully grown plantation without incident. Still Barbara would not allow them to stop but made them push on for another two hundred paces until they came to another overgrown fire trail. About a hundred metres down it she saw the main road, so the group was settled under cover amongst the trees.

4:25. Time for a rest, she thought.

But what was really nagging at her was that it was only an hour or so to dark.

What will we do then?

Chapter 33

A HORRIFYING DISCOVERY

As the long, straggling, and exhausted group closed up, Barbara counted them: 7 cadets, 30 slaves, and one injured prisoner, a total of 38 people! She was astonished.

Karen joined her, "Most of these people can't go much further. They are all too weak and sick," she said.

"They don't have to. I'm planning on finding a nice safe harbour position for the night," Barbara replied.

"Where?"

"About another kilometre," Barbara answered.

She had the germ of an idea, suggested to her by the map, but she didn't want to mention it until she had seen the ground and thought it out fully.

Wendy sighed with relief at the news. She looked utterly exhausted. "Thank God!" she said. "I couldn't go much further."

"You've done a mighty job Wendy," Barbara said. "You should be very proud of yourself." She felt a surge of affection and patted her shoulder. Wendy gave a tired smile and dropped her pack, then slumped down on it. Her expression changed back to one of worry and she added, "I'll be okay. It's just that I am very worried about Lofty."

Barbara glanced at Roger, but his face remained composed. He said, "He will be okay. Lofty can look after himself."

Barbara looked at the slaves as they lay or sat in the long grass. Satisfied all was temporarily under control she said, "I am just going off to do a quick recce of the road junction. Keep these people quiet while I am gone."

Roger had just sat down on his pack. He stood up and said, "You shouldn't be going off on your own. It isn't safe. I will come with you."

Barbara smiled. "No you won't. I'm really going away to do something else."

Roger's cheeks tinged red. "Oh... er... I see." Embarrassed, he sat down again.

321

Barbara dropped her own pack and walked along between a row of trees until she was out of sight of the others and could just see the main road. It came around in a curve from her right and then across her front. Off to her left the road curved away from her to the right to cross a small creek via a single lane concrete bridge. She trampled some of the grass, took off her webbing, unbuttoned her trousers and squatted down. From that position she could just see through a gap in the trees and over the long grass.

All the while her eyes and her brain were busy. *We could cross that bridge,* she reasoned, but it looked a good spot to set an ambush just on the other side. It would be a risk. Was it worth it? Anxious to avoid trouble she looked around for options.

The blowflies attracted her attention by their buzzing. She noted a swarm of them hovering noisily over the grass about ten metres away, on the side of the road. She wondered idly what might be attracting them, and then froze with shock when a terrible low groan sounded.

With her stomach churning from apprehension, Barbara hurriedly dressed, picked up her rifle and pushed cautiously forward through the grass to investigate. This brought her out beyond the last trees and in view of anyone lurking in the creek line or beyond it. Her mouth went dry with fear, and she had to consciously make herself move. She crouched in cover and carefully scanned likely enemy fire positions. By then her emotions were jumping up and down, with a sort of sickening dread battling with fear.

After two swift steps she could see what lay in the grass: two bodies, both slaves!

As her eyes took in the gaping wound in the shattered skull of the first one, Barbara reeled with nausea, for she knew instantly that it was death she was looking at. Her stomach turned and the world seemed to spin. She was about to rush back to the others when the second body groaned again.

Barbara nerved herself to go to him and to kneel down to check the man's pulse. All the while her eyes searched the opposite tree line, and her imagination went to work. One of the incidents the cadets used in training to test the reactions and leadership of section leaders was called 'The Body and the Sniper', where a body was positioned as bait to draw a patrol into the open.

Is this the bait? Am I about to become a body? Barbara fretted.

Fear, plus the stunning shock of the absolute reality of the situation, caused a surge of near panic. With an effort which left her trembling she controlled it. Her fingertips felt at the man's throat. Yes, a pulse! That made her reconsider the other man. With a conscious effort she made herself look at him. The first thing she noticed was that flies were walking on his open eyes and they did not flicker.

No. He is definitely dead.

Very conscious of her vulnerability, Barbara backed into the cover of the pines, then turned and walked quickly back to the others. As she got near them, she tried to call, but it came out as a strangled croak, "Roger! Dan! Gordon!" Her voice choked up and she could only hurry on.

But they had heard her. Roger appeared on the run, SMG ready. Dan and Gordon followed. Roger called, "What's the matter Barb? You are as white as a sheet? Here, it's alright."

She ran to Roger and put an arm around him. He did likewise and cried in worried astonishment, "Why, you are trembling like a leaf! What's the matter old girl?"

Barbara bit her lip and clung to him for a moment till she had control of her voice, then whispered hoarsely, "Two slaves. Just near the road. One is dead. The other is badly wounded."

Dan and Gordon started in that direction at once. Barbara called urgently after them, "Oh be careful! It might be The Body and the Sniper!"

Dan gave a thumbs-up. He understood exactly what she meant. Roger released her. "You go back to the others," he said gently. "We will look after this. And don't worry, we will be careful."

Barbara nodded, unable to speak. Her eyes misted up and she just stood and cried for a minute while Roger followed the other two. Jennifer, Karen, and a couple of slaves joined her and wanted to know what was going on. She composed herself enough to explain then insisted they all go back under cover.

There was a buzz of discussion as the news went round the slaves. That made Barbara angry, and she hissed at them for silence. Worry for the safety of the boys gnawed at her, and she told Karen and Jennifer to keep the slaves quiet and hurried after them. She joined Gordon under the cover of the last pines.

"Where are Roger and Dan?" she asked.

323

"They are just scouting the creek line and the scrub across the bridge," Gordon explained.

Barbara looked carefully and saw movement through the trees. She brought her rifle into the shoulder and clicked off the safety catch in case the boys needed covering fire. Out of the corner of her eye she spotted movement. It was Roger as he flitted across from tree to tree. Dan was further up the other slope.

"Did they cross the bridge?" she asked anxiously.

Gordon shook his head. "No, they went to the right and crossed the creek."

On hearing that Barbara relaxed slightly. *Good, their training is working,* she thought.

The cadets did not do much tactical training but at least they knew enough to be as safe as they could be. It only took them a few minutes to search the most likely places (coming in from the rear). They returned the way they had gone, by wading the small creek, and signalled all clear.

When Roger and Dan walked across the road to where the bodies lay Gordon said to Barbara, "You stay here and cover us."

Barbara nodded. She felt a bit of a coward at that but was glad to be spared. Roger and Gordon knelt in the grass beside the bodies while Dan remained on watch covering the creek and road. After a minute Roger walked over to her.

"They have both been shot in the back of the head," he said.

Barbara swallowed as bile rose into her throat. "I know. I saw," she whispered.

"The one who is still alive looks as though the bullet struck at an angle and didn't penetrate the bone. The bullet has torn right across to here." Roger used his finger to show her on his own head the path of the bullet. "He is obviously concussed and has lost a fair amount of blood, but the wound shouldn't be fatal if we can get him to a doctor quickly. Would you mind going back and organizing some slaves into a stretcher party?"

Barbara nodded and hurried back into the trees, returning a few minutes later with four slaves. This time she went forward with them to where the bodies lay. One of the slaves looked at them and said, "These are the two who were in the Land Rover when it drove off: Bruce and Pederson. Pederson is the one who is alive."

Roger quickly organised them to construct a stretcher while he and Gordon carried out what limited First Aid they could. While they did this Barbara crouched further back, feeling sick and very guilty.

This has all happened because we have attacked the Smilies, she thought. *And it was my idea and my pushing that made it happen!*

To take her mind off the horror, and the guilty thought that it was her actions which had caused the man's death, she again studied the captured map. She noted the locations of the Slave Groups. They had now freed three groups: C2, C3 and C4. That only left Group C1.

Fiona must be with them, she thought.

She saw that C1 were located up a side road which went North-East towards Mt Burton. The turnoff was only about another kilometre further on. She saw in fact that there were two side roads, a second one forking off the first only a hundred metres from the turnoff. This second side road led to an airstrip.

An airstrip! Yes! All these slaves said they were flown here, and Inspector Sharpe said that the man who escaped had also been flown in.

It came to her that the airstrip was a possible escape route for the Smileys, and she had a rapid series of ideas on how they might make it unusable to prevent this. Then she bit her lip and sighed.

No good thinking like that. My first job is to get all these people to safety, and the casualties to hospital. Then we can look for Fiona. She checked the time. Almost 5pm. Only an hour of daylight left. *I will have to make up my mind quickly what to do!* she told herself.

A feeling of almost sick despair constricted her stomach and chest. She bent to study the map more carefully, this time noting little red circles with Xs in them. There was one drawn just north of the bridge at Silky Oak, another at the Sandy Creek bridge, one near the southern end of the road they were on just before it re-joined the Black Mountain Road, and one on the side road to Mt Burton at the far side of Macalistairs Pocket. She saw it was where the road left relatively flat ground to climb up onto the crest of the mountain.

Those might be gates, with armed guards, she decided. *Now, we have to avoid them. Which is the best way to do it?*

She bit her lip when it became obvious it was a choice between going over Mt Burton and down to the sea, or over the southern end of Mildew Mountain through several kilometres of jungle.

Roger came to speak to her. "The wounded man, Pederson, he came to for a few minutes. We asked him what had happened. You aren't going to believe this, but he said that he and his friend laughed at the Smileys for running away from us. So the Smileys in the Land Rover pulled up, made them get out, and just shot them."

Wendy was horrified, "But that's just cold-blooded murder!"

Barbara felt an icy chill grip her. She suddenly sensed that the nightmare might just be beginning. It hardened her resolve. She hoisted herself up. "We can't wait any longer. Detail eight more slaves to carry Pederson's stretcher. Karen, you supervise them. Jenn, you keep watch on the Smiley prisoner. I'm going on ahead to select a harbour area. I will take Dan and Wendy with me. Be ready to move as quickly as you can."

"Are you going far?" Roger asked with a worried frown.

Barbara shook her head. "No. Just across the creek and up onto the next ridge."

She pulled on her webbing and pack and helped Wendy with hers, then hoisted Dan's on her front. As she did, the slaves began to cry out and ask questions and had to be reassured they weren't being abandoned. Some began to whine: they were hungry, they were too tired, why hadn't the police arrived? Barbara cast a withering glance at them. Hungry? Yes, she did feel hungry. It had been a long time since breakfast. Tired? She had slogged nearly 30 kilometres since 2 am!

Out at the road she explained to Roger and Gordon where to go and Dan was given his pack and told to cover them across the bridge then follow. She did not go over to look at either the wounded slave, nor at the dead one.

Barbara had decided that using the bridge was a fair risk as the other bank had been scouted and watched. So she led the way straight out onto the road and down across the bridge. As soon as she was across, she turned off the road, clambered over a drainage ditch and entered a forest composed of thickets of small paperbark trees and stands of large sheoaks. Underfoot was a springy carpet of ankle high grass.

This must have been the natural vegetation of Macalisters Pocket before all those horrible pine trees were planted, Barbara thought.

It was easy vegetation to walk through and confirmed what the map had indicated. There was plenty of cover and the road was soon lost to sight. She walked up a long, gentle slope until she was on the crest of a flat ridge. When she had counted 300 paces from the road on a compass bearing, she halted.

"This will do. Dump your gear. Dan, would you mind going back alone to guide the others here?" she said.

Dan shook his head. "No problem. See you in a while." He trotted off back the way he had come. Barbara warmed to him.

What a good sergeant he is! He had not uttered a single complaint.

Wendy dropped her pack with a sigh of relief then unslung the captured radio from around her neck. That gave Barbara an idea.

"Wendy, turn that radio on and see if there is anyone talking," she said.

She had in mind that they might be able to use it to contact the police, or a CB Radio Ham who could do it for them.

Wendy sat on her pack and clicked the 'On' switch. At once the radio began talking.

"Trigrams," Wendy cried. "Someone is talking in code."

"And we can guess who," Barbara replied. "Get out your notebook and copy the messages down. There is a captured code book in my bum pack, the one we got at the Yards this morning."

Was it only this morning? It seems like days ago! she thought.

Barbara left Wendy to it, feeling it was a good thing to keep her busy. *Poor Wendy! She looks so tired and so down. She is fretting: Where is Lofty? Is he alright? Where are the police?* Barbara thought. Then she shook her head. *I have to concentrate, not worry. We will have to save ourselves.*

She sat on her pack and studied the map intently, making notes from time to time. As she did, her overstrained muscles began to cramp and she had to keep changing position and rubbing them.

The sound of many voices announced the approach of the remainder of the group. Barbara was astounded and annoyed. When they arrived, she sat them in a group and snapped at them, "Now listen to me! If you people want to stay alive learn to shut up! Stop talking! Whisper if you have to communicate. And don't wander around. Now, we are going to camp here. After dark there will be no fires, no lights, no talking and no moving around. You will just lie down and sleep. We will run a nylon cord around the perimeter of the camp. It will be at waist height. If you move outside that in the dark we are liable to shoot you. Is that clear?"

There was a murmur of assent, some of it resentful. She went on, "We are still right in the middle of enemy territory. All our lives now depend on self-discipline, or we could end up like his mate." She pointed to the wounded slave. "So stop bellyaching. It is only for one night. We will eat now. Go to the toilet. Men that way and women that way, but don't go far, not more than fifty paces. Count them."

Barbara left the slaves and organised Roger and Gordon to run a perimeter cord around the 'harbour'. "Be quick. It will be dark in half an hour, and we need to eat and have a conference. Dan, you act as sentry, just over there on our track in will do. Wendy, you keep copying those messages and decoding them."

Wendy nodded. "They are going non-stop, so I haven't had a chance to decode any yet."

"We'll do it in a minute. Let's eat while it is still light," Barbara said, acutely conscious that the sun was gone and that twilight was setting in.

She sat on her pack and pulled out her stove and dixies, all the while looking around to see that the slaves weren't doing the wrong thing. The smell of burning hexamine lifted her spirits. So did the cup of hot coffee which followed. She put pre-cooked rice on to heat, the flames glowing brightly in the growing gloom.

Roger organised the slaves to sleep in two rows side by side. Barbara noticed them looking hungrily towards her as she ate but it didn't move her.

Too bad! she told herself. *We don't have enough food to share around, and we need the energy more if we are to win clear.*

Roger came and sat beside her. "Perimeter cord is done and all slaves accounted for," he reported. "Boy, am I hungry! I could eat the arse out of an Aardvark."

"Roger!" Barbara chided, but she smiled.

Good old Roger. Ever since she had been in Year 9, he had been a friend, nearly four years of trials and tribulations. And here he was, beaten, tortured, tired, but still able to joke. Good old Roger, dependable, good-natured, loyal.

And he is as brave as can be, and much tougher than he looks, she thought. *So why does Wendy prefer Lofty?*

But then she shrugged and smiled, knowing that love was beyond reason.

Chapter 34

CAPTURED CODES

"So what is the plan, Barbara?" Jennifer asked.

"Don't laugh when I say this, but I think we should stay here tonight and send two people to try to get help," Barbara replied.

"Hmmm," Roger said with a grin. "I've heard that story before. Yes. I will go."

"We will decide in a minute," Barbara answered. She still hadn't made her mind up.

"And what if help doesn't arrive?" Gordon asked.

"Then we head off cross-country on a compass bearing."

"Which way? Towards Kuranda?" Karen asked.

"No, east, over Mt Burton and down to the sea," Barbara replied.

Roger looked doubtful. He said, "We will never get those stretchers down that mountain. We had a bugger of a job just getting to here."

"We won't get them through ten kilometres of jungle either," Barbara said. "No, we will have to leave them with a couple of volunteers while we get the rest to safety."

Gordon frowned. "They could die by then," he pointed out.

Barbara shrugged. The idea made her sick. She answered, "I know. But whatever we do is liable to have that result."

Jennifer glanced across at the stretchers. "We'd better not leave a slave to guard that Smiley. They would cut his throat," she warned. "I've been watching them. They must have 'accidentally' dropped that stretcher fifty times."

"So who goes for help?" Roger said. "The sooner we start the better."

Barbara hesitated. To her own surprise she realised she did not want Roger to go. She told herself it was because he was more reliable in a tough spot and she needed him to help find Fiona, but she wasn't satisfied with that.

But I can't send any of the girls, she thought. *Or could I?*

Gordon's name popped into her mind, but she pushed it out and substituted Dan's. Then she shook her head.

"I think it is too late to go now. It will be dark in a few minutes and it won't be like at Silky Oak which was mostly open country. Apart from this pocket it is all rainforest for twenty kilometres. If we walk along the road in the dark, we could blunder into anything," she warned.

She flinched at that, having a clear idea of what 'anything' might now involve. A contact in the jungle at night would be at point-blank range, and deadly.

"I agree with you," Roger said. "Let's have a good night's sleep and decide in the morning."

"I think so too," Gordon agreed. "By then the police must surely have arrived."

"I hope so," Jennifer said doubtfully. "I overheard some of the slaves at the commune saying that the police had raided them yesterday afternoon and found nothing."

"We can only hope," Barbara said. "Jennifer, you take over from Dan as sentry so he can eat. I'll see how the slaves are... Argh!... Oooh!... Ouch! ...ah!" these last because of sore muscles as she stood up.

Slowly she hobbled along the first line of slaves. Most were lying down. They all seemed to have at least a blanket.

After she had asked them how they were, one elderly male slave replied, "We will be alright, Miss. This is how we have been sleeping for months now."

Barbara checked the two casualties. Both were still unconscious and felt clammy and feverish. It made her feel sick. She re-joined the others.

"The slaves seem very docile," she commented.

"I suppose they've had the stuffing knocked out of them," Karen said. "That's how I feel."

"Yes," agreed Roger. "I think after you've been whipped a lot when a person with a gun says to you 'lie down and go to sleep', you do. Ow!" He moved and adjusted his shirt.

"Are you okay? Does it hurt?" Barbara asked, remembering the whip and burn marks on his body.

"A bit. Dan is probably worse."

"Silly me. I've got some antiseptic cream in my webbing. Take off your shirts both of you. What about you, Karen? And Jennifer?"

"They didn't whip us," Karen replied. "But they did promise us worse if we didn't talk. Your arrival saved us from that."

Dan was still eating, his hexamine fire a bright glow. That made Barbara realise how dark it had become.

"Come on, Dan, shirt off, and you'd better finish with that fire... Ooh! There's another radio call, Wendy."

Wendy pulled out her pocket torch. "Dig out my sleeping bag somebody so I can hide this light." She turned the torch on and stuck it in her mouth and began writing, her notebook on her knee.

Karen unrolled her sleeping bag and draped it over Wendy while Barbara dug out her First Aid kit. Roger peeled off his shirt and sat on his pack. Even in the gloom Barbara could see the burn marks and bruises.

She squeezed antiseptic cream onto her fingertips and began to gently dab it on. Roger trembled and murmured a few low groans.

Barbara paused in her rubbing. "Am I hurting you?" she asked. She felt Roger's skin. He felt warm and yet shivered.

Roger nodded. "A bit," he replied. "Doesn't matter. Keep going."

Barbara continued rubbing. "Some of these blisters have had their tops rubbed off," she observed.

He has a temperature and a slight fever, she thought.

Roger nodded again. "Hmm. Yeah. My pack and webbing did that. They hurt a bit... Ow!" he gasped.

Barbara marvelled how Roger and Dan had gone all afternoon without complaint wearing shirts and webbing and carrying packs. She carefully dabbed cream on all the marks she could see in the gathering darkness.

"I'll put some Band Aids on those blisters on your shoulders," she said.

As she worked, Barbara noted that Roger wasn't as well built or as muscular as Gordon. *And his skin is much paler. He obviously doesn't go out in the sun as much. But he's not as pudgy as I thought. Well, he is a bit pudgy, but he is solid.*

Very carefully she rubbed down Roger's right side. "Now the front."

"I can do that," Roger replied.

"I'll do it. Move your arms out of the way, no, kneel," Barbara ordered.

"Yes Ma'am!" Roger quipped.

Barbara rubbed and dabbed for a few minutes. Roger began to squirm. "Ouch!... heh, heh, heh... that tickles... Ow!"

331

"Keep still." Barbara rubbed ointment onto another dark weal. "That should do. Dan's turn."

Dan also groaned a bit as she worked on his cuts and blisters. Jennifer came to help and put Band Aids on the raw scabs on the boy's shoulders.

Barbara shuddered as she contemplated the pain the boys must have endured. She gave Dan's shoulder a reassuring squeeze and he flinched.

Roger pulled on his shirt. "Could have been worse," he commented.

"How?" Dan asked.

"We could have been tortured by their Number Four Section," Roger replied.

Dan tried to laugh at that. "Oh my word yes! They are the mob to avoid: 'Kill the women and rape the men!' would be their motto."

"That's enough," Karen said in a shaky voice. She started to cry. "That was what they were going to do to Jennifer and me next," she went on. "That horrible woman was about to hand us over to those disgusting men." She began to sob.

Barbara stopped rubbing Dan and moved to comfort Karen. Wendy put her head out of the sleeping bag and stroked Karen's hand. She said, "Here Karen, help me decode these messages. You too Roger. Do something useful for a change."

After a minute Karen dried her eyes. Barbara took her hand away and Karen pulled out her own sleeping bag and torch.

"Do we have a sentry roster?" Dan asked.

"I'll work one out now," Barbara replied.

She also extracted her bedroll and burrowed headfirst into it, torch in mouth. It took her only five minutes as she used a simple timeline. She made a carbon copy then tore the page out of her notebook.

"Here. Jennifer till 2000hrs. Then I will do till 2200hrs. At 2100hrs Gordon can join me and we will then do the usual staggered reliefs, two hours on, changing every hour."

"Can you and Gordon be trusted together?" Roger asked teasingly.

"You just help Wendy decode that message Roger, before you get hit again," Barbara snorted. Only then did she realise that she had not spoken to Gordon for hours. He sat there beside her. She said very softly, "You are very quiet, Gordon."

"Hmmm! It's been a terrible day, that's all," Gordon replied in an off-hand tone.

"You aren't sure whether you still like me, are you?" Barbara stated.

Gordon shrugged. After a short pause, he answered, "You are certainly full of surprises." He paused for a few seconds, then went on, "I can't help thinking of that man we left lying back there in the grass."

Barbara reached over and squeezed his hand. At that moment, Wendy stuck her head out of the sleeping bag and said, "Barbara, some of these messages are really interesting. They are very important."

Barbara lay down and squeezed her head into the unzipped sleeping bag with Roger on her right and Wendy on her left. Gordon peered in beside Roger and Karen on the other side of Wendy. Dan also joined them but could not fit in. Wendy said, "These messages read as though the Smileys are in a bit of a dither."

Roger smiled. "That's to be expected. I'll bet they've been very worried boys since early this morning," he agreed.

"Certainly since we attacked the commune at lunch time," Barbara added. "What do they say Wendy?"

"Well, first of all there was this message, in clear. The Base Station, who I think is Mister Smiley, that is Call Sign Zulu One, has been trying to make contact with Call Sign Victor Hotel 136. He has tried three times in half an hour, but hasn't made contact." She pointed to the timings written at the top of each message.

"Then he sent this message to Call Sign Zulu Zulu in code." She pointed to the pencilled block letters:

MOVE TO MY LOCATION ASAP.

"That's no help,' grunted Roger. 'We don't know who Zulu Zulu is, or where the location of Zulu One is."

"What does ASAP mean?" Dan asked.

"As soon as possible," Karen replied.

"Oh!"

Wendy turned the page. "Then we got this one, from Zulu One to Call Sign Mike Victor 55."

CONFIRM TIME OF RENDEZVOUS.

"They are trying to escape," Roger said. "That will be their transport."

333

"Yes," Barbara agreed. "But is it a car or a plane?"

"Or a ship," Dan suggested. "Mike Victor. MV. Motor Vessel?"

"Could be," Barbara agreed. "That complicates things a bit." She bit her lip.

"Why? You weren't thinking of trying to stop them were you?" Gordon asked.

Barbara was but rather than admit it she said, "I was still hoping to rescue Fiona."

"No chance," Gordon replied. "Those crooks will be long gone by morning."

Barbara felt resentment bristle but said nothing. Roger did though. "Never say die!" he murmured.

"I don't think they will be," Wendy added. "Look at this message. It is from Call Sign Zulu Six."

POLICE HAVE PULLED BACK AND SET UP ROADBLOCK AT GRID REFERENCE 429506.

"Police!" Barbara cried. Her heart lifted and for a moment she felt lightheaded. She met Wendy's eyes, which were shining with delight. "Lofty must have made it!"

"Yes," Wendy said. Tears suddenly ran down her cheeks.

Roger pushed his map into the torchlight. "Where is that grid reference?"

"Here, where this gravel road we are near joins the Black Mountain Road. Near the Smiley's guard post at Sandy Creek, the one we detoured around," Wendy said.

"In that case there should be police at the southern gate too. They would hardly leave that uncovered," Roger said.

They all grinned and spirits rose. Barbara damped them, "They won't get here tonight," she said. "If there has been shooting they won't risk it in the dark."

Roger nodded. "No, you are right there," he agreed.

"Doesn't matter. We should be safe enough," Wendy added. "The Smileys probably haven't got a clue where we are. All we have to do is hide and wait to be rescued."

Roger agreed. "Even if the Smileys did know where we are I can't

334

see them tramping through the bush in the dark to try to find us, knowing we have guns and would shoot," he said. "Why would they try?"

"What other messages are there Wendy?" Barbara asked.

"That is all so far."

"Fine. Would you please keep listening?"

"Sure. Karen, would you mind helping me?" Wendy asked.

"Of course I'll help," Karen agreed.

Chapter 35

A CHANGE OF PLAN

Barbara moved out from under the sleeping bags.
"I'll take over from Jennifer now. It will give me a chance to think," she said.

She walked the ten paces to where Jennifer sat. It was now quite dark, with just enough starlight for her to avoid the trees.

Jennifer pointed upwards. "Starting to get overcast. It might rain."

Barbara shrugged. Just one more thing to put up with. She sat down with her back against a small tree and rested her rifle across her knees. She felt utterly exhausted and longed to go to sleep. And she would have except for her sense of duty, and a nagging feeling that there was something she should be doing.

So she sat in the darkness and listened. Apart from the murmur of the other's voices as they decoded the messages and a few groans from the slaves and wounded there was just the sighing of the wind in the sheoaks. It made her feel very isolated and far from help.

Then the radio began again, a man's harsh voice with a metallic tone. It sounded very loud.

"Oh we are a mob of idiots!" Barbara said softly to herself, striking herself on the forehead at the same time. She got painfully up and padded over to the others.

"The radio," she said. "Try to call the police with it, or someone who might help."

Roger smacked his forehead. "Oh! What drongos we are," he said. "Good idea."

"Hang on," Karen said. "Won't Mr Smiley hear us if we call?"

"Possibly not if we change frequencies. It's worth a try," Gordon said.

Barbara left them to it and went back to her place. She could hear clearly from there. They tried eight other channels but got no response. She heard Dan say, "These crooks probably don't use ordinary Citizen's Band frequencies. I'll bet they are using different ones."

"You could be right," Roger agreed. "Switch back again and let's see if Mr Smiley has got any more to say."

No sooner had this been done than another coded message started to transmit. Barbara half listened but her mind was trying to concentrate on the problem of how to rescue Fiona.

She has to be in that slave group C1. And that is only a couple of kilometres away up that side road, unless they have moved, she mused.

Would they have moved? The idea worried her. She speculated over what the Smileys would do next. And what would they do with their slaves?

Roger is right. If I was them, I'd be getting out as fast as I could.

Into her mind crept the sinister thought that if the Smileys could just shoot two slaves beside the road, they could easily shoot twenty. The image of the fly walking on the dead man's eye filled her with a terrible dread.

Poor Fiona!

Dan came over to her. "They want you there. Some really interesting stuff is coming through. I'll take over as sentry again."

Barbara re-joined the group. Roger had tied a nylon cord between three trees and hung the sleeping bags over them to form an L-shaped screen. This shielded their torch light from any observer on the road. Wendy was busy writing Trigrams as they came over the radio. Karen and Roger were using the codebook to decode another message. Gordon and Jennifer sat watching.

Roger looked up at her approach. "Here Barbara, it's from Zulu One to another Call Sign called Romeo Four."

Barbara took the notebook and read:

CONFIRM YOU ARE MOVING WITH IMPORTANT
DELIVERY TO THIS LOCATION VIA MILDEW TRACK.
WHAT IS YOUR ETA?

"Mildew Track?" Barbara asked.

Roger shrugged. "Search me. I looked on the map and couldn't find it," he answered.

"Ah! The captured map," Barbara said. Quickly she pulled it out and turned on her torch. She saw at once a double dotted line coming in from

337

the Black Mountain Road across the southern end of Mildew Mountain to link with the commune Road about two kilometres to the south of their present position.

Roger compared the two maps. "Not marked on the army topo map," he noted.

"Must be an old timber road they use as a secret entrance," Karen suggested.

"In which case the police won't be watching it." Roger said.

"No. But if there are police roadblocks to the North and South of it on the Black Mountain Road then they can't escape that way. I don't see any other roads leading out of the area, just a couple of farm tracks that don't lead anywhere much."

"So how did they get in?" Karen asked.

"They may have been in already. Or the Smileys may own other properties over to the west there?" Barbara suggested.

"That's possible," Roger agreed. "They have all that land over near Silky Oak."

"Here, read this message," Karen said, passing it to Barbara.

She read:

FROM CS R4 to CS Z1 ETA APPROX 2200 HOURS.
ADVISE YOUR LOCATION AND SAFE ROUTE

"Location and safe route!" Barbara cried. "That's what we want."

"This might be it now," Wendy said, handing Karen another page of Trigrams. Almost immediately the radio began again, and Wendy went back to writing. Barbara could hardly sit still as she watched Karen's pencil translating the codes into words.

Roger scanned the code book and called the meanings. "Alpha Alpha Lima? Ah! Here. Grid Reference, Alpha Juliet Kilo... that's 'Four', Kilo Foxtrot Foxtrot... that's 'Five'," he read out.

"These Smileys mustn't know that we have both a radio and a code book," Gordon observed.

Barbara nodded. "They probably do. But what other choice do they have? Send in clear? Besides they probably hope we aren't listening, or don't know how to use them," she replied. "Mr Smiley would just think we were troublesome kids and not appreciate that we are army cadets."

338

"Here it is," Roger cried. "You beauty!"

MOVE VIA ROAD JUNCTION GRID REFERENCE 453425 TO GRID REFERENCE 464446

Barbara quickly found the places on her map. "That is the road junction just over there, only five hundred metres away. And their HQ is up that side road that leads to Mt Burton."

As this knowledge sank in, she felt herself tingle with excitement as an idea half-formed earlier began to crystalise.

The radio began again: Zulu One to Call Signs 6 and 7.

"Seven? Who is Seven? I thought they only had six sections," Roger asked.

"Don't talk, decode," Karen said.

Jennifer frowned. "I wonder what the Important Delivery is that Call Sign Romeo Four is bringing?" she asked.

"Dial-a-Pizza," Dan called softly.

They all giggled. "Idiot!" Barbara laughed. But she was consumed by curiosity to know. Her thoughts were now in a ferment. The crooks HQ wasn't at the airstrip as she had expected. It was where Slave Group C1 was marked on the map. Why? What did it mean?

And was Fiona in Slave Group C1?

She must be, or she's dead, she thought grimly.

"Here's another," Karen said, offering her the next message.

Z1 to CS 6 WITHDRAW NOW TO ROAD JUNCTION GR 453425 AND SECURE UNTIL CS 7 AND CS R4 HAVE PASSED THROUGH. THEN WITHDRAW ON MY COMMAND TO THIS LOC. ACK.

Z1 to CS 7 WITHDRAW NOW TO SECURE EAST END OF MILDEW TRACK UNTIL CS R4 HAS PASSED THROUGH. THEN WITHDRAW TO THIS LOC. ACK.

"Ack?" Karen asked.

Roger looked up. "Acknowledge. To let them know they have received and understand the message," he explained.

"And did they?" Barbara asked.

"Yes."

Barbara studied the map and shook with excitement. "We've got their plan! They are concentrating up the Mt Burton Track."

"But why?"

"Waiting for the Special Delivery. Then they will bug out," Roger suggested.

"Yes, but by air or sea?" Jennifer said.

"Sea," Barbara replied emphatically. "If it was by air they would be at their airstrip."

"How?" Gordon asked.

"Same way we did, down Mt Burton to the beach, Casuarina Beach probably. Then onto a launch and away," Barbara said.

"Wouldn't they be seen?" Wendy asked.

"Maybe, but there are a lot more boats than aircraft," Barbara replied.

"I wouldn't like to go down that mountain in the dark," Wendy said.

"Nor would I, but they probably have a track, a secret back door," Barbara replied.

Gordon looked worried. "So what? We can't stop them," he put in.

"We can have a damned good try," Barbara said fiercely.

"Barbara! Don't be silly. People will get hurt. We don't want anyone else killed," Jennifer wailed.

At that Barbara's blood boiled. "People will get hurt alright! I've had these Smiley bastards. And Fiona's Slave Group is with them. What will happen to them? Will they take them with them as hostages? Or shoot them?"

That caused an uncomfortable silence.

"What is your plan?" Roger asked.

"First we are going to disorganise them, hit them a couple of times to throw them into a panic. Then I'm going to cut them off," Barbara answered.

"Why not wait for the police?" Jennifer asked anxiously.

"Because by the time they arrive the Smileys will be gone, and Fiona could be dead!" Barbara snapped. "You don't have to come. I only want volunteers. So, who is with me?"

Roger immediately put up his hand. "I'm your man," he said.

"Me too," Dan called.

340

Wendy nodded. "I'm with you," she said.

"Yes," Karen said.

"Yeah, okay," Gordon reluctantly agreed.

Jennifer nodded but looked very unhappy.

Barbara smiled. "Good. Now, we haven't much time. This is the plan." She quickly outlined it to them. When she had finished and dealt with their questions she said, "Now get your webbing and move fast. Leave your packs."

"What about these slaves?" Jennifer asked.

"Bugger the slaves! They are safe enough here. They are all adults! I'll just tell them to stay put," Barbara cried in exasperation. She strode over and woke the man who had seemed to be the strongest personality earlier and told him.

"We are leaving. We will be back in a few hours. You people just stay here and keep quiet."

"But... but you can't just leave us!" the man expostulated.

"Can't I? Just watch me. I came here to rescue a friend, not you. Now just be grateful and shut up," Barbara snapped. She was in no mood for arguments with people she considered weak-willed idiots.

Within five minutes the seven cadets were moving down the spine of the ridge on a compass course. Barbara led, pushing branches aside, ignoring the long grass and possible snakes. Once she walked through a spider's web and felt the loathsome thing scuttle up her arm. She flicked it off and pushed on, her body shuddering with reaction.

After another seven minutes the cadets were sliding down a low clay cutting onto the gravel road. The night was black. Low clouds were scudding overhead, and the only sound was the soft sighing of the winds in the trees and the crunch of their boots on the gravel. The temperature was warm enough for Barbara to perspire inside her field jacket.

"Okay Roger, off you go. We will join you as soon as we can," Barbara said.

"How long do you reckon?"

"Those Smileys at Sandy Creek had a 4WD. I'm surprised they haven't arrived here already," she said. She checked her watch. It was 20:45.

Roger reached over and squeezed her arm. "Good luck."

"Thanks, but I will depend on skill," she replied.

341

Roger chuckled and her heart warmed to him. He headed off south with Karen and Jennifer. Barbara led the others north.

A couple of hundred paces brought them to the bend which led across the narrow concrete bridge they had crossed earlier. Beyond it the road turned sharp left to where the body of the slave presumably still lay. A wall of pine trees, black and forbidding, provided the backdrop.

"This will do. Wendy, you hide in that washout there and keep listening to the radio. Gordon, you go to the other end of the bridge. Has everyone got their torch ready?"

They moved into ambush positions. Gordon went across the bridge and hid down under its far end on the left. Barbara crouched at the closer end on the same side of the road. Wendy vanished into the erosion gully nearby and Dan stood in the middle of the road with a powerful torch. Barbara had planned to do this, but Dan had insisted.

Barbara settled herself in long grass so that she could spring up quickly. After checking her torch and rifle there was nothing to do but sit and wait, and worry.

Am I being stupid? Immoral? Will there be more dead bodies in the grass like that poor man just over there? Have the ants replaced the flies? Don't dwell on that! Think about something else. The gypsy Fortune Teller. He said there would be misery and death, and he was not wrong! What else did he say? She couldn't remember so she continued to worry. *What will Mr Smiley do? Is it a trap? Have the Smileys sent those radio messages to lure us out?*

Time dragged slowly. 2100hrs. More waiting. *Getting cold, getting cramps... tired. I wish they would hurry up. Perhaps we are too late? If they don't come soon, we will have to give it up and move to support Roger. 2105hrs.*

More minutes dragged by. A spatter of raindrops made Barbara glance up the dark clouds which seemed to be shredding the treetops. Then the sound she had been hoping to hear came to her.

Is that a vehicle I can hear? Yes! Headlights!

"Get ready," she called in a low voice.

Then it all happened faster than she had visualized it. The vehicle was driving fast, rattling over the corrugations in the gravel road. Its headlights swept overhead then shone along the edge of the pines. Suddenly it was there, roaring around the bend.

342

Dan stood in the middle of the road 50 metres on. He clicked on his torch and waved it at the vehicle while holding up his other hand signalling it to stop. The headlights lit him up brightly as the vehicle turned onto the bridge.

Barbara heard the vehicle start to shudder and its brake lights glowed red as it bounced onto the bridge. She glimpsed the driver's face, a mixture of puzzlement and alarm. It was the Smileys. She aimed, ready to shoot the tyres. The vehicle skidded to a halt. Dust swirled around it.

By then Barbara was up and running. She glimpsed Dan jump into the ditch, his rifle swinging up to aim at the vehicle. Then she was beside the cab.

"Stop!" she shouted, levelling her rifle at the driver.

Gears grated and the driver swore. The vehicle's engine roared and it began to race backwards, wheels spraying up gravel. Only then did the driver become aware of Barbara. By the light from the dashboard she clearly saw his eyes dilate as they took in the barrel of the rifle.

"Stop!" she shouted again, almost a sob as she didn't want to shoot. It would be bloody murder at that range.

Crash! Tinkle. Crunch.

The vehicle hit the guidepost at the end of the bridge and jerked to a stop. The engine spluttered and died. There were yells and swearing. Barbara glimpsed a second man as she drew level with the cab again. The second man opened his door and hurled himself out. She tensed to shoot but he scrambled out of sight on the other side of the vehicle. She heard his boots running on the bridge.

"Gordon! Stop him! He's getting away!"

She heard Gordon yell at the man, glimpsed the running figure swerve and vanish into the long grass on the other side of the bridge. Wendy appeared beside Barbara, her rifle aimed at the driver.

"Get out you! Hands up!" she shrilled.

Barbara ran to the rear of the vehicle, checked there was no-one in the back, then turned to look. She glimpsed a flicker of movement and heard crashing in the undergrowth among the pines. Gordon stood at the other end of the bridge.

"You let him get away," Barbara said.

Gordon turned to her. "Yes. Sorry. I just couldn't shoot him."

"That's alright. Nor could I. Was he armed?"

"Don't think so. He didn't have a rifle. I'm sure of that," Gordon replied.

Bang! Bang!

Two shots rang out from the pines trees. Barbara clearly saw the muzzle flashes and her mind registered the sound of a pistol. One of the bullets struck the vehicle beside her. Despite a spasm of terror she quickly aimed and fired back, re-cocked and fired a second time. Dan joined in from the other side of the vehicle.

"Take cover!" Barbara cried.

She scrambled down beside the bridge. There was the sound of crashing in the pines. She aimed at this and fired again. The reek of hot gun oil and cordite filled her nostrils. She sniffed then inhaled. Her heart pounded as the adrenalin rushed. Then she was disgusted with herself.

I am enjoying this! What a thrill!

Trembling with excitement Barbara looked around. Wendy had the driver out and lying on the road in the glare of the headlights. Barbara yelled, "Gordon! Kill those headlights! Wendy, you stay under cover."

Gordon ran to the cab and reached in. After a few moments of fumbling the headlights snapped off. Barbara ran over to the man lying on the road.

"Are you Call Sign Six?" she snarled, holding the muzzle of her rifle near his right eye.

"Ye... Yes!" the man replied. He was badly frightened.

"Gordon, search the vehicle for the radio and any guns and documents. Dan, keep us covered," Barbara called. Then she turned back to face the prisoner and laid her rifle in the dust well away from him. "Wendy, cover me while I search," she instructed.

Wendy moved out to stand at right angles, her rifle aimed at the man's head. Barbara quickly searched the man. She could smell his fear and saw the sheen of his widely dilated eyes in the darkness. He made no attempt to resist. All she could find was a wallet. She pocketed this.

"Now, tell me what your plans are."

The man's eyes rolled to look at her, then away. He made no reply. She tried again. The man remained silent. In her desperation and fear Barbara felt her anger surge and had to restrain herself from kicking him. A dozen questions produced no answer.

A radio squawked. Wendy unhooked hers from her belt. Gordon held one up as well. Barbara clearly heard the voice of Mr Smiley. He was asking Call Sign Six if they had heard gunshots.

"Gordon, answer him. Pretend you are Call Sign Six. Tell him you have secured the road junction and that you haven't heard any gunshots."

Gordon nodded and grinned. He held the radio up to his mouth. "Hello Zulu One. This is Call Sign Six, message, over."

Mr Smiley answered at once and Gordon relayed Barbara's message, then signed off.

Dan indicated the captured driver. "What will we do with this joker?" he asked. Even as he spoke Barbara noted that Dan still faced the pines, rifle at the ready.

"Tie him up and dump him in the ditch beside the road. Make sure you have the ignition keys," Barbara answered.

Gordon did the tying and he and Dan then dragged the man to the side of the road and placed him in the drain. Dan held up the vehicle's ignition keys. Gordon indicated two rifles he had removed from the vehicle.

"Bring them, and that radio," Barbara said. "Now, let's go and join Roger and the others."

As she moved, she glanced at her watch. 2125hrs. In a fret of anxiety she strode off along the road. She was confident that the man who had escaped would not give them any trouble and that if any more enemy arrived from that direction they would be very cautious and slow to react.

Earlier she had considered having just one roadblock to save splitting her force but now she saw she had made the right decision. Now any enemy coming from the north would be delayed a good kilometre away from the others.

And in the dark and the confusion it will take the Smileys quite a while to work out what is going on, she reasoned.

Barbara smiled grimly. "Now for Romeo Four," she muttered.

Chapter 36

FAST AND FURIOUS

Barbara walked as fast as she could in the starlight, ignoring sore muscles and aching feet. The others followed in silence, the only sound the scrunch of their boots on the gravel. A second small concrete bridge was reached after eight minutes.

No danger of ambush, she thought.

Roger's patrol had already checked and crossed it. Just beyond was the dark edge of the rainforest and a road junction on the left. She led the way along this.

The side road, which she knew led northeast to Mt Burton, actually went through an inky-black tunnel in the rainforest. It was so dark she had trouble keeping on the road and several times blundered onto the verge. For safety she slowed down.

Roger should be just here somewhere, she thought.

Even as she did Roger spoke from the darkness beside her and she jumped with fright.

"Halt! Hands up!"

A torch shone on her briefly, then flicked off.

"Good," Roger said, relief evident in his voice. "How did it go? It sounded like quite a battle from here."

"We caught one and blocked the road. The other got away. But Mr Smiley thinks those two are here securing the road junction for him. What is the layout here?" Barbara replied.

There was the rustling of leaves from the darkness and Roger appeared as a dark shadow and stood next to her. "I've got Karen and Jennifer here with me and we've pulled a log across the road about ten paces further on. Oh, and we saw a zombie."

Barbara felt her hair bristle as a wave of superstitious fear swept through here. "Saw a zombie! Roger!"

"We did," Roger insisted. "About half an hour ago. We saw torches coming from the main road. As they got closer we saw that it was a Smiley with a torch leading a zombie on a chain. A second Smiley walked behind

346

holding the other end of the chain and he had a stick and a hurricane lantern. We let them go past."

"Oh Roger! Fair go!" Wendy said. "You are just trying to frighten us. How did you know he was a zombie?"

"Because of the way he walked, a stumbling shuffle, and his flesh had a sort of rotting, greenish colour," Roger replied.

Barbara felt herself break out in 'goose bumps' and that irritated her. "Rot! There's no such thing," she snapped.

"Have it your own way. Anyway, what is the plan now?" Roger asked. "I mean, if we are trying to cut-off the Smiley's escape, why aren't we getting around behind them?"

"Fair enough question," Barbara said. "Two reasons. No, three. First, we aren't sure which way they will go but this road junction here, including another road junction another hundred metres up this side road, controls all the vehicle movement and the airstrip. Second, I think this 'Special Delivery' is important. If it wasn't why haven't they already left? And third, it is going to be very difficult to get around behind them in the dark. I can show you on the map, but I assure you I have thought about it."

"And what about Fiona?"

"I'm going to look for her now."

"Now!"

"Yes. I'm going to divide us into two groups again. One will stay here and hold the road junction. The other will move with me to the Smiley HQ."

"Who goes.... Hey! Vehicle coming!" Roger cried.

"Quick! Dan, Gordon, run up the track until you come to a road junction. It should only be about a hundred metres. Act as cut-off and early warning. Go!" Barbara ordered.

They began to move. There was a stumbling crash and a cry of pain from Dan.

"Mind the log across the road," Roger called.

Dan swore. "Now he bloody tells us!"

At that moment, the glow of headlights from a vehicle coming from the south along the main road lit up the road junction fifty paces behind them.

"Too late! Hide, left hand side!" Barbara yelled.

They scuttled and stumbled into the blackness, blundering through vines and foliage. Only the rapidly increasing glow saved Barbara from crashing into a tree. There was the sound of breaking twigs and then the clang of metal on metal.

Gordon cried out, "Blast! Dropped a rifle."

"Too late. Lie still!" Barbara called as the vehicle slowed at the junction.

Its headlights came into view and it turned along the side road. The car began to accelerate. Then the driver obviously saw the log and braked violently, skidding on loose gravel and dead leaves. The vehicle, a white Range Rover, stopped almost in front of Barbara. She peered around the tree she was hiding behind and saw that it contained four people.

The door closest to her opened and a man got out. She had to stifle a gasp. It was the Reverend Simon Ditchburn. He wore his shiny grey suit she noted as he moved into the beam of the headlights to move the log.

Barbara didn't wait. She tapped Roger and stepped forward. Five steps took her to the vehicle, and she put the rifle barrel right in through the open door.

"Switch off! Put your hands up!" she barked at the driver.

The people in the vehicle gasped in fright. Roger poked his submachine gun in the rear window. "No tricks. Hands up!" he ordered.

Karen and Jennifer started to move out. Barbara called to them without taking her eyes off the driver, "Karen. Jennifer. Stay under cover and watch the main road. Now turn the motor off you and get out."

Gordon and Dan appeared in the beam of the car's headlights just beyond the log. The Reverend Simon yelled in fear and sprang back. The driver, an African American, sat with his eyes goggling and his mouth working soundlessly.

Barbara repeated her order, "Switch off I said!"

The driver nodded and did so. He seemed mesmerised by the rifle muzzle. Something clicked in Barbara's memory. "Good boy, Pedro. Now put your hands up. This thing is loaded and I know how to use it."

Even as she said it, Barbara thought, *Did I reload after that last action?* The worry made her break into a cold sweat and for a moment her voice quavered. *What will I do if he moves? No. Act tough. Bluff!* she told herself.

She rasped at him, "Now get out of the car, slowly, and keep your hands up. Jennifer, come out and cover him. Make him lie on the road on his back. Keep well clear of him."

As soon as Jennifer appeared, Barbara turned her attention to the two people in the back, and got a surprise. One was a middle-aged woman with dark complexion. A name hovered at the back of Barbara's memory but all she could think was, *We've caught a big fish, an Oojoombie.*

Next to the woman sat a middle-aged Caucasian male with a crew cut. He wore a check sports coat, tie, white shirt and chequered slacks.

The woman recovered first. "What is the meaning of this outrage? Who are you? Stop pointing those guns at us!"

Kadumpi or something. The Third Oojoombie! Barbara remembered.

"Shut up!" she snapped. "Save it all for the court case. Get out and lie down on the road."

"I refuse. I demand you let us go!" the woman shrilled.

"Get out before I drag you out!" Barbara snarled.

She walked around the car to the door beside the woman and jerked it open. The woman evidently believed her because she did as she was told, still muttering and grumbling.

Barbara turned to the other man. "Who are you?"

"I am Pastor Smith," the man replied with an American drawl. "And this is monstrous. We are religious people on God's business and haven't done anything wrong."

"We didn't say you had," Barbara replied tartly. "Now keep your hands away from that jacket and get out. Lean on the car. Cover him, Wendy. Roger, you search him. No! No! Wendy. Stand back where he can't reach your rifle and aim lower. Aim at his stomach."

Barbara stepped back to take stock of the situation. Then she walked around to the front of the vehicle into the beam of the headlights. The Reverend Simon lay there on his back covered by Dan. Gordon was standing nearby.

"Gordon, watch up the road," she ordered. Once he had moved to do this she looked down at the Reverend. "Hello Reverend Simon. Fancy meeting you here." she said. She took off her hat so he could see her face and hair.

For a moment he was puzzled and didn't recognise her. He was clearly very frightened.

Barbara gave him a savage smile. "You don't remember?" she said.

349

"I am Fiona Davies' friend. But of course you never met her, just visited her house a dozen times. Now where is she?"

The Reverend Simon goggled at her, his face a pasty mask of fear. "I don't know what you are talking about," he croaked. His eyes bulged and sweat beaded his brow.

"Right first time. You don't know, at the moment. I'll tell you what, Mister Reverend, she'd better not be like the man back up the road there who was shot dead by one of your Smiley men, or you will join him," Barbara grated.

"D... dead man! I don't know what you are talking about," the Reverend Simon gabbled.

Barbara grunted. "Hmmmpf. We'll see. Search him, Dan. I will cover you. Then roll the slimy bastard on his front and tie him up. Hey Roger! This is the Reverend Simon. Look at the funny colour he's gone. Does he look like your zombie?"

"Worse," Roger called. "Maybe we could trade him in. He could start a new career."

Dan chuckled. "Now there's an idea," he said. "Swap him for Fiona."

"Good thinking Sergeant Russell," Barbara replied.

Roger called out again, "Look what this nice religious man was carrying." He held up a silver-plated, pearl-handled six gun.

"And the Reverend Simon here has a snub-nosed Beretta," Dan added, examining an automatic pistol in the vehicle's headlights.

"Pedro here didn't have a gun," Karen added. "Just two knives."

Dan grumbled, "I've tied up so many people today I'm running out of nylon cord."

He finished lashing the Reverend Simon's feet to his wrists then rolled him face down in the dust.

Barbara nodded with satisfaction. "Okay, now tie up Pedro, then the gun-toting pastor. I'll tie up the nice lady," she instructed.

"You can't do that! That's assault," the woman screamed. "I know my rights. I'll see you in court!"

"I hope so. Now put your arms behind your back before I knock you out," Barbara ordered harshly. The woman reluctantly did so. To hold her down Barbara knelt with one knee on the woman's spine. She said, "I'm surprised you haven't asked who we are. We might just be bandits who are going to rob you."

The woman went silent. *She knows who we are alright,* Barbara thought. In a minute she had trussed the woman securely. Then she retrieved her rifle and stood up.

"Now, Gordon, search the vehicle and lay everything out on the road in the headlights. Dan, drag the good Reverend over next to his mate Pedro, then get up to that next road junction and keep watch." She walked around and looked in the vehicle.

"Hello! Here's a nice gun," Barbara said, picking up an Uzi Sub-machine gun off the front seat. "Is this yours, Pedro?" she asked as she checked it. "Not on safe, Pedro. Very sloppy! I'm glad you aren't in my platoon." She engaged the safety catch and slung the weapon over her shoulder by its strap.

By this time all four people had been tied up and lay in a row beside the vehicle. Barbara thought for a moment, then said, "Jennifer, you guard them. Roger, help Gordon search. Wendy, bring me that radio."

As Wendy went to pass the radio to Barbara, Karen called out, "Another vehicle coming!"

Barbara looked. It was coming from the same direction, from the south along the main road. "Karen, take cover on the right. I'll join you. Roger and Gordon, on the left. Jennifer, you get in the trees and keep guard on the prisoners."

They scrambled into cover just in time. A Land Cruiser roared into view, slowed to turn up the side road, then screeched to a halt amidst shouts of alarm and oaths as its headlights lit up the first vehicle and the litter of gear and people around it.

Barbara heard a man yell, "What the bloody hell?" as she stepped out from behind a tree.

"Police!" she shouted. "Stop and get out!"

There was a tongue of red flame from the back of the vehicle. The bullet snapped past so close Barbara felt the shock wave from it. She dived for cover as Roger's SMG stuttered from across the road.

There was the thud and whine of bullets striking metal, the smash and tinkle of breaking glass and a medley of screams and shouts. The vehicle's gears grated and its engine roared, then began to splutter with a metallic flailing sound.

"Cease fire! Cease fire!" Barbara screamed. She didn't want a massacre.

Oh my God! It has all gotten out of control, she thought.

There were more shots, but the vehicle's headlights suddenly went out and it stopped moving. By then it had crashed backwards into the trees on the far side of the T-junction. Barbara heard the thuds of men jumping out and of running footsteps. As one of the Smileys ran back down the road, he opened fire with a sub-machine gun. The stutter hammered in Barbara's ears. The winking red flames seemed to be pointing directly at her. She reacted instinctively.

She raised the rifle and fired, but when she pulled the trigger it just went 'click'. *Bugger! I didn't reload!* she thought. She dropped the rifle and reefed the Uzi around. *Blast it! Won't go off! Ah! Safety catch.*

Suddenly the SMG did go off, just as the man fired again. Barbara was startled by the noise and vibration and held the trigger too long.

"Stop!" she yelled at herself. "Bursts of three to five and aim! Oooh! I've never fired a sub-machine gun before. Oooh! That was good!"

With an effort she mastered her excitement, aware that the men were running off south down the main road the way they had come. At least one was whimpering and groaning. The hot gun-oil and cordite smell wafted over her, along with the odours of diesoline and hot motor car.

"Is anyone hit?" she called. "Roger? Gordon? Karen? Wendy?"

They all answered. Roger came out, gun at the ready, and looked in the vehicle. "Here's one. I thought I got him," he said. He bent down to a dark form lying on the road. As he knelt to examine the man he reached down and tossed a rifle aside.

"Is he dead?" Barbara asked as she walked forward. She started to shake and shiver as the awful reality of what they had just done began to sink in.

"No," Roger replied with a sigh of relief. "He was the bastard who shot at you," he added. He bent back to the wounded man. "Where are you hit?"

"Stomach," the man groaned.

"Are you part of Section Six? What's your name?"

"Ye... Yes. I... I'm Mick Mer... Mercer. Aargh! Do something! Get me a doctor! Oh it hurts! Aargh!"

"Who is Call Sign Seven?" Barbara asked as she knelt next to the wounded man.

"That... That's us. Aargh! Ow! It hurts."

"How many of you are there?" Roger asked harshly.

"Fix me up! I'm bleeding!" the Smiley shrieked.

"Not till you answer the questions," Roger replied grimly.

"F... four," the man gasped between clenched teeth.

Barbara did a quick calculation. "Two left then. I heard one moaning as they ran away," she said.

Reaction caused her to shiver. *Oh Christ! What to do now?* She bit her lip and shook herself. *Act! Too late now for regrets! Save Fiona!*

Barbara looked up and saw Gordon looking down at her. He said, shaking his head, "You don't do things by halves do you?" Barbara didn't know if his comment was in admiration or dismay, and realised she didn't care!

She pointed south along the road. "Keep watch down the road. If you hear movement challenge them, and this time shoot. You won't hit them in the dark. But it will scare them off," she said.

Karen joined them. Barbara stood up. "Drag him over near the others and give him First Aid," she ordered. "We daren't use a torch here. They could shoot us from further down the road."

While they did that, she had a quick look in the vehicle. It was full of personal gear and boxes. *No point in trying to search that in the dark,* she decided.

"Wendy, bring that man's rifle," Barbara said. She walked back and found her own where she had dropped it. As she walked slowly back to the Range Rover she opened her basic pouch, took out some bullets and began reloading the rifle.

Wendy called, "Barb. Mr Smiley is calling on the radio. He sounds a bit worried."

"Ah yes! The radio. Here, put all these rifles in a row on the road. Give me the radio."

Barbara took it and held it to her ear. On an impulse she pressed the 'transmit' switch. "Hello Mr Smiley, this is Barbara, over."

There was a silence for a moment then Mr Smiley called again asking, "Say again, over."

Barbara repeated what she had said. There was no response but she was sure had heard her, so she went on, "This is Barbara. You know, the girl with the red hair. I've got a deal to make with you. Over."

"...crackle... N... eal you bitch! What's going on?"

"Be polite!" Barbara snapped. "We have captured some of your people: a nice lady named Pandami or something. The Third Jumbo anyway. And Pastor Smith. And also Slick Simon, the Shiny Reverend. You can have them back if you give me what I want."

"What do you want?" Mr Smiley snarled.

"He's angry," Barbara said to the others. Into the radio she said, "All your slaves, alive and well."

There was silence for a minute. Then Mr Smiley replied, "I don't believe you. It's a trick."

"Okay, I'll put them on, wait, out."

Barbara walked over to the woman and held the radio near her mouth. The woman at once began to speak rapidly in a foreign language. *Hindi? Spanish?* It didn't matter. Barbara released the pressel switch and walked away. Then she called Mr Smiley again.

"Are you convinced now? I want all the slaves. Oh. I don't mean Groups C2, C3 and C4. We have them safe already. I mean C1. Over."

There was heavy breathing on the radio when Mr Smiley replied. He began negotiating, wanting details: When? Where? How? How could he be sure it wasn't a trap? Barbara heard the radio die away to a whisper. Then it came back stronger. She began to feel uneasy. Mr Smiley sounded as though he was gasping for breath.

Wendy had been listening. She commented, "He is walking with that radio, or running."

Alarm bells rang in Barbara's brain. "Jennifer, Karen, stay here and watch these people and help Gordon guard this road junction. Roger, Wendy, come with me."

With her heart in her mouth from apprehension Barbara started running up the side road. The dying headlights of the Range Rover picked out the log and she jumped it. "I think Mr Smiley is coming down the track on foot," she explained as they pounded up the rutted slope. "And he won't be alone."

"What if that mob we just had the shoot-out with attack again?" Roger asked between puffs. "We will be under attack from both front and rear."

"I don't think they will. They've had a bad fright, and 50 per cent casualties. Besides, we've got their radio. I saw it in their truck," Barbara replied. "Now don't talk, run!"

Chapter 37

MOVE FAST!

They arrived at the second road junction just as Mr Smiley started calling again. He wanted to know why they did not answer. The signal was loud and clear.

At the last tree on the left Dan stepped out to meet them. Barbara stopped and looked around. In front was a triangular grassy clearing about fifty paces wide. The Mt Burton road ran across it as two wheel tracks and vanished in the blackness between a pine forest on the left and jungle on the right. A side-track, overgrown with knee high grass, went off at right angles to the left.

The track to the airfield, Barbara decided.

She stared along it and was disappointed. She had hoped they would be able to see the landing ground from this point, but a large stand of pine trees blocked it from view.

On either side of the Mt Burton road was a tangle of waist high blady grass and weeds. After a moment's thought Barbara pointed left. "In here, in the edge of this bit of jungle."

That placed the Mt Burton road and thick jungle on their right flank and the clearing and airfield track on their front. To the left and rear was the patch of jungle extending down to the small creek on the edge of Macalisters Pocket. Barbara gave rapid instructions and ignored Mr Smiley's repeated calls for an answer. She placed Wendy on her right facing the road and the others on her left facing the clearing. Then she pushed in behind the tree right at the corner of the patch of jungle.

No sooner had she taken cover than Mr Smiley called again. She wiped sweat from her face and placed the radio to her ear. Then she lifted it clear. "I can hear him talking! He is just across the clearing," she hissed to the others. Clicking off the radio she moved the butt of the Uzi into her shoulder. She was gulping deep breaths from both exertion and fear.

The visibility was very poor. Not only was there no moon but the overcast seemed even thicker.

Rain before morning, she thought.

She checked her watch. 2230hrs. What a hectic hour it had been!

Suddenly, figures appeared in the gloom along the Mt Burton Road: one, two, three.

"Halt!" Barbara shouted. "That is far enough! We can..."

She never finished the sentence. The figures dived into cover. There were several shattering *Booms!* and she saw spluttering red flashes. It took her numbed mind a moment to register that she was being shot at.

They aren't going to negotiate! she thought.

For a stunned moment she didn't react, was only aware of shotgun pellets and bullets peppering the leaves and thunking into tree trunks.

But Roger and Dan did. Both opened fire from her left. Then Wendy joined in from her right rear, the lighter *snap!* of her .22 very distinctive. Barbara aimed at winking gun flashes and fired a short burst. This time she was ready for the recoil and kept the SMG under control. Five rounds only. She released the trigger and blinked to clear her vision. The firing she had aimed at stopped but she had no idea of whether she had hit anyone or not.

For half a minute it was bedlam. Shots cracked past, tore through leaves, struck trees, snickered through the grass and struck sparks on the gravel. Barbara heard thrashing in the long grass across the road to her right front over on the edge of the jungle. She steadied the gun against the tree and fired another burst at the sounds.

A man screamed, "Aaargh! I'm hit!"

There was crashing and stumbling in the grass and the shooting died down. Barbara felt simultaneously exultant and nauseous. She looked around, trying to sort out what was going on.

Two on my right on the other side of the road. Two or three in the pine trees across the clearing. And they've all gone to ground, she decided.

"Cease fire," she called.

They did so. In the resulting silence she clearly heard Mr Smiley yelling at his men in an angry voice, exhorting them to attack. There were a few scattered shots but no apparent movement.

"They aren't very keen," Roger said, and raised his voice, "Come on, you bastards! Mr Smiley said attack! Don't just skulk in the forest."

This drew a burst of fire to which both Dan and Wendy replied with single shots. Roger called out again, "Come on, attack! Mr Smiley will lead you!"

From across the clearing Mr Smiley's voice could be heard calling obscenities and instructions. His men did not move. Dan chuckled and said, "No he won't. He's gone back to change his underpants." He called out, "Come on Happy People, your God will protect you. Mr Smiley is right behind you!"

"About a hundred metres behind!" Roger added. Then he laughed out loud.

From the pine forest came a shouted string of obscenities. Barbara sighted at the area and fired another burst. "Don't swear, you bad mannered pig. There are ladies over here."

There was more swearing so she fired again. The Uzi suddenly stopped firing. *Out of ammo!* Barbara realised.

She had not brought the rifle and the Smileys now opened up a steady fire. She winced as a bullet struck the tree next to her face with a thud that made the trunk quiver. Trembling with anxiety and fear she crouched behind it. For the first time she really feared they might be attacked and overrun.

I didn't think these crooks would do it, she told herself. *I thought they would just run!*

Swallowing to quell rising panic she forced herself to be calm. "Save your ammo," she called to the others. "Just an occasional aimed... Shit! That was close!... aimed shot."

Then Barbara remembered the pistol. She slung the Uzi and dug out the pistol. It worried her as she wasn't sure how to use it. She gripped it firmly and pulled back the slide to cock it, then aimed it around the side of the tree.

Blat!

Good. It works, Barbara thought.

She took stock. No attack had developed. Over to the right she could hear groaning, but it was further away.

"Wendy, crawl back and bring up a couple of those rifles and ammo for them, and see if there are any magazines for this Uzi in the car," she ordered.

Wendy started back, rustling, and crunching on the deadfall and getting snagged by vines. The shooting died down. Barbara strained her ears.

"I think they are pulling back," she whispered to Roger.

"I think so too," Roger agreed. "Listen."

Barbara did, noting that she was having trouble hearing above the thudding of her heart. *No doubt about it, judging by the noises in the undergrowth and the mutter of voices over where the Mt Burton road goes into the forest,* she decided.

So what now? She picked up the radio and turned it on. "That wasn't in the deal Mr Smiley," she said.

An obscenity crackled back.

Barbara replied, "Crude peasant! But I'm still willing to negotiate."

Instead she heard Mr Smiley calling Call Signs Six and Seven. She smiled. "I won't tell him. Let him worry!" she muttered.

She waited for a gap in the transmissions and pressed in the transmit button and held it in to 'jam' the net. After a minute she released it.

"What now, Babs?" Roger asked.

"Wait for Wendy to bring us more ammo. Then I'm going back to sort things out at the vehicles. After that, I think we should move to strike at their HQ."

"Good idea," Roger agreed. "That was CUO Kirk's recipe. Hit the bastards and then hit 'em again. Keep them off balance."

Barbara realised her throat was so dry she was going hoarse. She had a big drink and passed the canteen to Roger. "Here."

"Thanks," Roger replied. Their hands met and Barbara felt Roger shaking.

"You alright?" she whispered.

"Apart from being scared witless, yes," Roger replied lightly. "Actually I'm shivering like a dog with two lots of fleas. Some sort of fever."

Barbara moved closer and put her hand to Roger's cheek. "Ooh! Yes. You are burning hot," she said.

"Just reaction I think," Roger replied. "It's not every day you get whipped and tortured. I'm bloody sore all over."

"Good old Roger," Barbara said, squeezing his shoulder.

"What about me? Don't I get any sympathy?" Dan asked.

Barbara's heart went out to them. "No," she answered, her voice almost choking up. "Sergeants only get extra duties."

Dan grumbled but she knew he was alright. She leaned over and gave his ankle a squeeze.

Ten minutes dragged by. Barbara again held down the radio transmit button. There was a spatter of raindrops and the wind increased, rustling the leaves and making it hard to hear. Then the wind died away and they distinctly heard the mutter of angry voices in the forest on the other side of the clearing. One voice was louder than the others.

Roger chuckled and whispered, "Sounds as though Mr Smiley is having a bit of a leadership problem."

Barbara smiled. "Good!" she muttered. That idea cheered her enormously. She released the radio switch and listened to it but there was nothing to hear. She checked the time. Just after 23:00.

"God I'm tired," she whispered.

"You're tired! Did you get any sleep last night?" Roger asked.

Barbara had a sharp memory of kissing Gordon. She flushed and bit her lip. *Was it only last night!* she marvelled. It seemed like a week ago.

"Not much," she mumbled.

There was movement behind them on the track and Wendy groped her way up to join them. "Here," she said. "This is the rifle you had Barbara. There are two magazines for the sub-machine gun, and here's an AK47. It's got a full magazine."

Barbara unslung the Uzi and took the rifle. "Here Roger, you have this Uzi and the fresh magazines. Dan, you take the AK47."

"You wouldn't believe the collection of guns we've now got," Wendy went on. "I spread them all out and counted them. Including that Uzi we've captured seven guns tonight. That includes another fancy little pistol I discovered in that woman's briefcase."

Barbara did a quick calculation. "That makes 16 guns in 24 hours," she said.

"Lofty had a shotgun," Wendy said.

"I counted that."

"Jennifer's got a whopping great automatic pistol," Wendy added. "Oh! And she and Karen have searched the luggage. It's enough to make your eyes pop. There is a suitcase stuffed with money, American dollars mostly. It must be a million bucks! And there are lots of important looking legal papers in a couple of briefcases, and a lot of gold and jewellery in that lady's gear."

Roger grunted softly. "That must be the 'Special Delivery' Mr Smiley was waiting for," he suggested.

359

"And why Mr Smiley attacked us," Dan added.

"Yes," Barbara agreed.

She bit her lip. That was bad news really. It meant he didn't care about the Third Oojoombie or the Pastor. *He wants the loot. So he won't negotiate to swap slaves for prisoners. Maybe he will accept a ransom, money for slaves?*

Barbara unhooked the radio and tried calling him, but got no response. She started to call again when Roger touched her on the arm.

"Sssh! Someone moving over in the pine trees."

"Another attack. Get ready. Spread out. Wendy, you cover the right. Dan, move further down to the left," she whispered.

They moved slowly and as quietly as possible into better fire positions. Barbara leaned on the tree and aimed the rifle at the noise. The rustle of grass and the occasional crackle of snapping twigs came to her clearly. She felt her stomach churn.

If this is a real attack it means kill or be killed, she thought. *If they had pressed the last one, they would have overrun us.*

She contemplated whether or not to try to withdraw while there was time but somehow it went against the grain and she stood her ground and kept the orders unsaid.

She strained her eyes and ears and cursed silently as the wind gusted again. There was another spatter of raindrops. Was that a movement? She bit her lip and steadied the rifle, her finger curled to take the 'First Pressure'.

Suddenly a man called out, "Hey! You, over there! Don't shoot. I want to give myself up."

Was it a trick? "Walk out where we can see you with your hands up," Barbara answered quietly.

There was a crackling in the undergrowth across the airfield track on her left front. The man called again, his voice quavering with fear.

"Don't shoot!" he said.

He materialised from the blackness under the pines and walked out onto the track, his hands held high, a rifle in one.

"Stop and put down the gun," Barbara commanded when he was in the middle of the track.

The man did so. Barbara listened. She could not hear any other movement. "Now walk over here and lie down on your front," she said.

The man obeyed. Barbara said to him, "If you move, I will blow your brains out. Tie him up, Roger."

Roger stood up. "I'm out of cord."

"There's some in my bumpack," Barbara said.

Roger slung the Uzi, groped his way through the vines, fumbled with the straps on her combat pack and began digging around in it.

"Hurry up! You can play with my bum some other time," Barbara muttered irritably.

Roger chuckled. He found the roll of cord and tied the man's hands behind his back. Then he frisked him.

"Nothing," he said. Very cautiously he walked out to pick up the gun then moved back. "Seventeen. An automatic shotgun."

Barbara said, "Okay, Dan and Wendy, you stay here on guard. Roger, bring the prisoner down the track so we can question him."

"Wait," Roger hissed.

He made his way over, returned the rest of the cord to her pack and did it up. The man was hauled to his feet by Roger, and they made their way back into the tunnel of jungle. When Barbara judged they were safely down the slope and out of sight of anyone across the clearing she had the man sit down and shone her torch on him. He looked to be in his forties. She had never seen him before.

"Okay buster, who are you, and what's the story?" she asked.

"Me name's 'Spider' Carey an' I don't want no more trouble," the man said.

"Spider?"

"Yeah. That's what everyone calls me, even the cops. I'm a burglar, yer see. I'm one of them people wot is described as being 'known to the police'. I reckon this Smiley mob's goose is cooked an' I don't want ter be involved in wot they is talkin' about. I'll get enough time as it is," he said. He sighed, then added gloomily, "Ah well. I've bin inside before often enough, bugger it!"

"What are the Smileys talking about doing?" Barbara asked. As she did, she felt her scalp tingle as a terrible feeling of dread gripped her.

"They'se gunna shoot the slaves so they can't blab, then make a run for it. Well, not all the slaves. Mr Smiley said they are gunna keep a few special ones as hostages."

Barbara felt her blood run cold. *Shoot the slaves! Poor Fiona! They*

361

will do it too! she thought. Her mind raced. *We have to move fast if we are to save them.*

"How many Smileys are there?" she asked.

"There woz ten of us. Be only nine now I've given meself up," Spider replied.

"Nine? Hmmm." Barbara dug in her map pocket for the captured Roll Book. "Mr Smiley is there. What about Kowalski, Crane and Bragg?"

"Yep. That's Headquarters."

"Okay, you are in Section C1. There should be four of you."

"Nope. Only three. Me, 'Nasty' Cramp an' 'Banger' Blandford. But Blandford yer can strike orf. He's just had his hip broken by a bullet. They're callin' up a vehicle now ter take 'im back ter camp."

"Calling? I haven't heard."

"Nah. Mr Smiley, he changed frequencies. 'E don't wanta talk ter ya no more. 'E don't like you, no fear!"

Barbara checked the names. "So where are Van Dorkle and Ziggenheim? They are in Section C1."

"Are they? I didn't know that. We don't see much of them. They're the pair of mongrels wot guard the track up over the mountain."

"So they aren't with you?"

"They weren't when I left camp."

Barbara turned the pages. "Are there three blokes from Section C3 with you, Markham, Fells, and Bellamy?"

"Yeah."

"What about Krinkle from C4?"

"No, ain't seen 'im at all. 'E should be over at Silky Oak."

Barbara added them up then compiled a pencil list. "What about the two men who brought the zombie?"

"That woz Cramp and Blandford. They woz sent ter get 'im, the poor bastard!"

Roger asked, "Tell us about the zombie."

Spider snorted. "'E ain't no zombie! That's just crap ter scare the shit outa these idiot religos. They swallow it too. The zombie's just a looney named Boris Brosnik. They do 'im up with make-up, drug 'im, then stir 'im up with an electric cattle prod. It's a real good act."

Barbara was revolted. "You disgusting animals!" she hissed.

"Aw, not me. I didn't do it," Spider whined.

"No. Not you! Of course not!" Barbara snarled. "Okay. How many slaves in Group C1?"

"Nineteen."

"Is there a blonde girl named Fiona?"

"Might be. I didn't learn their names. But there is a blonde sheila. They come an' they go yer see. I mean, one girl died last week. An' Mr Smiley sometimes takes the real pretty ones away. We... we heard that Pastor Smith keeps 'em at his house near Kuranda, if yer know wot I mean."

"I do," Barbara grated between clenched teeth.

What revolting creatures! Poor Fiona! We must act, she thought. She said, "So there are only eight Smileys left. Will they fight?"

"A couple will. Kowalski will, an' Mr Smiley."

"Tell me about this headquarters. What sort of place is it? Describe the layout."

"Aw, it ain't the real HQ. That's somewhere over near Kuranda. Only the people from HQ are here. It's just a temporary camp, a few tarpaulins and tents. It's just a temporary hideout. It's at a road junction where a side-track, one of these fire trails, leads down to the airfield."

"What is going on over there now?"

"Mr Smiley left Fells and Bellamy at the camp ter guard the slaves. Watch out fer that Bellamy. 'E's a bad bastard. It woz 'im wot shot them two slaves this arvo."

"Describe him."

"Big bloke. Beer gut, beard."

"Go on."

"All the rest of us come ter attack yez. Now three of us were left ter watch yer while they clear the camp out. Mr Smiley took the rest back, including Blandford. My job was ter cover the airfield track, which suited me as it got me far enough away from Bragg and Markham so I could give meself up safely like," Spider explained.

"Are they going to escape by air?"

"Nah! The aircraft is in Brisbane, eh! An' it won't fly up. They is gunna git out by boat."

Barbara unfolded the captured map and studied it. There were two tracks. "Which way? Do you mean along this track down to Casuarina Beach?"

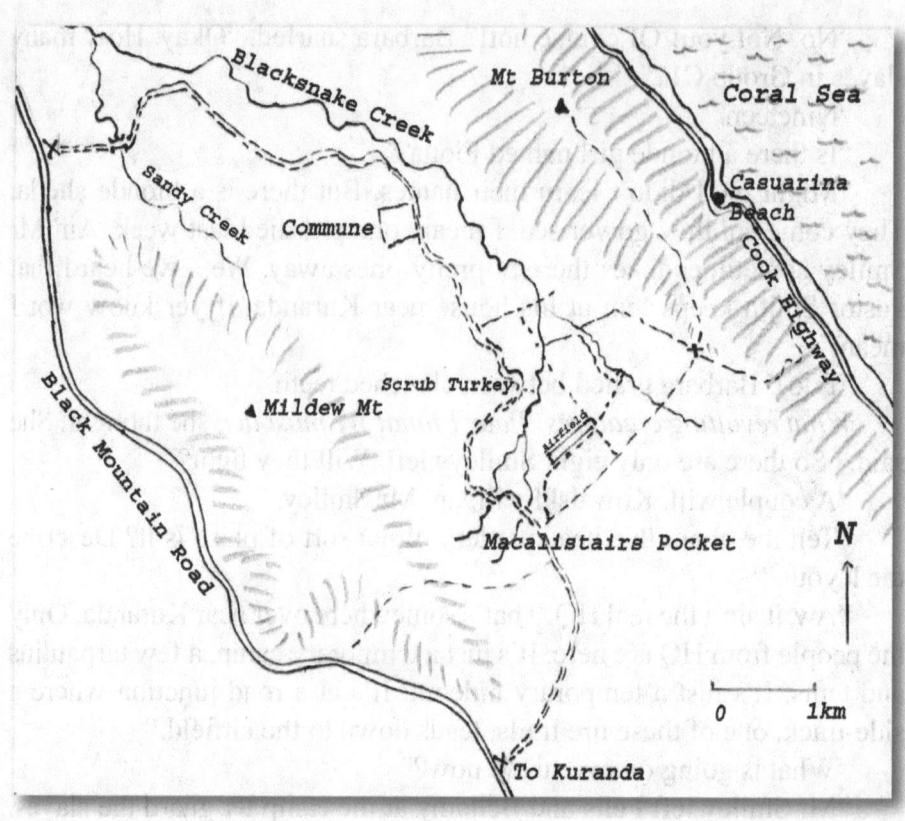

"Dunno. Never bin past the gate with the 'Keep Out' sign," Spider replied.

"Where is that?" Barbara asked.

"There, where the road goes up outa the pines onto Mt Burton," Spider indicated.

Barbara stood up and stretched. Time to get moving. But what was the best plan? There seemed to be too many problems to solve.

How do I hold this roadblock now? Do I need to? Does it cover our rear? How do I guard the prisoners? And the wounded? And what to do with the captured evidence? And the money? And the slaves? she wondered, as a feeling of being overwhelmed swept over her. But she shook her head. *I am the leader. They depend on me. I must get this right,* she told herself.

To help her she used the problem-solving technique of the Military Appreciation that she had been taught at cadets. *Aim?* she asked herself.

But it had not changed. *To rescue Fiona,* she thought. Except now there were serious limitations: the safety of the slaves and securing evidence for any court cases to follow. One thing was crystal clear to her. *This road junction is the hub of the Smiley's road network. If we hold it then we keep them split up and unable to drive out. Also, we are getting too spread out. We need to draw up our tail and concentrate.*

Driven by a feeling of desperate apprehension she made her mind up. She didn't like the plan, but it would just have to do.

"Roger, take this guy down and put him with the other prisoners. Tie his feet as well. Then go back up to Dan and Wendy. I'm going to send Gordon to bring all the slaves here."

"It would be safer to move everyone back to our harbour in the scrub," Roger replied.

Barbara nodded. That was what bothered her, but she had considered the options. "It is, but getting the wounded Smiley there without another stretcher is going to be very difficult."

"The other Smileys can carry him," Dan suggested.

Barbara shook her head. "That means they have to have their hands and feet untied. No. That is even more dangerous. They might jump whoever is guarding them or might just escape. Better to bring them all here."

Roger nodded. "You are right. So here it is then."

He got up and moved to collect the prisoner. Barbara walked down the road slowly ahead of him, thinking hard, and stumbled over the log. She fell heavily, dropping the rifle and skinning her palms. She also barked her shins painfully.

"And shift this bloody log!" she cried as she got to her feet. She rubbed vigorously. The pain brought tears to her eyes. "Gordon, Jennifer, Karen," she called when she reached the Range Rover.

They joined her. Crouched in the bush just off the road she opened her map and shone her torch on it. As quickly as she could, she outlined what had happened, then went on, "I want two of you to go back and bring the slaves here. You've got a compass Gordon? And a map? No, have mine. Bring them all here as quickly as you can and sort them out, and our gear. Those who can use a gun split into three groups: one group to guard the prisoners and loot, one to hold this road junction and one to guard the top road junction. No, we will hide the loot in the jungle first so it doesn't go missing. Warn the slaves not to harm the prisoners. We need them alive as evidence. And make sure they don't shoot us or the police."

"Or each other by accident," Karen added.

Barbara went on, "The other slaves can bed down in the jungle on the left here. Now be as quick as you can because then I want two of you to move via the airfield track to this bridge here." She circled it on his map with a pencil. "Then follow Blacksnake Creek east to where it crosses the Mt Burton Road here. I want you to set up a cut-off to stop the enemy escaping."

She paused and looked up into Gordon's eyes. "Shoot at them. You don't have to aim to hit them. Just make them take cover and pin them down. If they take to the scrub to go around you that's fine. I just want to delay them till daylight. Then the police can round them up. We will meet you there. I want you there by 0200 to 0230hrs at the latest, so you will have to move fast. That will leave one of you here with the slaves. Who wants to stay?"

"I will," Karen said. "I will go with Gordon to collect them then stay here with them. I can look after the wounded."

"Thanks. Okay, I am heading off now with Roger and Dan. I will leave Wendy on guard up there Jennifer, till Gordon gets back. Then she can move with you," Barbara said.

"What are you going to do?" Gordon asked.

"First a recon of their camp. Then I'm going to rescue the slaves," Barbara replied.

"For heaven's sake be careful! We don't want anyone shot," Gordon said.

Barbara grunted. "Hmmm. Bit late for that. Okay, password is 'Happy' and the countersign is 'Holiday'. Any questions? No? Let's move!"

As Gordon and Karen headed slowly off along the main road in the darkness, Barbara got up and walked over to the vehicles. She used her torch to examine the captured gear and then arranged for Roger and Dan to help her carry it all. After a final check that Jennifer was alright guarding the prisoners she slowly and stiffly hobbled up the track. Roger was just shifting the log when she got to it. She helped him and they walked up together, both puffing from the weight of the suitcases and briefcases they were carrying. At the track junction Dan and Wendy were called in and the plan explained.

When she had finished Barbara asked, "Will you be Ok here on your own Wendy?"

Wendy nodded. "Yes. I'm not on my own. I've got a gun! If they attack, I will just withdraw. I mean I will keep shooting and pull back. I'll be alright."

"Good girl! Now, it's nearly midnight. We need to move fast. These Smiley mongrels might move at any time."

If they haven't gone already, she added mentally.

She did not put it past Mr Smiley to abandon his rearguard without telling them. She now felt an all-consuming feeling of dread which made her itch to move. The image of the fly walking on the dead man's eye, of his shattered skull, hovered on the edge of her consciousness.

They checked their weapons, had a drink and then she led them off to the left along the airfield track.

"Take care!" Wendy called softly.

"We will. Now let's move fast!" Barbara said.

Chapter 38

THE NIGHTMARE CONTINUES

It was 0015hrs when they set off. As they walked, a fine drizzle began to fall. Barbara ignored it. She led them left along the airstrip track, walking as fast as she safely could while encumbered by two briefcases and the rifle. The fear of snakes she determinedly thrust aside as she strode through the knee-high grass. Roger followed ten paces behind with Dan ten behind him.

After fifty paces Barbara halted. "In here," she instructed. She turned left and forced her way into the dark wall of jungle, snagging her left sleeve badly on wait-a-while as she did. Quickly she shoved the briefcases behind the nearest tree. Roger and Dan followed her example and quickly hid the suitcases in the thick foliage and long grass.

Barbara freed herself from the snagging vines, swearing softly as she did. She made her way back out to the track, aware that her arm was stinging and that the warm feeling was almost certainly blood. Shrugging at the annoyance of the pain she looked carefully around in the darkness. As soon as Roger and Dan were back on the track she turned and continued on along it, walking as fast as she could. Without a word the other two followed, weapons at the ready.

After rounding a bend fifty metres on the cadets had the open ground of the grass airstrip on their left and pine forest on their right. It looked dark and forbidding. The night was thoroughly depressing, made worse by Barbara's black forebodings.

She walked through the wet grass with her heart in her mouth, accepting that there was some risk of encountering Smileys but felt sure they lacked the manpower to cover all approaches.

Besides, Mr Smiley thinks he has one of his men guarding this track!

It was about a kilometre to a track junction near the north end of the airstrip. They covered this in 15 minutes. As they halted for Barbara to check her navigation a heavy shower of rain swept over them. She tried to shield her map with her hat, but numerous drops spattered on it.

Doesn't matter, she shrugged.

She slid the map into a plastic bag and pushed it back into her trouser map pocket. In an attempt to keep the trickle of cold water out, Barbara pulled her jacket up around her neck. Her trousers and boots were already soaked from the wet grass. In the blackness she squinted to study the side-track. It was similar to the one they were on, just two wheel tracks in long grass, except these were more recent. The track went on across the airfield into a black belt of pines beyond.

"I know where this track goes," she whispered to Roger. "We crossed it last Friday on our way to the commune."

That meant the Smiley camp was about 700 metres to the right. Barbara checked her rifle and consciously summoned up her resolve to keep going then started walking that way. The rain eased then stopped. A cold wind sprang up, whistling through the tops of the pines. This quickly chilled them, and Barbara began to shiver. Then the clouds rolled away and stars appeared.

Barbara counted her paces. At 0700hrs she slowed down from a brisk walk to a careful patrolling speed. *At 120 paces to the 100 metres I should have about 150 to go,* she reasoned.

To her own annoyance, she found that growing fear was making it harder to move. Her eyes began to play tricks as they searched the darkness.

The track went up a gently rising wide ridge with pine trees on both sides. After another hundred paces Barbara slowed down even more. *If it was me, I would have a sentry watching this track,* she reasoned.

So she edged over to the left to 'ghost walk' along the fringe of the pines, one careful step at a time, eyes and ears questing for the sentry who might be there.

It was nerve-wracking, as much because going slow meant wasting valuable time as because of the risk of sudden, violent death. Her heart thumped. Her mouth was dry. Her eyes felt scratchy and hot. Her bodily aches had all coalesced into one vast numbness which she ignored.

Voices.

And a light.

A torch flickered through the trees off to her left front. Not far ahead of her a vehicle door was slammed. *At least someone is still here!* she thought with relative relief.

She had feared to find the Smileys all gone and only dead slaves

369

to mark their passing. Carefully she stepped off the track on the left and began moving forward. She bit her lip then cursed silently as she encountered a clump of lantana. It crackled and rustled. All she could do was back off and edge around it, losing sight of the others as she went under a pine tree.

After about ten minutes, although she lost all track of time and it seemed much longer, Barbara reached a point where she had a clear view. At the road junction three vehicles were parked, all facing north. Two men were loading one of them with haversacks and bundles. Across the road beyond them was a tent fly or tarpaulin spread between some trees. Under it was a table which was illuminated by a kerosene pressure lantern. Three men stood beside it talking.

One was Mr Smiley. He was very angry. Another had a hatchet face and a long, bristling moustache. The third had his back to her. *Five men,* she counted.

Plus the two back along the main track watching our roadblock. That is seven. Where is the eighth? And where are the slaves? Is Number Eight on sentry, or is he guarding the slaves? Barbara made out the dim shapes of two tents to the right of the fly. *Too dark. I will have to move around to have a look,* she decided.

She was now worried about losing contact with Roger and Dan, and of the deadly confusion which might result, so she back-tracked around the lantana to the airfield track. Here she found Roger and Dan crouched under cover on either side of the track.

Roger gestured to the camp. "We could hit them now, one good attack," he suggested, whispering in her ear.

"No. We need to find the slaves and make sure they are safe first. Besides we would only win if we shot people in a surprise attack," Barbara replied. Her battered emotions quailed at the thought.

"They might already be..." Roger began. He didn't finish.

Dead! thought Barbara. It made her feel sick, and she swallowed. "I'm going to look in those tents," she said.

"No, I'll do it," Roger replied.

"I said I will," Barbara insisted.

Dan tapped her shoulder. "Stop arguing. I will."

"We will cover you," Barbara said. "Roger, you come with me, then move out to my right. I will move up to the corner."

Both whispered okay and Dan glided off into the pines to the right. Barbara edged into the trees on her right with Roger following. Knowing they were moving back towards extreme danger sent her heart rate soaring and her mouth went dry with fear. Suddenly she felt exhausted and found she was shivering but hot, as though she had a fever. It took her an effort of willpower to keep moving.

As carefully as she could she skirted a clump of lantana and then edged in closer to the junction of the two tracks. On hands and knees she crept through the grass and ferns until she was only one tree from the corner. Very cautiously she moved to a kneeling position and aimed her rifle around the right-hand side of the tree in the way she had been trained to use tree trunks for cover.

As she did a movement out of the corner of her eye made her glance to her right, and she froze in heart pounding shock!

A person was sitting at the next tree on her right. The person was sitting with their back against the tree and facing the tents. Even as Barbara looked, she saw the person's head slowly turn in her direction. Barbara was about to jump up and cry a warning to Roger, who was even then creeping up behind that tree, when she got an even bigger fright. Realisation of what she was looking at seemed to freeze her blood.

It was the zombie!

There could be no doubt. In the faint light from the lantern Barbara saw that the person's eyes were unnaturally large and that the whole face and head looked too big and too long. Even in the half-light Barbara saw that the zombie's face was horrible. It was misshapen and had ugly warts and lumps on it, some of which appeared to be green. The zombie was clad in black clothing and his hands also looked huge and rotten with lumps and patches of luminous green.

Then Barbara noted that the zombie had a chain wrapped around his body and around the tree behind him and her initial spasm of terror subsided slightly. By this time all the hairs on the back of her neck were standing up and her skin had gone cold and come out in goose bumps. Her breathing was ragged gasps from anxiety.

Now she saw that the horrible face was actually some sort of mask and that the repulsive looking hands were gloves. But she was still scared, and her mind raced over what to do. She had no doubt that the zombie was looking at her.

If he calls out what will I do? she worried. *By now Dan should be across the track further along and he could end up cut-off and out of touch. He might have trouble re-joining us.*

There was also the strong probability of a gun battle with Mr Smiley and his thugs. That would spoil her plan to find the slaves.

But the zombie did not call out. He just seemed to stare at her, which she found very unnerving. Then she saw that the big staring eyes were actually part of the mask.

He can only see through those small holes, she decided.

A faint crackling in the grass behind the zombie caused him to turn his whole body to look back. As he did, Roger's face appeared beside the tree trunk the zombie was leaning on and only half a metre from the zombie's.

Barbara tensed ready for action. She saw Roger's eyes widen and heard him gasp in fright. Then she hissed and called softly. "Roger, back off! It is the zombie."

She saw Roger lick his lips and raise his Uzi. For several tense seconds he stared at the zombie. The zombie stared back. But he did not cry out or do anything else. Then Roger began to back away. To Barbara's enormous relief the zombie did nothing but lean around the tree to watch him go.

Time I was gone too, Barbara decided.

She began creeping back the way she had come. But the moment she moved the zombie's head swivelled to look in her direction. Once again her hair stood on end, and she found it quite disturbing to have him staring at her. Still he did not make any sound, so Barbara resumed moving, taking the risk of him calling out at any moment.

But he didn't and a couple of minutes later Barbara had moved out of his sight, deeper into the pine forest. She found Roger kneeling behind a tree and aiming his Uzi towards the zombie.

Barbara rubbed her eyes and crouched beside Roger. "The zombie," she whispered.

"I know!" Roger whispered back with feeling. "I nearly crapped myself."

"We will move a bit further along," Barbara said. She felt confident now that the zombie would not call out and thought that, even if he did, the men might ignore him. "Follow me," she whispered.

372

She carefully crept ten metres along to the right and then forward to the track again. As she did, she kept glancing to her left but several trees hid the zombie from sight. Thankfully she reached a position beside the track and lay down in the grass to watch.

From where she was Barbara could just see into the tent fly. *I could kill Mr Smiley now,* she mused.

She aimed the rifle and settled the man squarely in her sights. Then she shivered, and was appalled at herself. She lowered the rifle and shook with emotion. Roger patted her shoulder. She leaned against him and sighed softly.

Good old Roger! I can depend on him.

From time to time the wind dropped and they overheard snatches of the conversation, such as, "I hope they wait for us," and, "They must be bloody finished by now!" but not enough to work out what was going on.

The two men finished loading the vehicle and went over to sit at the table. They looked thoroughly depressed. The third man under the fly moved out into the darkness and stood in the centre of the track junction only twenty metres from them and faced south, apparently listening.

Barbara slid back her sleeve and checked her watch. She was amazed. *01:30! Hurry up, Dan! What's keeping him?*

Five long minutes later there was a rustling in the grass behind them. Roger turned, SMG ready. "Hsst! Here we are," he called softly.

Dan re-joined them. "Four tents," he whispered. "One has a wounded bloke on a stretcher. The others are all empty. And I thought I heard voices down that way." he pointed off to the North, diagonally between the two roads.

"Let's investigate," Barbara decided.

The trio moved cautiously back to the airfield track and down it for 50 paces, then crossed the track and entered the forest. After a few paces Barbara stopped to listen.

Yes, there are noises. What was that? A thud? A voice? That way for sure, she told herself.

She moved on at a slow walk-through waist high grass and weeds. The lower branches of pines were so low in places that she had to crouch and push through underneath them and once went through a spider web and had to suppress a yelp. Shuddering with reaction she clawed the sticky mass off her face.

The friends went down a gentle slope. Definite thuds. *Digging noises,* Barbara decided. She pushed slowly on. A faint glow appeared through the trees. Another fifty cautious paces revealed the scene.

A line of slaves was digging a long pit between the rows of pine trees. A lantern at either end provided illumination. Other slaves sat in a huddle, chained to a tree, and one was a fair-haired girl. She sat with her grimy head resting on a man's shoulder. Barbara could not see her face, but her hair style was like Fiona's. Standing at the far end facing them was a Smiley with a sub-machine gun, a big man with a beard.

Bellamy the murderer! Barbara thought.

Roger crouched beside her. "They are digging a grave," he whispered.

"Yes, their own. And from the look of them they know it. We are just in time."

"What will we do?"

"Hush! Someone coming."

A man with a torch and a gun came walking down between the rows of pines. He stopped at the top end of the pit and looked at it. "That's bloody deep enough. I'll go and get the others," he said.

Bellamy grunted and said, "I'll make a start."

The man shrugged and curled his lip. "If you like," he replied. Then he turned and walked back towards the camp.

Barbara felt a surge of sheer panic as the implications of what the man had said struck her. *They are all going to come down here to shoot the slaves! We must save them immediately. But how?*

She bit her lip. Her whole body trembled with intense emotion. In her anxiety she gripped the rifle so hard her hand hurt. But in a few seconds she had made her decision.

"Dan, Roger, cover up towards the camp to stop any other Smileys arriving. I will deal with this guy," she whispered.

She didn't want to argue, and didn't wait. The rifle butt came up into her shoulder and she aimed right at the centre of the man's chest.

Twenty-five metres. I can't miss, she thought grimly. That was too much for her. *I can't do it! I'll shoot him in the legs.* So she lowered her point of aim, then bit her lip. She paused to steady her breathing. *No, that won't do. He has that sub-machine gun pointed right at all those people. Even if I hit him, he might still open fire and kill some.*

Barbara chewed her lip in indecision. A memory of an incident she

374

had seen on the TV news came to her. It had been a hostage drama in America where a man had been holding a gun to a woman's head. The police Chief had asked the marksman beside him: 'Can you kill him before he can pull that trigger?' 'Yes sir,' the marksman replied. 'Do it!' and he had. *Whack!* Right in the head. The gunman had dropped instantly.

Barbara raised her sights to the Smiley's head. She calmed her breathing, took the first pressure, and hesitated. Once again, she could not make herself pull the trigger.

Then the situation dramatically worsened. Bellamy slung the SMG and pulled an automatic pistol from his belt and cocked it, then snarled at the slaves to throw the tools out. They did so, their faces a mask of apprehension. Picks and shovels were tossed up into the grass. Bellamy grabbed at the nearest slave, a bald-headed man, gripping him by his yellow cloak. He shoved the muzzle of the pistol into the man's sweating face and turned him around.

As he did, he snarled, "You religious wierdos had better start hoping there really is a God. So start prayin'!"

The slave began to jibber and beg for his life. Bellamy just jeered and gave a harsh laugh. "Stop snivellin', ya git! If you really believe in heaven, you should be keen to get there."

To Barbara's horror Bellamy thumbed back the hammer of the pistol and moved to aim it at the back of the man's head. Gripped by desperation Barbara lowered her aim, to the man's right hand.

It isn't in line with his stomach and there is no-one else in the line of fire. she thought.

But she was shaking and knew she was having trouble aiming. Then she saw Bellamy's hand tighten and knew she must act.

Bang!

Bellamy spun round and fell, the gun flying through the air. As he went down he let out a terrible scream which melded with the screams of fear from the slaves and shouts of dismay from some approaching Smileys.

Roger's sub-machine gun let rip a shattering burst up the hill through the pines. Dan's rifle added to the din: *crack! crack! crack!*

Barbara found herself running forward, oblivious to the bullets which snapped through the pine needles. The wounded Smiley was thrashing about in the long grass. As she reached him, he struggled to his knees. In the light of the lantern she saw that his right hand was now just a ghastly mess of shattered flesh and bone. Blood seemed to be spattering everywhere. The bullet had badly mangled the hand and the man appeared to be missing several fingers. One dangled by threads of sinew and skin.

Bellamy screamed and screamed, each one a pitch higher and more spine-chilling. Barbara stood transfixed by the horror of what she had done. Aghast she stared at him. He saw her but his eyes did not register. His face contorted with agony, and he shrilled again. His SMG hung loosely from the crook of his arm, but she hesitated to try to take it off him as he was holding his shattered right hand with his left.

Barbara felt the bile rise to choke her. "Oh my God! What have I done? What will I do?" she cried.

Strong arms grabbed her and pulled her over into the grass. "Down!" Roger yelled in her ear.

Barbara's mind registered the terrified faces of the slaves just near her, and the fusillade of gunshots. Roger reached across and wrenched the SMG from Bellamy, injuring his hand again.

Bellamy fainted.

"Thank God! Oh God... forgive me!" Barbara cried.

Roger put his arms around her and held her tight, a comforting press of sweaty wet uniform, webbing and warm flesh. She shook with emotion and buried her face in his shirt.

Crack! Crack! Thud!

Pine needles rained down on them. Dan's rifle banged twice more. There were distant yells. Slaves screamed and whimpered. Barbara's mind registered Mr Smiley shouting, "Do what I say! Now move!"

Mr Smiley! The Smileys! They were attacking! Fear hit Barbara like a bucket of ice water. *I'm letting everyone down!* she berated herself. She struggled to free herself.

"I'm alright, Roger. Let me up. Where's my rifle?" she cried.

Then it dawned on her: the Smileys weren't attacking. They were running. Dan fired again from further up the hill. A vehicle started up. There were more shouts and a sporadic crackle of return fire which came nowhere near them.

Barbara picked up her rifle as the vehicle roared off northwards. She saw its headlights flickering through the trees. Dan gave it two parting shots which drew return fire from at least two Smileys retiring on foot along the road. Barbara turned to the slaves.

No. Not Fiona.

Some other blonde girl with lots of freckles.

Barbara looked frantically at all the other slaves. No, Fiona wasn't there. Barbara's shoulders sagged in defeat.

All that, and I failed! she groaned.

By this time the slaves were starting to recover from their shock and were chattering and crying out in delight as their minds registered the uniforms. Barbara turned to Roger who was bending over the wounded Smiley.

"She's not here Roger," she cried in a broken voice.

Then she choked up and tears flowed freely. In a blur she saw Roger walk towards her. He enfolded her in his arms and she sobbed as she had never sobbed before.

"It's okay. We will find her," Roger said. He hugged her and she put her head on his shoulder and cried. He went on, "That was bloody marvellous what you just did. I couldn't have done it."

"Oh what have I done!" Barbara wailed.

"Given that murdering bastard his just deserts," Roger replied grimly. "No. A life for a life would have been better." He hugged her again, patted her back and stroked her hair.

Slowly Barbara calmed down. The slaves were demanding attention. Roger's SMG was digging into her. Her own right hand was getting cramp from gripping her rifle. The wounded Smiley began to groan. Dan reappeared.

"Bloody top stuff!" he cried excitedly. "That shifted those mongrels in a hurry." He laughed gleefully and patted his assault rifle.

"Have they gone?" Roger asked, releasing Barbara.

Dan nodded. "I think they are just up the road a few hundred metres," he replied. "The vehicle stopped and I heard voices. Then the Rover drove on."

"Protect us while we sort this out," Roger said.

Barbara dried her eyes with Roger's damp handkerchief then blew her nose. "I'm alright. I'm just a bit upset," she said. In truth she was appalled and disgusted and feeling very guilty.

"That's okay," Roger said, patting her shoulder. Then he turned to the slaves and bellowed, "Shut up and sit down! You are safe now, or nearly. Now, do any of you know where a girl named Fiona Davies might be?"

"Yes," a woman answered.

Barbara lifted her head. *At last! News!*

The woman continued, "She and her father were in this group, but the Smileys took them both away yesterday afternoon."

Disappointment stabbed through Barbara.

Roger asked, "Do you know where to? Which way did they go?"

"That way," a man answered, pointing northeast. "They went in a Land Rover. I heard they were going to join the special prisoners."

"Special prisoners! Who are they?" Roger asked. "You mean there are more slaves?"

"Yes, so we heard."

Barbara rubbed her face. She was so tired her mind seemed numb. It was there in her memory. *If only... Ah!*

"I know! What fools we are! That man... Jeremiah Somebody. He was kept in a concrete building on a mountain near the sea."

She pulled out the captured map and held it to the light. "There! Right on top of Mt Burton."

Roger looked at it. "Then this must be the vehicle track we crossed on top of that ridge last Friday," he said. Then he groaned. "We were within a kilometre of the place a week ago!"

"Well, we know where it is now," Barbara cried. "Come on! We must hurry!"

Roger grinned and held up a hand. "Whoa! Slow down. Let's sort this mess out first. See if you can find some keys to free these slaves. I'll do some First Aid on this murdering mongrel."

"Tie his legs first," Barbara cautioned.

While Roger tied Bellamy's legs with a length of rope Barbara reluctantly searched the man's pockets and belt but found no keys. One of the slaves called to her, "He hasn't got them. The section commander, 'Nasty', has them."

While Roger secured a field dressing firmly over Bellamy's wounds Barbara seated the slaves and counted them. 19. So Spider had told the truth. Eight in one chain gang, the grave diggers, and eleven in the other. They were chained to the tree.

378

When Roger had finished tying the bandages, tying Bellamy's wrists together in the process, he took a mattock from the unfinished grave side and tried to chop through the chain where it passed around the tree. All he succeeded in doing was have it bounce off and bruise his knee.

"I need bolt cutters or an axe or something. I'll go and look in the camp," he said.

"Be careful. There might still be some Smileys there," Barbara cautioned.

Roger waved to indicate he understood and walked off up the hill. Barbara quietened the slaves and quickly explained what the situation was.

A shot away up the track made her jump. Dan fired back from near the Mt Burton road. There were three more shots from further along the road in reply. Silence fell.

Roger! He went to the Smiley's camp. I hope he is alright, Barbara thought in horror.

She peered anxiously into the darkness and heaved a sigh of relief when Roger came striding cheerfully back through the trees carrying an axe.

"What was that shooting?" she asked.

"Bastards took a pot shot at me when I went near the lantern at the camp. Silly of me. I should know better," Roger replied.

"So they are still there," Barbara stated.

"Seems so."

"Why? Why don't they just run away while they can?" Barbara wondered aloud.

Roger shrugged. "Rear guard? To hold us up?" he suggested.

Barbara shook her head. "Yes and no. These blokes are just crooks. They won't sacrifice themselves just for Mr Smiley so he can get away."

Roger shook his head. "I reckon they might. I think they are more scared of the Oojoombies than they are of us or the police. I suspect that they know the Smileys will hunt them down if they don't obey orders. They are better off in jail."

Barbara considered this. She remembered the others who had been captured and their fear. No, their terror. "You might be right," she conceded. "So they are buying time, but why? Ah! I'll bet they are waiting for the Special Prisoners to arrive so they can use them as hostages."

She looked at the map. "There is a road junction marked at the base of the ridge leading up to Mt Burton. There is a gate or guard post there. I wondered why it was there. Obviously, it was to separate the special prisoners from the others. The left-hand road leads up to Mt Burton but the right hand track leads to a much lower part of the coastal range. There is a nice spur leading down to the sea."

Roger leaned over to study the map. "I saw that ridge the other day. We should have come up it."

Barbara nodded. "Yes, but we were taking the shortest route to the commune. I'll bet that Mr Smiley has had to go left up to Mt Burton to collect the Special Prisoners. Then he must come back down to that junction to go along the other track. These jokers just up the road are holding us well forward of the junction until he has done that. They will fall back at some time to join him."

"Could be," Roger agreed.

Barbara bit her lip. That meant they couldn't use the road. They would have to by-pass through the forest. In the dark that meant the pine forest. It would be almost an impossibility in the jungle.

If only I hadn't told Gordon to position that cut-off! she thought.

It was really annoying as he would be only a kilometre from the road junction at the gate when he was in position. She looked at her watch. 0215hrs.

No. Gordon would have been too late to cut them off, except this rear guard, and it is too late for us to try to catch him at the airstrip.

Roger left her to puzzle it out and went to chop through the chain. After several attempts he had made no apparent progress.

"I'll have to chop the bloody tree down," he grumbled. It was a poor joke, but it raised a laugh.

"Get some steel backing behind that chain," a man suggested.

A mattock blade was inserted between the trunk and the chain. That did the trick. Roger snapped the chain with two solid blows. He then picked up Bellamy's sub-machine gun and examined it. It was the same type as the one he had so he extracted the magazine and stuffed it into his basic pouch. The SMG he leaned against a tree.

Then he returned to Barbara. "So what's the plan, Barb?"

"Send these slaves back via the airfield track to join the others at the roadblock. We will go on and try to rescue Fiona," Barbara answered.

Chapter 39

PUSHED TO THE LIMIT

Barbara turned to Roger. "Go and call Dan. We will lead these people to the airfield." To the slaves, she said, "Get ready to move. We are leaving here in two minutes time."

Within a minute Roger reappeared with Dan. Dan looked scared and was puffing. He cried, "The zombie is loose up there. He jumped out and nearly got me. Scared the crap out of me."

The thought of the zombie roaming free in the dark bothered Barbara. "Loose? He was chained to a tree when we saw him. I wonder how he got loose?" she said.

Dan shrugged. "Don't know. I suppose those Smiley mongrels let him go. He was pretty stirred up, growling and trying to grab me by the throat," he answered.

"Which way did he go?" Barbara asked.

"Not sure. I just bolted and heard him grunting and growling around the camp. He might still be there," Dan replied.

Barbara shivered with apprehension. "I hope he doesn't hurt someone," she said.

Roger gave a short laugh and said, "Well I'm not going to try to recapture a maniac in a monster suit in the dark. He will just have to be rounded up tomorrow."

Barbara shuddered at the thought and nodded. Then she bit her lip. There was nothing to be done about the zombie now. She turned to the slaves. "Right you lot, pick up that Smiley and carry him, and make sure he arrives alive. We want to see him in court for murder. Let's go!"

Barbara did not wait but set off through the trees. Roger ensured the wounded Smiley was picked up. Dan came last as rear guard. They made their way through the dark pines to the airfield track, the slaves grumbling and stumbling. Barbara didn't care what their problems were. They were saved and that was enough. Her mind was concentrated on how to save the Special Prisoners and the problem of how to do this had her in a lather of indecision.

Which way should we go? Where is the best place to intercept the hostages? What will we do when we do? she worried as she pushed herself along with fretful urgency, ignoring her bodily weakness and pains.

It took them seven minutes to reach the airstrip. 0242hrs. They stopped for a minute to allow the line of slaves to close up.

Barbara pointed left. "Go that way and you will meet more of our people at a road junction about a kilometre along. And make sure that Smiley arrives there. Now get going."

"Aren't you coming with us?" queried a slave, his voice cracking with anxiety.

"No. Stop wasting time and go!"

"But you can't abandon us out here in the middle of nowhere!" the man cried.

"I can and I'm going to. It isn't the middle of nowhere. It is only Macalisters Pocket. You can walk to Kuranda if you like. Now get moving. Come on Roger, Dan," Barbara replied.

Without waiting to argue she turned on her heel and strode off to the right, ignoring the pleas and complaints of the slaves.

Her irritation with them helped her make a basic decision about which way to go. She walked for 50 paces until she was clear of the slaves, then halted to allow Roger and Dan to catch up. While they did, she took out her map, then crouched in the long grass and turned on her pencil torch to study it.

"Where to?" Roger asked as he joined her.

Barbara pointed to the map. "To this bridge across Blackwater Creek, then northeast, say 45 degrees magnetic until we hit the track on the ridge top south of Mt Burton," she replied. She pointed to a place about a kilometre west of the gate and junction at the bottom of the ridge.

"Hmmm. About two kilometres," Roger said. "Will we make it in time? It will be mostly jungle don't forget."

Barbara bit her lip and shook her head. "We won't if they move fast, but we have to try," she said.

While she talked, she placed the lighted torch on her compass to irradiate the luminous markings.

Dan crouched to study the map. "Why not go the other way, to cut the track down to the sea?"

"We would have to zigzag to get around their rear guard, then pass between it and the guard post at the gate. That is about 3 kilometres at least. And we run the risk of bumping into Gordon's patrol in the dark. Besides, we don't know that the Smileys will go that way. The house on Mt Burton is almost directly above Casuarina Beach and we know there are yachts there. For all we know there might be a track straight down," Barbara explained.

She bit her lip. It was the cruellest dilemma she had ever faced. She set her compass on the bearing she had worked out, switched off her torch and stood up. For a moment she was seized by cramp in the legs, and she had to cling onto Roger to straighten up. To her dismay, she realised that her leg muscles were all trembling and she feared she was about to collapse.

Oh don't give up on me now! Please God, give me strength! she prayed.

"You okay?" Roger asked, taking her arm and helping her up.

"Yes. Just a bit tired that's all," she replied.

For a few moments she stood to recover. As she did, she looked around in the blackness, noting that the thick grey overcast was breaking up. A fresh breeze caused her to shiver.

"I will lead for a while," Roger said firmly. "You navigate. Dan, you put your safety catch on and don't shoot us in the bum."

"It is on!" Dan cried indignantly.

Roger set off at a brisk walk. Barbara forced her tired legs into motion and followed. She found it easier once they were moving and was relieved that Roger was in front. At least the fear of snakes receded somewhat.

Unless you subscribe to the theory that the first person stirs it up so it bites the second! she thought gloomily.

They covered the 500 metres to Blacksnake Creek in just over five minutes. The crossing was not a bridge. It was a concrete floodway. Beyond it was more pine forest. For a moment Barbara hesitated.

Should we try to find the track we cut on Friday? She wondered. Then she shook her head. *No, we didn't really cut a track. We will waste more time looking for it than it will take to make another.*

Roger paused and queried the course. Barbara indicated the direction and he immediately plunged off the overgrown track into waist-high grass and lantana. This led them into the pine trees. They made no attempt

383

to move silently but crashed along as fast as they could walk. It was almost totally black, with just enough starlight for them to avoid the pine branches. The grass was wet and they were soon soaked through. Barbara was now so exhausted it took her a conscious effort to lift each boot.

For a time fear took an almost paralysing grip on Barbara. *Oh my God! The snakes come out at night to hunt. There have to be snakes in this long grass.* She pictured some of the reptiles she had seen in the past: huge, red-bellied blacks as thick as her arm and two metres in length. *That is Blacksnake Creek back there,* she told herself. She prayed as she walked. *Please God, no snakes, or at least not a Taipan. Good old Roger. I'm glad he is in front of me to scare them away. Oh, I hope he doesn't get bitten. Please God, no snakes!*

The march developed into a nightmare of stumbling in the weeds with sweat stinging in numerous lantana scratches on hands and face. Nerves were stretched taut by the darkness and the fear. Muscles were strained with constant tripping, bending and walking. Pine needles and grass found their way down the back of their necks into their shirts.

As she pushed under a low branch Barbara felt her head. *Where's my hat?* she wondered. She could not remember losing it. But there was no point in worrying about it so she shrugged and kept going.

The undergrowth thickened to include clumps of wild raspberries which grew higher than a person. These had vicious thorns several centimetres in length. After the first few painful encounters, which drew blood, they slowed down. Roger used his secateurs to snip a path. Even so they still got scratched and their clothes were torn. Barbara could never remember a worse time in her whole life. Her temper got rapidly shorter and when a thorn ripped open her right cheek, narrowly missing her eye, she let rip with a burst of muttered swearing.

The boys made no comment. They were busy swearing themselves. It seemed they had made a serious error and Barbara became more and more desperate.

Suddenly they emerged on a cleared lane of waist-high grass. Beyond was a black wall of jungle.

Roger stopped. "Bloody hell! We will never get through that," he gasped.

Barbara checked the time. 0320hrs. "We have to try. It is only about half a kilometre."

384

"If it's like what we just came through it will be the death of me," Roger gasped. "This looks like an old fire trail. I reckon if we follow it to the right we should come to that road junction at the bottom of the ridge."

"That is where the guard post is marked on the map," Barbara pointed out.

"Might be."

"We can't take the risk. If we stumble into a gun battle, how can we sneak up to rescue hostages?"

"How will we rescue them anyway?" Roger asked.

But he didn't wait for an answer. He turned and deliberately walked into the tangle of rainforest. He began to push, swear, tear down vines and cut and battle his way in.

The others followed. It was worse than Barbara had imagined possible. In 15 minutes they progressed barely 50 metres. They were continually snagged by unseen wait-a-while, entangled by vines of all thicknesses, blundered into trees, tripped over logs, had sticks poke them in the eye and generally found their character being tested to the limit. It was so dark that Barbara proved the theory about not being able to see her hand in front of her face.

They came to a sweating, cursing halt. A sickening sense of having made a stupid decision came over Barbara. She bit her lip and held back the tears with an effort. Her whole body trembled with fatigue and over-exertion. The only heartening thing was that the ground was getting perceptibly steeper.

"We will have to go back," she said with a sniffle. She wiped sweat from her face and tears from her eyes.

"We can use our torches," Roger said. "That is how CUO Kirk led us to safety up on the Herberton Range when we were being hunted by those Kosarian Partisans."

"But we might be seen. We are heading towards the enemy, not away from them," Barbara said.

"It's a risk, but they will hear us anyway," Roger replied. He had a drink. So did Barbara and she was dismayed to find she was out of water. She couldn't remember drinking it.

Roger took out his torch and flicked it on. "Keep me on the compass bearing," he instructed as he resumed his onslaught on the jungle.

The torch certainly helped, and Barbara noted that it was barely visible at 20 paces. In the next ten minutes they covered nearly a hundred metres and by then they were starting to climb a steep slope. Roger halted to get his breath. "My torch is starting to die," he muttered. That was obvious by its feeble yellow glow. Barbara took out her own but Roger stopped her.

"Save it," he said. "Here comes the moon."

Barbara looked up and offered a silent prayer of thanks. A pale glow began to light the sky through the foliage. She realised she could actually distinguish tree trunks and clumps of palms.

Roger rose and attacked the forest with renewed vigour. The friends hauled themselves up the slope from tree to tree, ignoring bumps and scratches. At one stage Roger got wedged between two trees and had to back up. As he did, he slipped on the leaf mould and scrabbled for a minute before regaining his feet.

"We would go faster if we dumped our webbing," he said.

Barbara thought about it. They would certainly make better time. But then, Capt Conkey always insisted they wear it. It contained things they, or the hostages, might need: water, First Aid stores, food, torches.

"No."

Roger didn't argue but resumed the climb. Moonbeams began to stab through, producing a dapple of light and shade. The slope became steeper and steeper until it was as easy to crawl as it was to walk. They had to haul themselves up from tree to tree and continually slipped and slithered on the loose deadfall. The wait-a-while became even thicker so that Roger stopped for minutes at a time cutting at it. It seemed that the ordeal would never end. Barbara struggled to keep going. She knew she was being pushed to the limits of her endurance. Gritting her teeth she struggled on.

And suddenly they were there, standing on the muddy vehicle track in the moonlight.

But were they in time?

Barbara pulled out her torch and flicked it on, pointing it at the ground.

"One set of tyre tracks. No footprints," Dan said, kneeling for a better look. Barbara did not dare kneel. She was afraid she might not be able to get up again. It seemed that every muscle in her body was quivering from over-exertion.

"So they haven't come back yet!" she croaked, gulping air into her heaving lungs.

"Or they aren't coming back this way," Roger added soberly. "So what do we do now?"

"We must go up the mountain," Barbara said. "All the way to the top of Mt Burton. We will either meet them coming back down, or we will chase them down to the sea."

"Bloody hell!" Roger groaned. "You wait till you see the other side of this bloody mountain Dan. You'll want to become my platoon sergeant then."

"Anything to escape from the current slave driver," Dan replied banteringly.

"I'm not a slave driver!" Barbara said, bristling with resentment. "Anyway, better the devil you know. Now let's get moving."

Barbara did not want to waste time and felt that if she stopped too long her muscles would seize up. She began slogging up the road, her pace almost a totter.

"Ow!" Dan cried as he lurched into motion. "Am I sore!"

They struggled up over a low rise, then trudged down across a shallow dip. The road then went up a steep pinch for a hundred paces. Barbara tried to make it up without stopping but couldn't. She laboured to a gasping stop. Dan slogged on past her.

"I'll go scout," he said. "Give you a break."

Roger reached Barbara and gripped her arm. She took hold of his and resumed plodding up. The road was greasy from the rain and it was hard going. It was also dark, despite the moon. The road was narrow and the trees met overhead to form a gloomy tunnel.

On top of the crest Dan halted to get his breath. "What will we do if we meet them coming the other way?" he asked.

"Hide and let them go past," Barbara gasped. "Then we will follow them and wait for a favourable opportunity."

On they went. The road wound up and down along the spine of the 'razorback' ridge, gradually gaining height. From time to time one or the other would stumble on a rut or a rock or slip in the slush and mud underfoot. It was hard work for all of them. Barbara had to make a conscious effort of willpower to summon up her last resources of strength to push herself up the hills.

As she summoned up the last of her reserves of energy, Barbara calculated that she had been marching and fighting for over 24 hours and she was afraid that the end of her endurance was close. Several times she had to stop, heart pounding, gasping for breath, leg muscles shaking. Once she was brought to a halt by an agonising cramp in her left leg.

"Ow!" she moaned softly. "Cramp. Ow! Hit it Roger, hit it! Punch it!" she moaned.

Roger knelt with a groan and began pummelling her leg. She moaned softly in pain. Roger them used both hands to squeeze and massage the calf muscles.

Dan came back to see what the delay was. He peered in the shadows. "Not now you two. Save that for later."

Barbara laughed and cried at the same time. "Shut up, Dan. It hurts. If you get too cheeky, I'll make you carry me," she said.

That sobered them. Barbara relaxed her muscles and stood trembling. She helped Roger up while Dan scouted on ahead. They resumed their plod. Another steep slope slowed them. Once over the crest they started down a steep slope which was greasy from the rain.

Dan halted and waited for them. He pointed down the road.

"There is a vehicle just there at the bend at the bottom. It's not moving," he whispered.

Barbara could just make out a white shape in the moonlight. They stood and listened for a minute, but the only sound was the wind in the trees and a gentle swashing sound which had Barbara puzzled until she realised it was the surf on the beach down to their right.

"I'll check it out," Dan said. Roger moved to a fire position to cover him while he ghosted on down the side of the road. Two minutes later his dark form came flitting back, clearly visible as he broke the dappled moonbeams.

"It is Mr Smiley's," Dan reported. "It looks like he lost control on the mud going down and slid off the track. It is wedged against a tree. There is no-one there."

They walked cautiously past. The vehicle lay half on its side with two wheels off the track and one up in the air. It wasn't badly damaged but was plainly stuck. That cheered Barbara up.

Now they have to walk!

Another two minutes of steady walking went by. At times the

brilliance of the moon made it seem as though a spotlight was on them as the crossed open patches. The dapple pattern made visibility confusing and difficult. Barbara kept rubbing her eyes and wondering if she was starting to hallucinate from fatigue.

"How much further?" Roger asked when next they halted on an up-slope.

Barbara shrugged. "Not sure. Can't be more than one or two kilometres. It is Five o'clock. Only an hour to daylight," she answered.

Dan made a sharp hiss. "Someone coming!"

As quietly as possible they moved off the road into the jungle, the thud and squelch of approaching footsteps causing Barbara's heart to start pounding with excitement. She crouched behind a fern beside a big tree. Gently she eased off her safety catch.

Down the road, heading in the opposite direction, came a slithering, stumbling line of people. They were led by the hatchet-faced Smiley with the bushy moustache. He was carrying an M16. Barbara saw him clearly as he passed through a beam of moonlight. The harshness of his face made her shiver. It was like a nightmare.

Mr Smiley followed next, a sub-machine gun in one hand and a briefcase in the other. Next came a Smiley Barbara had never seen before and he was holding the end of a chain which secured a line of hostages. As each hostage passed through the moonbeam Barbara got a clear view of them.

Fiona's father was the third one.

And Fiona was fourth!

No doubt about it. Fiona!

She looked haggard and unkempt. In the moonlight her fair hair looked unreal, a silver-grey. Like her father she wore the yellow robes of a slave. All the other hostages wore a variety of civilian clothes. Barbara counted them. Nine. And two more guards.

Once the group had passed out of earshot Barbara exhaled a slow stream of air. She felt dizzy and had to lean on the tree.

Roger nudged her. "You okay, Barb?"

"Yes. Just held my breath too long. It was Fiona."

"I know. I saw her. Now all we have to do is rescue her."

"Ah! That's the tricky bit," whispered Dan from the other side of the tree. "As my dear old dad often says: 'First catch your chicken!'."

They moved back onto the track. Barbara remembered to slip her safety catch back on. Roger snicked his off. "I'll go first."

"Don't blunder into them if they stop for a rest," Dan cautioned.

Roger gave a disdainful sniff. "It'll be bloody Corporal Russell if there are any more insults," he said.

He tried to make it light and bantering but underneath Barbara could tell he was nettled, and also deadly serious. So was she.

And she was elated. The hunt was nearly over. They had found Fiona. *Somehow, we will rescue her,* she told herself.

They commenced the pursuit. Now Barbara became even more concerned that she would be forced to give up from physical collapse. Several times she staggered and Dan grabbed her elbow to steady her. The dappled patterns of moonlight and shadow began to play tricks with her eyes, and she knew she was starting to hallucinate.

At least it is mostly downhill, she thought thankfully.

Three times they stopped when the group in front stopped. During one of these halts they heard angry murmurs and what might have been blows. The next time they heard a savage command quite distinctly, "Get up! Get up and move!", and the slash of a whip, followed by a cry of pain.

Barbara felt her anger move to a simmer. She forced herself on. Once they nearly walked into view of the group ahead, but Roger was careful. He waited at each bend until the last person of the group in front had rounded the next bend. Then he walked quickly forward to it, followed by the others.

Grey half-light began to merge with the moonlight. By the time they passed the crashed vehicle they could clearly see each other. Barbara became aware of a pink glow through the foliage off to her left. She looked that way and got a glimpse through a gap in the trees of a silver-grey sea with the flush of dawn lighting the undersides of distant clouds.

Soon be daylight. Thank God! she thought. But she knew with bowel gripping fear that with the dawn would come the hour of decision and she braced herself for it.

The track began to go down steeply and curved westward. Barbara started to fret. They would soon be down the mountain and back in the pine forests of Macalisters Pocket and no opportunity had yet presented itself to try to carry out a rescue.

We need to get around in front of them somehow, she thought. *But how? Perhaps we can surprise them next time they stop for a rest?*

It was a horrible problem, with terrible consequences if they made a mistake. Barbara had no illusions that Mr Smiley and his cronies would kill to save themselves. It made her sick to her very core, but did not weaken her resolution to act.

Suddenly Roger stopped and listened. He held up his hand for them to halt. It was getting beyond first light by then, details were clearly visible and Barbara could see both her rifle sights.

Down the slope ahead someone yelled out. Barbara and her friends stiffened in surprise and crouched against trees. Roger gave her a quizzical glance.

A single gunshot broke the stillness. It was followed by a savage burst of automatic fire.

Barbara felt her stomach turn over with anxiety. "Oh no! They must have run into Gordon's patrol," she cried.

She was appalled at the rapidly mounting volume of gunfire from ahead. It sounded like a full-scale battle. Poor Gordon! Poor Wendy! And Fiona was still a hostage.

Determined to save her friends Barbara stood up. "Come on!" she snapped. Slipping off her safety catch she took the lead. The gunfire further down the slope was fast and furious. It sounded like dozens of weapons. The shots came so fast they became an almost continuous roar. The noise rolled up the mountainside and, though muffled by the jungle, was like a solid force. Barbara's heart quickened as the adrenalin pumped. She gripped the rifle at the ready as she doubled forward.

At the next bend in the track, Barbara came to a halt and cautiously looked around. A glance showed that they were at the bottom of the mountain. The road curved left through a gap between big rocks and a low cutting, then down to the right to where a grassy clearing could just be seen. Huddled against the bank beside the rocks were the hostages. A single Smiley was guarding them, and he was looking down over a boulder towards the clearing. All the other Smileys were below that on both sides of the track. Puffs of gun smoke showed where two of them were.

In an instant Barbara made her decision. She began walking straight down the middle of the road, rifle at the ready. The others followed. Only then did she realise that bullets fired by the 'friendlies' were cracking around her and thudding into trees. She flinched but kept walking, her eyes on the Smiley.

As Barbara got closer she saw the eyes of the hostages widen as they saw her. *They will give me away!* she thought in alarm.

So she raised a finger to her lips and kept walking. Her gaze locked momentarily with Fiona's. She saw her gasp in disbelief as recognition occurred. By then she was only ten paces from them.

The Smiley sensed something and turned his head. His eyes bulged in astonishment and fear. Barbara saw his muscles tense, preparatory to springing around.

"Move and you are dead!" she snarled, aiming directly at his chest.

The man's eyes flickered from her face to the rifle and back to her face.

"Drop you gun!" Barbara snapped. "Hands up!"

To her intense relief he obeyed. Barbara moved sideways to cover him. She realised that the firing had all died down. In the silence someone was shouting.

"Grab his gun Roger. Give it to Fiona," Barbara ordered. Then she pointed at the Smiley. "Lie down on the track you!"

She again motioned to the goggle-eyed hostages to stay silent and moved past them to the bend as Dan took over covering the Smiley. All the shooting had now stopped and Barbara was able to understand the shouting down at the clearing.

Mr Smiley was yelling, and it wasn't at Gordon's patrol.

It was at the police!

Chapter 40

THE PROBLEMS RESOLVED

Barbara heard Mr Smiley yell, "I've got nine hostages here. You coppers back off and let us go or I'll start killing them. If you don't start moving back in one minute, I will shoot a hostage just to prove that I mean business."

Barbara peered through the jungle looking for him. *He is somewhere down to the left,* she thought, her eyes blurring with tiredness and strain as she scanned the undergrowth.

Then her gaze focused on a hand and arm lying on the grass out in the open at the base of the slope. Moving slightly she was able to look through a gap in the trees. Sprawled in a bloodstained heap on the edge of the clearing was the Smiley with the bushy moustache.

Only three left, including Mr Smiley, Barbara counted.

One was down the slope on the left of the track. She could just see his legs behind a tree. Another was below to her right somewhere.

Mr Smiley yelled again. "Ziggy, bring one of those hostages down here. Start moving back coppers!"

Barbara took a deep breath and called at the top of her voice, "Don't believe him. The hostages are safe!"

Mr Smiley swore and yelled, "Who the hell is that?"

A voice from in the jungle down to her left answered, "A soldier. No! The girl with red hair."

"That bloody interfering red-headed bitch!" Mr Smiley screamed.

By then Barbara had moved behind a tree as she saw a flicker of movement. A bullet tore up the earth near her feet. She hastily aimed and snapped a shot back.

No good. He's got the drop on me! she realised.

She reloaded and rolled out onto the track, then scrambled to the other side. As she did, firing broke out all over the place. She glimpsed Dan stand up to fire down over the rocks.

"Got the bastard!" Dan cried exultantly.

"Did you kill him?" Barbara called in dismay.

"Nah! The mongrel's still wriggling so I can't have," Dan replied, a tinge of regret clear in his voice. A ricochet whined viciously off the rocks near him, causing him to flinch and duck down. He went on, "He's out of the fight though. He's dropped his gun and is busy with trying to stop the bleeding."

Barbara assessed the situation. Fiona was crouched in a firing position with the Smiley's sub machine gun. Her eyes were blazing with hatred and her lips were drawn back to reveal her teeth. Fiona cocked the gun and clicked off the safety catch. Then she raised the weapon to the shoulder and sighted at the man as he lay on the track. The Smiley stared back in obvious fear and began pleading for his life.

Barbara sprang up. "No, Fiona! Don't kill him!" she shouted.

Roger also sprang up. Fiona hesitated. Her eyes met Barbara's and her face twisted with emotion. Then she lowered the gun.

"Sorry, Barb. But if you'd seen what these animals are like!"

"We have," Barbara snapped. "Now, let's get back somewhere safer."

Fiona pointed. "Roger, get those keys off his belt and set us free, quick!"

As Roger raced out and knelt beside the man, he was almost hit by a shot from down the track. Barbara swung round and fired back. Her mind raced as it took in the ground.

If that bloke, or Mr Smiley, moves even a few metres they will be able to fire right along this section of road, enfilade it, she thought.

She aimed and fired again as she glimpsed movement amongst the trees. Then she shouted: "Roger, don't wait to unlock them here. Get them all back over into that gully behind us." She turned and shouted at the slaves, "Get up! Move! Move! Get up and bloody run!"

To cover them, Barbara fired again, and so did Dan. Roger raced across and hauled the end slave to his feet and pointed the way. The man was terrified and in panic. He tripped and fell, bringing down two others. Roger hauled them to their feet and dragged them back up the track past the rocks and into the jungle. The others followed in a struggling mob.

Barbara became aware that a storm of fire was lashing the jungle where Mr Smiley was. The police were on the other side of the clearing.

There must be a dozen or more, she judged by the volume of fire. *That is where we need to get to.*

Suddenly, a movement in the jungle on her left attracted her attention. Out of the corner of her eye Barbara saw what was causing it. It was the zombie! The zombie stepped out of the undergrowth, his clawing hands reaching towards her. For a fraction of a second Barbara stood rooted to the spot in shock. The sight of the revolting grey and green face caused a wave of intense fright. Instinctively she swung up her rifle to shoot but could not bring herself to fire. She stepped back, and stumbled on the rough track.

As she fell, she screamed in fear. The zombie stepped forward to try to grab her. Then he stopped, his hands grasping at her but just out of reach. Barbara twitched in terror, flicking her body out of his reach and rolling onto her front. In the process she gave her knee a painful bump and she scratched herself some more. But she clung onto her rifle and was able to scramble to her feet.

Through eyes that were misted with sweat and terror she saw that the zombie was held by his chain. It was caught on something in the jungle, and he turned and began pulling and flicking at it, uttering spine chilling growls while he did. Then it came loose and he gathered it in. Barbara sprang back to try to get away. As she did, the Smiley they had disarmed went to get up. He was looking at the zombie with a look of absolute terror. The man got as far as his hands and knees before the zombie struck. The zombie lashed out with a length of his chain. The heavy steel links whacked into the side of the Smiley's head and he flopped down into the mud and lay still.

Barbara stared in horror, then moved to the far side of the track. As she did a bullet smashed into the tree trunk a centimetre from her head. She saw, in instant focus, Mr Smiley's face over his rifle barrel. He was down among the trees at the bend.

He screamed, "You bitch! I'll kill you!"

At that moment, the zombie turned towards Barbara again, his horrible hands raised in a strangler's grasp. But on hearing Mr Smiley his head swivelled to look in that direction and he gave another animal growl before stumbling and crashing back into the jungle. Barbara recovered from her fright sufficiently to fire back then dodged behind the tree, even as the next shot struck it. The bullet punched through the edge of the trunk, throwing out jagged splinters.

Barbara sprang up and hurled herself over a large rock, to sprawl in the leaf mould beyond on her back. She grimly kept a grip on her rifle and ignored the pain of another banged knee. A shot whacked off the rock as she struggled to her feet. Dan was near her and returned the fire. Barbara scrambled further into the forest.

Mr Smiley's voice rose above the roar of gunfire, "You bitch! I'll get you!"

Barbara rose to her knees and aimed at where she thought he was. "I'll cover you Dan. Run!" she commanded.

She fired, re-cocked and fired again as Dan scrambled back past her. Several shots cracked past. She fired again then scuttled back over a low crest. As she ran, she sucked in frantic gasps of air, her heart hammering in cringing fear of the bullets. The others were huddled there in the top of a small gully. Dan stood guard, covering the way they had come, while Roger was busy unlocking the chain.

Barbara flopped down gasping. Fiona dashed over and embraced her, "Oh Barbara! I can't believe it! Thank you! How did you find us?"

Barbara hugged her and laughed, a mixture of nervous tension and hysteria. "It's a long story. Tell you later. We aren't out of the woods yet. Face up the hill and cover our rear."

Fiona was crying. They both were. Fiona hugged Barbara again and shuddered. Barbara met Roger's eye and suddenly felt self-conscious. When Fiona began to slobber her with tears and kisses Barbara held her away.

"Save it for later. Cover up the hill!"

Barbara disentangled herself and got up. She checked and reloaded her rifle and looked around. The firing had all stopped. Fiona wiped her tears and picked up the SMG. Roger pointed where she had to face. By this time he had freed all the slaves and they were all crouching in the small gully.

As Barbara recovered her breath, she reloaded the rifle and took stock of the position. Over the track she could hear Mr Smiley calling to the other Smiley, but she could not hear enough to follow what he was planning. She didn't care. All she wanted to do now was get Fiona and the other hostages to safety.

Twenty metres down the slope was the grassy clearing. Beyond was a thick belt of wild raspberries. Down at the bottom of the small gully, beyond the clearing, was what looked like a swamp: pandanus and thick bushes. The police were over there somewhere but she couldn't see any of them.

We had better be careful, Barbara thought. *We don't want to be shot by mistake.* She noted that, if they could get across the clearing, they would be safe. *It will be a fire trail around the pine trees, or an old logging track,* she decided. *If we go along to our right for a hundred metres or so we will be safe enough to cross.*

She explained her plan to the others. Dan nodded and said, "We'd better be careful. There is someone moving up the slope on the other side of the road. I can't see him but I can hear him. If he gets much further around it will be dangerous to leave this dip."

"Then let's get moving," Barbara said. "Follow me."

She rose and moved at a slow walk out of the dip and away from the road above them. Fiona followed her. Roger ushered the other hostages after her. Dan came last as rear-guard.

Barbara angled downhill to put a large dead log between them and the Smileys. This brought them almost to the edge of the clearing. When all were under cover of the log, she held up her hand.

"I'll just have a quick look along the clearing," she said.

She wanted to make contact with the police if she could, so they could help. Quickly but cautiously she crawled down through waist-high weeds and grass to the edge of the clearing. From behind a tree she cautiously raised her head and looked right and left.

Fifty metres to her left was the road junction, and on a tree just near it was a white painted sign, which said,

KEEP OUT TRESPASSERS PROSECUTED.
DANGER. GUARD DOGS.

The Mt Burton road crossed the clearing to vanish into the pandanus swamp. The track in front of her was all overgrown with knee-high grass.

Movement away to her left, beyond the road junction, caught her eye. Someone was walking towards her along the side-track. Three people. Then Barbara gasped in dismay. It was Gordon, Karen and Jennifer, and they were walking straight into the area in front of Mr Smiley!

Afraid they would blunder into a trap, Barbara sprang up, stepped out into the open and yelled, "Gordon! Go back! Get under cover!"

Bang! Bang!

To her horror, Barbara saw Gordon knocked over by a shot, the rifle he held flying from his grasp.

Mr Smiley!

There he was, just in the edge of the jungle. Barbara brought her rifle up. At the same moment, Mr Smiley stood up behind a tree and turned to aim at her. Thirty metres? Things seemed to happen in slow motion: Butt in the shoulder, raise the foresight to the base of the target—he is starting to aim at me!—steady the breathing, take the first pressure—the muzzle of Mr Smiley's rifle now just a black dot-raise the foresight to the point of aim—a puff of smoke from Mr Smiley's rifle, a vicious *Crack!* right beside her head—his mouth twisting in fury as he cocks and re-aims—steady the breathing, hold, squeeze the shot.

Bang!

Mr Smiley went over backwards. Barbara felt instant relief, exultation, and revulsion. She was also aware of other shots from off to her right. She crouched back under cover and worked the bolt. A fit of trembling shook her.

"Oh my God! I've shot him!" she cried.

"Bloody good!" Roger called, but she barely noticed.

A man was shouting up in the forest to the left, "I give up! Stop shooting! I give up. Don't shoot!"

"Cease fire!" yelled a loud voice across the clearing.

Inspector Sharpe, Barbara recognised. The firing stopped.

Inspector Sharpe called loudly, "Come out with your hands up."

A Smiley appeared on the edge of the jungle with his hands up. Barbara sprang up and started running. Roger yelled out, "Barbara! Stay down."

But she ignored him and ran across the Mt Burton road towards where Gordon lay.

Roger yelled again, "Dan! Cover this mongrel. Inspector Sharpe! He is the last Smiley." Then he was running too.

Barbara ran to where Wendy and Jennifer were kneeling in the long grass. She felt utterly wretched and sick at heart. Poor Gordon! It was all her fault. Jennifer reached him first and cradled his head on her lap. Barbara saw that he had blood all over his chest, but he was alive.

"Thank God!" Barbara cried.

She cast her rifle down and knelt beside him. Gordon saw her and tried to get up. He gave a weak smile which then twisted into a grimace of pain. Wendy joined them, pulling frantically at her webbing to get it undone to extract a field dressing. Suddenly she stared past Barbara and screamed:

"Barbara!"

Barbara turned.

It was Mr Smiley, the shoulder of his shirt soaked with blood. He had hauled himself upright and was raising his rifle to aim at her from ten metres away.

I'm dead! she thought.

There was a flicker of movement in the jungle behind Mr Smiley. Barbara saw him glance that way and then his mouth opened in fright. He tried to swing his rifle around but bushes blocked the movement. There was a flurry of movement in the bushes and a black shape sprang out and grabbed him by the throat.

The zombie!

Barbara knelt in the grass, one hand scrabbling for her rifle and the other gripping Gordon's sleeve. But she could only watch in horror. The zombie flicked his chain around Mr Smiley's neck and began hauling it tight. Mr Smiley let out a strangled grunt and tried to pull away. His face became red, then purple. To her dismay Barbara saw Mr Smiley get his rifle in between him and the zombie. There was a muffled bang. The zombie twitched and let out a moan of rage and pain. Then he went berserk and grabbed at Mr Smiley's throat and head and wrenched and twisted violently.

Mr Smiley struggled frantically to re-cock his rifle but was unable to. He suddenly went limp and buckled at the knees. Both he and the zombie went down in a writhing heap, which then went still.

Roger raced over to Mr Smiley and aimed down at him. Then he relaxed and seemed to slump. His face a mask of satisfaction and distress he turned and walked slowly towards Barbara.

"I think he's dead," he said.

Barbara rose and went to join Roger. She knew that what she was going to see might haunt her for the rest of her life, but she just had to look. It was awful. Mr Smiley's neck was bent at an odd angle and he looked a waxy-blue colour. There was no doubt he was dead. The zombie lay on him, quite still and the back of his shirt blasted open and all soaked in blood.

Roger knelt and pulled the zombie's mask clear of his neck and felt for a pulse. Then he stood up and shook his head. "I think he is dead too."

Might be for the best if he was insane, Barbara thought.

Then she shuddered. Roger turned and wrapped his arms around her. She responded and kissed him on the cheek, hugging him tight. Good old Roger!

They stood holding each other. Armed police in blue and black uniforms swarmed everywhere. Barbara shivered and clung to Roger. Tears came and she closed her eyes. She nestled her face into his neck and felt the comfort of his arms around her. She sighed and opened her eyes.

Lofty!

"Lofty! At last!" she cried. She and Roger released each other and turned to him. "Lofty, where have you been?"

"Don't ask. Not now," Lofty said. He looked embarrassed. "It's a long story. We got chased and had to hide and got a bit lost." He turned and held out his arms. Wendy rushed forward and threw herself into them. They kissed passionately.

But? Barbara thought. *But Lofty loves Fiona? Fiona! Where is she?*

She looked around. Fiona was standing with her father and the other freed hostages talking to that awful Superintendent Blunt and Inspector Sharpe.

I must speak to her, Barbara thought. *But first Gordon.*

Barbara turned back to where Gordon lay with his head cradled on Jennifer's lap. "How is he?" she asked anxiously.

"Look!" Jennifer said. She had torn open Gordon's shirt. Blood trickled from a long gash right across his ribs. "The bullet didn't go in," Jennifer explained with tears of joy in her eyes. "Here's why."

She held up the Monk's Amulet. It had a deep dent in it. The bullet had been deflected by it.

Gordon gave a weak grin. "I'll be right. It stings like buggery, but I'll live."

"How do you know what buggery feels like Gordon?" Roger asked, relief evident in his voice.

"Roger!" Barbara scolded.

But it was Roger's hand she took. He put his arm around her and she smiled at him, aware that tears were streaming down her face.

Two paramedics elbowed them aside. Barbara looked around and saw Fiona walking towards them. Barbara released Roger and stepped out to meet her. The two girls embraced and hugged each other.

"Fiona! Oh I'm so glad you are safe!"

"Oh Barbara, was I glad to see you! Hello Roger. Hello Lofty. Hi gang!" Fiona greeted. She trembled with emotion and her cheeks were wet with tears. "It's been a nightmare," she said.

"Amen to that!" Roger added.

"Thanks for saving us," Fiona said.

Her father joined her and added his thanks. He looked haggard and broken. Two more paramedics arrived and insisted on Fiona and her father moving over to the vehicle which had just driven in.

"Oh! Here's trouble!" Dan called.

Barbara looked. Capt Conkey was walking towards them with Superintendent Blunt and Inspector Sharpe. Capt Conkey was in uniform and the two senior policemen wore their grey suits, looking somewhat incongruous in the jungle setting.

Capt Conkey raised an eyebrow as he reached them. "Keeping out of trouble as usual?" he said with heavy sarcasm.

"Sir! It's not like that. It's..." Barbara stammered.

Inspector Sharpe shook his head. "I've seen you lot at work before, but this takes the cake. We've been following a trail of destruction and bodies for days. Bloody well done!" He shook Barbara's hand, then Roger's.

Superintendent Blunt stood scratching his head. He put on his hat and hitched up his trousers. "Bloody hell! You kids have captured more crooks, rescued more hostages and shot more people in two days than I've seen in twenty years! I think it's time I turned my bloody badge in."

He walked off muttering to where two more detectives were taking photos of the bodies of Mr Smiley and the zombie.

Barbara looked at Roger and smiled. Their eyes met. They turned to face each other and held each other at arm's length.

"Roger, I think you are wonderful," Barbara said.

She stepped forward and kissed him gently on the mouth, then drew back. Roger blushed bright pink, beamed with pleasure and for a moment struggled to speak. Then he said huskily, "That is the nicest thing I've ever heard. It was worth shooting Smileys just to hear that. In fact, I'll kill anyone who ever tries to harm you."

He hugged Barbara to him, and they kissed again. The others looked on, smiling with delight. After a minute the pair drew apart.

Oh dear! Barbara thought. *Poor Gordon!*

The paramedics had him on a stretcher and were swabbing the wound. Jennifer stroked his cheek and held his hand. Gordon looked up at Barbara.

"You are too deadly for me," he muttered.

He turned to Jennifer and smiled. She pressed his head to her bosom and kissed him.

Special Thanks to

To the staff who made it possible to plan and conduct the 130 Regional Cadet Unit/Army Cadet Unit 'Senior Exercises' which provided the inspiration for this story, and the Cadet Under-Officers and cadets who had the grit and ability to make the exercises happen. They are:

1992: Staff: CAPT(ACC) C. R. Cummings (OC 130RCU Heatley), LT(ACC) Warwick Hamilton (130RCU), CUO Tracey Beatty (130RCU), CPL(ACC) Maurice Shephard (15RCU-Ignatius Park College), Cadets: CUO Hal Tucker (15RCU), CWO2 Jason Furze (15RCU), CUO Amanda Johnson (122RCU Mackay), CUO Leisa Kenny (130RCU), CUO Warren Bartholomew (130RCU), CUO Zak Wright (130RCU), CWO2 Trudi Lenon (130RCU), CWO2 Derek Whalley (130RCU), SSGT Len Beatty (130RCU-the zombie), CUO Tamara Briggs (131RCU Sarina), CWO2 Hambley (131RCU)

2002: Staff: MAJ(AAC) C. R. Cummings (OC 130ACU Heatley), CAPT(AAC) Warwick Hamilton (130ACU), LT(AAC) Duncan Forster (130ACU), 2LT(AAC) Cheryl Matthews (130ACU-Charters Towers), CUO Tracy Batt (130ACU), CUO Danielle Phillips (130ACU), CUO Laura Roberts (130ACU), SSGT Matthew Trewern (140ACU William Ross SHS-the zombie), PTE Ben McCulkin (Army driver): Cadets: CUO Marshal Lawrence (130ACU), CUO Chris Picone (130ACU), CSgt Chandell Kemper (130ACU), CWO2 Fapani (134ACU-Cairns).

2009: Staff: LTCOL(AAC) C. R. Cummings (OC 130ACU Heatley), MAJ(AAC) Warwick Hamilton (130ACU), CAPT(AAC) Duncan Forster (130ACU), MAJ(AAC) John Zimmermann (OC 122ACU Mackay), CAPT(AAC) Andrew Hansen (122ACU), LT(AAC) Cheryl Matthews (130ACU-Charters Towers), LT Graham Cummings (4 Fd Regt RAA), LT Marshal Lawrence (2RAR), Cadets: CUO Megan Rockley (130ACU-CT), CDTWO2 Tiffany Barrett (130ACU-CT), CDTSGT Hayward (130ACU), CDTSGT Callum Hogg (130ACU-CT- the zombie).

Enjoy more C.R. Cummings stories

The Air Cadets

The Navy Cadets

The Army Cadets

 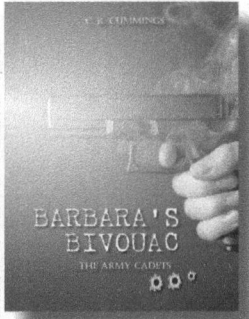